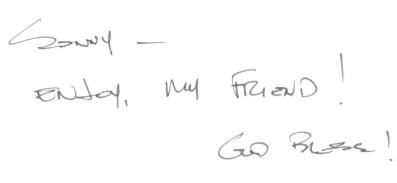

Sonny —
Enjoy, my friend!
God Bless!
Danny

THE OUTLAW

A RICH FARRIS DETECTIVE NOVEL

DANNY R. SMITH

D0556047

ISBN-13: 978-1-7349794-3-5

Cover by Jon Schuler

www.schulercreativelab.com

❀ Created with Vellum

You'll eventually resolve your last family dispute, book your final felony arrest, and break down your last of countless crime scenes. And when you finally turn in your gun and badge, you'll do so with a heaviness you might not have expected.

But you will always be part of a family. My family.

This is for those who have served.

PROLOGUE

The way it worked in the joint, you hit the ground when the siren sounded or you took your chances with the man in the tower. You couldn't count on a warning shot, though protocol dictated one be fired. The reality was, it depended on who stood watch at that moment. Was it a young prison cop with a hard-on to see some action, or a veteran hack just doing his time too?

On the streets it was different, and that was something not all convicts understood. Sirens served as warnings, signals that the cops were on their way and it was time to move out. There were no guards shouting orders, no crosshairs on your state-issued denims, and no walls or bars or razor wire fences to restrict your movement.

Seventeen years of incarceration could ruin a man, change his way of thinking and maybe slow him down at times like this. Some convicts became institutionalized, preferring structure and mandates over personal freedom. In the pen, the only decisions a convict made were where to stand in the yard to minimize personal risk, and whom to avoid. With that simplicity, a man could stop thinking for himself, and then he wouldn't know how to handle a bad situation when it arose out on the streets. He'd freeze up at the sounds of sirens, maybe hit the ground and wait for further orders from The Man.

Not Buddy Frantelli. He never hesitated. At the first sound of sirens, he moved off quickly, instinctively. Because nothing good could come from a white convict being caught in an alley with a black girl—especially a dead one.

1

The black girls had moves Buddy couldn't believe, their hips in low-rise jeans or short skirts moving effortlessly with the rhythm, rapid thrusts keeping time with certain beats. They were out there getting it on, grooving with different partners, blacks or whites, men or women, sometimes both. Buddy had never seen anything like it.

Now that he thought about it, he'd never seen black girls dance before at all. Well, he'd seen them a few times on television, *Soul Train* maybe, when the blacks had control of the dayroom television, something that occurred more frequently lately as more of them came to Idaho and ended up in prison. But he had never seen them like this, live, up close and personal, close enough to feel the moist heat from their bodies and to breathe in the collage of perfumes as he moved through the crowd, bumping into some and rubbing across others, nobody seeming to care. It was the type of incidental contact that would have a very different result in prison.

Before Buddy had gone away, he'd sometimes get out for a drink, see if he could find a little action if he felt like it or otherwise just get away from the house, still living at home back then. But in those days, there weren't any clubs where blacks and whites would hang out together. Shit, he didn't think there had been even a handful of blacks in Boise before he went away, not enough to irritate a guy anyway. Not enough to make the streets unsafe, raise the crime rate, change the dynamics of the city night life. Man, how times had changed. Now look at this place, he thought, all these *dudes* dancing with the white girls, these guys who looked like pimps in their leather jackets and slacks. It made Buddy sick to see everyone catering to them. White boys kissing their asses, trying to emulate them, calling them *bro* and shit like that. Yeah, sure, they were *the shit* now, these slick-acting, jive-talking brothers.

Buddy heard enough conversation—mostly from the two white broads a few stools down—to realize that most of these dudes played ball at the university. It figured, Buddy thought; he couldn't see any other reason they'd be living in Boise. Twenty years ago, well, seventeen years and three months to be exact, the few who were here knew their places. Now look at them, parading around like they owned the goddamn town. Maybe Buddy would show them something about respecting another man's space, understanding boundaries, keeping to themselves rather than mixing with other races. Teach them about the cardinal rule he'd seen reinforced on the yard: wait your turn for the weight pile when the whites were there first—that's how we'll get along.

But there was the light-skinned one, a little watered down he might say, there in the tight white pants, a skinny little jig with light brown skin and straightened hair. Man, Buddy thought, she'd be the one if he were to cross that line. Jesus, look at the way he was thinking now. Too much time away, he supposed. Being locked up not only left a man hungry for a woman, it could change his appetite, make him less discriminating about what he devoured.

As much as Buddy enjoyed the show, he decided he just couldn't stand to stay. If that dude down the bar kept looking his way there would be trouble, Buddy being the type to never back down from confrontation. He had too much pride in his skin for that bullshit. And that would be all he needed, he thought, to catch an assault case less than two days out of the pen. Sometimes it was better to move along and avoid the drama.

Buddy stood and reached into his pocket, digging for a wad of bills while keeping his eye on the spade with the plastic-looking jacket, seeing him through a clouded mirror behind the barmaid. Also seeing two dumb white bitches twirling their hair, adjusting their little asses on circular stools as the dark-skinned Kojak told them how he had been out of the lineup most of last season due to an injury, otherwise he would have had a record-breaking year. But even with that, he'd been scouted by the pros and would probably be playing in the NFL before long if he could stay healthy, he said. And the white girls swooned.

Buddy's eyes shifted to the image he'd only seen in polished aluminum for nearly two decades, comfortable with the hardened man looking back at him. He liked the shaved head and full, heavy mustache that had blossomed during his time away. He looked hard now, no longer the baby-faced kid he was when he went inside and had been forced to prove himself at just over twenty-two years of age. He reached to unbutton the top of his denim shirt, but the faded blue ink on his neck—a vulture on one side and an hourglass on the other —caused him to button back up.

Buddy caught the spook's eyes in the mirror and held his stare until the dude looked away. He felt his jaw clench and muscles tighten, reminding him of the feeling he'd get when something was about to go down on the yard or in the chow hall and he could feel it coming or see it starting to happen. He pictured himself sticking this dude in the throat, jabbing him a few times in the liver, maybe hit him in the kidney with a homemade shank and watch the dude's gold-toothed grin fade to that stupid look Buddy had seen on other men, that look of disbelief—nobody ever expecting it would happen to him. All he would need was a piece of sharpened metal, part of a bed frame or maybe a spoon, a shoestring or some tape wrapped around one end for a grip. Any type of weapon at all, and in a split second—with Kojak not watching his own ass, too busy looking at all the pretty little white ones—it'd be over. Hit him hard and fast, drop the shank and walk away. Just like that.

Some people were lucky Buddy had restraint.

The bartender, a woman about the age of Buddy's mother, but not thin as a twig like Mrs. Frantelli, picked up Buddy's five and the empty tumbler, swiping a wet rag across the bar in the same swift move. Buddy waited until she turned back to him, seeming to realize now he was expecting his change. She turned to the register with the five, came back around and dropped a buck and a quarter on the bar, never making eye contact with him. Buddy collected his money and backed off the stool, giving the spade another glance before heading for the door.

Maybe he'd try down the road, see if he could find a place where a white man could get a drink *and* a little respect. Someplace a lonely convict might find some company, maybe a lady with a soft spot for outlaws. Somewhere without the drama, he thought, as he stepped onto the sidewalk under neon lights, the sounds of traffic replacing the music, voices, and laughter spilling from the club as the heavy wood door closed behind him. He looked one direction and then the other, taking in the various neon signs scattered throughout the block, all within walking distance and still not far from home.

He liked the flashing arrow and the name of one just a short distance from where he stood, and he headed to the Lucky Seven.

2

Rich Farris buttoned and then unbuttoned the jacket of his new Hickey Freeman suit, straightening his posture as he studied his image in the mirror. The brunette at Nordstrom had put the ensemble together, this dark blue one with a white shirt and gray necktie with specks of green and blue. Rich had chosen it over two others, a gray pinstriped and a solid black, each by Joseph Abboud. She had said any of the three would be perfect, but since it was now spring, he could get away with a lighter color too. Her gaze met his in the mirror as her hands came to rest on his shoulders. She told him he'd look good in just about anything, with his slender frame and beautiful brown skin. Rich saw her now, in his mind, as he studied his pose in the mirror, remembering the young lady with provocative hazel eyes working her charm. Keeping customers like Rich coming back, spending more on threads than they could afford.

Rich came out of his bathroom, silently questioning his decision to buy a new suit and wear it on a day like today. Still, he'd get his shoes shined on the way in, stop by Chambers in Watts—his old stomping grounds—to have his wingtips polished for five bucks including the tip. Maybe today he'd give Fuller a ten, show some appreciation for the master of his trade, the best shine man in the business. Rich could have bought a new pair for the occasion, now that he thought about it, but the suit had nearly killed him, seven-fifty out the door.

He pulled out of the darkness of his parking garage into the bright spring morning, and paused to see in his mirror the wrought-iron gate close behind him. He pulled his sunglasses from the visor then tuned his radio to the news to catch a traffic report, which was more of a habit than a necessity early on a Sunday morning, or perhaps just a distraction from his thoughts. Traffic into L.A. would be light until later in the morning when Southern Californians began flocking to the various attractions spread across the southland: Olvera Street, Chinatown, Universal Studios, Farmers Market, Hollywood–Grauman's Chinese Theatre, beaches to the south or west, mountains to the north or east, amusement parks, sand dunes, equestrian centers, skating parks, lakes—just about anything one desired could be found in or near the City of Angels.

Right now, however, the roads were primarily occupied by family sedans headed to church, joggers in nylon shorts and tank tops, and neon bicyclists traveling in packs while continuously fighting for their right of way. Rich slowed for a Starbucks but opted to continue past when he saw the crowded parking lot and a long line for the drive-thru. Maybe he'd swing through a Jack-in-the-Box instead, pick up a breakfast sandwich and black coffee. He set his sights on the bright red sign on his right just before the freeway but past a sports bar, two or three restaurants, and a couple of burger joints—a row of culinary conveniences he would pass almost daily before getting onto the northbound Long Beach Freeway.

A Hispanic woman with limited English but a pleasant smile greeted him at the drive-up window, handing him a cup of coffee and telling him, the best he could figure, it'd be a couple minutes for the sandwich.

"*Gracias*," he said.

Rich thought about the drive ahead, plotting how he'd take the Long Beach to the 405 to the Harbor so he could swing by Chambers, get back on at Florence Avenue and have an easy commute downtown from there. He glanced at his watch: 8:20. Then he wondered if

Chambers would even be open; he couldn't recall having ever gone there on a Sunday. He also wondered if he should stop by the office, see who was working the desk today. But what would be the reason? It didn't really matter... or did it? Would it make a difference if it were someone he knew? Suddenly there seemed to be more to consider than what he had anticipated.

Rich handed the smiling cashier a ten and drove off; she could keep the change.

Nothing had changed as far as Rich could tell when he arrived at the coroner's office. But, he thought, why would it have? It had only been a couple years, not quite two, actually. It wasn't like driving past his childhood home in Inglewood, something he'd do from time to time when he was still on the job. He'd drive through the streets where he and Tommy Newman rode bikes or played at the park when the only concern was to have your ass home before the streetlights came on. Now the homes sat fortified with security bars over doors and windows as citizens took refuge behind stucco walls from the violence outside their front doors, the street gangs and drug dealers who had changed a middle-class black neighborhood into a war zone.

But at the coroner's office white vans still lined the driveway to the service floor where the stiffs displayed the results of varying degrees of violence, often of the sort that led to death. The recently arrived would wait their turn to be stripped, washed, photographed and x-rayed before being rolled into one of two windowless, concrete rooms with stainless steel tables that butted against stainless steel sinks, designed for the ease of washing everything away except the odor and maybe the memories.

Rich could smell the death as he swung his 1969 Corvette Stingray into an empty space. Or was it his imagination? Either way, there it was, the pungent stench of decomposing flesh and blood, an all too familiar recollection. This is where it had all begun, Rich thought, as he parked and got out of his car, the morning sun warming his shoulders. A couple of years ago, he had felt on top of the world on mornings like these. Today, he only felt regret and sorrow. Maybe he was just feeling sorry for himself, as the shrink had once suggested, but nonetheless he hadn't been able to shake it. The drinking no longer dulled the pain, and it seemed to make everything that much darker.

He reflected on those days of glory when a beautiful morning like this one would brighten his day and energize him. And the thoughts of those days naturally included memories of his last partner, Lizzy, who had recently succumbed to cancer. With that, he walked away from his car, leaving the keys in the ignition and the windows rolled down. *Fuck it*, he thought, as he headed toward the door.

Rich expected to avoid cops at this time of day, almost eleven now. Especially on a Sunday. He knew, after spending twelve years assigned to the elite Sheriff's Homicide Bureau, that most detectives would have arrived for autopsies around nine—if they had come at all—and that they would be done and gone by now, in most cases.

In the early days, the first couple of years Rich had worked Homicide, he had attended the autopsies of every case he was assigned. As time passed, he adapted the old-timer style of calling in for the results of suicides and accidental deaths in order to give himself a break. Eventually, he only attended the cases he viewed as important, dead cops and kids, and cases sure to draw attention, like celebrity murders. Especially when the celebrity was the one who did the killing.

Dead kids. Jesus, Rich thought, as he began his walk to the service door. The dead kids—and there had been a steady stream of them— had probably been a big part of why he was here today. That and the cops, like his friend Ron Bowman, a street cop in East L.A. who took one in the throat during a family disturbance call. The asshole husband, armed with a snub-nosed revolver with a missing front sight and duct-taped grips, nails a cop in the jugular at thirty feet. Luck of the bad guy, Ron had always said. Rich recalled standing over the metal table that day, his friend staring back at him through dull eyes that told him nothing, not even goodbye. Rich had stood solemnly that day as the medical examiner opened the dead cop's chest, peeled back his scalp, removed his brain and dropped it in a bucket.

And later he drank.

He continued to drink, more each day it seemed, and every day without fail or prejudice. But it hadn't helped. Rich continued to struggle with the images and the scars of that one and the others, and the passage of time seemed to do little or nothing to ease the pain. Day after day, night after night, the memories would make the gears squeak inside his head, and the only relief was lubrication. Scotch seemed to work the best.

But the kids, for Christ's sake, they had come in all sizes, shapes, and colors. There was no discrimination when it came to the abuse of children. Their fragile bodies would lie on the cold steel, broken in a variety of ways: beaten, shot, strangled, stabbed, drowned, suffocated... A baby drowned in a bathtub as her crackhead mother lay passed out on the couch, half a dozen more shaken to death. There were two occasions when he had spent the day sifting trash at a recycling plant, newborns discarded at birth. Another had been thrown off a goddamn bridge.

Yet the ex would wonder why he hated people. His former bride, who had gladly received half of his paychecks for the last ten years and now took a generous portion of his retirement too, would tell him he should branch out, socialize with people other than cops, people who were normal. *Normal.* Maybe she meant people who had never seen a child or close friend dissected, or who had never sifted through trash for evidence of a dead baby. People who had never experienced tragedy beyond a dip in the stock market, this circle of friends she had asked him to embrace. Have a cocktail and discuss the index, wait for some asshole with manicured nails to ask, *What was it you said you do?... Oh really?... Well, that just sounds so—interesting. Do you have to see real dead people?* Maybe Rich would tell the asshole about the teenaged girl beaten to death with a tire iron by her drunken stepdad, how her skull was shattered and they never found one of her eyeballs. Say to him: Listen, Skip, why don't you be a sport now and fetch me another drink. Or shall I tell you more about the little girl?

Rich paused to watch two coroner's technicians working at the rear of a van backed into a space reserved for the *loading and unloading of passengers only.* By the bulk beneath the white sheet, Rich assumed the passenger to be an adult male coming in for final service, another statistic in the City of Angels where premature death was an accepted risk of life.

Rich walked in and nodded, saying good morning to a young man in scrubs while making his way to the sign-in sheet. He felt comfortable, confident he could walk in without confrontation or concern. He'd been here hundreds of times and remained a familiar face, even several years later. If he hadn't been personally recognized, he knew he still bore the look of a homicide cop with his tired, distant stare, the eyes of a man comfortable in the presence of death, the face of a man who had witnessed unspeakable violence.

Rich dropped the pen onto the clipboard and strolled through the reception area into the main hallway, where the stench of death blended with an acrid odor of formaldehyde. Comfortable among the scores of cadavers lining the halls, Rich took his time to study the human remains as he made his way to the autopsy room. He surmised the various causes of death, seeing obvious homicide victims: a gang member with multiple gunshot wounds, a woman with stab wounds, an obese man with a bullet hole in his forehead, jail tattoos all over his body. Rich smirked at the look of surprise on the dead man's face; death had been sudden and unexpected. He pictured the man holding his stance, letting everyone know he was the toughest *hombre* on the block, maybe in the neighborhood. It had probably been a fourteen-year-old who pulled the trigger on him, putting the big man down. Maybe the youngster having been disrespected, called a *puto*, or he might have been from a rival gang and was just making his bones.

Rich paused at the sight of a middle-aged man with a single gunshot wound to the right side of his temple, the impression of a gun barrel and front sight tattooed on the flesh. It was a classic indication of a contact wound, no doubt a suicide. Rich reflected on the many suicides he had seen over the years, some of the strangest cases ever. There were hangers, jumpers, and those who slit their wrists. Some consumed large quantities of booze and pills, some chose asphyxiation. There had been a few who had lain on railroad tracks and just waited, exemplifying the commitment some had to ending their lives.

Rich thought of a young lady who had shot herself in the chest, too vain to put a bullet in her head.

What had often bothered him were the locations some chose to end their lives, doing the deed where loved ones would make the discovery. Maybe it was their way of getting in the last word, punishing those who drove them to that fatal point. Rich had always wondered why they wouldn't go someplace where a stranger would find them, a construction site or parking lot, maybe out in the woods. A citizen could make the discovery and call it in, and then a cop who couldn't care less would be dispatched to clean it up. Let the loved ones hear about it in a sterile environment, see them after the mortician completed the makeover and had dressed them up in a nice suit.

Or go ahead and dress for the occasion. Maybe do it right where you'd end up anyway for the postmortem examination.

This one did it right though, this old man with a single gunshot to the head; he wouldn't have felt a thing. The lady who shot herself in the chest would have suffered for a few minutes, Rich surmised. She would have lain there wondering what the hell she had done, but it would have been too late then to reverse her course. Some actions were irreversible; that was a law of nature Rich had come to know as an absolute. Proper shot placement and a quality firearm meant everything. Straight through the temple, under the chin, or in the mouth with an upward trajectory, and nothing smaller than a thirty-eight. Forty-fives were reliable, as were .357s, 9mms and everything in the vicinity. Don't screw around with .22, .25 or .32 auto calibers. Never a .380; Rich had seen too many of these caliber gunshot wounds result in only bad headaches. When it came to shot placement, Rich figured the mouth would be best, which seemed to be the preferred method of cops who checked out early. One every day was the national average, or at least that's what the department's shrink had told Rich not long before the department gave him his papers. Post-Traumatic Stress Disorder commonly went undiagnosed in cops, the good doctor had explained, and Rich wondered what the hell was the benefit of knowing it. On the bright side, the doc had said, there was a tremendous effort being put forth to help cops deal with readjustment, much in the same way such effort was made with returning combat veterans. That was the good news. Soon, if he continued his therapy, continued his medication, discontinued the booze and solitary lifestyle to which he had become accustomed, he would no longer feel the urge to punch every dipshit who asked him why cops don't shoot people in the arm or leg like they do in the movies.

But the prescription seemed worse than the ailment, Rich concluded, and he had continued to self-medicate in the manner which pleased him most.

He moved on through two sets of double doors, past the dressing room—he wouldn't need protective clothing today—past the photo room, the property room, and into the examination room on the left.

There were six examination tables, four of which were occupied. A crispy critter lay curled into a ball on one table, an elderly woman on the next, then a man and—shit, a kid at the far table. Three doctors and two techs huddled around the toddler-aged child with unusual interest. Rich heard one of them say, his words muffled through the protective face mask, "I'll be goddamned, it's a quarter." The physician then removed a coin from the child's esophagus with forceps, for Christ's sake, and held it up for all to see.

It kept the interest of all in attendance, which suited Rich just fine.

Rich looked at one of the two unoccupied stainless steel tables and saw it happen in his head like he had hundreds of times before. He would hoist himself onto a table, face up, stare into the overhead light and say a final prayer. Ask the big guy for mercy, or whatever bullshit came to mind at the time, if anything at all. Then get it done, make it quick before some asshole tried stopping him. That was the plan.

He remembered telling the new guys, you always wanted to remain vertical in this place. He'd walk them in for their first time through the back door, onto the service elevator, headed for the autopsy room, telling them that every day above ground was a good day. And he often reminded them of it, almost every time he left this place.

What the hell had happened?

Richard James Farris saw himself remove from his waistband the

Colt .45 Auto, Model 1911, and stuff the barrel into his mouth. He would be careful to maintain an upward trajectory, sending the bullet through the roof of his mouth and into his brain. Instant death. He pictured the hammer back, cocked and locked as they called it, using his thumb to depress the safety and then push the trigger. He had never shot a gun that way, but imagined it couldn't be too difficult or awkward, once you set it in motion. Then he pictured Jesus from portraits he had seen, the white man with long brown hair and a beard, welcoming arms protruding from draping garments. He saw his mother now, standing next to Jesus, looking down on him with a worried look, or maybe a pitiful one. He tried seeing Jesus as a black man, standing there next to Mama, but it didn't work for him, Jesus with the long brown hair.

Rich reached for the pistol beneath his jacket, figuring it best to remove the gun before climbing onto the table. But as he did, the relative silence was suddenly pierced by a ringing cell phone.

Jesus, he thought, seeing that everyone now looked his way. He fumbled for the phone on his belt, just behind the pistol tucked into his waistband, while offering a nod and a smile toward the other men in the room, men wearing paper gowns and caps and rubber gloves. Men nonchalantly gathered around cadavers.

Nothing to see here, folks.

Rich, standing inside the doorway beneath an electric fly zapper, sweat beading on his forehead and nose while the others stood watching, said into his cell, *"Hello?"*

3

Boise Police Detective Jeremy Cross couldn't believe it, seven months of waiting for someone to die, practically begging for his first call-out, and here it came on a Sunday morning, the first day of April. Or was it an April Fools' prank? The other guys in the unit, seven of them if you included his lieutenant, were just the kind to pull his chain. His partner, Steve Troy, had told him he needed to keep his phone with him and turned on at all times, even during church. He could put it on vibrate if he wanted, but he had warned him not to leave it at home or in the car. First time you do, Troy had said, that will be the time they need to call you out.

It occurred to Jeremy that someone could be messing with him as he made his way toward the back of the church, feeling a hundred eyes upon him, and his wife's scowl, and the kids watching as he excused himself and left his seat. This had better be the real deal, he thought, as he pushed through the first set of double doors.

"This's Cross," he whispered into his cell as he hurried through the foyer into the daylight of a brisk spring morning, the first day in weeks it hadn't rained. He only waited a second—all of the silence he could stand—before saying, "*Hello?*"

"You a little excited this morning, Jeremy?"

He recognized the voice of his lieutenant, Ryan Fitzpatrick. "No sir. Well, maybe a little. Do we have a case?" he asked, hoping to hear there had been a murder.

It could have been any number of deaths: suicide, accidental, industrial—even just an unattended death, a natural death but with no doctor to sign the death certificate. Or maybe something else, an investigation unrelated to death, some type of case that required the response of a detective during the off hours. It wasn't uncommon to be called out on evenings and weekends at the request of a patrol supervisor, and all too often, it would be for something far less exciting than a death investigation. Jeremy didn't mind; he relished the excitement of it all and looked forward to each new case. But each time the call had come, he had secretly hoped for a murder. So far, he had been disappointed. Not that he wished death on anyone—quite the contrary—but if he were going to fancy himself a homicide detective, he needed to investigate an actual murder: *the unlawful killing of a human being with malice aforethought.*

The lieutenant said, "There's been a murder, Jeremy. You and Troy will have the handle on it."

Cross ended the call and glanced behind him at the closed doors of the chapel, then took a deep breath and let it out slowly.

BUDDY LAY STRETCHED ACROSS A STAINED, FLORAL-PATTERNED bedspread, flipping channels with a remote control. Getting it figured out, the arrows left or right to change the channels, up or down to adjust the volume. But he couldn't focus on anything showing on the tube this morning; he was still thinking about last night, how one thing had led to another and the next thing he knew, man, there he was again, mixed up in some shit. His luck was horrible like that. On the one hand he'd made what he believed to be the right choice for a fresh-out-of-the-joint convict, and got the hell out of that one place before some racial drama went down. If these white girls wanted to have their black men, what business was it of his? It made more sense to find a better place to drink, surround himself with better company. Like in the joint, it was always best to keep with your people: whites with whites and blacks with blacks. Less drama.

But there was his bad luck. It turned out the joint downtown, *Lucky Seven*—though now he knew there was nothing lucky about it— a place he had remembered his old man would frequent when Buddy was just a kid, had turned into a trendy goddamn place just like the other. "Seven" had been a no frills joint, the type of place where cowboys, bikers, and working stiffs coexisted with little more than an occasional fistfight out back. Now the place blasted rap music and the white girls dug it and the brothers would bust their moves on the dance floor, working themselves into a sweat. Man, he'd had enough of those dudes and their bullshit in the joint. Now he had to deal with them on the streets?

Buddy had learned at an early age that the blacks would try to run things if they outnumbered the white boys; otherwise, they kept to themselves. Buddy had seen it firsthand in the joint, how when there were plenty of brothers they'd make girlfriends of the white boys. But only the *soft* white boys, not the ones who were connected with the brand, the *white power peckerwoods* who weren't afraid to fight back. They'd tell the new guys—*fish* is what they were called in the joint— they could be somebody's bitch, or they'd have to pay rent, their choice. Tell them it was up to them, one of the two, or maybe they'd rather get stuck. They'd put it that way and see how the fish handled it.

The way Buddy had handled it was he balled up a solid fist, big and strong from years of hard work as a kid, and hit the man on the bridge of his nose with a big sweeping overhand right. Then he kept punching as the sweaty dude folded onto the ground and the siren sounded and it was time to hit the deck or take your chances with the man in the tower. After thirty days of doing pushups and sit-ups in the hole, Buddy returned to general population, now a target to the blacks but a man with respect from the white boys.

Shortly after his return, Buddy got in with a man called Big John Wilson who was known as a heavyweight among the white boys. He was doing twenty-five to life for a hate crime, shooting a spade who Wilson had said tried to commit a crime in the wrong neighborhood. Buddy approached the shot-caller on the yard and hit him up, calling him *brother* but giving the man his respect. Buddy told him he needed a *piece* so he could tame an ape, put it like that and waited. Told Wilson he'd take out the jig who had wanted to make him his bitch, and if he was able, he'd stick one or two more before the guards stopped him. He'd do it for the *fellas*, the other white boys on the yard. Buddy figured it to be an offer the big man couldn't refuse. Big John had sized him up for a minute, looking at him through dark shades with large plastic frames, then he told the young Buddy Frantelli who to see on the yard—*his* yard—for the hardware, and let him know he was on his own until he proved solid. Wilson told him take out a nigger and maybe then he could kick it with the white boys, enjoy the privileges of brotherhood: protection and camaraderie.

Buddy caught the queer dude coming back from the shower the next night and stuck him in his dark flabby gut. In and out and in and out until Buddy couldn't feel anything but warmth and sticky wetness, and then he realized he had dropped the shank. Fatboy was still on his feet, looking at Buddy with wide-open eyes but not doing shit, just standing there gasping, holding his belly with a stupid look on his face. Buddy moved quickly and mixed into a crowd of convicts who were gathered in the recreation room. He stripped off one of his two denim shirts, used it to wipe the blood from his hands, and then tossed it into a trash can and kept moving. He continued to distance himself from the bleeding brother until the siren sounded and he hit the deck. He lay prone among the masses of convicts and concentrated on his breathing, doing his best to control himself so he had a chance to go unnoticed. And he waited. Buddy waited for the cops to come and pull him out, where he would then be identified and taken back to the hole.

But it never happened; Buddy never went to the hole. He was eventually questioned, as were all the other inmates in his housing unit, but then he was returned to his cell and never heard another word about it. He never saw the queer again either, and he could only hope the man had died from his wounds or maybe infection, the rusted piece of metal doing more than just making a few jagged holes.

Buddy flipped through the channels trying to get his mind off of prison and off of last night. He needed some smokes and something to drink, thinking of it now, maybe a box of beer or some grapefruit and vodka. He hated like hell to go out just yet, with all the action still going on just up the street from his motel. But what else could he do, lay around all day dying of thirst? Wait for the cops to come and take him back to the hole?

4

Men, women, and children had gathered at the yellow tape, gawking and likely speculating about what might have happened. Buddy considered joining them. He could blend in with his ball cap and dark shades, both of which he'd just picked up at the convenience store along with a morning paper, a fifth of vodka, and a pack of non-filtered Camels. There was nothing in the paper about last night, but that was okay; he'd mostly picked it up to look at the classifieds, see what types of jobs were available. If he was going to stay out of the joint, he was going to have to avoid these little mishaps that got people killed. The way you did that was to work hard during the day and to be home at night—wherever home might be.

Buddy had learned to weld in the joint and how to turn wrenches from his old man, at a very early age. It had been the extent of the family income, the old man fixing neighbors' cars in their driveway and front yard whenever he was sober enough to do so. Up until the day he left. Which was the second best thing that had ever happened to his mama, she would say. The first best was the old man turning up dead a short time later. The cops had knocked on her door to give her the news, and she had thanked them and gone back to watching the television, no emotion involved. But a month or so later she showed some emotion when she learned about the benefits she would receive from social security.

Buddy stood outside the market under a bright morning sun, not giving much more thought to Ma or to the late *Mister* Frantelli. He was more concerned with the activity up the street, cop cars and a crowd of onlookers half a block away to his right. The red and yellow motel sign over an otherwise unremarkable gray building a block to his left was the place he had called home since his release. He stood with a paper sack in one hand and a newspaper folded under his arm as he lit a Camel with his free hand. The cigarette dangled under the brushy mass that covered his mouth, and smoke drifted up past his eyes as Buddy stood contemplating. Go have a look, or play it safe?

If there was one thing Buddy could appreciate more than the morning sun, it was the freedom of choice he now had. Wake up when he wanted, choose what he wanted to eat or drink, change the channel on the television and never watch that *Soul Train* shit again.

A black Ford Explorer raced up the road. Buddy watched it go by, recognizing it as a cop car even though he'd been off the streets most of his adult life. He had watched television and had seen the news and movies and read the paper while incarcerated, and he had seen the cop cars change from Caprices and Crown Vics to these midsized SUVs, and there was just something about the way cops drove—like they owned the goddamn roads.

The driver was young, clean-cut, wearing a white dress shirt and tie. He appeared focused and intense as he sped past Buddy without so much as a glance in his direction. As the cop neared the crowd, he hit the brakes and came to a stop near a group of similar SUVs of different makes and colors: a brown Dodge Journey, a blue Nissan Pathfinder, a charcoal gray Ford Explorer. Buddy liked the charcoal one the best, thinking that shade of gray would look nice on a chopper or maybe a restored truck, something that rode low and showed some chrome. The large, athletic-looking man unfolded himself from the black Explorer, then opened the back door and pulled a suit jacket from its hanger. He shrugged it over broad shoulders and the holstered pistol that sat high on his hip as he walked through the crowd toward the yellow tape. Buddy appreciated the size of the man, at first just seeing him as a big white boy who parted the crowd with no effort behind his movement. But then he thought about how he hated cops, and thought, *what a waste of talent.*

Buddy's curiosity got the better of him, so he turned to the right and headed for the crowd.

JEREMY CROSS DUCKED UNDER THE YELLOW TAPE AND STEPPED INTO HIS first crime scene with a body still there and onlookers gawking. It gave him a real sense of having arrived in the big leagues now, joining the ranks of homicide investigators. It reminded him of being a rookie and walking to the mound the afternoon of his first profesional baseball game, playing Single-A ball for the Boise Hawks, a minor-league farm team for the Colorado Rockies. He felt the familiar jitters in his stomach and the pressure that came with a crowd focused upon him, or so it seemed. This was no major league debut, but the magnitude of investigating death had not escaped him.

"Careful where you step," Steve Troy said, coming toward Jeremy with tired eyes and a bored expression, as if the man saw death every day. He was dressed casually in a light blue dress shirt, its collar unbuttoned and a striped tie hanging loosely around his neck. His brown slacks rode a little high over scuffed brown cowboy boots.

Jeremy felt his training officer was somewhat of a blowhard, a guy who might have been a little over-impressed with himself. What did he have, a dozen homicides under his belt? Maybe that was a dozen more homicide cases than Jeremy had, but the man overacted his part, playing the big city detective. Sure, he'd been in this assignment for over a decade now, but this wasn't Chicago, D.C., or even L.A. for that matter; this was Boise, Idaho, a city of just a couple hundred-thousand mostly law-abiding citizens.

When Jeremy first promoted to Detectives, he had worked several assault cases, a few rapes, and finally his first death case, a suicide. In the following months there had been a couple of other suicides, a suspicious death that turned out to be a natural, and several overdoses. Detective Troy had accompanied him on each of those cases, of course, and had treated him like a child, demeaning him in front of patrol officers, coroner's investigators, and civilians. At the first suicide, Troy had warned him not to toss his cookies on the victim if he was going to throw up, and he had had a good laugh about it with a couple of the patrol cops.

Jeremy had hoped a homicide case would be different, that it would be too important and the atmosphere too intense to worry about harassment from his partner, but he had hoped in vain. He proceeded beyond the yellow tape with caution, aware of every inch around him and taking extra precautions not to alter the scene by inadvertently stepping on evidence. As he did, his partner asked what took him so long, did he have second thoughts about coming to his first murder scene, and then asked was he feeling nauseated yet, did he need a barf bag.

"I had to get a ride home from church to pick up my city car," Jeremy said.

"*Church?*" Steve Troy stood with his hands planted on his hips, the right one just in front of a seasoned leather pancake holster. It was black, matching his belt, but not his boots. "A real homicide dick would've responded from a bar."

Jeremy grinned, doing his best to conceal the contempt he had for the man while remaining silent and awaiting further instruction or insult. He often wondered how this man had been selected to train new detectives. His personality made it difficult for anyone to respect him. Jeremy had kept his thoughts to himself, for the most part, only occasionally venting to his wife, who was less than sympathetic about it. His thoughts had ranged from stepping down from his newly attained rank of Detective, to punching out his training officer in the parking lot. These were only thoughts built on frustration, though, and Jeremy knew he could make it through the training process without resorting to either one. Besides, he hadn't been in a fight since junior high.

Now, stepping into his first homicide scene, he felt the uncertainty and apprehension of the unknown, the mysterious world of death investigation, and he didn't need additional pressure from this jerk. He would do his best to ignore the hazing and focus on the task at hand, while trying to not second-guess himself about his chosen profession. Did a baby-faced Mormon really have any business being a cop, much less a homicide detective? He didn't exactly fit in with the other cops who drank and cursed or cheated on their wives or lied to their captains about how things went down sometimes. Not that all of them were that way, but plenty were, or so it seemed. Jeremy had never really been embraced by the others, and when he made Detective after only four years on the job, he had heard about complaints from some of his peers. Not directly, of course, only behind his back or second-hand from the few friends he had on the job. The subject matter would often cite Jeremy's straitlaced style as evidence that he was the *golden boy*, the type of young cop the brass would favor, making him their pet and grooming him for swift movement through the ranks. He was the type of cop who would present well on camera, in front of crowds, and in the local news. A tall, physically fit young man with an honest smile and an impeccable background to match. Jeremy tried to dismiss the criticism, having felt he had made the grade based on merit and education. He had been one of the top cadets in his academy class and excelled in each assignment he had held since becoming a sworn officer. He was also in the minority of street cops to have earned a college degree, thanks in part to a left-handed 95 mph fastball. He took pride in his work and had collected more than a few commendations for his efforts along the way, and he would apologize to nobody for that. Although he did, at times, question whether or not he fit in, regardless of his accomplishments to date as a cop.

"Isn't that right, junior?" his partner said, still amused by his own comment. "A real dick would be swigging the rest of his beer, looking to pay his tab or beat a bartender out of it, not hurrying to finish a prayer, right?"

"No doubt, sir."

BUDDY COULDN'T BELIEVE THE WAY THEY LEFT THE POOR THING LYING IN the alley, exposed to public view. It occurred to him, as he looked at her now in the light of day, the little chocolate bunny lying there with her skirt hiked up to reveal skimpy red panties, that it didn't have to go down the way it had. It had been her own damned fault, and look at her now.

There was his bad luck.

Here he had tried to change the way he felt about colored people after meeting her in the bar the night before, having been drawn to her light brown skin and straight hair that had given her more of an islander appearance or some type of exotic mix. She had hardly appeared African at all, to look at her with the green, almond-shaped eyes and smaller lips. He had watched her for a while, he recalled, now reflecting on the moments of last night, and he remembered thinking that maybe it'd be interesting to try something a little different, even though it didn't feel right to him deep down inside. But he had never seen girls move the way these colored girls did, and he couldn't deny that it had really turned him on.

It had been awkward when he approached her and asked if she needed a beer. She had giggled a little, then cracked a bright smile and said why yes, she'd have a drink, maybe *Sex on the Beach*.

The hell you say, Buddy had exclaimed, and she giggled more and told him it was the name of a drink, and yes, he could buy her one if he would like. She said her name was Lacy Jane. He liked that, *Lacy Jane*, and for the first time in a long time he had had a silly feeling come over him that he didn't quite recognize or understand. They had a couple of drinks and then she talked him into dancing with her. The song was slow so they came together and Buddy held her tightly while barely moving his feet—maybe a little too tightly, she had hinted.

Things seemed to be going well and then she said she needed to get some air, and asked if he wanted to go for a walk. They went out the back where an alley ran behind the club, and Buddy knew she had more on her mind than just taking a stroll. He may have been gone a while, but he certainly knew when a girl liked him and what she had in mind when she asked him to get away from a crowd.

Once they were outside, alone in the alley, she had skipped ahead, twirling and giggling and flipping her hair about. Her skirt had lifted once or twice, enough to reveal those red panties, and Buddy now pictured her with that devilish grin as she asked if he saw anything he liked. Well, hell yes he had, the hell'd she think?

Then he had tried to kiss her but it seemed awkward and she turned her head and tried to pull back. Her expression had quickly changed to one of fear as his hands gripped her bare arms. She had tried again to move away, so he guided her against the wall and blocked her there. He again tried kissing her, but she had jerked her head away as if he had done something wrong or somehow offended her.

Looking at her now, Buddy felt no guilt for how it had ended. The dead black girl hadn't had any patience with a man who had been away too long and might have been a little overzealous. Instead, she had completely shut down, and then she had told him she wasn't the kind of girl to kiss on the first date. Oh, was that right? Then she told him she wanted nothing to do with him after he grabbed her again, this time with a better grip, a good hold on her so she couldn't pull away as he pushed his body against her, trapping her against the brick wall. He was going to finish what she had started.

What the little bitch shouldn't have done was call him a freak, say he was a crazy white boy with her nostrils flared and a wild look in her eyes. Buddy had then seen the African in her, and realized he should have known better than to think this one would be any different than any other, the damned savages that they were apt to be at times. And then it was too late, it seemed, everything happening very quickly as it sometimes did out on the yard or when some shit got started in the chow hall. His instinct that had never failed him in the joint had told him that trouble had come to him yet again, and he knew there was no way to avoid it once it arrived; you just had to handle your shit. Man up and take care of your business.

When she screamed, Buddy knew it was too late to let her go. Who knew what she'd tell the cops? One thing for sure, whatever she told them would have been enough for the pigs; it would be her word against his. Her young, uncontested word versus the word of a convicted felon and parolee.

Buddy stood at the edge of the crowd, recalling every detail of the night before, seeing her the way he had seen her last night and again this morning in his head while gazing through smoke at the small television beyond the foot of his bed. He relived the moments from the bar to the alley, the skirt, the light brown skin, her pulling away and starting to scream. He could see her mouth open and he could feel the warmth of her breath as her eyes filled with fury, starting the whole goddamned ruckus that had caused all this unnecessary violence. Then he thought about the big man in the joint, the one who had thought Buddy would be his bitch, and he pictured him with that same look in *his* eyes, the same disbelief he saw in the eyes of this colored girl at the moment it went bad. From fun to scared, then to that dull, lifeless look as he squeezed her neck to make her shut up and behave.

Buddy thought of his childhood puppy, the way it had wiggled and squirmed and pawed his arm as he taught it a lesson for nipping him on the nose. He compared how both had seemed so cute until that moment when they became vicious, and then they weren't cute at all and he had to deal with them the best way he knew how. He remembered how he had tossed the dead puppy into the bushes of a nearby empty field to conceal it from his mom, Buddy having been blessed with good instincts even at that early age. He had gone back the next day to have a look, and then the next day, and then the day after that one and several more times until it smelled bad. Eventually the hide turned to leather and the dark and dampened soil beneath it had dried and the bugs had moved on, having picked the meat clean. The dead puppy had lost its appeal by then but Buddy still visited it every so often, if only to relive the moment or maybe pay his respects.

Buddy stood with the crowd, fragrances of soap and shampoo and cologne wafting from various onlookers who stood in front of him and to his sides, people speaking to one another in hushed tones, discussing violence as if they understood anything about it. There with the dead girl in front of him and the dead puppy on his mind, Buddy wished it could have been an empty field, just him and her, none of the strangers intruding on their moment. Someplace more private where he'd be able to come back to see her again and again, day after day, until she smelled bad and until she no longer did.

Buddy grew tired of the people gawking, talking about it, surmising how it had happened, asking one another if they knew her. Was she a hooker? Shit, *was she a hooker…* What the hell did these people know about anything? What the hell did they know about violence and death or hookers or black bitches with red panties who got their jollies teasing white boys? Buddy needed to go before he decided to straighten somebody out, explain to them how little they knew about any of the things Buddy knew about, explain to them how minding your own fucking business kept you alive longer in the joint. More people needed to have that education, spend some time inside where you learned about respect or you got beaten or stabbed and maybe killed. Learn to stay off another man's bunk, stay out of his locker, keep your distance in the chow line so as to not crowd the brother in front of you. You didn't want to bump into him or touch him or breathe on his neck. You learned to respect a man's privacy at moments like these or in the shower.

Someone needed to cover the bitch up.

THE FACT THAT HER PANTIES WERE INTACT MEANT SHE PROBABLY HAD not been sexually assaulted, Steve Troy explained to Jeremy as they stood a few feet from her remains. Unless the offender—that was the word they used in the Bureau, Troy explained, reminding Jeremy he had been to the FBI academy in Virginia—dressed her posthumously. He liked that word too, using it twice now in the thirty minutes Jeremy had been on scene. Probably a hooker, Detective Troy surmised, a trick gone bad. "You see that shit all the time nowadays, the city not being what it used to be."

Jeremy asked, "You don't think it could have had something to do with the nightclub?"

Detective Troy glanced at the back of the building, looked up and down the alley, seeming to consider it for a moment. But he turned back to the young detective with a contemptuous smirk, his gray eyes covered by wire-rimmed sunglasses. "What, you're a seasoned dick now? Got this all figured out?"

Jeremy didn't reply.

She didn't appear to be a hooker, not to Jeremy. Not in her designer clothing, manicured nails, and elegant jewelry: a gold cross on a small chain around her neck, gold hoop earrings, a gold stud in the side of her nose. Jeremy figured her for a college girl out on the town, not a working girl. Maybe it was a generational thing, Detective Troy unaccustomed to seeing women dressed this way unless they were selling their bodies on the street. Jeremy had seen the way young ladies dressed in college, and to his partner's credit, there wasn't much difference between the two, some college girls and the ladies of the night.

Steve Troy was saying, "Only thing bothers me about this—her being a hooker—is the location. I don't recall ever seeing street-walkers in this part of town, but I could be wrong."

Thinking it over, second-guessing himself maybe, his voice a little quieter now.

Jeremy watched his partner study the scene, the surrounding area, and the crowd. The short, stocky cop with his grayish-brown brush hiding his mouth, an overweight man with a flat-top haircut, mostly dark but peppered with gray. Jeremy wanted to connect with the guy but often wondered why he bothered, why it mattered—he really didn't like anything about the man. It would make the working relationship more comfortable, and the training process less stressful if they did connect on some level, but Jeremy doubted it would happen.

Steve Troy took in a breath, forced it out through a sigh and looked up at Jeremy. "You ready to document the scene, junior?"

Jeremy pulled a pen and notebook from the inside pocket of his suit jacket, excited but nervous as he waited for the great knowledge and trade secrets his partner would impart to him along the way. He thought the veteran would have a few processes that differed from what he had learned in the classroom, the various detective training classes, and the advanced crime scene analysis he had been exposed to since promoting to Detectives. This would be the magical stuff, knowledge bestowed by a veteran who had honed his skills over many years of training and crime scene experience. Jeremy said, "Yes sir," and waited.

Detective Steve Troy paused, looked around again and came back to the young detective who awaited his guidance. He said, "Good, have at it. I'm going to go talk to the uniforms, see if they've found any witnesses. Don't screw anything up, don't miss anything important, and don't throw up on our girl."

5

herie Lewis had no idea what she would say when he answered the phone; she had never even spoken with the man. Aunty Louisa had told her the man was a drunk with anger management issues. But that hardly mattered to Cherie; he was a cop, a homicide detective in Los Angeles, and that meant something. It meant that regardless of whatever flaws he may or may not have had, he was Cherie's best bet, if not her only option. Aunty Louisa had warned her not to expect much, not to get her hopes too high. She had said the guy was a loser, a real piece of work, a cheating, lying so-and-so, and she hoped he rotted in hell for his sins.

But Cherie Lewis didn't care.

He answered the phone on the third or fourth ring. Was he asleep? No, Cherie decided, he sounded alert, not groggy. Maybe even excited, almost panicked, she thought, and she wondered if he too was frantic over Lacy Jane. Then she realized there was no way he could know; nobody from her family had had any contact with him for years. Cherie pictured him in her head, the image of a man she had never met, based on a few fundamentals: black, clean-cut, professional. After he answered, she paused, maybe froze for a moment, and at one point almost disconnected the line. Then she heard his voice again, this time less intense, less intimidating.

"*Hello?*"

"Uncle Richie?"

RICH'S HEART POUNDED. SWEAT BEADED ON HIS FOREHEAD. HE TOOK deep breaths to calm himself, trying to come down from an adrenaline high as his mind replayed the voice, searching for recognition. *Uncle Richie?* She spoke with a southern drawl. *Uncle Richie?*

Coroner's examiners and technicians stared as Rich held the cell phone to the side of his head, eyebrows crowded over questioning eyes. "Who's this?" he asked.

"This's Cherie Lewis. My mama's Florence Lewis, your ex-wife's sister. I don't mean to bother you, but..."

Jesus. He couldn't process any of it. He could barely speak coherently. "Yes... hello... um, yes, honey, what do you need? I mean, what can I do for you?"

"Well, I have this little situation," she began.

Rich listened as she told him about her missing daughter and the cops who weren't doing much to find her, while men in paper gowns returned to their gruesome duties on the other side of the chilled room. He needed to get out of there.

DIVINE INTERVENTION WAS A PHRASE HE HAD HEARD BEFORE, PERHAPS A cliché, but now Rich had to seriously consider it a possibility as he merged the Stingray into traffic on the southbound Golden State Freeway, light traffic under a midday sun, the Santa Ana Mountains to the east barely visible now through the smothering smog. This made twice now he had sought to carry out an exit strategy—not counting the times he had played with his gun over a bottle of scotch—and both times the craziest shit had happened. Rich heard the girl's voice in his head over the throaty V-8, the pleading voice of a young southern woman in despair. He pictured her with a coy smile, smooth skin, and a nice figure. Or maybe she was homely, phoning from the projects or a single-wide trailer surrounded by weeds, dirty feet beneath soiled sweats, a cigarette dangling from her mouth. Rich returned to the former image, a pretty young lady, even though she was his niece. Pretty, but simple, maybe even plain. The hero and the downtrodden.

Then he wondered what could he do? He was a *retired* homicide detective, which meant almost nothing. Not here in L.A., and certainly not in Shreveport, Louisiana, where Cherie's sixteen-year-old daughter, Lacy Jane Lewis, had gone missing five days ago. Rich detested Cherie's mother, but he had no reason to dislike Cherie. Her Aunt Louisa, the woman now collecting half his retirement salary, was Satan as far as he was concerned, and her sister, Cherie's mama, Florence, wasn't much better. Still, Rich knew himself well enough to know he would slide into rescue mode, do what he could for the young woman, because, well, that's what he did. That's what he had always done, and according to the shrink, that's what cops tended to do. Then after thinking about it, counting the number of buddies on one hand and then the other who had *rescued* their brides, Rich thought, okay, maybe. Yeah, okay, shit, so that's what we do. Some were war brides, plucked straight from the barrios or ghettos or trailer courts north and east of civilization, places where people dropped out of society. Cops all over seemed to find the strays, or maybe the strays found them, a steady check and a dental plan, citizenship in some cases.

What's the point?

Rich thought about the situation, then thought about his morning plans and how they had completely imploded. He had felt certain today was going to be the day; he had truly believed he was prepared for the final act. But it didn't happen, and maybe now he had something to live for, if only temporarily. Maybe it was a kind of karma, or destiny, or maybe it was just prolonging the inevitable. Rich stepped on the gas to go around a slower-moving vehicle, and as the wind funneled through the opened windows and T-top of his classic muscle car, he felt alive—perhaps more alive than he ever had felt before. He brought the Stingray up to cruising speed and settled into the deep leather seat, thankful that his prize possession hadn't been stolen. It would have been, had the day had gone as planned. Some lucky punk would have had a hot car that would have never been reported as stolen.

BUDDY COULDN'T BELIEVE IT. RIGHT BEFORE HE LEFT, TWO COPS WALKED past him in the crowd without as much as a glance. For a moment, he thought his arteries would explode. It gave Buddy hope, the cops not focusing on him. Maybe his luck had finally begun to change, he thought, watching the two cops in their white shirts and colorful ties climb into their unmarked cars. Buddy watched as they caravanned down the street toward the motel sign hanging over the sidewalk. Seeing the sign made Buddy think maybe he should head back to his room, get off the street for a while. There was no sense pushing his luck, as bad as it could be at times.

Then both goddamn cars with the two cops, a fat white guy in one and a beaner in the other, turned right into the driveway of his motel, for Christ's sake. What the hell were they doing? His mind raced to find a reason for them going into the motel that was unrelated to the dead girl, but he couldn't come up with one. Buddy didn't believe in coincidences.

The one thing Buddy had going for him was superior intelligence, which he considered a gift, maybe God-given, an offering of sorts to offset all the bad luck sent his way. Right now, Buddy's keen mind and sense of survival told him to head the other direction and to not look back. So that's what he did, thanking the good Lord he hadn't left anything in the room. Like his prison-issued state I.D.

6

Elwood Johnston pulled his Peterbilt 379 onto a paved lot behind the Flying J truck stop, and brought the nose of the red rig around until it was parallel with four or five semis to his right, eyeing the other trucks through the passenger's window to line her up. He'd leave the old girl running while he went inside to pay for the 378 gallons of fuel he had just finished pumping, and grab a couple of cheeseburger snacks for the road. He stepped off the rig and headed for the wall of darkened glass, pictures of half-pound burgers and all-beef wieners—*April Specials*—painted in bright colors, and beer posters on two glass doors. He could hear the rumble behind him, 550 horses waiting at the gate, 900 miles ahead of her. He figured he'd be in L.A. by morning, glancing at the *Timex* stretched over his giant left wrist, especially if he kept the nap to a couple of hours. Couple of cheeseburgers and a coke, two, maybe three hours of shuteye in the sleeper, and he'd be headed south.

Elwood rubbed the stubble on his chin as he approached two glass doors reflecting three-hundred and some-odd pounds in jeans and a red t-shirt, *Old Glory* waving over the breast pocket. He tightened his stomach muscles as he reached for the handle, not seeing much change in the mirrored image as the door came open toward him with force.

"Pard'n me," Elwood said, nodding to the man with a shaved head, tattoos on his neck, and a bushy mustache and goatee.

The man brushed past him without a word in return, just a look through hazy smoke, a burning cigarette dangling from the corner of his mouth. Elwood glanced back toward the lot as he stepped inside, the sound of idling diesels giving way to country music and friendly chatter inside. He saw the tattooed man headed across the pavement, a dozen or so rigs in the background. One of them rock 'n rollers, speed-freaks on wheels, the new breed of drivers nowadays, Elwood thought. The kind of asshole who doesn't have any courtesy for his fellow truckers, teamster brothers, and no respect for his elders. Elwood told himself he should've backhanded the boy. *Pard'n me, my ass.*

Elwood set two foil-wrapped double cheeseburgers, a family-sized bag of *Doritos*, two liters of *Coke* and his *Flying J* card on the counter, telling the woman in her short hair and mustache, yes ma'am, that'll be all, 'cept maybe a *Powerball*. Actually, he said, five would be better, increase the odds of an early retirement. Or maybe he would stay on the road a few more years and use the money to fix up the rig, give her a custom paint job, something patriotic. He told the woman to put all but one burger in a bag, and moments later he was out the door with his groceries in one hand, a cheeseburger snack in the other.

Crossing the parking lot, Elwood squinted to see the tattooed asshole leaning against a fender of his rig while lighting another cigarette. Elwood had a bad feeling about the guy, and as he continued walking slowly toward his truck, he realized this punk was waiting for *him*. Elwood wondered why, and the more he watched the man staring at him, the more convinced he was that this rough-looking fella was going to be trouble.

What Elwood figured he'd do, running it through his head as he continued toward his rig in no hurry, chewing his burger and taking bigger bites to finish it off, was give the man another chance to be friendly. Try the nod again, say, *Hey, how's it going?... Hey, how ya' doin',* buddy? Maybe, *Hey asshole, get the hell off my fender.* No, not with all this shit in his hands and the bad heart. But if he were ten years younger...

What Elwood actually said was: "Pard'n me, sir." Saying the same damn thing he had said when this punk had bumped him in the doorway, and wondering why the hell he had. Where was that tough voice he had in his head?

"Where're you headed, old-timer?"

Old-timer? The scrawny little bastard. "Who, me?" Elwood's mind raced to stay ahead of him. The man looking for a free ride. Elwood knew the type and should have seen it coming. He knew better than to take on hitchhikers like this guy. He'd pick up a passenger every now and again, usually ladies down on their luck, his experience telling him the company was usually better as long as they weren't too crazy. But never the likes of this guy, these jailbird types, dope-smokers and communists.

The guy said, "I was wondering—if it wouldn't be too much of a bother—maybe I could get a ride somewhere. Where'd you say you was headed?"

Man, this guy. "Oh, well, I'm just goin' on back home now—"

"You put 400 gallons of fuel in your rig to go home, pops?" the youngster said, pushing off the fender now, closing his distance on Elwood with a wild look in his eyes.

"Well, actually, I—"

The man with his tattoos was up close now, close enough that Elwood could smell the stench of liquor and cigarettes and sweat coming off him. The dude glanced around the parking lot, looked over his shoulder, and then came back to Elwood, leaning into him now, right in his face, coming at him with a low tone, making it sound cool but getting his point across: "Here's the deal, pops... you offer me a ride and I don't kill you right here in this parking lot. How's that sound?"

The slime ball grinned, showing his crooked and tobacco-stained teeth. His eyes were dark and distant, revealing only the emptiness inside the man.

Elwood followed the movement of the youngster's hand to see the handle of a hunting knife stuffed into his waistband, the guy lifting his shirt just enough to give him a peek. Elwood's mouth was dry and his mind seemed to be stuck between gears, unable to process it all and respond with words. He looked back over one shoulder and then the other, seeing nobody who could be of any help. He stood alone with this convict as the Peterbilt chattered in rhythm with its neighboring rigs spread across the concrete field, masses of steel outlined by small orange and yellow lights in the early evening hours.

Elwood looked back at the man with the knife in his waistband and the evil in his eyes but still found nothing to say, no way to respond.

The convict said, "Well, pops?"

And the two of them loaded up in Elwood's rig.

7

Detective Richard James Farris, Los Angeles County Sheriff's Homicide Bureau, Retired, pulled into the parking structure below his condominium complex. He removed his Ray-Bans and tossed them onto the dash as he swung the front of his Corvette into its designated space, the tires squealing against the oil-stained concrete. He took the stairs from the structure to a landing deck halfway to the second-floor walkway, paused briefly to look over the pool area—there were two moms with young children splashing in the shallow end—then finished his climb to his unit. He keyed open the door, stepped inside and paused again, glancing around the kitchen to his left and the living room beyond it. *Home sweet home.*

He felt strange in the stillness as if he were an unexpected guest. But nobody noticed. No wife, no kids, no dog, cat, or fish. At least not now—not any longer. The wife had been gone more than fifteen years, and Orlando, the blue betta who had previously inhabited a small tank near the kitchen window with a partial view of the pool, had passed away a month ago, the cause of death undetermined. There were no signs of trauma, no indication of foul play, and no suicide note. Rich assumed it to be a natural, the least imposing of all determinations. Still, it remained an unsolved case. *Another* unsolved case. But Orlando was probably better off, Rich decided, now somewhere in betta heaven, swimming freely through golden waters, or however it was for fish who believed.

Rich tossed his suit jacket over the back of a brown leather-covered couch, eyed the scotch at the bar but silently declined. Right now he needed a clear mind. He needed to stay focused, or what was the point? Cherie, the damsel in distress, had told him that her teenaged girl was missing. Lacy Jane was not the type to run away, she said. How many times had he heard that? There was no boyfriend—as far as she knew—and the child was not involved in drugs or gangs. Maybe she drank at times, but Cherie didn't know for sure. Don't all the kids?

Rich had gone through the basics:

Lacy Jane Lewis. 16 years old, will be 17 in July. Looks like she's 25. Good-looking girl with her daddy's light complexion and her mother's almond-shaped eyes, only green not brown. Attends continuation school, as does her friend, Tanika Edwards, who was missing as well. She was another smart but sassy teen with an adventurous streak that once landed her in jail for MIP: Minor in Possession of alcohol. And she had just turned 18.

Rich opened his laptop on the kitchen table and powered it up, anticipating the email Cherie promised would be forthcoming with the requested information: photos of the girls, contact information for the detective assigned to the case, a list of Lacy Jane's friends and their contact information: phone numbers, links to their social websites—Facebook, Twitter, etcetera—and all of Cherie's contact information. Rich had asked that she send it, and provided his email address, explaining as he was walking out of the coroner's office that he was not in a position to take notes at that time.

The computer came to life slowly, as it usually did, which Rich believed was due to the quality of wireless internet he "borrowed" from a neighbor whose access was unsecured. He was certain his computer had been infected by spyware and malware, which might have been the price he paid for being cheap at times. While waiting, he grabbed a bottle of water from the fridge and looked out over the pool. He stood near Orlando's vacated home watching the few who gathered in their swimwear and shades under the bright Southern California sky. He looked for the flight attendant from 103 but didn't see her, and he wondered if she was working over the weekend. He pictured her serving cocktails in First Class, or walking from the cockpit as two pilots turned to watch her go. One of these days he would get the courage to introduce himself, he thought. Rich noticed the homeowners association president, an uncontested, elected member of what Rich called the condo Nazis. The dweeb unfolded a chair near the shallow end and took a spot not far from the moms and kids. Rich wondered which of them had drawn Mr. HOA President to that location. *The pervert.* The little bald weirdo with his button-up shirt, shorts, and flip-flops, taking a break from busting balls to enjoy the scenery. Rich saw himself drowning the man. Walking past him and grabbing his collar and dragging him into the pool without pause, and then holding him under water. Not until he died, just until he begged and then cried and scurried back to his room to write up another violation for the man in 211, this time a pool violation. Excessive violence at the pool.

Maybe the mothers would applaud him.

Rich walked into the adjacent dining area and slid into a chair behind his computer, the screen now filled with icons over a picture of his Corvette parked at the beach, the sun setting in the background. He opened his email account and logged in to find six emails from Cherie, each with photographs of a teenaged girl who did appear much older as described. Rich thought the girl could easily pass for twenty-two, and she was pretty enough and fit enough to be a swim-suit model. Her shoulder-length, brown hair had streaks of dark and light highlights and it carelessly fell over golden-brown shoulders. Her hazel eyes were full of adventure or maybe mischief. Rich clicked on a link that took him to a Facebook page with more photos of the young lady in different poses, some natural and some that appeared to be professional portraits. He viewed the profiles of a couple of her friends, but quickly realized it was a shot in the dark, the page indicating there were more than a thousand. Rich had about twenty, including his deceased ex-partner, and his daughter, Shayla, who worked as a prosecutor in Las Vegas, and with whom he seldom spoke.

Rich sent the various emails to his printer, then got up from the table as he unlocked his cell phone. His first call would be to Sheriff Jonathan Walker of the Caddo Parish Sheriff's Office in Shreveport, Louisiana. Cherie had provided his cell phone number, saying he was the one to speak with. She didn't know of any detectives working the case.

"Good afternoon, Sheriff," Rich said, calculating the time in Louisiana to be close to three or four o'clock now, not sure if they were two or three hours ahead.

"Good afternoon to you."

"My name is Rich Farris, and I'm a deputy sheriff out here in L.A. County," Rich said, fudging slightly on his status.

"Uh-huh."

"I apologize for bothering you on a Sunday, sir, but I understand you're working a missing persons case involving two girls, Lacy—"

The Louisiana lawman interrupted, his words slow and thick: "Where'd you say you was from, son?"

"Los Angeles. I work Homicide with the SO out here. Name's Farris, Rich Farris."

"Oh, okay then, California uh?"

"Yes sir."

"Now about these girls, you was asking—"

"One of the two, Lacy Jane Lewis, she's my niece's daughter, whatever that makes her to me. I don't know the girl, but family is family, if you know what I mean."

"Yessuh, I do."

"Well, I just wanted to check in with you, let you know who I am, see if maybe there was anything I could help with on the case, or maybe you could give me some information about your investigation, let me know what you have so far."

The sheriff said, "If you could call the office tomorrow, my assistant Mary Jo will be happy to put you through to me, or you could just call my cell again, either way, Deputy—uh, was it Harris?"

"Farris, sir... Rich Farris. *Frank Adam Robert, Robert Ida Sam,*" he said, spelling it out phonetically.

"Okay, well, if y'all can call us tomorrow, I'd surely appreciate it. I'm a bit tied up here this afternoon, got myself entered up in a bass tournament. And to be real honest with ya, I'd prefer to not talk business on the Lord's day."

RICH STARED AT THE PHONE, BUT NOT IN DISBELIEF. HE HAD TRAVELED the country working homicides and was well acquainted with some of the slower-paced agencies and their very different styles. He considered the source, then the situation, and moments later he had a plan.

He hurried into his bedroom, on the phone again but now with the airlines, as he pulled a travel bag from the closet and began filling it with pants, shirts, socks, undershirts and shorts, belts and shoes. He then put two pairs of slacks and a jacket in a garment bag and zipped it up, while asking a lady on the other end if there were any direct flights into Shreveport, and then saying, fine, whatever you have in the next couple of hours. Rich pushed a rack of clothes in his closet to one side to reveal a safe concealed on a corner shelf, and retrieved a Glock 9mm along with two extra magazines loaded to capacity, and two boxes of ammunition. He traded the .45 in his waistband for the more modern, smaller and lighter pistol. He paused briefly and stared at the .45 before putting it away, and thought about the insane day he was having.

The lady on the other end was asking for a credit card. Rich hurried back to his dresser and took one from his wallet. He read her the numbers and continued packing, placing his weapon and its accessories in a soft-sided leather briefcase, along with his Los Angeles County Sheriff's Department badge, a six-point gold star with a blue inlay and a bear that had been polished until it had no hair and looked like a pig. The badge had been reported *lost or stolen* two years before his retirement, the report vague as to the time and place or circumstances of the theft. It would come in handy now, having more weight than the one issued to him when he left the department that had a banner with the word *RETIRED* prominently displayed across the top.

While he finished packing and gathering his toiletries, he looked around to be certain he hadn't forgotten anything. Then he thought about how he would get his gun on the plane. It took more than a stolen badge after 9-11, with all the extra security, and knowing what Rich knew about some airport employees and theft of personal belongings, generally reported only as *lost* luggage, he would never consider packing it in his checked bag.

Under the afternoon sun, Detectives Steve Troy and Jeremy Cross watched as the last of the crime scene investigation concluded. Crime scene technicians placed paper bags of evidence into a white panel van. The bags included everything from discarded cigarette butts to hairs and fibers and swabs of blood, all of which would be taken to the state's crime lab. The coroner's investigator departed with evidence from the decedent, including samples of hair and fingernail clippings, and his notes of the crime scene investigation. He was followed by the transport van carrying the remains of an unidentified female adult, Jane Doe Number 2, her temporary identity, the second unidentified female corpse of the year. Uniformed police officers pulled the yellow tape from light poles and fences, and gathered it all along with the empty Styrofoam coffee cups from the hoods of their vehicles. The items were placed in the trunks of their patrol cars to be properly disposed of at the station.

The crowds of onlookers disappeared around corners and into nearby vehicles, homes and businesses, none of which seemed as secure as they had the day before.

Detective Troy stood near the mouth of the alley, his shirt sleeves turned up, dark sunglasses nestled in his flattop, the detective looking around as if something was missing or lost, or maybe forgotten. Detective Jeremy Cross stood beside him, looking around also, thinking this was what great minds of crime scene investigation must do before releasing the scene. He'd been told several times in class and once or twice by Troy that you only get one shot at the crime scene.

Cross felt fatigued and was surprised that his feet were sore and his legs ached. It didn't make sense, as he stayed in good physical condition, still running and lifting weights on a regular basis. So he figured it must have been the long hours standing and walking in dress shoes, a practice to which he was not accustomed.

Detective Troy finally said, "Be at the office tomorrow at about nine. We'll go in a little later than usual, given the hours we put in today. We'll get started on the reports and evidence until they call us for the autopsy, then we'll start working on leads."

Jeremy replied, "Yes sir." With that, he stepped away from his first homicide scene, a little disappointed if he had to be honest about it.

8

Elwood Johnston steadied the wheel with his left hand, his left elbow braced in the frame of the driver's window as his rig rumbled south through Nevada headed to California; Idaho and Oregon were both behind him now. He had made the trip a hundred times, but not as a hostage or kidnap victim or whatever you called it when some asshole pulled a knife on you and said take him to California. Elwood thinking, man, if this punk hadn't had a weapon... Elwood was also thinking of the various ways he could get out of the situation. He thought about putting some type of code out on the CB radio, something secret that truckers used to alert one another, but he couldn't think of any such duress calls if they had them. He also figured if he did know one, and he used it, nobody else would know what the hell it meant and ignore him anyway. The only CB lingo he could think of was a code to warn other truckers about cops working radar—a smokey with a camera—but everyone knew that after the movie *Smokey and the Bandit* came out several decades back.

Elwood thought about stopping to use the head, maybe find a place he could slip out and disappear, let the asshole figure out how to drive a semi pulling 80,000 pounds of weight, two trailers stacked high with alfalfa hay. See how far he gets. The rig was insured, though Elwood wasn't sure about the cargo, $8,000 worth of hay once delivered in California.

Then it occurred to him that nobody could make that trip without resting up, especially when they had started late in the day. Now that it was dark and they'd been on the road for more than a few hours, Elwood felt certain his passenger would start to fade. That's when Elwood would ease his Buck knife out of the center console pocket— the damn knife there this whole time and Elwood just now thinking about it—and slice this dude across his neck the way you bled a lamb. Elwood glanced over at the man and thought about the distance between them, and realized he couldn't do it while moving down the road and still maintain control of the rig.

But he would come up with something, now that he was on the right track, 300-some miles behind him and more than 600 to go. Elwood would just have to be diligent to see the opportunity when it presented itself. This boy's time was coming.

Buddy enjoyed the ride, seeing sights he hadn't seen for nearly two decades, the vast deserts stretching out to meet the faraway mountains painted red and brown and at times blue and purple. The mountaintops still held snow that reflected the morning sun across the horizon in front of him, accentuating the freedom of the road, moving across open and untamed country without restriction or limitation. He could go wherever he wanted now, whenever he chose to go, and all he had to do was point his recently acquired *Made in China* hunting knife toward the gut of Elwood to alter their course. Buddy reflected on the intelligent decision to purchase the cheap knife at the liquor store before fleeing Boise, and he was thankful for the street smarts that guided him.

Buddy thought California would be perfect, all the beautiful women and good weather and big crowds where he could hide in plain sight. A sense of excitement came over him, but then he thought about the trucker and wondered what he would do with him once they arrived. He looked over at Elwood, considering, and he couldn't help thinking of the Elwood from *The Blues Brothers*, a movie he had seen in prison. The big man pushed his rig slow but steady through the great northwest, a master behind the wheel, still alert after driving all night. Buddy admired that, as the thought came to him that maybe he could learn to drive a truck himself. Hell, maybe fat boy here could teach him. He studied the poor bastard in his worn out red t-shirt and faded blue jeans, and wondered if he would be able to let the man walk away or would the trucker represent too much risk of him being identified and captured? If the trucker was found dead in L.A., there would be no link to Buddy. Or would there? Chances were the cops would think it had been a robbery gone bad; everyone knew the savages in L.A. were always robbing, raping, and killing white folks. He remembered a scene from the news where a white truck driver was pulled from his rig and beaten by negroes to start the L.A. Riots. He also remembered a couple of beatings he and some of the other peckerwoods had put on some of the brothers in the joint, a way of retaliation afterwards. The whites outnumbered the blacks significantly back then, at least in the Boise pen.

Buddy watched the man behind the wheel, this pitiful idiot with nothing but the road and his trailers full of hay back there, nothing else going for the man. He decided he'd get to know him a little, thinking maybe it would help him decide what to do with him when they parted ways. Buddy said, "Mr. Elwood, what's your story, man?"

Elwood glanced over from the road, and then back. "What d'ya mean, my story?"

"You married, got kids, what?"

He looked over again, hesitated a moment before answering. "Kids are grown and gone, Mom is all that's left."

"She gonna worry, you don't make it home on schedule?"

"Yeah, I'd say Mom's probably worried by now, since she ain't heard from me. I usually check in every now and again."

Buddy let that hang there a moment. "What if you don't ever make it home, Mr. Elwood?"

Elwood glared at Buddy but didn't answer.

Buddy chuckled and returned his gaze to the horizon, the sun now above the mountains casting shadows across the valley floor.

9

Rich Farris had no problem boarding the plane armed after presenting a letter with a slightly revised date and destination and which bore his prior captain's signature on a sheriff's department letterhead. It had been fairly simple to make the changes, and when he presented a photocopy to the boarding agent, he kept her busy with flirtatious chatter. Farris could be good at that when he applied himself. She had thanked him for flying United and then he was pre-boarded, a common procedure for LEOs who travel armed.

When he landed in Shreveport later that evening, Farris couldn't believe the size of the airport; he was certain he'd been in bigger barrooms. It was easy navigating through the terminal to the baggage claim and then to the rental car counter where he picked up the sedan he had reserved for a week. He wasn't disappointed to find a black Toyota Camry had been assigned to him; he liked black cars, and the Camry was better than a Taurus. Those were his two options for a *full-sized* sedan.

After loading his luggage, he plugged the address of the Holiday Inn Express into his phone's GPS, and headed for what he would soon declare to be his southern command post. He arrived within a few minutes, and when he walked through the sliding glass doors, he was greeted by two friendly faces at the counter, one of whom addressed him in an unmistakable southern drawl, saying, "Good evening, sir, how may I help you?"

"Good evening, young lady. I have a reservation for a king, non-smoker. Name's Richard Farris."

The flickering light of her computer screen reflected in her dark round eyes beneath a cloud of natural hair. Her colleague, a white male probably ten years her senior, turned and disappeared into a room behind the counter. After a moment, the clerk looked up and smiled as she asked to see his ID and credit card. Rich opened his wallet to retrieve his driver's license and the American Express he had used to book the room, and as he did, the badge in his wallet was inadvertently displayed.

"Oh, you're an officer?" she asked, sounding surprised.

He saw her name tag and made his reply a personal one, designed to detract from the line of questioning that always followed the question, *are you a cop?* He said, "Yes, Odessa, I am. That's an awful pretty name, by the way. Were you named after that little town in West Texas, by chance?"

Her eyes seemed to brighten the room when she smiled and said, "Well, as a matter of fact, I am. That's where I was born and raised. What about you? You're a long way from home, Mr. Farris—or should I call you, Officer?"

"You can call me Rich."

"Well, Rich, what brings you to Bossier City?"

"Business, Odessa. But I thought this was Shreveport."

"No sir," she said, still smiling—maybe too much, Rich thought, given the twenty year age difference. "This is Bossier City; Shreveport is right over there, across the river, but most people don't know the difference."

Rich turned and looked through the glass doors in the direction she had pointed. "I see."

"I can give you a government rate," she offered, "since you're apparently here on business. What, may I ask, might a detective from Los Angeles be doing all the way down here?"

Rich was caught off guard by her question. He hadn't meant to reveal his badge to her—he certainly hadn't been trying to get a discount on his room—but neither had he expected her to be so inquisitive. His mind raced to come up with a cover story, but he couldn't think of anything on the spot so he just told her the truth. "A family member—my niece—is in some trouble. She's missing and I'm here to see if I can help find her."

Odessa's smile disappeared and she went back to work on the computer without a reply, suddenly all business. Rich found it to be a peculiar response, and he wondered if she knew about Lacy Jane. It was a small town, after all, and the story might've been in the paper. She placed a keycard in a small paper envelope, wrote the number *202* on it, and handed it to him. She said, "Mr. Farris, your room is two-oh-two, and the elevator is right around the corner." She pointed to her left.

Mr. Farris. All professional.

Something about what he had said caused a reaction, and Rich wanted to know why. But the other clerk reappeared, so Rich accepted his room key, thanked her, then picked up his luggage and made his way to his second floor room with a view of the kidney-shaped pool.

RICH SAT ON THE BED IN HIS HOTEL ROOM SEARCHING THROUGH LACY Jane's Facebook page, scouring it for any information or leads, killing time since the sheriff said he could see him tomorrow morning and until then, there was nothing Rich could do. He had thought about calling Cherie, maybe seeing about getting together with her this evening to garner more information, but decided it'd be best to speak with the sheriff first. He was dreading meeting with her in the first place, not knowing how he might be received or if his ex-wife would be around.

He glanced at the clock and saw it was almost seven, and realized he hadn't eaten dinner. Actually, he hadn't eaten since breakfast, what was intended to be his last meal, collected at a drive-through window earlier that day. It seemed like weeks ago, truthfully—or maybe a lifetime ago. Maybe he would go out and get some dinner and a couple drinks. As he thought about where he might go for those things, there was knock at the door. It wasn't heavy like the cops nor the light taps of a timid maid, checking before using a passkey. This was more businesslike, official, but not as if there were a problem. He stood up from the bed and started toward the door, wondering if his credit card had been declined or if they needed to put him in a different room. Rich looked through the peephole to see it was the young lady from the front counter now standing at his door. Rich opened the door and smiled. "Hi, Odessa."

His smile was not returned. She stood silent for a moment.

Rich said, "Can I help you?"

Odessa brushed past Rich, making her way into his room uninvited, and walked directly to the bed and had a seat on the end of it. "Lacy Jane is my friend. That's who you're here for, isn't it?"

Odessa Brown said, "Tanika is nothing but trouble, I knew it from the start. Lacy Jane started running around with her after her mama sent her to that continuation school. That's where they met. Tanika's into dope and she's a trampy little thing, likes to share her cookies all over town, if you follow me."

Rich said, "How do you know Lacy Jane?"

"I knew her through church."

"How close to her were you?"

"We were pretty close until she met Tanika. Then she started avoiding me, probably because she was living a sinful life."

"Sinful?"

She shrugged. "I'm just saying."

"How did you find out she was missing?"

"I heard about it somewhere and then I called her mama, Miss Cherie. She's the one who told me that Tanika was also gone. She had spoken with Tanika's mama, who told her that Lacy Jane had stayed the night before the two of them disappeared, and she hasn't seen either of them since. And Miss Cherie told me that Tanika's mama said that they're probably just out having fun somewhere, that they'll show back up. Not too concerned about it, I guess. But Miss Cherie's sure been worried about it. I can't believe you're her uncle; that's just crazy."

"How old are you, Odessa?"

A moment passed before she answered. "Twenty-one."

Twenty-four years younger than he, Rich quickly calculated. He would have put her a few years older than that, maybe twenty-four, twenty-five, mature and professional dressed in slacks and a blouse and with the appropriate touch of makeup for work. Rich said, "Who knows how we can get in touch with Tanika? I understand Lacy Jane didn't have a cell."

"I've been trying. Miss Cherie has a cell number that Tanika's mama gave her, and she gave it to me. We've both been trying. But when you call, it says the subscriber is not accepting incoming calls. That usually means she hasn't paid for her minutes, just uses her phone with wifi. I've texted her too, but she hasn't replied."

"Where do you suppose they could be?"

She shook her head. "No idea."

He waited as Odessa seemed to be thinking of the possibilities.

She said, "Maybe New Orleans?... Texas? Where *would* they be? Maybe just over there across town, the other side of Shreveport where the gangsters sell dope and act like fools. I have no idea where she could be. But I've got a bad feeling about it."

Rich, standing near where she sat on the end of the bed, reached over and lightly touched her shoulder. "I'll do my best to find her."

Odessa didn't look up when she nodded.

10

The postmortem examination, referred to simply as a "post" by those in the business, was scheduled to begin at 9:30 am according to the text message on Detective Jeremy Cross's cell phone, sent by his lieutenant just after 8:00 am, Monday, the second day of April. Jeremy sat sweating on the edge of his bed in shorts and running shoes as he read the message a second time. He noted the message in his case notebook, the exact time he received the message, who sent it, and what he had been instructed to do. Note everything, he recalled being told on more than a few occasions, and be detailed and accurate; time notations were critical.

His wife had just left the house. She was headed to two different schools to drop off the kids, and then to the gym, and then maybe coffee with girlfriends, she said. The good news was that she would be home when he returned from work tonight, regardless of the time. Home taking care of the kids and household chores and waiting for her hubby to return from a long day of investigating death and fighting crime. He was proud of who he was and what he had achieved, despite the fact that his wife had had higher expectations.

He reflected on when they had met in college, how everything seemed perfect between them. And then after they married, when Jeremy decided he wanted to be a cop, she had frowned and said, "Seriously?" She had said, "Why did you waste your time getting a degree if all you're going to be is a cop?" He remembered her words, saying, "Jeremy, listen... it's not that I won't support you in what you want to do with yourself, but come on, you're not twelve anymore, this isn't playtime or make-believe."

One kid already and another on the way, it had been an inconvenient time to discover this distasteful side of his wife. But life could be funny like that, Jeremy thought, and that was as far as he had gone with those contemplations.

Jeremy got up off the bed and began preparing for his day. As he shaved, he thought about the day ahead of him. He had been around dead people plenty now, mostly natural deaths, a few traffic-related deaths, and others, but standing table-side for an autopsy would be a whole other experience. But it was part of the job, and he'd take it on like every other challenge he'd faced in life: football's hell week, spring training for baseball, finals weeks throughout college, and now an unpleasant marriage that he concealed from his family, his bishop, and even himself at times.

Jeremy noted his forced smile reflected in the mirror, and as with all matters throughout his life, he told himself that God had a plan for him, that he only needed to be true to his church, himself, and his family—in that order. He could feel that a bigger calling awaited him.

He turned up the radio and stepped into a steaming shower.

DETECTIVE STEVE TROY WALKED INTO THE SQUAD ROOM, A SPACIOUS area filled with a dozen or so desks, file cabinets lining the walls. The room was busy at 8:30 on a Monday morning, men and women in slacks and dress shirts, some wearing ties, walking to and from the desks and file cabinets. There was a kitchenette off to one side where a coffeemaker held two pots of supplemental energy for those who did partake. Troy headed straight over and picked up the pot with the brown handle, avoiding the orange-handled one used for decaf. As he filled a mug, Lieutenant Fitzpatrick approached him from behind and placed a hand on the detective's left shoulder.

"You get the message?"

Troy glanced back. "What message is that, Lou?" addressing his lieutenant casually, careful not to show him too much respect.

"Your post is scheduled for nine-thirty. I sent a text out after they called, sent it to both you and Cross."

Troy reflected on his cell phone chiming only twice before it had stopped. He remembered thinking it had been a hang up, still not having the new iPhone quite figured out. Now he remembered that the text messages have a different tone and he should have recognized it as such. He said, "Oh yeah, that message. I thought you meant something else. You bet, we'll be there. Figured I'd stop by for my file and grab a cup before heading over."

"You have an I.D. on your victim yet?"

"Not yet," Steve said, turning now to face his supervisor, a fresh cup steaming between them. "Hoping for something today after the post. Should get prints back and she'll probably be in the system, probably with a couple arrests for prostitution, maybe drugs."

The lieutenant nodded. "Keep me posted."

He watched his lieutenant walk away. He hated Fitzpatrick, the young lieutenant with his perfect blond hair and perfect little wife and three kids. The man had promoted to sergeant after only four years on the job, then to lieutenant three years after that. Much like his current partner, Cross, who had made detective before he had the experience. It was no surprise to Troy, since the both of them were Mormon.

Troy had six years to go, which would give him 34 years on the job on his fifty-fifth birthday, and that would be it. No more bullshit from the brass or the public. No more dealing with pompous lawyers and liberal judges, the two working harder to let criminals back out on the street than the cops worked to put them away. No more waiting till five for a drink and no more Mormon mafia.

It was going to be a long week.

MONDAY AFTERNOON, ELWOOD JOHNSTON WOKE FROM A FEW HOURS OF shuteye in the sleeper of his Peterbilt 379. Normally he slept comfortably, sprawled out diagonally, the bed more than spacious enough even for the big man. But this afternoon, as the truck sat parked on a large flat of gravel somewhere between Winnemucca and Hawthorne, Nevada, Elwood awoke crowded along the back wall of the sleeper cab with the tattooed biker trash asshole on the other side of him. The man lay in the opposite direction, his body blocking the only escape route from the cab, and he slept with a knife clenched in his right hand across his chest.

Elwood sat thinking of ways he could disarm the man, grab his knife and stab him with it, then throw him out on the bare ground in the Nevada desert, leave him on the sand and rocks where he could wait for the spiders and snakes to eat his flesh. Thinking that back in the day, back when Elwood played high school football, middle linebacker, hitting with 230 pounds of solid beef and brawn to put his opponents on the turf, and later when he wrestled steers in small town rodeos throughout the northwest, dropping off galloping horses to twist 500 pound steers into the ground, back in those days, things would have been a lot different. A fit Elwood, a hundred pounds lighter and twenty years younger. Elwood had to admit he was now older, slower, and not in anywhere near the shape he had been back then. And he hadn't been in good shape for quite some time, but he bet he could still use some of that country boy strength to whip this young outlaw, and maybe he'd have to see. Elwood was still running it all through his head when the man looked up and grinned, looking right at him as if he read Elwood's mind.

Elwood said, "I'm starving."

"You're not going to die, fat boy," Buddy said, and then closed his eyes again. After a moment, he said, "But then again, maybe you are. You never know."

Elwood thought of a few things to say in return, things like, *Who are you calling fat boy?*, and *We'll see who's going to die*, and, *Go to hell, punk*, but he held his tongue instead. Then he thought to himself that he'd put up with enough of this smartass and it was about time he did something about it, about time he made a move. He pictured the two of them coming out of the sleeper, this asshole having to go first and then probably watching him closely as he came out behind him, and the punk would probably go to the passenger's seat, and turn to watch him, probably still holding the knife. And Elwood thought, that's when he could make his move, come out of the sleeper like he was coming off a horse and grab that son of a bitch around his skinny neck with one arm while grabbing the hand holding his knife with the other, almost like grabbing a steer around the neck with one arm and its horn with the other to twist him into the dirt. Yeah, twist the little cockroach into the... into... but there wouldn't be room in the cab for all of that action, he realized.

Or maybe he would wait, because surely the dirtbag would have to take a piss before they hit the road again. He'd have Elwood come out first and then he'd crawl down after, still showing that knife—the pussy—and then he'd say, *Have a piss, pops*, or some shit like that. And that's when the little bastard would be vulnerable with his zipper down. There's no man who uses his weak hand to pull down his zipper and handle himself, if he doesn't have to. Elwood remembered an old rodeo buddy, a team roper who had lost his right thumb at a rodeo, the thumb being caught in his rope as he dallied it around the saddle horn while a six-hundred-pound steer ran the opposite direction with the loop of the rope cinched around his head. Elwood remembered the man telling how difficult it was to piss with his left hand, which he had had to do after losing his right thumb, and telling him there were other difficulties as well, private matters he didn't go into too much. The roper had said, "You wouldn't believe how much you need a thumb, until you lose one."

Elwood figured if the outlaw held the knife in his left hand to take a piss with his right, that'd give him a second or two to make his move. Catch the man with his johnson out and whip his scrawny ass for him. Clobber him just once with all of his weight behind a big ol' haymaker, and see just how much fight junior would have left in him after that.

Buddy said, "Pull over right there, pops," and pointed Elwood toward an empty parking lot that held an abandoned motel-casino. They were at the top of the Montgomery Pass in Nevada, a gateway to California that sits more than seven-thousand feet above sea level.

Elwood thought to himself, it's now or never, believing the asshole intended to kill him once they got to wherever they were going—Elwood knew he'd never make it to his planned destination. He eyeballed a small area of debris and parked with the driver's side near it, seeing rocks and boards and other potential weapons that he would try to utilize if the opportunity presented itself. He came to a stop and set his brake, the shrill sound of pressurized air accentuating the process. The convict told Elwood to turn off the truck and to wait right there in his seat, then he jumped down from the passenger's door and hurried around to the driver's door. He was there before Elwood had a chance to look for his Buck knife in the center console.

"Come on out, pops, but do it slowly."

Elwood opened the door and swung around, grabbing the handrail and turning his back to Buddy as he lowered himself from the truck. At the last step, he pushed off and propelled himself toward the convict with his arms stretched out to grab the man as if he were a steer to be twisted into the ground. But the outlaw slipped to the side, and Elwood saw the flash of a blade as it sliced across his forearm. Elwood hit the ground and Buddy came down after him, his knife blade leading the way. Elwood grabbed the convict by his arm and diverted the knife away, while rolling to his side and flipping Buddy off of him.

Elwood scurried to grab a nearby scrap of wood, a 2x4 that was splintered and weathered and had nails protruding from one end. Before he could reach it, the outlaw came down on him, plunging his knife into Elwood's side. His temperature skyrocketed and sweat poured from his body as Buddy stabbed him repeatedly. This was the end, Elwood realized then. He was going to be killed on the top of this mountain, five hundred miles from home. His body wilted and he collapsed in the dirt, an image of Mrs. Johnston fading in his mind.

BUDDY FRANTELLI STOOD ATOP THE MONTGOMERY PASS IN NEVADA, A brisk wind washing over him. It felt good as it cooled the sweat that now dripped from his head and arms and soaked his blue denim shirt. He glanced at the big man on the ground who made gurgling noises, his face planted in the dirt.

"Fuck!" he said, first to the dying man on the ground, and then to the abandoned casino, and then to the truck that stood next to him and hid him from the view of any motorist that might pass by. "Fuck, fuck, fuck!"

After looking around for several minutes, and realizing where he was—out in the middle of no-fucking-place—he realized he had to move, and he had to move quick. He had to think, come up with a plan and get the hell out of there and away from this dead lump of shit. So he climbed into the cab of the Peterbilt and closed the door, looked down once again at Mr. Elwood, this trucker who seemed like a decent guy but maybe a little annoying, and certainly a guy with bad luck—which was something Buddy could relate to—and said, "Look at you now, you big dummy."

AFTER IDENTIFYING THE VICTIM AS LACY JANE LEWIS OF SHREVEPORT, Louisiana, and discovering that she was a reported missing person, and then learning that she was only sixteen and not a prostitute, Detective Steve Troy had nothing to say. In fact, he had tossed the report on his partner's desk and walked out of the squad room without a word, which was fine with Jeremy.

Jeremy picked up the report, a printed copy of the data that had been indexed in the National Crime Information Center database, a law enforcement application referred to as NCIC, which indicated that Lacy Jane Lewis was missing from Shreveport, Louisiana. She was considered a runaway, and it was suspected that she was in the company of another young lady named Tanika Edwards. However, Tanika Edwards wasn't a reported missing person or a runaway because she was eighteen. And when you're eighteen, you can leave or run away or be missing or dead and it's nobody else's business.

Jeremy walked out of the squad room with the report in his hand and found his partner outside having a cigarette, just where he figured the veteran detective would be. He said, "Did you see on here she was supposed to be in the company of another girl?"

Troy squinted at his partner through a puff of exhaled smoke and said, "What's that?"

"The girl, our victim... she's a reported runaway—"

"Yeah I saw that."

"—who was thought to be with this other girl, an eighteen-year-old named Tanika Edwards."

"And?"

"Well, don't you think we should try to find *her*? She might be a witness or have some information about who our victim was with that night."

Troy rolled his eyes, dropped the cigarette butt to the ground near a canister ashtray and smashed it with the toe of his shoe. He said, "No shit, Sherlock. Yeah, we need to find her, that's what I'm out here thinking about. That and we need to decide who's going to notify the next of kin."

BUDDY KNEW FROM ROAD SIGNS AND FROM AN EARLIER CONVERSATION with the dumb trucker who got himself killed, that Bishop was the next town he would come to. But he didn't know that it was fifty miles away. What he did know was that the old man had made driving the rig look pretty easy, yet here Buddy couldn't even figure out how to start the goddamn thing. After thirty minutes of trying to figure it out, and watching as half-a-dozen cars traveled by, Buddy had just about had it. When a passing car slowed as if it were going to turn in, he nearly panicked. If anyone came fifty feet off of the road, they would see Elwood lying dead in the dirt next to the truck and not far from the old casino. He had to get away from the dead trucker, and he concluded he'd never get the damn truck started. He hit the steering wheel with his fist and cursed the truck, then he thought, that fat prick probably has a switch in here or something that he flipped when he got out, just to prevent Buddy from starting it.

Buddy climbed down and kicked Elwood in the side, immediately regretting it as blood spattered his boot and pants leg. Then he cursed the man again and kicked dirt at his cooling body.

He removed a wallet from Elwood's pocket and took the cash that amounted to just over a hundred dollars, and a credit card. He started to take the *Timex*, but saw that the crystal was broken and the hands were frozen. It had stopped at about the same time the trucker's heart had stopped, judging from his last grunt. Buddy dropped Elwood's heavy arm and stepped away from the body. Then he looked around once more, said, "fuck it," and walked out toward the road and headed west into the cool mountaintop wind.

12

Monday afternoon Richard Farris sat across the desk from Sheriff Jonathan Walker, who wore tan pants and a blue uniform shirt, a sheriff's star on the chest and four smaller stars on each epaulet, Caddo Parish Sheriff's Office patches on his sleeves. He was a big man across the shoulders and chest and he was full in the waistline but not a fat man by any means. He appeared strong—corn-fed and hard-work strong—and his eyes showed confidence but also skepticism.

Rich began, "I appreciate you meeting with me, Sheriff. I don't know what I can do to help, but if nothing else, I'd like to be a liaison for the family, keep them in the loop and help them to understand the process. Her mama reached out to me on this."

"Well, son," Sheriff Walker said, "there ain't much process on these here runaway deals. I don't know how y'all do things out there in the land of fruits and nuts, but 'round here, when kids run off and they're damn near of age anyway, there ain't a whole lot we can do about it."

"Sixteen?"

"Hell, boy, there's fifteen-, sixteen-year-olds 'round these parts done started families. She ain't no spring chicken, now."

Rich chewed on the "boy" part for a moment before continuing. He said, "What about the cell phone? My understanding is the other girl, Tanika, has a cell but nobody's getting through to her. Can you at least run a trace on cell sites, see if we can locate her that way?"

The sheriff leaned back and pushed a thick, calloused hand across his forehead and back through a dark head of thick hair. He smiled a little and said, "I don't think you're hearing me, son. We don't run active investigations on runaways down here. She's in the system, and that's the best we can do."

"But if you just ran a check, to maybe see where they are…"

He seemed to frown a bit, and Rich wondered if Walker even understood what he was asking, if he knew that the cellular provider could triangulate cell sites and tell them where the subscriber was generally located. In most cases, it would take a court order, but that wasn't a difficult process either, not for a law enforcement officer with any experience at all. Rich said, "I've written plenty of affidavits for this type of cell search, and I'd be more than happy to help out—"

"You don't have no authority down here, son," the sheriff said, making his point, "not here in this office and not at the courthouse. You're more than welcome to be a liaison for the family, but that's about all I expect from you. You hear me now?"

There was a knock on his door and the sheriff responded in an agitated tone, "Yeah?"

The door was opened slightly and a plump, gray-haired lady stuck her head in, tentatively.

The sheriff said, "Yes, Mary Jo, what is it?"

"You're going to want to take this call, sheriff."

He glanced at the light blinking on his desk phone as Mary Jo disappeared and quietly closed the door behind her.

STEVE TROY WAITED ON HOLD, STARING AT THE MORMON KID WHO SAT in the desk across from him. The kid was starting to piss him off, but

Troy didn't know why. Maybe it was his uptight Mormon bullshit. He didn't cuss, drink, smoke or chase tail—he didn't even talk about tail. Or maybe it was his know-it-all attitude, the kid suggesting shit Troy already had in the works, trying to show off, or maybe just being a pain in the balls. Whatever. Either way, he was tired of the rookie's shit already.

There was a man's voice now on the other end of the line. Troy said, "Yes sir, Steve Troy here, Boise P.D. out in Idaho… how are you today, sir?"

Troy looked down at the papers on his desk as the sheriff replied, saying he'd been better, how could he help him?

Troy said, "Your agency has a missing person, a runaway juvenile by the name of Lacy Jane Lewis."

RICH FARRIS WATCHED CLOSELY AS THE SHERIFF LOOKED UP AT HIM, making eye contact but showing no emotion. The sheriff said into the phone, "Yessir, we do have her as a missing person, put her in the NCIC just a couple days ago."

Rich's eyes narrowed as he studied the sheriff. His ability to read people through their expressions had always been a gift, though sometimes also a curse. The sheriff looked down, away from Rich's watchful eyes. He no longer looked strong or confident; rather, he now appeared solemn, maybe even distraught as he gently rocked his chair, listening carefully. The sheriff nodded and grunted into the phone, "Uh-huh… yeah… yessir… okay, yes… yes, I can take care of that for you." And then he said, "Will I be able to get copies of your reports?"

Rich took in a big breath and held it, closed his eyes and said under his breath, "Damnit."

AFTER PLACING HIS PHONE BACK IN ITS CRADLE, THE SHERIFF LOOKED AT Rich and studied him for a moment. He said, "I'm sorry to tell you this, son, but that was the Boise Poh-lees Department, over there in Idaho, and, well, it seems your niece has been killed."

13

B uddy had put out a thumb the first couple of times a car passed by as he walked along Highway 6 toward Bishop. He could see lights in the distance after he topped the pass and began walking downhill as daylight gave way to dusk. The lights were a ways off but it seemed to be all downhill from here. What the hell, he thought, he was young and fit, and there weren't any other options at this point.

After being passed over by several motorists, it occurred to Buddy that nobody in their right mind was going to pick up a stranger who looked like a convict. Especially if they saw the blood on his hands, his arms, his boots and jeans. Especially at this time of evening when the sun began dropping behind the mountains to the west and darkness was soon to follow. And he also thought that at any time, some do-gooder could stop and check on the rig and find the trucker's fat ass dead on the gravel, and they would call it in. Then some other do-gooder would get stopped at a checkpoint or some goddamn thing and mention that there was a convict walking on the highway.

So Buddy developed a habit of listening for the distant traffic and ducking into the brush until the road was clear again, just to be safe. It wasn't long before he heard a truck winding downhill, the gears holding its weight back from being a runaway on the steep grade, the powerful diesel engine barking and growling as it worked hard to slow the big freighter. He waited until it was necessary, just before the truck would be in view, then ducked twenty feet off the highway and took a seat in the brush near a cluster of rocks. Just as the truck was coming up on him, Buddy caught movement and looked to his right to see a rattlesnake eyeing him malevolently. The snake was coiled in the rocky sand just a few feet from him at the base of the rocks, barely visible as it blended with the terrain. But he heard him, the serpent's tail now buzzing, letting Buddy know he wasn't welcome, that he had sat down in the wrong spot. The truck's lights now washed over the ground where Buddy and the snake were sizing each other up, and Buddy couldn't move. So he said to the snake, in a low and calm voice, "Easy, now, Mr. Rattler... Easy there, big guy..."

The Western Diamondback lashed out and nailed Buddy's arm. At first there was a tingling sensation—not that bad at all, really—but then an intense pain ensued, a fire burning under his skin. He rolled away from the snake as it coiled back and struck at him again, this time nicking his hand.

"FUCK!"

The truck rolled past and Buddy jumped up and yelled again. "Goddamn!" He couldn't believe his bad luck. He could feel his arm swelling, and it throbbed like a son of a bitch.

The rattler was coiled again, but Buddy was out of reach. He took another step back as he watched the snake closely, his new enemy that he would kill and enjoy killing the way he had enjoyed killing the fat trucker who wrecked his whole fucking plan of getting to California without having to walk through the desert at night and get bitten by a goddamn snake. He leaned over slowly and picked up a rock, only glancing quickly to see it was a good sized rock, a little bigger than a softball. But his arm throbbed and he didn't think he could throw it. So he switched it over to his left hand and gave it a try. He missed the snake by three feet and it struck out again. Buddy couldn't believe how close the snake had come to nailing him once more, given the distance he had put between them.

The growl of another truck coming down the hill told Buddy he had to do something quick. The snake had coiled up again, ready for more fight if Buddy had it in him. And he did.

He picked up a stick, about four feet long and as big as his wrist, and he began beating the hissing and striking snake while jumping around to avoid its fangs, yelling and cursing at it while he did. When the snake began to retreat, Buddy pinned its diamond-shaped head to the ground with his stick, and held it there for a long moment as it writhed and rattled. Then Buddy went to work on the son of a bitch with his knife.

———

ODESSA BROWN HAD ARRIVED AT THE HOME OF CHERIE LEWIS LATE that afternoon and caught Cherie and her mama, Florence, and Cherie's Aunty Louisa Farris—she still used Rich's name because that's the name that was on the monthly checks the sheriff's department sent her—starting supper. The house smelled of fried fish and cigarette smoke. The three ladies seemed to be in a great mood, until Odessa told them that Rich Farris was in town.

"The hell's he doing here, anyway?" Louisa asked, first looking at Odessa but then shifting her questioning gaze to her niece, Cherie.

Cherie looked away.

Louisa said, "Tell me you didn't call him about Lacy Jane."

Cherie stood silent in her cutoff jeans and halter top, her gaze directed at her bare feet. Her mom stood nearby in slippers beneath an oversized flowery nightgown with a lot of wear. She was a large lady and found nightwear to be the most comfortable clothing, and she wore it all the time. She stood silent as her sister was now waving a finger at Cherie.

Louisa said, "You did call him, di'n't you? Oh my God, woman, what in the hell do you think an old washed-up womanizing drunk like him is going to do to help us find Lacy Jane? Have y'all got any sense at all?"

Cherie began to answer, but stopped. Odessa turned to follow her gaze through the front screen door toward the street, where a police cruiser had pulled up and parked. Farris and Sheriff Walker exited the vehicle.

Louisa stormed through the modest living room and shoved past Odessa. On the front porch, Louisa pointed her finger and shouted, "That motherfucker ain't comin' up in here! Y'all can jus' turn around now and go on back to wherever it was you picked up that trash."

BUDDY WAS PISSED.

Pissed at the snake, pissed at the trucker coming down the hill whose timing had put him in the bush with the snake, pissed at the dead trucker back there leaking on the gravel and dirt near the abandoned motel-casino because the fat son of a bitch couldn't just go along with the program and give a man a lift to California without trying to be a hero. Pissed and walking down this hill that seemed to get longer with every step, and the faraway town lights he had been able to see during the night as he slept beneath the stars—freezing his goddamn ass off—were now nowhere to be found. He had to come up with a plan to catch a ride, or he'd likely die out here in this godforsaken desert from his hand and arm that were swollen up with snake poison, or from the goddamn heat during the day or the goddamn cold during the night.

Then he stopped dead in his tracks. The pity-party ceased—if only for a moment—as Buddy stared in disbelief at four eyes staring back at him. "The fuck are you doing out here?" he said.

They held their gaze but remained silent.

Buddy said, "I can tell you one thing, you're sure a sight for sore eyes. And feet."

The burros, with their long ears and sad, droopy faces, watched, but they didn't answer.

Buddy looked around. For what, he didn't know. Maybe more burros, maybe riders, or Mexicans herding them around the desert or whatever. He didn't know why they were there or who would have brought them. Then he wondered if they were wild—wild donkeys or burros or whatever the hell it was the Bureau of Land Management called them. There had been efforts to preserve these creatures as a part of history, for the enjoyment of passersby, tourists and motorists and such, or maybe for emergency transportation for a guy in need. Buddy had read about them or had seen a program on the TV, and he recalled now that there were said to be thousands of these creatures roaming around on the vast deserts of government-owned land throughout the northwest. But he never thought he would actually see one, or two, and truthfully it might have never crossed his mind again until these two showed up, right when he needed them most.

As the standoff continued, Buddy began thinking about how to approach them without scaring them off. He wished he'd had a goddamn carrot or something, remembering how the program he saw, or maybe it had been something he read, mentioned that people were feeding the animals, and they shouldn't. The problem was that the burros were now starting to come right up to people, and that was not the best thing for the survival of wild animals. But it was the best thing for Buddy, that was for sure.

But he didn't have a carrot.

Now that Buddy thought about it, he wished he had anything to eat at all, and he sure as hell wouldn't be feeding it to these jackasses. Maybe he'd use something to bring them in close, trick them with the food and capture one to ride, maybe eat the other. Stab the bastard in his throat and skin him out, have him cooking over an open fire in no time. But he didn't have matches. Like a dummy, he had thrown his lighter across the sandy mountain when he discovered his pack of cigarettes was empty. That now pissed him off too. Now he had no way to make a fire to stay warm or to eat a donkey, so he decided it would be best to just figure out how to ride the burro to the next town where he'd stab the first fucker he came across who had a car or a bottle of water or a Snickers bar in his pocket.

DETECTIVES STEVE TROY AND JEREMY CROSS WERE NOT HAVING ANY luck finding Tanika Edwards. Nor did they find anyone who remembered seeing either of the girls leave the bar that night. The bartender remembered Lacy Jane, tapping his finger on the photograph as he said it, because she reminded him a little of Nicki Minaj, or maybe Tyra Banks. "Pretty little thing," he said.

The detectives were canvassing the nightclub near the crime scene, the club that Jeremy had mentioned on Sunday and Troy had scoffed at the idea of it being related to the murder. There were several people who remembered seeing a man that night who stood out from the others. Some had described him as a rough-looking character, uncivilized, and wild-eyed—the dangerous type. A black patron remembered the guy and figured him for a white supremacist type. A white woman in her late twenties said the dude was a pervert, that he rubbed against her ass as he brushed by her. She described him as bald with tattoos on his neck, and when she turned to give him a dirty look, he just grinned. "The guy really creeped me out, so I went over and hung out with Jamal, a friend who plays football at BSU. I didn't say anything to him, but I didn't worry about being felt up anymore either."

When Troy and Cross left the nightclub, Troy said he had to make a call, told him the lieutenant had tried calling while they were inside. They stood outside of Troy's detective car while he called Lieutenant Fitzpatrick. After a brief conversation, Troy said, "Thanks, Lou." He pushed a button and put the cell back in his pocket, then grinned at his partner. "Tanika Edwards just walked into the lobby to report that her friend is missing."

14

After the deadly snake encounter, Buddy had removed his t-shirt, and, using the hunting knife he had bought in Boise, cut thin strips of it to wrap his hand and to tie a tourniquet higher on his arm, almost at the elbow, hoping to stop the flow of poison. Buddy reflected on just how handy the knife had been, several times already. He had used it to persuade a trucker to give him a ride to California, but that didn't work out that well, so eventually he used it to gut the big dummy named Elwood who had tried to attack him, thinking he was smarter and tougher. After that, Buddy had wiped the knife on his jeans to remove the blood and sanitize it, and shortly thereafter he had to use it once again to cut the head off of a rattlesnake and then to skin it out—the goddamn rattlesnake that had bitten him on the arm and hand. Buddy hadn't eaten snake before, but he had heard it wasn't bad, so he ate some of it but it had been difficult to choke down raw.

Now he stood staring at these two donkeys with their sad eyes and big ears, his trusted knife held in his left hand because his right was throbbing with pain. He said, "Nice, donkey," and started inching toward the pair of jackasses that stood watching. He held out his empty hand, wrapped and swollen, and pretended he had something to feed them. The stupid donkeys were falling for it, and Buddy admired his cleverness as he inched even closer. Continuing to say, "Nice donkeys... Here ya go, now, Mr. and Mrs. Jackass."

When he was almost close enough to touch the nearest one, the one more brown than gray, the donkey stretched his neck to put his nose closer to the extended hand that offered nothing to the donkey but the smell of blood and poison. The donkey opened his mouth and let out a loud sound like a foghorn, something that should have never come from an animal, and in the same instant, much faster than Buddy could react, the son of a bitch spun around and kicked at him. The hoof of the goddamn creature that the government should've let die from starvation or thirst struck him on the wrapped and swollen, throbbing hand, and Buddy screamed in pain.

He swiped at the donkey with the knife but the goddamn creature was now hauling ass across the desert with his girlfriend in tow, the two of them braying as they kicked up a cloud of dust.

ODESSA HAD FOLLOWED THE SHERIFF OUT TO HIS CAR SO SHE COULD speak with Rich, who had waited outside. She had tears running down her cheeks and could hear the wailing behind her, Cherie Lewis out of control with grief and sorrow, hurt and anger. Odessa walked straight up to Rich and looked him in the eyes and said, "I'm going with you."

He glanced at the sheriff who now stood by the driver's door, ready to leave. Rich said, "Going where? I'm not going anywhere, honey, other than home. Back to Los Angeles. There's nothing I can do now."

"You're telling me you aren't going to Idaho, Mr. L.A. Detective? You aren't going to go see what happened to your niece and make sure that whoever did this is brought to justice? Is that what you're telling me?"

He didn't respond.

Sheriff Walker said, "Come on, Mr. Farris, we should go."

Rich stepped toward her, his hands held out as if to welcome her for a hug. He said, "Honey, I'm sorry."

Odessa stood her ground, not accepting his embrace. She shook her head, shocked at the news of Lacy Jane's death and now stunned at Rich's disposition on the matter, his apparent indifference to the terrible news.

The sheriff closed his door and started the car. Rich glanced over at him and then turned back to meet Odessa's gaze. "I'm sorry," he said.

She watched silently as he folded himself into the car without looking back.

Tanika Edwards paced the lobby, checking her phone every few seconds and watching through the glass doors as if expecting someone to arrive soon. The two detectives entered through a private back entrance. They walked directly to her, the only person in the lobby.

The shorter, older one said, "Ms. Edwards?"

"Yes," she said, "that's me."

"Follow us," he said, and turned to walk back the way the two detectives had come.

She followed him through the door that the younger, taller, and quite handsome detective held open for her. As she passed him, she asked, "Where are we going?"

The young one said, "Just back to an interview room, somewhere we can talk in private."

She nodded.

When they entered a small room with bare walls and a small table with four chairs around it, the older detective motioned toward a chair and said, "Have a seat, ma'am."

Then he introduced himself as Detective Troy, and nodded toward his partner and said, "This is my trainee, Detective Cross."

The two detectives sat across from her and the older one said, "So you came to report your friend missing?"

She told them the story, not the whole story, but the parts she thought they needed to know: "We were here visiting friends and a couple of nights ago we went clubbing and, well, my friend, Lacy Jane, was doing her own thing, dancing with different guys, having drinks and whatnot, and I lost track of her. When the end of the night came and I couldn't find her, I didn't worry too much because I figured she'd just hooked up, and you know, she'd probably text me later or the next day or whatever from some dude's phone and say come get me.

"I haven't heard from her, and now I'm starting to worry. She doesn't have a cell phone, but she knows how to get ahold of me, and she would have by now if everything was okay. At least I think she would have. Maybe she's mad at me, I don't know. But I'm really starting to worry."

Detective Troy sat listening with his arms folded and a bored expression. When she finished, he said, "Your friend was murdered."

Tanika's jaw dropped and she looked from one detective to another, trying to understand what she had just been told. How could she have been murdered? Here? In Boise? She said, "Where? What happened?" Her eyes overflowed with tears and paintied streaks of mascara down her cheeks. "What do you mean, she's been murdered? How is that possible?"

Detective Troy told her they didn't know much, that they were still investigating, but that Lacy Jane had been found dead behind the club. Then he asked her for details about where they had gone, where they were staying, when they had come to Boise—and why—and where were they staying? Had she talked to anyone in Louisiana since they'd been here? And finally, "Did you see her dancing or hanging out with a white guy, maybe a baldheaded one?"

Tanika Edward's eyes widened and she said, "Oh my God!"

FIVE MINUTES AFTER BEING KICKED BY THE GODDAMN BURRO, BUDDY had lost sight of the dust trail that followed the pair downhill toward the next town, or where Buddy presumed it to be. His hand now hurt worse than anything he'd ever felt, other than the day he'd lost his man virginity to Big John Wilson in the joint. But he didn't ever think about that day, or if he did, he'd deny it to himself. He would never admit it to anyone, ever. As far as he was concerned, it never happened, not the first time or any of the times after. If it hadn't been the shot-caller for the white boys who had made him a bitch, he would have killed the bastard for what he did. But in order to survive in prison among the most heinous, vile, and violent people on earth, there were some things he had to accept and keep to himself. Every convict would eventually have experiences they'd never mention to anyone.

Buddy assessed his current situation and recognized it as a dire one. The sun baked down on his bald head and face and he was nowhere near making it to the next town. He had no water, and he hadn't eaten a thing since having a few bites of fresh raw snake, which had nearly made him vomit. The stupid donkeys were nowhere to be seen, and there didn't seem to be another living thing in this godforsaken country. Nothing could survive this treacherous land, not even a motel-casino that had probably also been a whorehouse.

The fucking desert. This was just Buddy's luck. He'd die out here under the hot sun and freezing nights, and his skin would turn to leather and his bones to dust until the howling winds blew his ashes to Arizona.

For the first time since he'd been released from prison, Buddy wished he were back in the comfort of his cell where it was safe and sane. A place where there was always food and water and he could get medical care when a rattlesnake bit his fucking hand, or when a donkey kicked him, or when he was dying of starvation or thirst or heatstroke during the day or freezing to death at night. Prison wasn't all bad.

RICH HAD PARTED WAYS WITH THE SHERIFF AND DRIVEN BACK TO HIS hotel. He tried to nap but his mind wouldn't allow him to rest as he pondered his next move, if there would be one. There was a knock on the door and it wasn't a friendly one. Rich picked up his pistol from the nightstand and looked through the peephole as he had the day before. It was Odessa again, and she was frowning at the door.

He opened up partway. She pushed the door wide open, brushed past him, and stood near the end of his bed with her hands on her hips. She said, "Come on, *Uncle* Richie, you're going to Idaho to find out who killed Lacy Jane Lewis, and I'm going with you."

Rich looked into her big brown eyes and saw the pain and anger, felt it deep inside him. He had stood before hundreds of grieving friends and siblings and parents of murder victims, and he had never become dulled to the anguish of it. He didn't know Lacy Jane; he had never met her and never heard her name until tragedy fell upon the family. But she *was* family, in a sense, and to that degree he felt a part of the same sorrow he could see in Odessa's eyes. He said, "I'll go see what I can do, see what I can find out and maybe see if I can help. But you're not going with me, Odessa, and that's the final word on that."

15

Rich checked out of the Holiday Inn Express, dropped his rental off at the airport, and walked to the ticketing counter with Odessa at his side. And she wouldn't shut up.

"When my parents moved from Odessa to Shreveport, everyone would ask me about my name. Nobody ever even heard of the town, Odessa, and I would say it's next to Midland, and they'd just look at me with a blank stare, so I'd say it was a cattle town that became an oil town and then it became famous for its *Kiss and Tell Murder* in the sixties, where some guy killed a lady and told the police she had begged him to do it and they let him off because they found him to be insane, if you can believe that. But all of that was before I was even born, and in fact I don't even know that my parents had been born at that time, though I suppose they probably were. There was a movie about it."

They walked away from the counter with checked bags and boarding passes, and started for security.

Odessa still telling her story as they shuffled along: "It was a big deal, that killing, but now there's so much crime in that part of Texas, it's no longer a shock to anyone. We never go back to visit. My mom and dad moved here when I was twelve and my brother was already off to college. Dad had taken a job over there at the W.K."

Rich looked over at her. "The W.K.?"

"Willis-Knighton."

He stopped and said, "The hospital?"

"Uh-huh. You've heard of it?"

Rich remembered the name from doctor's bills he had received after the ex had moved to Louisiana but before they were divorced, when she was still on his medical plan. He never knew why she had been admitted to the hospital because she wouldn't take his calls, but he had done some research and learned it was a cancer center. "Yes, I have," he said. And after a moment he said, "Louisa—my ex—she had some treatments there quite a few years ago."

She said, "Uh huh," and left it at that.

They began walking again. He saw they were closer to security and that the line was short. He said, "What's your dad do at the hospital?"

She looked up at him. "He cures cancer."

When they went through Security, Rich had to use his silver tongue and the brass badge in his pocket to explain that this nice young lady—he called her his niece—had made an honest mistake having a locked-blade knife in her purse. He said, "She's never flown before," and then he whispered to the security man that she was also a little *simple*.

When they settled into their seats—Odessa had taken the window while Rich placed his carry-on overhead—she slugged him in the arm, and it hurt.

He said, "The hell is wrong with you, girl?"

"*Simple?*"

"You'd prefer to get locked up?"

"You didn't have to say I was simple, that's all I'm saying."

Rich looked past her through the oval window to see men and

women in blue jumpsuits with orange vests, helmets and earmuffs, moving about busily below them. Some were driving carts and others were directing the flow of traffic, various vehicles and carts trundling around below the plane.

He said to Odessa, "And I don't even want to think about why you had that knife with you."

Odessa was fishing through her bag, a large canvas carryall with handles like a purse, the LSU logo in block letters across the side. When she pulled a set of headphones from the bag and began untangling the wires, she looked at Rich and said, "It's better to be prepared, *Uncle Richie.*"

"Don't call me that," he said, "I'm not your damn uncle."

TANIKA WALKED OUT OF THE STATION WITH GUILT ON HER SHOULDERS. She had known the bald man from the club was dangerous, and way out of Lacy Jane's realm of adventure. Hell, she was nothing more than a little flirt, still a virgin who talked a big game. Yet Tanika had chosen not to interfere. She hadn't thought much of it really, at the time. She had been busy with the guy she had first met on the internet and had now hooked up with in Boise. He played football at the college, and Tanika thought it could be the start of something good, an athlete with a future and an education to boot. She had gone home with him that night, and had stayed with him ever since. *Tank.* Now she didn't have much choice because she was out of money, and quite honestly, she had no intention of going home. How could she, especially *now*?

She considered calling Cherie Lewis, Lacy Jane's mama, but the detectives had told her that she had already been notified of her daughter's death by the local sheriff. Tanika knew she would be blamed for Lacy Jane being killed. This was all too much to handle sober. In fact, life was too much to handle sober. But she had no money.

So when Tanika got back to the apartment of Maurice Sherman, the middle linebacker for the university who went by "Tank," she touched up her makeup and did her hair, and after putting on the appropriate clothing, she started what turned out to be an hour-long selfie session until she was happy with a couple of fairly seductive poses. Then she placed an ad on *Craigslist* advertising escort services and erotic massages. And she waited.

———

LATER THAT EVENING DETECTIVES STEVE TROY AND JEREMY CROSS returned to the lobby to take another missing person report. When the lieutenant had stepped out of his office and told the two to handle it, Troy said, to no one in particular, "The fuck's going on around here?"

Jeremy did a mental eye-roll at his partner's comment and demeanor and thought to himself, how long can I deal with this guy?

They met the woman in the lobby and Detective Troy introduced himself, ignoring his partner, and asked how he could help. Jeremy stood in the room, no more or less important than the plastic chairs that lined one wall or the mirrored glass built into another. He noticed the badly worn tennis shoes beneath old pants and the sloppy top on the woman who stood there with mussed gray hair and worry on her face.

She said, "Something's happened to Elwood."

They went back into the same interview room where earlier that day they had spent a half-hour with Tanika Edwards hearing about the two adventurous young ladies who had come from Louisiana to have a good time, and one ended up dead. As they settled into their seats, Jeremy wondered if this would be a similar situation, and he thought to himself, this is the most interesting work a cop can do, being a detective. And he was grateful for being out of uniform and done with handling family disturbances and drunken patrons.

Steve Troy looked at the woman with his bored, tired face, and said, "So *who* exactly is this *Elwood*?"

Carolina Johnston said, "Well, he's my husband of thirty-two years, last June. His name's Elwood Lee Johnston, and he drives truck."

Troy said, "He *drives truck?*"

"That's what he does for a living."

"Drives *a* truck."

"Drives truck."

Jeremy paused from his note taking and glanced over to see his partner roll his eyes.

Mrs. Johnston said she'd been worried but didn't know what to do. She said, "He hauls hay down to California. He left yesterday and I ain't heard from him."

Troy asked, "Is that unusual?"

"No, it's what he usually does. He also hauls cattle, and he has different trailers for that, but no it ain't unusual at all."

Steve Troy was impatient with her, which didn't surprise Jeremy. He said, "I'm not asking you about what he hauls, I'm asking whether or not it's unusual not to hear from him."

"Oh," she said, and seemed to retreat a little after being chastised by Troy. "I'm sorry, I didn't understand your question."

Troy tapped his pen on the table and leaned back in his chair and waited.

After a moment of uncomfortable silence, she continued: "Elwood don't have a phone, and he don't want one neither, says he don't need one cause he's got the CB radio plus what other drivers tell him them phones don't work half the time anyhow, not where they drive 'cross the deserts. But what he usually does is he leaves here in the afternoon or early evenin' cause he likes to drive all night. He fills his rig up right over here at the Flying J, and that'll get him all the way to California without refueling, even if he leaves her running while he sleeps. So he don't usually go anywheres they have a phone until he gets to where he's going. He'll stop in the middle of the desert to sleep and then maybe again somewheres along the road for a snack or some coffee. But he takes food and pop and some water with him and he don't very often go around where a lot of them other truckers go and congregate theirselves together and whatnot."

Jeremy asked, "Who's he drive for?"

Troy shot him a look of contempt.

She said, "He's independent. You know, owns his own rig and drives for whoever hires him, different ones. Well, he don't own it, you know, we make payments like you do for your house and whatnot."

Detective Troy to his partner: "What the hell would that matter?"

Jeremy Cross said to him, "Well, a lot of companies have GPS trackers on their rigs. I was just thinking—"

"Well there was your problem, you were thinking again. How about you let me finish asking the lady questions related to her missing husband, and then when I'm done, if you want to chitchat about who he works for and other unrelated shit like that, you just feel free to do so. But you can do it on your own time."

Jeremy's jaw tightened as he stared at Troy, seeing himself knocking the jerk out of his chair and then sitting on his chest, punching him in the face. He had done it once to a kid named Doug Rodriguez who had bullied him one time too many in junior high. Jeremy looked away from his partner and back at Carolina who also sat frowning, staring at Detective Troy until she looked over at Jeremy. Then her eyes softened and she showed a slight smile, maybe one of condolences for what Jeremy had to tolerate from this other detective. Though aside from a slight smile and compassionate eyes, Jeremy still saw the worry she had about her husband of thirty-two years who had gone missing.

She said, "Maybe he's had a wreck, went off the side of the mountain over there in Oregon, down by Rome or while going through Jordan Valley. How would I ever know?"

Jeremy had a bad feeling about the missing trucker, but didn't say so. Although she addressed him with her last question, he deferred to his partner as a way of self-preservation. He looked at him and waited.

Troy said, "We'll make some calls, check with the state police to see if there's been any accidents. Outside a that, there's not a lot we can do." Then he stood and looked over at Jeremy. "Give her your card, would ya? That way she can call *you* if she has any questions."

Jeremy and Mrs. Johnston both stood, and Jeremy reached across the small table and handed her his business card. They walked out together without either of them speaking another word.

16

He couldn't believe there was water in the middle of the desert, a steady trickle coming straight out of the side of a hill through a formation of rocks. He recognized it to be a fresh spring and knew it would be safe to drink from, and so he did. Buddy sat and drank until his belly was full, and then he sloshed the cool spring water over his body and it felt good. After a few minutes of enjoying the refreshment, he unwrapped his throbbing hand and arm and saw that both were now purple and black and green, and oozing puss where the fangs had punctured his skin. Two holes right through the dagger that decorated his right arm with a banner wrapped around it twice and the words *Peckerwood by Birth* and *Outlaw by Choice*. It was a tattoo that had been inked by his *cellie* who went by the name *Angel Charlie*, who had been able to get some red ink inside through a dirty cop, so he tattooed a little blood dripping from the bottom of the dagger's blade. Now there was blood that hadn't been tattooed by Angel Charlie and it was dried and crusted against the dying skin, and Buddy thought about how awful his luck seemed to be ever since he got out of the joint.

He leaned against the rock and let the cold water run over his throbbing hand and arm, and then closed his eyes and went to sleep.

He slept soundly, not knowing that Bishop was only another eight miles down the hill and that between here and there were several ranches with food and water and old men who carried rifles in their pickups.

Buddy also didn't know that a Nevada State Trooper had stretched yellow tape across the parking lot of the abandoned motel-casino atop the Montgomery Pass, after finding the stiffening remains of Elwood Johnston, a big man whom a preacher would later describe—to a small group of friends gathered beneath a popup canopy—as a good and decent man who had lived an honorable and peaceful life. Peaceful until the end.

By the time Rich and Odessa changed planes in Seattle, had lunch during their layover, and then boarded their next plane, Rich had learned just about everything he imagined he would ever need to know about Odessa Brown: her brother graduated from Louisiana State University where he had attended on a full-ride scholarship to play baseball for the Tigers. She had started her education there also, having earned an academic scholarship, and she had planned to go to the School of Medicine, following in her father's footsteps. But she found that biology—a subject she had enjoyed in high school—was very different and much more challenging in college, and she no longer enjoyed it. At all. She also had wanted to be back in Shreveport where she had originally promised her parents she would work to enter the LSU School of Medicine, but instead she shocked them with a declaration that she had been called into the ministry.

Rich said, *"Called into?"*

"Yes, called into."

So, she left LSU after two years and now attended the Louisiana Baptist University and Seminary in Shreveport where she lived with her parents so she could save the money she earned working at the hotel. She explained that after getting her Bachelor of Arts, she would continue on to pursue a Master of Theological Studies. She wasn't sure if she wanted to be the pastor of a church, or go into the prison ministries.

"Jesus Christ," Rich said, and then flinched when she balled up her fist again.

He said, "I mean... well, I don't know what I mean. My view of prison and inmates and jailhouse religion would probably be about as welcomed as one of politics."

"How do you know I'm not a conservative?" she asked.

"Well how do you know I'm not a liberal?"

Odessa rolled her eyes and said, "Really, Rich?"

After they deplaned in Boise, they picked up a rental car and drove downtown where they checked into a hotel not far from the airport. Neither had been to Idaho before and both were surprised to see how pretty the city was with the surrounding mountains that still held snow on the high peaks and a river that ran right through the center of downtown and wasn't muddy.

They went inside, and Rich asked for two rooms. He thought, if he were only twenty years younger, or if she were ten years older... He was thinking that and looking at her flawless skin and bright eyes when she said to the clerk, "If you have something adjoining, that would be preferable. And if there's anything with a view of the river, or the mountains, that would be marvelous."

They walked away from the counter with Rich thinking, she *is* ten years older... ten years older than her age in maturity and intelligence and... well, he left it there, and for a moment he felt ashamed for his thoughts. But he found himself attracted to her, and it had started when he first saw her at the hotel in Bossier City. He really enjoyed her company, and for the first time in a long while, he felt as if he wasn't alone.

JEREMY TOOK THE CALL BECAUSE HIS PARTNER WAS OUTSIDE HAVING A smoke. He listened as the cop from Los Angeles explained his relationship to the decedent, and told him that he happened to have some time off work and he and his—well, actually, a friend of Lacy Jane's, had come to Boise with the intention of liaising with the family. He also thought he'd see if there was any way he could help, without getting in the way of their investigation, of course. Jeremy said he would be happy to meet the detective and his companion, and gave them directions to their office.

When Steve Troy came back and learned of the meeting his partner had set up, which would take place in about thirty minutes, he acted as if he were going to have a stroke. "Are you fucking kidding me, Cross? You told this L.A. cop to come on down and show us how to do our job, like we need his fucking help?"

Jeremy tugged at his tie and said, "They're family of our victim. Wouldn't it be customary to meet with the family?"

Troy threw a file folder from six feet away that landed on Jeremy's desk, the contents of which scattered across it, some of it spilling onto the floor. His voice raised, he said, "When you're done sucking up to Mr. Bigshot from the city, you can start working on this file. It's a simple assault. See if you can figure it out without bringing in help from the outside. For Christ's sake, I'm surprised you haven't called the fucking FBI."

Lt. Fitzpatrick yelled from his office door, "Troy, in my office, now!"

Detective Troy's jaw tightened and his face became red, and he glared at his partner as he began slowly moving that direction. He said in a low voice, "You're on thin ice with me, Cross."

WHEN RICH AND ODESSA ARRIVED IN THE LOBBY THIRTY MINUTES later, Jeremy Cross came out to meet them and introduced himself, saying, "I'm Detective Cross, we spoke on the phone."

Farris offered his hand. "I'm Rich, this is Odessa."

Jeremy was immediately struck by Rich Farris, a man who projected strength and knowledge through a simple gaze. His eyes didn't intimidate; rather, there was a depth to them that seemed to harbor the thoughts of a sagacious man. Jeremy felt as if Farris could read his very thoughts. His companion, Odessa, warmed the room with her bright eyes and easy smile.

He invited them into the back, and for the third time in a day and a half, took a seat at the table with his guests. This time, his partner wasn't present. Jeremy placed a file on the table, looked at Odessa who sat poised and serious, and then into the eyes of the L.A. detective. Jeremy felt nervous but was determined not to show it. He said, "First, I want to tell you how sorry I am for your loss."

They each thanked him.

He then briefed them on what he knew so far about the case: "Tanika Edwards and Lacy Jane Lewis drove here from Shreveport, Louisiana, arriving the thirtieth day of March. Tanika had met a man online who plays ball for the university, and he had talked her into coming out to meet him in person. She talked Lacy Jane into coming with her. According to Tanika, Lacy Jane wasn't very happy at home—typical teenage girl stuff.

"Tanika is currently staying with this ball player, a guy named Maurice Sherman, also known as 'Tank.' He's a middle linebacker for BSU, and he lives in an apartment near the campus. I can provide you with his address if you would like to meet with her.

"Saturday night, that would be the thirty-first of March, the two girls went out. They ended up at a nightclub right here on the edge of downtown, a place that can be a little wild on the weekends. It's a hotspot for the college kids, including some of the football players, and at times it can draw quite an interesting mix, including bikers and cowboys. This Tank guy was there to meet Tanika, as planned, and she ended up hanging with him all night and lost track of her friend. We found a few people—the bartender, a waitress, and a couple of patrons—who remembered seeing Lacy Jane, and said she was hanging out with a rough-looking white guy."

Odessa huffed and shook her head.

"He's been described as a bald-headed guy with tattoos, and one of the witnesses said he looked like a white supremacist."

Odessa said, "What on earth was she thinking?"

Rich reached over and placed a hand on her arm, apparently trying to comfort her. She glanced at him and then refocused on Jeremy, waiting for more.

He continued, "She was found in the alley, but not until almost dawn. Nobody saw her as they were leaving the club that night, which is likely because at the other side of the building, out on the street, there had been a traffic accident with injuries, and that became a spectacle for most of the patrons of the club. The cops were out there along with fire and an ambulance, so it was sort of a big attraction. It's likely that the murder happened at about the same time, or maybe a little before, but of course we couldn't know with any certainty, not at this point. Her body was found early the next morning by someone out for a walk."

Jeremy studied each of them for a moment, and after assessing the situation, and giving careful thought to how much he should say, and how it should be said, he finally explained, "She was strangled. Manual strangulation, likely by bare hands."

Odessa seemed to be trying to hold back her emotions, but it was of no use; tears began rolling down her cheeks. Jeremy waited while she composed herself, taking a tissue from her purse and dabbing at the corners of her eyes. She looked at him and said, "I'm sorry. Go ahead, please."

"We haven't had much information to work with, so that's about all we have for the time being. I would like to canvass the nightclub again this Saturday night, talk to the regulars, and also have a look around for this white boy with the tattoos."

Rich, still watching Jeremy very intently, finally spoke. "He won't be there."

Jeremy nodded. "I don't think so either, but it's something I figure needs to be done. If I didn't at least try, someone would ask why I hadn't at some point."

"You're right about that, Detective."

Jeremy said, "We checked for surveillance video, but there isn't any outside the location. The nearest traffic camera is a block away, and there was nothing of interest there. Of course, what would we look for?"

Rich thought for a minute, and shrugged.

"Our best hope is forensics, at this point. We hope they come up with something from the trace evidence, maybe DNA."

Rich said, "This isn't your first rodeo, is it?"

He chuckled and said, "Actually, it is. First homicide case since I made detective a few months ago."

"Well, you have an intuition for this type of work. I can see that. Do you have a partner?"

"Yes, Steve Troy. He's breaking me in, what you'd call a training officer I guess, for detectives."

"Where is he?"

Jeremy raised his brows and said, "I'm not sure."

Rich seemed to ponder the answer for a moment. Then he stood and said, "If you need any help, I would be more than happy—in fact I'd be honored—to lend a hand. I won't get in your way, and I'm not here to tell anyone how to do their job, like some know-it-all from the city. I'm sure you guys know what you're doing here. But I'd really like to see this case solved, and if I can offer any help, it would be my pleasure to do so."

Jeremy said, "Thank you, Detective, I appreciate that. I'm sure I'll be in touch."

The three of them walked out of the room, through the lobby, and outside into a beautiful spring day. Rich and Jeremy shook hands before they started in separate directions.

Jeremy said, "Detective Farris?"

He stopped and turned to face him. "Please, call me 'Rich.'"

"I'm just curious, how many of these cases have you handled? Homicides that is."

"No idea."

The answer stunned him. He grinned a little and said, "Really, you have no idea?"

Rich shook his head. "More than a hundred, I know that. A guy gets to the point where he doesn't want to remember."

1 7

Nancy Cross bustled through her kitchen, having separate conversations with each of her three children while unpacking and cleaning lunch boxes and preparing dinner. She glanced toward the doorway to see her husband walk in, a smile across his face. It was the first time she had seen him come home in a good mood in weeks.

He said, "Hi honey, what's for supper?"

She stopped for a second and surveyed the room, making sure all kids were accounted for and nothing was on fire before answering. "Chicken."

Even that couldn't dampen his mood. He said, "Guess what happened at work today?"

Nancy directed her four-year-old through the kitchen with a hand on the back of his head, saying, "Out, out, out." Then she turned to her husband, sighed, and said, "Tell me."

"Lieutenant benched my partner."

"Steve?"

"Yeah, can you believe it?"

She leaned against the counter after tossing a towel to the side and glancing at the timer on her stove. This actually was interesting, unlike most of what he told her about his work, which was mainly complaining about his partner, lately. She said, "What'd he do?"

"Same thing he always does, only this time Fitzpatrick overheard him cussing me, and saw him throw a file folder at me too. Well, not at me, but at my desk. He flung it from twenty feet away."

"Good. I hope they fire him, the jerk."

"Apparently, Lieutenant Fitzpatrick had just handled a complaint about him before it happened."

"Oh?"

"Yeah, about the way he treated a woman who came in to report her husband missing. She complained about how he spoke to her and also how he treated me in front of her. She said she was real disappointed."

"Good riddance."

"They won't fire him, at least I don't think they will. But apparently, the LT sat him down to discuss the complaint and also brought up what he has seen, how Steve treats me and other detectives, and Steve didn't handle it right."

"How do you know all this?"

"Lieutenant Fitzpatrick told me."

She glanced toward the living room at the sounds of squabbling kids, though she couldn't see them from where she stood. She said, "Why would he tell you that?"

"I don't know, maybe just to explain why my partner would be benched. He told me to go ahead and interview the relatives—some family of our victim came up from Louisiana—and said to follow up on whatever leads we have on the case. He said to just ask him or one of the other detectives if I need any guidance."

Nancy thought, *because your job is just so complex.*

He said, "That's not even the best part."

Nancy listened while moving to the threshold of the living room to check on the kids who were suddenly too quiet. She saw that they were huddled on the floor, playing harmlessly. She walked back to the stove, where she pulled the chicken from the oven and turned two burners off. She grabbed plates and silverware from the cupboards and drawers and yelled to the kids to get washed up. She nodded to her husband who continued telling his story and said, "Can you make the drinks?"

Jeremy grabbed a gallon of milk from the refrigerator and a stack of cups from a cupboard. He said, "So the uncle of this girl who was killed, Lacy Jane, he's a homicide detective in Los Angeles—"

"Yeah?"

"—and it's weird, and you may not understand this, but I look into his eyes, and it's mesmerizing. There's something about this guy, like you can tell by just looking at him that he has this wealth of knowledge, like he's seen more and done more than anyone ever should, maybe more than most ever have, as far as death investigation. And it's not like a thousand-yard stare, either, you know, like they say the crazy guys get. It's more like a thousand-mile-deep sea of knowledge. But he's also charismatic, if that makes sense. That's the best way I can put it, but I don't want to sound gay about it."

She said, "Too late."

"Real nice."

"Can we finish this later?"

"One more thing real quick—"

She turned and shouted toward all areas beyond the kitchen, "Kids, let's go!"

"—after our meeting, when I briefed him on the case and told him some of my thoughts as far as direction of the case, and so forth, he said to me, something like, 'This isn't your first rodeo, is it?', and basically gave me the idea he thought I was doing a good job. How crazy is that? I told him, well, actually, yes, this was my first murder case, and that I've only been a detective for a few months. He said, 'Well, kid, you've got a good intuition for this type of work.' "

"He called you kid?"

"No, not kid. I don't know, I don't remember… it's not even the point. You're missing the whole point here."

Nancy forced a smile and began ushering the kids into their seats. Then she took a seat at the opposite end of the table from her husband.

She was fussing with her daughter's hair, pushing it behind her ear for her when she said without making eye contact, "Will you say the blessing, Jeremy?"

As the sun began to set beyond the range of jagged mountains to the west, Buddy rewrapped his hand and arm and headed downhill with a belly full of water and a powerful hunger. He wished he'd had a canteen, or a bottle, or something else he could fill with water, but he didn't. Which was just his luck. He shrugged at the thought of it, and then, addressing the sage and sand and faraway lights and even farther away mountains, he said, "It's do or die now, bitches."

Rich and Odessa were discussing what they wanted to eat. Odessa said, "Something with some local culture, not Outback or Olive Garden, or any of those other types of places you can find just about anywhere."

Rich said, "You have any ideas? How would we find out about the *local culture* around here? Should I stop and ask someone, or call that detective, or what?"

They were standing in the hallway outside of her room, about to go their separate ways so they could both settle in and freshen up before dinner. Odessa said, "We can ask the clerk downstairs. I *always* have good recommendations for out-of-town guests back home; it's what competent hotel staff do. There's more to that job than checking people in and handing out keys. Also, I could do a Google search on my phone. Either way."

Rich shrugged and said, "I'll drive, and I'll buy, but that's as much as I'm willing to do. The rest is on you."

She smiled and turned to open her door. Rich walked away, hearing her door open and close behind him. He unlocked his own door and walked in, glancing at a second door, the one that separated their rooms. It was locked, of course, but he pictured her behind it. He saw her walking through the room, maybe already searching for places to eat on her phone, maybe having a seat on the bed and calling downstairs to ask about the *local culture*. Then he saw her glance at the door also, before walking into the bathroom and closing that door behind her. That's what he saw in his head as he walked into his own bathroom and looked at the man in the mirror who was too old to be having those thoughts about that girl.

AT SEVEN, ODESSA KNOCKED ON THE DOOR BETWEEN THE TWO ROOMS and waited. Rich opened his door, bare chested. She looked at him for a long moment, trying to maintain eye contact, and then she stepped past him and into his room. She looked around and settled her gaze on the view of the mountains outside. "You're not ready?"

From her peripheral vision, she could see him moving through the room, and she glanced over to see him pull a blue- and yellow-checked button-up shirt from a hanger. She turned away as he slipped it on, but she could feel his eyes on her. "I am now."

Odessa turned to face him as he buttoned his shirt, the image of his bare chest and solid shoulders remaining in her mind. He was fairly muscular for his age, which she assumed to be mid-forties. His mid-section wasn't too flabby either, especially for someone who probably drank a bit. Or a lot. She didn't know, but she had an idea of how a single man from the big city might behave. But maybe she shouldn't stereotype, she thought.

The two stood facing each other for an awkward moment until Rich said, "Did you figure out where to eat?"

She held up her phone. "A place we can walk to from here, so wear comfy shoes."

He glanced down at his chukka boots. "I think I'm good, unless we're crossing any rivers."

She smiled and turned toward the door, and the two walked silently through the long narrow hotel hallway. She led them into the stairwell, mentioning that she didn't like elevators, and he followed without comment. Finally they stepped outside into a perfect evening as the sun dropped slowly beyond the buildings and trees to the west, and the city came to life. There were lights and music and the cozy sounds of chatter and laughter as people gathered in and around the various clubs and restaurants and street vendors and entertainers. It was the friendliest-feeling city she had ever experienced.

18

As the full moon hung over the Rocky Mountains, Jeremy and Nancy finished bathing the kids and put them to bed. Then they retired to the living room where Nancy read a romance novel and Jeremy watched baseball with the volume low, per her request.

STEVE TROY BORED A BARTENDER TO DEATH WITH HIS PISSING AND moaning while he sat at the bar at Sheehy's, a little Irish pub where cops used to drink back when cops drank and didn't hurry home to their pretty little wives and perfect families.

TWO BLOCKS AWAY RICH AND ODESSA SMILED INTO EACH OTHER'S EYES and felt euphoric on the patio of an 8th Street bar and grill, where friendly people gathered to dine and drink and dance to sidewalk musicians on a perfect spring evening.

JUST OUTSIDE OF DOWNTOWN, TANIKA EDWARDS STARED AT THE ceiling, thinking about her first trick earlier that afternoon, and coming to terms with being a whore. Tank was on top of her, holding her arms down as he parted her silky-smooth legs and had his way with her savagely, but only for a couple of minutes.

BIG JOHN WILSON STOOD NAKED AND HANDCUFFED ON THE CONCRETE walk outside his cell at the Idaho State Penitentiary while two guards searched his bunk and personal property for evidence related to the stabbing of a white boy they called Eddie the Rat, an informant to the guards.

TO THE WEST, THE COPS WERE REMOVING YELLOW CRIME SCENE TAPE from the parking lot of an abandoned Nevada motel-casino, as the coroner carted away the remains of Elwood Johnston.

THE SAME MOON LIGHTED THE SKIES SOUTH AND EAST, AND ABOVE Jonathan Walker's five acres of tall Louisiana grass. The sheriff sat on his porch sipping moonshine, thinking about the charismatic cop from Los Angeles with his provocative eyes, and the dead girl, whose disappearance the L.A. cop had come to investigate. She had been just another runaway, after all, and it wasn't the sheriff's doing that got her killed. He took another sip and watched his cows graze with newborn calves at their sides, a testament to the cycle of life.

AND ON THE OTHER SIDE OF THE RED RIVER, CHERIE LEWIS AND HER sister, Louisa Farris, drank gin and grapefruit juice as they mourned the loss of the beautiful and vivacious Lacy Jane Lewis. They had no idea that the plane buzzing overhead was an American Airlines cargo jet bringing home the remains of their precious loved one.

19

S ix years earlier, almost to the day, Travis and Katrina Jacobson retired from their civil service careers in Los Angeles and bought a ten-acre spread outside of Bishop, north on Highway 6 where it was peaceful and they had room for their horses and goats and dogs and cats. Travis had bought a Dodge pickup that had four-wheel drive for the winter, and he put a flatbed on the back for hauling hay or horse trailers or his gooseneck camping trailer which he grudgingly used to take the wife back to the big city to spend time with the grandkids. Having been a cop in L.A., he hated returning. Having been a nurse, Kat—as she was called by family and friends—never could fill her need for nurturing, and the grand-babies were always pulling her back.

When they did leave for the week, for however long they'd be gone, the girl next door—which was actually a half-mile away—would come over to feed and water the animals and keep an eye on every-thing. They knew they could depend on the born-and-raised country girl who could buck hay side-by-side with the boys and shoot pistols and rifles, and who had killed her share of game and predators in her fifteen years. They paid her twenty-five bucks a day and she was welcome to stay there if her parents didn't mind. Her name was Samantha Wright but everyone called her Sam.

Everyone other than Dusty McBride, that is, who was sweet on her and called her Sammie, or Sammie Jo. He came around as often as he could, and even more when she housesat for the Jacobsons. He was seventeen and drove an old flatbed Ford pickup that he had been driving since he was twelve. That was when his father gave it to him so he'd have his own ranch truck, something to drive across their two-hundred acres of hay and pastures and down to the neighbors when need be, delivering hay or helping with chores or just to visit. Wherever Dusty went, so did his blue heeler he called "Blue." Her spot was on the flatbed where she'd roam from side to side, drinking in the gusts of wind and taking in the sights. When Dusty would start toward the truck, she'd *load up* without waiting to hear him give the command. Then she'd stay on the bed of that truck come hell or high water, waiting for him and watching for him to come back to the truck no matter where he had stopped. She'd sit there until the cows came home or until Dusty would say, "Okay."

When Dusty finished helping Sam feed and muck stalls at the Jacobson place this morning, the two of them stood near the corrals enjoying the morning sun and visiting while the horses chomped their hay and their tails swooshed at flies. Sam told him that Mr. and Mrs. Jacobson wouldn't be coming home until tomorrow morning, and she thought maybe she'd stay the night on their property. She asked if he thought maybe he'd want to come back tonight, that they could go for a ride or cook something on an open fire in the pit, and sit out under the stars.

He said, "Yes ma'am, you bet I would."

She watched as he wiggled into his long-sleeved western shirt, her gaze roaming his lean and muscular build, tanned and now wet with perspiration. He snapped up his shirt and tucked it into his jeans behind a silver buckle that had a bronc and a banner that read *California Circuit High School Rodeo Champion*. He barely whispered "load up" to the heeler who stood at his side and stared at him with adoring eyes, waiting for instruction. Blue jumped onto the bed of the truck and stood wagging her butt that had no tail.

———————

DUSTY MCBRIDE WATCHED HIS DREAM GIRL WALK AWAY, BACK TOWARD the barn. Her jeans were tight and long and their dusty legs bunched up against her spurs. He couldn't be sure, but it seemed she might have been wiggling her cute butt a little more than usual. Blue stood on the bed of the truck, wiggling hers too.

He sped down the half-mile dirt road with his windows down and his country music turned up loud, a cloud of dust rising behind him and drifting across the morning sky. When he reached the highway, he turned left and headed toward town, where his cousin who worked at a market could supply him with beer for tonight.

———————

BUDDY HAD MADE IT ALMOST ALL THE WAY TO THE LIGHTS JUST AS THE dawn allowed him to see the activity below, maybe just a half-mile away now. It seemed busy. There were dogs running around, barking, horses neighing and goats bleating, and there were a couple of people with cowboy hats milling about, maybe doing their morning chores. He had stopped to settle his throbbing hand and arm, and now sat on a rock in the shade of a juniper. His hunger had passed, or maybe his mind had disconnected that signal, but he was thirsty again and would no doubt need water as the day warmed up under the big desert sky.

Then he saw one of the cowboys leave in a truck. He thought maybe he shouldn't wait, thinking he had only seen the two so far. But not long after, the other cowboy was mounted on a horse and loping circles in a corral. So he decided it would be best to wait until at least that was over, having the good instinct to not take on a man who was mounted on a horse.

Buddy would wait. Sit in the shade and observe the activity below and come up with a plan. He would be patient, and think it through carefully, knowing he was at a significant disadvantage without the use of his strong hand and arm. He also knew that ranchers were tougher men than those in the city. They worked hard every day with their hands and their bodies and most were handy with firearms too. He would need a good plan to be perfectly executed, and that would take patience.

LIEUTENANT FITZPATRICK HAD PLACED A CALL ON HOLD AND STEPPED out of his office to find Jeremy Cross sitting at his desk. He said, "Cross, my office."

When the young detective came in, Fitzpatrick asked him to close the door and have a seat. "You're going to want to hear this."

The lieutenant, his white shirt crisp and his gold cufflinks polished, pushed a button and said to the phone that sat on his desk, "Okay, Detective Cross is here with me now, would you mind starting over from the beginning?"

JEREMY LISTENED AS THE WOMAN'S VOICE OVER THE SPEAKER SAID, "Okay, you bet... So my name is Sylvia Cordova and I'm a supervising agent with state parole. We just had a call from a Nevada State Trooper, a Detective Miller, who is looking at one of our recent parolees as a possible suspect in a murder case. The parolee's name is Buddy Frantelli, and it so happens he was a *parolee at large* because he didn't fulfill the mandatory check-in that's required within forty-eight hours of a prisoner's release. We've put a warrant for his arrest into the system due to the violation."

Jeremy shifted his eyes from the phone to the face of his lieutenant as Fitzpatrick said to the woman on the speaker, "So how does this connect to us?"

She said, "His mother lives in Boise, so I thought you'd better know. I know the detective I spoke with from Nevada said he'd be calling you at some point today to ask for some help. I told him I'd give you a heads up."

As the lieutenant started to say goodbye, Jeremy spoke up: "Excuse me."

Fitzpatrick nodded and said, "Go ahead."

"Ma'am, this is Detective Jeremy Cross. Do you happen to know where in Nevada this murder occurred?"

She said, "Almost in California, some deserted town near Bishop."

"Highway six?"

"Yes, as a matter of fact, that's what he said."

"Do we know who was killed, or any other circumstances of the murder?"

"I don't," she said, "other than that the victim was a truck driver. Apparently they lifted a print from the driver's door that came back to Frantelli."

Jeremy locked eyes with Fitzpatrick, but could see he hadn't connected the dots. He said with intensity in his voice, "Our missing person, Johnston, he was a truck driver."

The call ended and the two of them sat in the office with the door closed, the lieutenant chewing on the end of a pen. Jeremy said, "This Frantelli guy gets out of the joint but doesn't check in. His mother lives here yet he's headed to California, and he kills a truck driver along the way. Or at least one would have to assume it was he who did it, his prints having been lifted from the truck."

"Yeah, and?..."

"Well, our missing person, the trucker, Elwood Johnston, had filled up at the Flying J, according to his wife. That's not far from our crime scene."

"The girl?"

"Yeah, the murder case, Lacy Jane Lewis. She was seen with a guy who fits the general description of a convict. We need to get a photo of this Frantelli guy and go from there. I wouldn't be surprised if he hijacked the trucker in order to flee Idaho after killing Lewis."

"So why would he kill the trucker, out in the middle of nowhere? And where the heck would he have gone? Why not take the truck?"

Jeremy considered the questions for a moment, and replied, "Something went wrong. Maybe Johnston tried to make a move, tried to get away from him. As far as leaving the truck, maybe he didn't know how to drive it. I know I wouldn't know where to start."

"I don't know," said the lieutenant, "something doesn't quite fit. It's not like he's going to kill a guy out in the middle of nowhere and what, walk through the desert to the next town?"

"Maybe he carjacked a passing motorist. Again, it may have not been his choice of time or place to ditch the trucker, but he's our guy —I can feel it. This is him, Lieutenant, I'd bet on it."

2 0

When Jeremy called Rich Farris on his cell phone and told him he'd like to meet right away, Rich said, "Name the place." Jeremy gave him the address of a Maverick Station that sat two blocks from the home of Mrs. Frantelli.

When they met, Rich said, "You seem excited this morning."

Jeremy smiled at Odessa and then addressed Rich. "It's all unravelling, right now as we speak."

"They sell coffee inside?" Rich asked, and nodded toward the front of the store.

"I think so, yes."

"Let's grab a cup, relax a minute, then go over everything slowly. What do you say?"

When they came back out of the Maverick, Rich was sipping on a tall cup of strong, black coffee. Odessa had some sort of latte, and Jeremy had a Coke. Rich said, "Not a coffee drinker?"

"Well, I'm Mormon," he said.

"No shit, huh?"

"Yes sir."

"Now, don't take this the wrong way, because I don't know any

Mormons to speak of—not sure there's many of them in Los Angeles —but how many wives do you have?"

Jeremy grinned and said, "Just one. How's your game?"

Rich said, "How's that?"

"Don't take this the wrong way," he said, grinning widely as he said it, "but I don't know many black guys to speak of. We don't have a lot of them here in Idaho. I was just wondering how good you are at playing hoops."

Rich laughed and said, "Touché, my man, touché. I like your style."

They both chuckled and Odessa stood smiling. She said, "He probably could have a bunch of them, if he wanted."

They both looked at her quizzically.

She said, "Wives."

BUDDY WATCHED AS THE LONE COWBOY FINISHED RIDING ONE HORSE, then soon after began riding another. He wished he had something to enhance his view, or maybe he could move somewhere closer to see better. But he didn't want to leave the shade of one of the few trees he had seen out in this barren country. His hand and arm throbbed and he was hungry again, and thirsty for that spring water he'd left the night before. Besides, he was still working on his plan, studying the layout of the ranch below. He said, "Take your time, cowboy."

JEREMY TOLD RICH AND ODESSA ABOUT THE IDENTIFICATION OF THIS convict named Buddy Frantelli, believed to be related to a murder in Nevada. He explained that the victim turned out to be Elwood Johnston, who was a reported missing person here in Boise. Johnston was a trucker, and according to the trucker's wife, Elwood's last known location was the Flying J, which just happened to be a couple of blocks from where Lacy Jane was murdered. Jeremy argued that it only made sense that Frantelli had hijacked the truck and driver to get the heck out of Idaho after killing Lacy Jane. He was going to get a photograph of Frantelli from the Department of Corrections, and try to get an identification of him from someone who saw Lacy Jane on the night of the murder with a man who matched Frantelli's description.

Now he was just waiting for the Flying J management to see if they had surveillance video going back to the day of the murder.

Rich said, "You still running solo?"

Jeremy nodded.

"You're doing a hell of a job," he said. "What's next, Detective?"

"His mom lives around the corner. I think we should pay her a visit."

"We?"

"Well, since I'm without a partner, and you wanted to help out... I was thinking maybe you guys could give me a hand."

"Your lieutenant okay with that?"

Jeremy finished his coke and looked him in his eyes. "I don't know why he wouldn't be."

21

———

Sam finished riding the red roan Hancock-bred colt that Travis Jacobson had been worried would be a bucker. When she had agreed to start the two colts for him, get them both broke to saddle and ride, he had told her his concerns about this one, saying, "Those Hancocks are known to buck." He told her he didn't want to see her hurt, and that at the first offer to buck, she needed to back off and they would send him out to someone more apt to ride the rough ones.

But Sam liked the challenge and said that her daddy had shown her a better way with young horses than riding the rough off of them the way some cowboys do. It was a matter of learning to communicate with the horse in subtle ways, and learning to get through to them without too much pressure. You'd never use any more pressure than just what was needed, and your timing had to be good so that you released all pressure the moment there was a positive response. It was something they called *feel*, in the horse world, or in part of the horse world, anyway. She had smiled and told Mr. Jacobson, "We'll get along just fine, me and that roan colt."

She unsaddled the colt and looked into his brown eyes and saw the softness of the gentle but powerful athlete, and whispered her thanks for the nice ride he had given her. She then hosed him and the other one off, careful to wash the sweat and dirt from their bodies. Once she finished washing them, she scraped the excess water off and left them standing tied to dry in the morning sun. Sam pulled her felt hat off and used it to brush the dust off her britches before she sat down in a folding chair next to the barn. Just a few feet from the horses, she jotted notes in her journal about her 22nd ride on the Hancock colt and her 28th on the gray filly. The notes weren't much different from the day before or the day before that, or really for the last seven rides over the past two weeks. Both of the two-year-olds were off to a great start and it was almost time to turn them out, meaning to put them out on the pasture. It was best to put about thirty rides on them as two-year-olds, and then to leave them alone for a year. That would allow them the time they needed for maturing in their bodies and minds before more training is presented to them. That's what Sam's daddy had always said.

These were the first two she had started without her dad there to help her, and she was proud of herself, almost giddy with the accomplishments she logged in her journal.

She finished the other chores, and when the horses were dry, she turned them out in their stalls to fresh water and tubs of hay. Then she started up the Polaris four-wheeler—an all-terrain vehicle that in these parts was considered a ranch or farm vehicle and could be driven on the road by unlicensed drivers—and headed off for home where she would help her dad with their chores and tell him all about the colts and how they were progressing. Then she'd have to go inside the house and do her studies, because that's where she went to school.

BUDDY SAW THE SECOND COWBOY LEAVE THE RANCH RIDING THE FOUR-wheeler ATV. He'd been watching all morning now and hadn't seen a single other human being, though there were critters scattered everywhere.

His hand and arm were now numb, no longer throbbing though

the arm was oozing pus and blood through the bandaging he had made of strips from his t-shirt. Buddy felt weak and nauseated, and he was sweating while sitting still in the shade of the tree. His vision was blurred at times, and his breathing could be labored without effort. Buddy wondered about the snake's venom and what it was doing to him inside, and he cursed his luck again.

But this was not the time for self-pity; it was time to move.

———

A SMALL, FADED YELLOW HOME SAT ON AN OVERSIZED STREET IN OLD Boise, just two blocks from the Historical District where expansive homes sprawled across large-acre lots of manicured lawns under the canopies of hundred-year oaks and towering poplars.

Jeremy parked in front of the ramshackle home with its peeling paint and rotted wooden trim and eaves. The place looked to have barely survived the hundred years of hard winters and sweltering summers of the northwest desert region that saw the city's population explode. While many other century-old structures had either been bulldozed and replaced by stylish duplexes that were perfect for child-less professionals with their designer eyewear and electric cars, or they had been refurbished as quaint cottages where discerning thirty-somethings sat near gas fireplaces grasping oversized mugs of lattes, Mrs. Frantelli's home stood unabashedly in its original form, a patch of crabgrass and relentless weeds surrounding a driveway consisting of two parallel strips of broken concrete, the final resting place of several old cars and trucks that hadn't been moved—or perhaps even noticed—for decades.

Rich parked two houses west, which was customary for cops who had been shot at—or knew of others who had—while approaching homes for the mundane purposes of resolving family disturbances or talking to witnesses or looking for suspects. And as they met somewhere between their vehicles, Jeremy took notice, and it registered. He said, "I guess I shouldn't have parked right in front, huh?"

Rich shrugged as if it were no big deal. "It's how we learn. They call it *experience*."

It had become a habit of Jeremy's to watch the subtle processes of the veteran detective who seemed to glide effortlessly through life, from Jeremy's brief view. He hadn't shared his personal life with Jeremy, other than that he was the uncle of Lacy Jane, and his delightful companion, Odessa, was a close family friend. But Jeremy had a good idea of who this man was, and he imagined what his life back home was probably like, this knowledgeable, contemplative man with his orderly yet amenable ways.

Jeremy pictured Rich with a large and loving family and a wife of twenty years or more, though he hadn't mentioned one. He would be the private type who wouldn't discuss such things with relative strangers, and the absence of a ring meant nothing on a lifelong cop from the city. Jeremy knew that. He probably lived in a large, comfortable home that sat on a fair-sized lot with an immaculately manicured lawn with shrubbery and large shade trees that he enjoyed while sitting on the porch. He would sit and visit with his friendly neighbors who embraced the black man they lived next to in their otherwise all-white neighborhood. Jeremy would enjoy being Rich's neighbor himself.

Rich said, "Looks a little rundown, unkempt... gives you a good idea of the type of person who lives here."

Jeremy nodded, silently admiring the way Farris studied and analyzed everything and everyone, and seemed to be constantly planning ahead, seeing the future in short and narrow frames directly related to his mission.

The three of them approached the door. Rich stood to the side, and without looking back, gently ushered Odessa to a position behind him and away from the path to the door. Jeremy followed suit and stood to the opposite side. They looked at one another and Rich nodded, giving Jeremy the silent okay for proceeding.

Jeremy knocked on the door but there was no response. After a moment of silence, he looked at Rich, who only shrugged. He knocked again, this time more forcefully. Then he announced, "Police department," and quickly regretted it, wondering if it was what Rich would have done. But he had done it, and Rich showed no response one way or the other, so he continued, "Anybody home?"

Only the sounds of birds chirping and distant traffic could be heard on the otherwise quiet morning. After a moment, Jeremy looked at Rich and shrugged. "Well?"

Rich said, "Let's have a look around."

The trio walked slowly and cautiously around the side of the house, along the dilapidated driveway and past the abandoned cars and trucks, with Jeremy leading the way and Odessa bringing up the rear. Rich paused at each window to peek inside before walking past it, and after the second time he did so, Jeremy began doing the same. When they rounded the corner they were met by a fat calico cat who arched her back and turned in a circle as she meowed at the sight of them.

Odessa knelt down and was saying to the kitty, "Ahh, kitty-kitty..." and Jeremy was surveying the backyard, when Rich drew his pistol from beneath his sport coat and stepped in front of Odessa, yelling, "Don't shoot! Don't shoot! Don't shoot!"

Jeremy looked around to see Rich pointing his pistol toward the house. An old woman dressed in a nightgown had stepped onto the back porch with a shotgun in her hands.

22

Steve Troy stepped into Sheehy's, leaving the bright sky and busy day behind him as the dark, solid door settled into its closed position. He stood still for a moment, allowing his eyes to adjust to the dark room that held a dozen small tables along three of the walls. The fourth was lined with mirrors and shelves behind a dark wood bar with a padded leather edge.

There were three others present when Steve walked in: an elderly local man everyone called Woody, an old hag everyone called The Stork, and Dave, the former Marine who worked the bar on weekdays from ten in the morning until eight at night, at which time he usually became a patron.

Dave said, "In a little early today, Steve. Day off?"

"Yeah, I'm taking a little vacation time, and couldn't think of a better place to spend it."

The bartender didn't ask what he was having; rather, he turned a tumbler over in front him and poured him a double Jameson.

Steve lifted his drink and admired the liquid gold as he held it up with the light of the bar behind it. He said to no one and everyone, "To the Irish."

BUDDY LIFTED HIS OWN LIBATION AT THE SAME TIME, AN UNOPENED bottle of Pendleton that he had removed from the liquor cabinet of the ranch house, which he had walked right into through an unlocked back door. The interior was decorated in heavy woods and dark leather and it was cool and quiet, the sounds of dogs and goats and horses outside barely audible. He smiled for the first time in a long while, maybe two weeks, and then he opened the bottle and had a long pull. The whiskey felt good going down his throat and filling his stomach. He took another swig and then carried the bottle with him to the fridge, where he was pleased to see there was cold beer and plenty of food. He was just in time for lunch, he thought, and grinned again. He would probably have the place to himself until the cowboys returned, at which time he would kill them and continue to enjoy the privacy and seclusion of this ranch that sat on a hill just a few miles or so from the town of Bishop.

MRS. FRANTELLI HAD NO IDEA WHERE HER SON WAS, SHE SAID, AND SHE hadn't seen hide nor hair of the boy since just after he was released from prison. She said he had come through that back door just a few days before, and he'd gotten smart with her and rough with her too. She had sat on her couch while Buddy looked through her drawers and cabinets for money and valuables. She didn't know what he thought she would have, she told the detectives, avoiding any mention of things they didn't need to know, such as her stash of cash that was beneath the floor just about where the black girl stood listening. She told them that the rotten boy she'd raised was plumb mean and ornery, calling her an old wretch who'd outlived her usefulness while he trashed her place looking for who-knows-what.

Buddy had been quite surprised when she worked the action of her shotgun and put a live round in the chamber and told him she'd shoot and kill him if he didn't leave then, or if she ever saw him again.

He had turned back with a look of disbelief, and then he'd looked around as if he couldn't believe she had been able to arm herself right under his nose. He tried to change his tune then, she told them, saying he was sorry and he was glad to see her and wasn't she glad to see him after all these years? But when he stepped toward her, she let one fly, pulled the trigger on ol' Betsy and blasted that hole right there in the wall.

All three of her guests turned to look at the interior wall near the hallway behind them that featured a ten inch pattern of buckshot two feet above the floor. There were small pieces of drywall and wood on the carpet beneath it. She said, "And that's the last I seen of that son of a bitch."

<hr />

RICH AND ODESSA STOOD BENEATH THE SHADE OF AN OLD OAK IN FRONT of the small bungalow where the feisty old lady and her calico cat seemed to be getting by just fine without much help or money or fuss. Jeremy was telling them that a gunshot in Idaho didn't alarm many folks, and that it most likely wouldn't be called in and reported. He said, "People shoot guns all the time in these parts, even in the city limits, without worrying that someone else might think something bad happened." He said, "Around here, nobody thinks there's been a drive-by shooting or a murder just because they heard a gunshot. They don't assume the worst. Most people would probably think that old lady Frantelli had just shot another skunk, or maybe a badger getting into her chickens."

Odessa said, "Badgers?"

"You bet, they're around, and they can be mean too. But what I'm trying to say is, there's a completely different type of mentality around here than what I think you're used to."

Rich soaked it in, thinking how odd it sounded but realizing too that it made sense. A gunshot in *his* neighborhood would warrant a dozen 9-1-1 calls, and a shotgun blast would bring a SWAT team. He shook his head and said, "Too bad old Ma Frantelli didn't kill the bastard."

"I wish she had been able to narrow it down, what day this all happened," Jeremy said. "I'd like to know if it was when he first got out—was mom his first stop for some domestic abuse and financial aid—or did he come here after killing Lacy Jane, looking for the means to get out of town?"

Those were good questions, and Rich stood processing them, thinking of the possibilities and probabilities, but ultimately concluding it didn't change anything now.

Odessa, the young lady who loved to talk and who had worn Rich out as they traveled across the country, had been very quiet as she accompanied the detectives these last few days. She would have plenty to talk about in the evenings, during meals or drinks at the hotel or downtown on the festive streets of Boise, but she seemed to be all business during their *working hours*. So Rich was surprised and Jeremy appeared a bit taken aback as well when she said in her melodious southern drawl, "Do y'all wonder if maybe she isn't telling the truth?"

"What do you mean?" Jeremy asked.

"Well, down south we have a saying that blood is thicker than water, and I just couldn't help but wonder if she'd tell us anything about where he's gone even if she knew."

Rich said, "You saw the hole in the wall."

"Right, I did. But there's other explanations for that also."

"Like?"

"Like maybe that happened when she was sitting over there fiddling with that old shotgun and it went off without her expecting it or even knowing why. Or maybe that happened a month ago, or a year ago, I don't know."

"The parts of wood and wall on the floor tell me it was more recent," Rich said.

"How could you tell? The house hasn't been vacuumed in years, by the look and smell of it," she argued. "I'm not saying I'm right, I'm just saying that there's something about that woman I don't like, and I'm a woman. We have something that y'all don't have when it comes to knowing other women."

Rich and Jeremy looked at each other but didn't say anything.

She said, "Another thing, what do you suppose he could have been looking for? What would give him the idea she had anything at all worth stealing?"

Rich nodded. "That's a good point."

She said, "There's more to her than what meets the eye. That's all I'm saying.

The three stood silent for a moment and then Odessa said, "Anyone other than me ready for lunch?"

23

Buddy had enjoyed the cold beers and spicy whiskey in the cool house with its comfortable furnishings and plenty of food. He had also enjoyed the pain meds he found in the medicine cabinet. As he sat on the leather sofa with a first-aid kit on the table next to the pills and booze, he thought that with just a little more numbness, he'd do it. He'd remove the swaths of shirt that he had wrapped his arm, and he'd use the contents of the first-aid kit to doctor it up. He'd leave the tourniquet on because he had heard somewhere that once you applied one, you needed to leave it until you made it to a hospital.

Which brought up a new dilemma that he didn't want to contemplate, and that was how the hell was he going to get to a hospital and have his arm taken care of without drawing any attention? He'd have to think about that later, because for now he felt good for the first time in a long time, with his arm and hand no longer throbbing and his belly full and a foggy daze coming over him. He lifted the bottle and took another long pull, saw that he was half done with it, and thought he'd better rest now while he could. He leaned back into the cushions and closed his eyes with the .44 Magnum he'd found in the closet held in his left hand.

After a short time, Buddy passed out.

He was still passed out two hours later and didn't hear the four-wheeler or the truck that came up the drive, passed by the house, and stopped in front of the barn. Nor did he hear the laughter and the playful conversation of the gleeful adolescents who had a ranch to themselves for the night and an ice chest full of beer to help them enjoy it.

―――――――――

WHEN THE EVENING CHORES WERE DONE AND THE SUN BEGAN TO DROP behind the jagged mountaintops that sat across the highway from the hillside ranch, Samantha Wright drifted from the barn toward her *friend's* pickup with Dusty McBride following along, his eyes glued to her tight Wrangler jeans. Blue brought up the rear.

Dusty said, "Where're you headed, Sammie Jo?"

"I've worked up a little bit of a thirst doing these chores," she said, "and I just thought maybe I'd have a look and see what you hauled up here in that cooler."

He was looking at the long brown hair flowing from beneath her straw cowboy hat when he said, "Well maybe that's a surprise for later on."

She turned quickly and he almost ran into her. Face to face, staring into each other's eyes, she said, "It's later now, cowboy. I say we have a beer and go for a ride, see how you are on a colt."

"Shit," he said with a wide grin, as he pushed the front of his hat up high on his head, his careless blond hair now jutting out all sides, "I'd ride the rough off both them colts and have 'em lined out before breakfast the first day, had Mr. Jacobson hired me instead of a girl."

She stepped into him, fiddled with the top buttons of his shirt, then gently touched his chin and then the tip of his nose. Then she flipped his hat back off of his head and took off running and giggling.

Dusty grabbed his hat and gave chase, yelling to her he would get her and she'd be sorry. She ran into the barn and climbed the ladder into the loft. He ran in behind her and as he started to climb the steps, he looked up to see her looking down at him. Her hat was gone and her long hair now draped over her head and face. Her mouth was closed but turned up into a grin and her eyes sparkled mischievously. She whispered, "Go get the beer and bring it up here. Also, there's a bottle of Pendleton in the house. Hurry up, cowboy."

JEREMY HAD SAID GOODBYE TO RICH AND ODESSA AFTER LUNCH AND they had agreed to meet early the next morning for breakfast at a little café not far from the hotel. Jeremy had some other cases he needed to work on through the afternoon, and until he heard back from the Flying J about the video, or unless another break came in on this case, he'd be otherwise occupied the rest of the day.

Odessa wanted to see the sights of the beautiful city and Jeremy suggested they go to the Idaho Botanical Garden, or the Old Idaho Penitentiary, or they could drive up to Bogus Basin—he had turned to the north and pointed northeast toward the mountains—which, he explained, was a ski resort during the season, and in the off-season there were trails to hike or bike, or you could just look out over the valley and enjoy the view. He said, "Or you could go to the aquarium, the zoo, the art museum, Barber Park or maybe the Basque Museum, or any of the Basque restaurants or shops downtown. There's a lot to see."

Rich wasn't normally the type to do much sightseeing, but he told Odessa he would enjoy doing whatever she wanted to do.

AT THE RANCH, LYING ON STRAW AND LOOKING UP AT OLD BOARDS THAT allowed the bright light of the moon to peek through cracks and small holes, Dusty was saying, "I didn't mean to upset you, Sammie Jo."

"You didn't *upset* me," she said, and then smiled with her mouth closed. "I'm fine. It's just that *no* means *no*, and you'd be smart to remember that from here on out."

"Yes ma'am," he said, sincere and apologetic.

"Now, how about that ride?"

"Whatever you want to do," he said.

"Well what I'd like to do is get those two colts out of the corral and away from the arena. I've been wanting to go outside on them for a while now, and they're more than ready for it. But I think they'd be more comfortable together, and I know I would be."

"Which do I get to ride?"

"The Hancock. If either of them's gonna buck, it'll be him. There's nothing I'd enjoy more than seeing a cocky cowboy bucked off a saddlehorse."

He smiled, and said, "Not a chance, little girl. Besides, that Hancock deal is overstated, if you ask me. Some of 'em buck, some never even offer to buck. I think it's more about how they're started than how they were bred. You seem to have done a pretty good job."

She smiled. Then she leaned over and kissed him on the mouth, but lightly. She backed off and said, "C'mon, let's go see."

As Sam climbed down from the loft, Dusty jumped. His legs buckled as he landed and tumbled over on the dirt floor. "Damnit!"

She laughed at him. "Too many beers?"

He looked up at her while gathering his hat, Sam still working her way down the ladder, ass first. He smiled and said, "Maybe. Probably a good thing I forgot to get that whiskey you mentioned."

They brushed the horses and picked their hooves clean, and then they saddled them under the light that hung high on the front of the barn, illuminating the hitching posts and parts of the dirt driveway and the nearby corral. The two young horses, a red roan colt and a gray filly—usually referred to by cowboys as just colts, regardless of their sex—stood patiently. They were relaxed, each of them with a hind leg cocked and occasionally licking their lips and chewing, though there was no food in their mouths. Sam stepped back into the tack room and came out with two headstalls, both equipped with snaffle bits. She said, "You'll want to keep your hands soft. These colts are light in the mouth and I intend on them staying that way."

"Yes, Miss Samantha, I *am* aware," he said slowly, with attitude. "I've rode colts."

"Yeah, but not nice ones like these, ones that have some feel to 'em. You ride them jug-headed cowboy horses that you've got to whip and spur to get 'em going, and then when they run off or go to bucking, you buckaroos go to yankin' on their mouths to get 'em stopped. *Cowboys.*"

He glared at her. "I don't ride that way, unless it's a bronc."

She said, "I'm mostly giving you a hard time. But seriously, I want these horses to stay soft, so no cowboy shit."

"Are we going to ride, or do you intend to stand there all night and lecture me about how it's done?"

Sam didn't answer. She had just finished putting the bit in the gray filly's mouth so she grabbed a handful of mane and stepped into a stirrup, swung her leg over the colt and settled softly into the saddle. She reached back and gently rubbed the top of the gray filly's rump while keeping her eyes on its head. The filly's ears perked up, and one of them twitched back at her, letting Sam know she was paying attention and ready for a cue. Dusty threw his leg over and came to rest on the back of the red roan without touching his stirrups, and the roan jumped a little but settled quickly. He looked over at Sammie Jo next to him, and grinned. They turned and started down the driveway, side by side, beyond the light of the barn and into the darkness. Blue silently followed along at the heels of the Hancock. It was midnight.

BUDDY DIDN'T HEAR THE HOOVES CRUNCHING ACROSS THE GRAVEL outside of the house as the two colts headed down the driveway. Nor did he hear the Jacobson's dogs barking at Blue, nor the coyotes yodeling and yipping from the mountains behind the house in the bright, moonlit night. He was out cold under a Navajo blanket, sleeping like a baby on the leather cushioned couch, the .44 at his side and a bottle of Pendleton in his hand.

24

When Buddy Frantelli woke up two hours later, he almost panicked in the stillness, having no idea for a long moment just where he was or how he got there. He looked around, allowing his eyes to adjust to the darkness, thankful for the moonlight shining through the windows. A half-empty bottle of whiskey in his hand helped him remember where he was and how he got there, and what he had planned for the cowboys who lived there once they came home. But how had he not been discovered? Or had he? Was he alone in the house? Maybe the whole place was surrounded by cops. That's what he needed to know. So he stood—unsteadily at first—and with the recently acquired gun in his left hand, he began a slow and methodical search of the home.

THE HANCOCK RELAXED IN THE GLOW OF THE BARN LIGHT WITH THE gray filly at his side. They stood head to tail, each with a cocked hind leg, relaxed after an easy and uneventful ride in the moonlight. His eyes drifted shut but bounced open each time the filly swooshed her tail across his face.

BLUE SLEPT NEXT TO THE LADDER AT THE FOOT OF THE HAY LOFT. SHE would perk her ears and open her eyes each time the boards squeaked above her or when the colt or filly neighed or stomped at the ground. She paid no attention to the yipping and yodeling coyotes, as she was accustomed to their song.

JUST ABOVE BLUE, A YOUNG COWBOY SLEPT SOUNDLY, THE GIRL OF HIS dreams at his side. It was a time and place they believed to be their paradise, a place where—as far as either of them knew—nothing in their world could go wrong.

TWO-HUNDRED MILES AWAY IN RENO, NEVADA, ELWOOD JOHNSTON LAY naked on a metal table with a white cloth covering his large body, as he chilled in a cold room at the Washoe County Coroner's Office awaiting his final medical examination. He had plenty of company as it was the final destiny of the recently departed from thirteen counties of rural Nevada and five others in California.

FURTHER EAST, A RETIRED HOMICIDE DETECTIVE SLEPT SOUNDLY IN A king-sized bed with a beautiful girl in the room next to his. He didn't dream, which meant he had no nightmares.

NOT FAR FROM THE HOTEL WHERE FARRIS PEACEFULLY SLEPT, STEVE Troy stumbled into his apartment where nobody awaited his return. There were no loved ones in his life, not even a pet. There weren't even pictures of family or friends on the walls or mantles or night-stands. But he didn't notice because he was accustomed to it the way a man is accustomed to sleeping in prison—locked away, with no escape and no choices, only living with the consequences of past ones.

NOT FAR FROM TROY'S APARTMENT, JEREMY AND NANCY SLEPT BACK TO back in a queen-sized bed as their three children were nested safely in the other two rooms. More consequences.

AND A FEW MILES FARTHER SOUTH THERE WAS ANOTHER COUPLE WHO slept back to back. Tank snored and Tanika stared into the darkness with tears trickling down her face. She didn't know where she had gone wrong, though generally she believed it was probably when she lost her virginity at thirteen and began drinking and using marijuana. Not long after, she had stepped up to cocaine, and eventually she made the leap to heroin. By then she had lost track of all the boys and men for whom she had opened her legs, and the heroin had become her best friend. She craved the numbness it provided better than anything else.

Tanika considered leaving while Tank slept, but she had no idea where to go. She couldn't go home—ever—and she didn't want to live on the streets or clean up in a shelter.

She wished it had all been different. And she closed her eyes.

A SHORT DRIVE FROM DOWNTOWN STOOD A FORTRESS IN THE DESERT called the Idaho Department of Corrections, and within the Maximum Security facility stood an area of small isolated rooms commonly referred to as *the hole*. Big John Wilson stared blankly at the ceiling above him, unable to sleep as he listened without emotion to the sounds of violence on the tier below.

BUDDY FINISHED HIS SEARCH OF THE HOME, SATISFIED THAT HE WAS alone and reveling in the idea of having a little bit of good luck for a change. He stripped the grungy clothing from his soiled body and stepped into a steaming shower with a renewed outlook on his future. He'd had a series of unavoidable conflicts—none of which were his fault—and now, rather than being able to adjust to society and live as a free man, he was an outlaw on the run. He needed to get medical attention for his hand and arm, and he needed to get the hell out of this area before they found the dead trucker and started looking for him.

Images of the trucker lingered in his mind for a moment, and then he flashed to the image of a black girl in the alley. As he revisited the timeline, he recalled the meeting he had with his mother. He had been so angered by her, he could have killed her. In fact, he might have, had the crazy bitch not tried blowing his nuts off with the goddamn shotgun.

The water cascaded over his bald head and down his lean, muscular frame, and across his hand and arm that throbbed again as he stood contemplating his future moves.

He had no idea that a young man stood a hundred feet away, pissing on a fence post under the moonlight while speaking softly to the colt who stood watching.

WHEN DUSTY TURNED AND BEGAN ZIPPING UP, HE WAS STARTLED AT THE sight of the bathroom light on in the house and the sound of water running in the shower. He rushed into the barn and scurried up the ladder and gave Sam a nudge on her leg. He said, "Sammie Jo, wake up. I think they're home."

She opened her eyes but her brows were low and she didn't seem to understand what he was saying.

"They're home," he repeated, "someone's in the shower."

"Oh shit!"

"Oh shit is right," he said. "What are we going to do? They had to have seen my truck out front, and your four-wheeler is here, and the horses are accounted for... they'd have to be wondering where we are, or what's going on."

Sam sat up and pushed her fingers through her hair, shaking loose the straw before reaching for her hat and putting it on her head. She said, "I don't know. Do you have any bright ideas? We're gonna get killed if they find us up here."

"Just one."

"Well, let's hear it."

"You're not going to like it," he said. "You're going to think it's dumb."

"Well try me, because I haven't a clue what to do. My dad's going to kill me if Mr. Jacobson figures this out and calls him. Flat kill me."

"Okay, well I say we get those beer cans out of here, get the cooler back to my truck, and then just go back to sleep."

She rolled her eyes. "That's your plan?"

"Listen, it might sound dumb, but what choice do we have? We're both dressed, and when Mr. Jacobson comes out in the morning to do the chores and check on his horses, he'll find us here sleeping innocently, nothing going on. We'll tell him that we went for a late night ride—which is the truth—and that after taking care of his horses, we just crashed. It's the only thing that's going to work. It's actually all true except maybe the beer, and I don't think he'd make a big deal of it if he found out. Mr. Jacobson's pretty cool."

She considered it for a moment. "Fine, you clean up the cans and get the beer out of here, I've got to go back behind the barn for a minute."

Buddy finished his shower and took another pain pill from the bottle and washed it down with a swig of Pendleton. He dressed in fresh jeans and a western shirt, all pressed and cleaned, straight from the closet in the master bedroom. Then he spent the next hour gathering some food, extra clothing, another firearm—a 30-30 lever-action saddle gun—and all the pain pills from the medicine cabinet, everything he recognized as a narcotic. He donned a baseball cap that said *Mule Days, Bishop, California*, and had a mule embroidered across the top. It reminded him of the damn burros he'd come across in the desert, and that had started to piss him off, but he figured the hat would help him fit in when he went into town. He found an old phone book, tattered and layered with dust, and several years out of date. But it was all he could find, so he used it to look up health clinics in Bishop and found one that opened at eight. The clock on the microwave told him he had another four hours so he lay back down and took another nap.

25

The next morning Rich jogged through downtown, running on sidewalks and bike paths while dodging around people who generally smiled and greeted him rather than snarling. When he arrived back at the hotel a little before eight, he grabbed a coffee and a couple bottles of water from the lobby and went up to his room. He chugged the water and started the shower. While the water heated, he shaved and brushed his teeth in front of the mirror. He looked up and studied his image, and he smiled. Life was good, and certainly better than the alternative. He was starting to see it again.

ODESSA HAD FINISHED SHOWERING AND WAS GETTING DRESSED WHEN she heard a knock on the door that adjoined her room and Rich's. She glanced in the mirror and saw that she was mostly decent, though not quite ready to go in her peach-colored capris and a sports bra. She smiled at the image in the mirror once her decision was made to open the door and give the man something to think about.

"Hey now, girl," Rich said, drawing back a step as she swung the door open. "It wasn't an emergency. You could've finished dressing."

"I'm dressed."

He looked her up and down twice before saying, "But you're wearing a bra."

"A sports bra," she said, and then tugged at the sides to provide a bit of a lift to her generous chest. "Some girls go out to clubs like this, and lots of 'em wear these to gyms or out jogging with nothing else."

He was staring at the bra now, or maybe beyond it. All he said was, "Damn."

"I'm putting a top on, so you can relax. I sure didn't think I'd give you a heart attack by letting you see me in a sports bra. My gosh, Richard."

She walked away from him but could feel his eyes upon her, the normally tenacious and questioning eyes that this morning seemed only appreciative. She selected a t-shirt from a drawer and pulled it over her head without turning back to him. She was looking out the window at the Rocky Mountains that were still dark against the fledgling morning skyline when she said, "I forget you're old." Then she turned around and met his gaze, and held it for a moment before she winked.

His smile never faltered as he took her all in once again, from head to toe. He said, "I forget it myself at times," and then the smile faded. Rich turned away and appeared to be studying a the unmade bed beside him.

Odessa remained silent as she processed the words, her smile now dissipated as well, and she wondered what he might have meant. Had it meant what she thought it might've, that maybe if he was younger or she older? She hoped that it hadn't. To her, the age gap meant nothing at all.

———

AT EIGHT O'CLOCK BUDDY WALKED OUT THE FRONT DOOR WITH A plastic shopping bag filled with clothes, pills, food, and a bottle of whiskey that was three-quarters empty. He carried all of it in his left hand along with the lever-action rifle. The pistol was tucked into his jeans. They were too big in the waist, but he had cinched them with a belt that had a beat-up, old silver buckle with a horse head and engraved flowers. He figured the cowboy look would help him fit in when he went to town.

He looked at the old Ford that was parked by the barn, and then at a Tahoe parked closer to the house. One was more comfortable, maybe more reliable, but the other fit in better with the way he was dressed and the rednecks he would encounter around here. He pondered it for a moment and then walked over to the Ford where he glanced through the passenger's window to see the keys were in the ignition, as he had expected they might be. He opened the passenger's door and set his rifle and bag of food down on the seat, then slammed the door closed and turned to walk around the back of the truck. That's when he was attacked from behind.

26

J eremy had a lot to tell them, so when they met for breakfast he could hardly contain himself. The waitress poured coffee for Rich and Odessa but Jeremy signaled for her to pass him by. He paused briefly to ask for a Coke, and then he continued. "...so he's positively identified by video as being at the Flying J at the same time the trucker was there, filling his rig. They damn near bumped into each other at the door, Frantelli heading out while Johnston was going in to pay for his fuel and pick up some snacks for the road.

"The prints they had made from Johnston's truck were not only lifted from the driver's door, but also the gear shift knob, the inside driver's door handle, and the passenger's door. My guess is that Frantelli tried to figure out how to drive the rig and get out of there after killing the trucker, but couldn't. Probably couldn't figure out how to start it"—then he looked at Odessa and said—"it's harder to figure out how to start a tractor than you'd think, if you've never driven one."

Rich seemed to be thinking it through, maybe picturing the scene the best he could from descriptions he had heard, and putting it together with Jeremy's theory.

"I just wish we had some evidence to put him at the scene," Jeremy said, "something to nail him down there in the alley with Lacy Jane. I'm certain he's the one who did it, that he's the one who killed her."

"We know he was in the bar," Odessa said.

"It's not enough," Rich opined. "The bar and the crime scene are two different places, though related. What Jeremy's saying—and he's right on track here—is we need more than people seeing this Frantelli dude in the nightclub, and even more than people seeing Lacy Jane with him in the nightclub. Hell, even if we find someone who saw them leave together, it's still circumstantial. Now, we can build a circumstantial case, rather, Jeremy can build a circumstantial case"— he nodded to Jeremy—"but I can tell you it's always tough to convict someone of murder without more than circumstantial evidence. It would be nice to have either physical evidence or a solid motive. Or a confession."

Jeremy thought about that, and it had never occurred to him that at some point, he might have an opportunity to interview her killer. It would be a first for him, and the thought of it seemed a bit over-whelming. He said, "What do you think the motive was, Rich?"

Rich paused but only for a moment. He said, "I actually don't think he had planned to kill her."

Jeremy was surprised to hear him say it. He glanced at Odessa, who also seemed a bit perplexed by the statement.

The waitress arrived with plates of omelets and toast and bacon and set them around the table, the sounds of dishes clanging together near and far. When she walked away, Rich continued: "I think he was on the hunt, having been locked up for so long. I think Lacy Jane had a wild streak, and like some young ladies, found it a bit thrilling to be with an outlaw. But this ain't the movies, folks, and with an asshole like Buddy Frantelli, a man who's spent his whole adult life locked up, a man who's had little to no sexual contact other than maybe prison rape, a man whose only female relationship is with his mother who tried to cut him in half with a twelve gauge shotgun, things can go south in a hurry. Lacy Jane likely became quickly offended or maybe frightened by him once they were alone and he started making his moves. He would likely have been very awkward and aggressive; he wouldn't know anything else. When those two forces meet, an overwhelmingly aggressive man and a young lady who is in over her head and becomes frightened, maybe terrified of this man she led on, a lot can go wrong. Terribly wrong. If she resisted or screamed or made any kind of a scene, a man like Frantelli is going to panic. He'd see himself back in the joint on a rape or attempted rape, or at the very least on a parole violation for being where alcohol is served. When a convict panics and sees himself being forced back into a cage, he's going to act like the wild animal he is. I've seen it many times, and it never ends well. I believe that's probably what happened in this case."

Rich added, "He had to shut her up, and there's only one way a man like him knows how to do that. And that's exactly why they should keep the animals locked up."

Jeremy hadn't picked up his fork nor his Coke and he hadn't blinked. He saw it all in his mind, thinking back to the crime scene, and he wondered how Farris so easily put it all together. He was probably right, Jeremy decided. He certainly was gifted. Rich was also extremely experienced, and Jeremy knew that much of his knowledge had been derived from his experiences, but he also had talent, a natural ability, a God-given gift like the ability to throw a 95 mph fastball and to know when to bring it inside on the batter. He wondered if Rich Farris had been born for the job, placed on earth for this exact reason and no other. Jeremy wished he could work with Farris as a regular partner, and wondered if he could talk him into staying. Or maybe he would go to L.A. Of course he couldn't, but the wistful thought had come as he realized this relationship, or perhaps internship, would be coming to an end. He dreaded the thought of it.

He said, "Rich, you need to keep talking. Tell me everything you can before you leave Idaho, because I've never had a better education at any time of my life, anywhere, in any circumstance."

Odessa looked at Rich with proud eyes and a smile. Rich sat solemnly over his omelet, emotionless and at ease. He said, "Jeremy, you're better at this than you know. Now, can you pass me that Tabasco sauce, please?"

WHEN BLUE SANK HER TEETH DEEP INTO THE CALF OF THE MAN WHO had violated the space of her master's pickup, she set the bite deep into the flesh as any good heeler would. She had nipped the heels of hundreds of cows who had defied her silent instructions of which way to go, or had turned back from the herd to try her. Some cows would get on the fight, and many had kicked at her or turned to chase and try to kill her. She'd had a few cow kicks to the head and she'd lost the occasional tooth as a result. But she never once had come off a bite until her master gave her the command to do so. Which sounded to her like, *attado*.

"FUCK!" BUDDY YELLED AT THE TOP OF HIS LUNGS AS HE SPUN IN A circle outside the pickup, a wild dog attached to his calf. He kicked his leg forward and backward as he hopped around, trying to free himself of this rabid creature. But the dog wouldn't let go. Buddy began thrusting the back of his leg against the truck, striking the dog against the metal, but the son of a bitch wouldn't let go. Buddy then began running and turning in circles, and at one point he fell, but got back to his feet in a cloud of dust. The fucking dog was still clamped on. He screamed in pain and cursed the dog, and finally he remembered the gun he had tucked in his pants.

THE TWO KIDS, WHO, AS KIDS WILL, HAD FALLEN BACK ASLEEP AFTER cleaning up beer cans and having a potty break behind the barn, shot straight up and stared briefly into each other's wide open eyes. Without a word, Dusty scrambled from the makeshift straw bed and moved toward the ladder. He took one step down and then jumped to the ground, landing on his feet and stopping his fall with his hands. He ran from the barn to see his dog locked onto Mr. Jacobson's leg.

As Dusty ran toward them, and just before he shouted *That'll do* at his heeler, Mr. Jacobson began spinning in circles while pointing his gun at the dog, and screaming words Dusty had never heard him use. That's when Dusty saw that it wasn't Mr. Jacobson at all.

Then there was an explosion, and flames erupted from the pistol this stranger held in his hand. A cloud of dust kicked up beneath the dog, but Blue held on. The man continued to scream as he fired his gun again, one blast and then another. Dirt was kicking up all around the man's feet and all around Blue, but she held on as she had been bred and trained to do, and growled fiercely through the bite, shaking her head as if trying to tear off a hunk of meat to chew on. Dusty stood still, helpless and clueless. Then a gunshot came from the other direction.

"The fuck?!" Buddy yelled. He stopped spinning but was dragging his leg behind him—the one with the dog attached to it—while looking away from where Dusty stood and away from where the truck sat parked. Dusty followed his gaze, and just as he spotted Sam near her four-wheeler, her rifle shouldered and pointed straight at the stranger, there was another blast, and then another, and the mirror of the four-wheeler exploded and Sam's rifle erupted as she fell backward and hit the ground.

Dusty yelled, *"Get 'em, Blue! Get 'em! Go on, get a'hold!"* and his heeler let go, but only for an instant, and then she reset her bite on the man's calf, this one deeper than the first.

Buddy spun and fired another shot from his pistol, this time pointed right at Dusty.

The blast and its sonic crack over Dusty's head drove him to the ground. As he looked up, he saw the man crawling into his truck with Blue still locked onto his leg.

Dusty yelled, "That'll do!"

The heeler released her bite and dropped to the ground below the truck. Dusty could see she was hurt. The truck, now running, shot toward him. Dusty rolled out of the way, just in time for the truck to pass by him. It clipped the barn door, knocking it off its tracks and sending pieces of wood and dust flying through the air.

The truck raced down the driveway and disappeared in a cloud of smoke that rose up behind it and lingered in the still mountain air. Dusty looked up from the ground to see both Sam and Blue lying motionless on the ground, thirty feet apart.

The colts ran and bucked in circles inside their corral, whinnying and snorting with their ears and tails high in the air.

27

R ich and Odessa remained at the diner after Jeremy left for the office. With the table cleared, Rich thumbed through the stack of reports that Jeremy had left with him: the initial crime report of Lacy Jane's murder, supplemental investigation reports, the coroner's protocol, and the Elwood Johnston missing person report. Rich knew that for him to come up to speed on the investigation, and if there was any hope of him offering some ideas about how to better tie Frantelli to the murder of Lacy Jane Lewis, he needed to study the case in its entirety. They were seemingly at a standstill while their prime suspect was on the run—and apparently on a killing spree—and Rich needed something to do. Odessa had brought a paperback to read.

There had been times during the trip when he pondered his purpose for being in Boise, and many more times when he questioned why Odessa had accompanied him. At those times, however, his thoughts always came back to the simplest conclusion: why they were there or what they were accomplishing mattered less than the fact that he was alive, and that in her company he was happier and more content than he had been for a long time. Rich didn't like to think about the arrangement ending, and maybe that's why he insisted on staying busy. Making busy work playing detective.

They remained in the corner booth with a view of friendly Idahoans wandering around the city. It wasn't like Los Angeles, or New York, where people moved quickly, always in a hurry, and without speaking to one another or even making eye contact. The people in Boise greeted strangers and spoke to one another as if they all were friends. It was the type of city Rich thought he could feel comfortable in without having a gun on his hip, and the type of place where he'd consider living if he ever left Southern California. After all, he had nothing left to keep him there. No wife, no kids, not even a fish at home with a view of the pool. His daughter, a prosecutor in Vegas, was a typical married professional who was busy with her own life. She didn't have a clue about Rich's struggles with life, and he didn't see her enough for it to matter how close to her he lived.

The waitress topped off their mugs of coffee and pointed to the near-empty Coke. "Is he gone?"

Odessa nodded. "Yes ma'am."

The waitress collected the glass and left. Rich said, "I thought Mormons didn't drink any kind of caffeinated drinks, coffee *or* soda."

Odessa shrugged. "Beats me."

It didn't matter, so he gave it no further thought, and continued reading.

Odessa closed her paperback novel and said, "I would like to read those reports."

He considered it for a moment. "Well, I guess you're a big girl."

"That's not what we *girls* love to hear, Richard, in case you were wondering."

"You know what I mean."

She smiled. "I know. Now let me see some of those reports."

BUDDY WAS QUICK ON HIS FEET, IF NOTHING ELSE. HE HAD HONED THAT skill in prison, learning to think fast and react quickly when something jumped off in the chow hall, or in the showers, or out on the yard. When he hit the highway and headed south, he second-guessed his idea of going into town. The boy was still alive, and there was no doubt he'd be calling the cops. He would describe Buddy and the truck he stole, and he'd probably be able to tell them that Buddy had turned south on the highway toward Bishop.

Although Buddy had never been in this part of the country, he knew how remote some of the highways were, and he realized that this highway with its signs advertising Bishop ahead would likely be the main thoroughfare through town. It would be an easy trap for the cops to head off a killer on the run. So when he drove into the north end of Bishop, he turned left on the first street he saw, and then into a large parking lot that featured a Kmart, a grocery store, and a few shops. The parking lot was large and crowded, which was perfect for Buddy. He pulled the stolen Ford between two other ranch-style flatbed pickups, and retrieved the bag of clothes, food, and whiskey. He left behind the empty pistol, and the rifle that would be hard to conceal, slammed the driver's side door, and began walking the lot. He went up and down the rows, between cars and trucks until he spotted a vehicle that sat unoccupied with its keys left in the ignition. Buddy smiled. *Small town shit.*

STEVE TROY SPENT THE MORNING TALKING TO THE RETIREMENT advisor, his union rep, and the police protective league's attorney. He asked the advisor what the numbers would look like if he took his pension a few years early. He asked the union rep, and then the PPL's attorney, if he had any recourse to the suspension he had been handed without an investigation, and if he could take legal action against the department, or maybe even Lieutenant Fitzpatrick personally. He'd had his share of the fucking Mormon mafia and said so to the attorney, who gave him a blank look in response. Then it occurred to the topnotch detective that he hadn't been offered a cup of coffee in the modest but comfortable attorney's office, nor had he seen anyone else with one.

The good news was he could retire at about seventy-five percent of his salary, which wasn't bad, he thought, other than the fact that his ex would get a sizable portion of it.

It was nearly noon, so he headed to Sheehy's where he could think it all over without having to worry about the Mormons or listen to any snarky attorneys.

ODESSA SOAKED UP EVERY WORD. SHE FOUND THE CRIME REPORTS AND investigative supplemental reports fascinating. She wondered what it would be like to work as a detective, and silently questioned whether the Lord was truly calling her into the ministry, or was this entire detour from her life's course actually a new sign from God. She would need to ponder that and pray about it.

The crime report was little more than a summary of the events surrounding the death of her friend, Lacy Jane Lewis. It was vague, intentionally so, Rich explained. It was what they considered the "first report," which would be available as a public record. A generic "Person Dead" report. No identification of the deceased. Jane Doe, Female, 18-25 years old. Unknown causes. And a description of where and how she was found. Not even the name of the person who discovered her body was mentioned in this first report.

Next came the detectives' report. This is where the details were found. The name of the victim. The name of the citizen informant. The details of how she appeared, from her manner of dress to the position of her body. There were notations of bruising on her arms, trauma to her neck, and the presence of postmortem lividity. It was noted that the lividity was consistent with her position, indicating she had not been moved since death. Which, Rich explained, meant she wasn't killed elsewhere and dumped in the alley. She was killed right where they found her, which was a significant detail in any case.

Odessa thought about shows like CSI and NCIS where she and most of the country seemed to learn about crime scene and death investigation. She had always enjoyed those shows but never really thought about them from the sense of *enjoying* the actual work; she just viewed them as entertainment. Now she saw the work as a science, a profession, and she was fascinated by it and drawn into it.

But this could be the last straw with her parents, should she pursue another change in career paths. From the medical profession to the ministry, and now crime scene investigation or maybe even police work. Or just being an investigator. Maybe work for the FBI or NCIS, even the local cops. Shreveport Police. Boise Police. Maybe LAPD or the Los Angeles County Sheriff's Department. She would have Rich to steer her in the right direction. *Her Richie.*

Her mother would flip. Her father would disown her.

She moved on to the supplemental reports which detailed all follow-up investigation, including a summary of the autopsy findings —even though a coroner's report provided the details of the post-mortem examination—interviews of potential witnesses, procedurals such as next of kin notification, property disposal, items of evidence and their chain of custody, and notable times of everything. Time seemed essential. Throughout all the reports there were times of noti-fications, times of arrivals, times of departures, times of noting times. She would remember to always check the time, and note it as needed.

This detective thing excited her. She couldn't wait for more.

She picked up the last report to be read, the coroner's protocol, and wondered if this would deter her from her newfound love of detective work.

RICH TOOK A MENTAL BREAK FROM THE REPORTS. ALTHOUGH HE appeared to be reading, he had stalled at the bottom of a page and was deep in thought a long way from Boise, Idaho. He was thinking about a day not long ago when he had planned to end his life and had gone further than any previous occasion with the implementation of that plan. He remembered the phone call that saved his life, Cherie Lewis asking for his help because her daughter was missing. If that wasn't divine intervention, he doubted such a thing existed. He considered the many times before when he had had suicidal ideations, though with far less resolve, and again it struck him that maybe there was a master plan for him over which he had no control.

It occurred to him now, as Rich sat in the small diner in the company of this lovely young lady who made him have peculiar thoughts about his future, that he hadn't thought about suicide, his dead partner, dead kids, or dead cops. A string of days and nights without those burdens and also without nightmares. He hadn't dwelled on booze, and he hadn't *needed* a drink. At all. Was it working the case, the fact he was now focused, preoccupied, doing what he was accomplished at doing? Or was it the girl? Which of these things had picked him up, and, at least for the time being, saved his life?

Maybe it was both.

He was very fond of each. Maybe more than he should have been. But this also might have been all there was, one last case, one last rescue of the downtrodden, one more victory over evil. One more *last call*. And the girl would be gone when the case was finished—he needn't kid himself about that.

Rich looked up to see Odessa immersed in her review of the coroner's protocol. She was striking, with her flawless skin, big brown eyes, and sparkling smile. And she was too young. He liked that she wore her hair natural, not straightened or colored like so many of the black girls now did. It reminded him of a time far behind him, and it made him feel young again. *She* made him feel young again. She exuded confidence, this determined young lady who was very comfortable in her skin.

And innocent.

Maybe pure.

She looked up to catch him staring. "What?"

"Nothing."

"You're staring at me, and you're thinking about something."

"Honestly, I think I was just zoned out."

"Rich, your eyes are very expressive and telling. I can see when you're thinking, or just looking."

"I think I was just contemplating the day, that's all."

"You do a lot of thinking and looking and analyzing, you do know that, right? In fact, it's constant. You never give it a break. You never just *zone*. I can tell when you're contemplating people or situations, and I can see when you're in a faraway place. At times I've wanted to ask what that place looks like, but I've resisted. I worry it might be too dark, or maybe that's just the impression I get. Maybe it's something preconceived, given your profession."

Rich listened as she read him as if he were an open book.

"I can also see when you are enjoying something you're looking at, maybe admiring it, or even lusting over it... in case you wondered."

"What! What do you mean, *lusting*?"

"Like in the room when you saw me dressed in that sports bra. Your eyes were lustful."

"You're nuts," he said, dismissively. He shifted his gaze back onto a report, though he couldn't see the words. Everything was a blur and his mind raced to find the words to defend himself. The indefensible, in this case.

"There've been other times too, and you know I'm not *nuts*, or lying about it either. Are you going to deny it?"

He couldn't believe it, the nerve this girl had. She was right, of course, but man, to just throw it out there, front him off like this. Where was all of this going? He dropped the report again and met her gaze. "I think you're off track, little sister. I'm twenty years your senior, and I *do not* look at you—or even *think* of you—that way."

She smiled and said, "Yes, you do."

Then she reached over and put her hand on his forearm. "It's okay, Richie. It's natural. Plus, I have to be honest, I'm very attracted to you, as well. I like you a lot, and I don't even know why. I can't quite put my finger on it even though I've given it a lot of thought. I've even prayed about it."

Rich didn't know what to say to that. To any of it. He looked off across the diner but didn't focus on any of the activity that surrounded them, others enjoying breakfast, waitresses buzzing around with trays of food or pots of coffee. He thought about Lizzy and wondered if he was trying to replace her, trying to find another smart and competent partner who also provided the female companionship he had avoided for so many years. Then he questioned if he had crossed the line with Lizzy, at least in his thoughts. Had he always secretly wished their relationship was more than just being partner and friends? No, of course not, he reasoned. She was happily married and Rich was not that type of man. But yes, he had found her attractive. Was that wrong? Was it wrong that he found Odessa sexually attractive? He didn't know.

She removed her hand from his arm and resumed her study of the material in silence.

Rich pushed his coffee away and lifted a glass of ice water, and chugged most of it down.

JEREMY SAT IN LIEUTENANT FITZPATRICK'S OFFICE, BRIEFING HIM ON the case. He methodically went through the evidence and the timelines, and then he tied it all together, the case of Lacy Jane Lewis and the kidnap and subsequent murder of Elwood Johnston. He explained how he was in communication with the Idaho Department of Corrections, who had issued a parole violation warrant for Buddy Frantelli, with the Nevada State Troopers, who were seeking a first-degree murder charge against Frantelli for the Johnston murder, and with the California Highway Patrol and the Inyo County Sheriff's Office in California, where the suspect would likely be by now, still on the run.

His cell phone rang and he looked to see it was a *760* area code phone number. He told his lieutenant he'd better take it, it was from California.

Jeremy listened to the voice on the other end of the line while maintaining eye contact with his lieutenant. The caller, a detective with the Inyo County Sheriff's Office, began telling him about a home invasion that had occurred just outside of Bishop. There had been a shootout, and the suspect got away. He said that based on the information Jeremy had provided him about the fugitive who was on a crime spree, they had a hunch this might have been him. The detective then asked if Jeremy had a photograph of this outlaw named Buddy Frantelli, something they could show to a couple of witnesses.

When he ended the call, Jeremy relayed the information about the shooting near Bishop to his lieutenant. Then he said, "I feel like I should be there."

INYO COUNTY DETECTIVE GERARDO HERRERA STOOD NEXT TO SHERIFF Alfred Reynolds, both dressed in green uniform pants and khaki shirts, along with Dusty McBride, Travis and Katrina Jacobson, and a weathered cowboy who stood with watery eyes. Dusty called him *Mr. Wright* but everyone else called him *Lou*. They were all waiting, looking down at Samantha Jo Wright who lay still on the ground in front of the barn with two paramedics attending to her.

As one of them stood and turned to face the waiting crowd, the other helped Samantha Wright to her feet. The first paramedic said, "Best we can figure, she'd been knocked out." He indicated the mirror of the four-wheeler that had been hit by gunfire and now lay on the ground near his foot. "Might've been the mirror. She's got a heck of a divot on her forehead."

There were sighs of relief as the onlookers let out volumes of air that had been compressed in their chests.

He continued, "She's going to be okay, but we need to run her down to the E.R., have them run some more tests and monitor her for a while, concussion protocol."

Lou nodded and then turned to the sheriff he'd known all his life. "Call up a posse, Al. I'm going home to get my long gun and more shells for everything I got in the truck. We need to find this scoundrel before he kills someone."

"It's done," Sheriff Reynolds responded. "The command post will be at the Kmart parking lot, briefing there in thirty minutes." He looked at his detective and said, "Gerry, let everyone know, and have dispatch notify the highway patrol."

Lou looked at Dusty and said, "Get your dog, boy, and we'll drop her off at the vet on the way into town. You'll ride with me."

2 8

Buddy drove out of the parking lot and started south on the main drag through town, then abruptly pulled over and stopped on the side of the road. It occurred to him that the cops would anticipate him heading south, and they'd be on the lookout. He needed to get some medical attention for the arm that no longer throbbed or even ached, but now had a very foul odor, and also for the calf that had numerous puncture wounds from that fucking Rottweiler or whatever the hell it was, and the gunshot wound right above the punctures. It had only grazed him, took some flesh but didn't hit muscle, bone or veins. The bullet must have just missed the rabid beast's ugly face, and that was just Buddy's luck. But now stopping in this town was out of the question, and continuing south on the highway would be driving straight into the arms of the cops.

He pulled a U-turn and headed north. The late model, nondescript, gray Buick—an old man's car by the look and smell of it—would attract little attention. The cops would be on the lookout for the truck he took from the ranch, at least until they discovered it abandoned once the old man reported his car stolen.

As he reached the north end of town, there was a sign indicating Reno was 206 miles. That sounded just about right to Buddy, far enough away from here and big enough for a hospital where he would go unnoticed.

———

Lou had his truck wound up, headed south on the highway toward Bishop. He'd stop at his ranch and get the guns and ammo, then get the boy's dog, Blue, to the town vet. Dusty sat nervously beside him, his dog on his lap, bloody bandages wrapped around her left hind leg. Dusty stroked her head, looking into her soft eyes and thinking of the loyalty she had shown him, and choking back his emotions while worrying they might have to put her down.

They turned off the highway onto a dirt road that headed west toward a house and barn that sat back a quarter-mile from the road. Neither Lou nor Dusty noticed the gray Buick that roared through their cloud of dust that drifted across the highway behind them.

———

Travis Jacobson rode in the back of the ambulance with Sam. The driver had stopped at the highway to wait for a gray Buick to pass by before turning toward town.

Sam looked up at him from the gurney. "Did I hit him?"

He took her hand and said, "Just rest now, honey. Let's not think about that."

———

The sheriff and his detective were in their vehicles, also waiting to pull out onto the highway, one and then the other backed up behind the ambulance. Katrina's Tahoe and a paramedic's truck brought up the rear.

Sheriff Reynolds noticed the gray Buick heading north and thought he recognized it from town. There were plenty of vehicles that passed through, tourists and vacationers and travelers of all sorts, but the local cars and trucks, vehicles he would see over and over, day after day, he would remember.

He watched it continue north and nodded as he thought, yep, it's a local vehicle. He'd seen it around town, probably belonged to someone who worked locally and lived up in the hills to the north, away from the congestion. But he couldn't think of who it was. If he wasn't tied up with all this other commotion, he'd stop and find out who it was driving it, maybe warn the man about speeding on his highway. He didn't very often cite a local.

Six-hundred miles away, Mrs. Frantelli sat on her back porch smoking her pipe and having a conversation with a calico cat who seemed to be in agreement that she'd raised a goddamn rotten kid.

29

Odessa Brown had balls, Rich thought, this crazy young girl next to him who smelled nice and spoke candidly and with the confidence of a worldly woman. His head was still spinning from the confrontation. That's how he thought of it, a confrontation. Like when he had taken on killers or other bad guys, looked them directly in their eyes and put it out there, daring them to deny it. He'd tell them straight what his theory was, how things had gone down and what their involvement in the whole deal had been, put it all out there and dare them to try lying to the human lie detector.

And that's exactly what she had just done to him. Looked him in his eyes and put it out there. Read him like a book and confronted him with the details. She knew he had lusted over her. She knew he liked her. She told him as much and dared him to lie to her.

Which he had.

Which meant she probably saw it in his eyes and knew it now for sure.

Damn, this girl.

But as if nothing had happened, Odessa reached over for his forearm again, at first still looking at a report, maybe finishing a paragraph or page, and then she lowered the papers and looked him in the eyes. "My butt's tired of this seat. Let's go for a walk or something, stretch our legs and take in some fresh air. Whad'ya think?"

Rich felt relieved that she was back to being casual, as if the talk of love and lust never happened. At least for now she was. He liked this version of her: the vivacious, beautiful, and engaging companion who made his head spin, not the interrogator who turned him inside out. He said, "Sounds like a plan."

They walked in silence for a short distance, taking in the shops and people on the streets and the snow-capped mountains to the east.

Rich had wondered on more than one occasion how Odessa was handling the situation with her work and school. What he really wondered was when she would say she had to get back to it. When would the ride come to an end and he'd be alone again? So he asked her.

She said, "Well, it's a family emergency leave, as far as work goes. They understand the situation and said no problem, take my time. They like me there and they're really good to me. As for school, my professors are emailing assignments. I'm in the top of my class, and I get along really well with each of my professors, and the administrators too. Everyone's been very understanding and supportive. I've been working on my assignments late at night—while you're sleeping—and in the mornings before we meet. I haven't been getting a lot of rest, to be honest, which is why I look terrible."

Rich didn't respond, just looked at her for a moment and thought, who *doesn't* like this girl?

"My parents are the only real problem."

That took him by surprise, and also reminded him of her age. He said, "Really?"

"Well, yeah. They're worried about my schooling, worried about my job, and worried about this man they know nothing about, with whom I've run off to the other side of the country."

They stopped and looked into each other's eyes.

Rich said, "You haven't *run off* with me."

She said, "Not yet."

FOUR HOURS LATER THE CALIFORNIA HIGHWAY PATROL CONTINUED TO watch every vehicle headed south coming out of Bishop. They had the two lanes merged into one and were slowing cars to just a crawl, taking a good look at the occupants of each one. If there was any question about who was in the vehicle, or if anyone appeared nervous, or if the vehicle could hold passengers that couldn't be seen, the officers would wave the vehicle over to the side of the road for further investigation. They had stopped or viewed hundreds of vehicles without finding anything even remotely interesting or related to the manhunt thus far.

Sheriff Alfred Reynolds had stayed at the command post back at the north end of town. He stood beneath the shade of an awning that had been opened from the side of the mobile emergency operations unit. The Pace Arrow motorhome had been converted to an office on wheels with police radios, maps on the walls, televisions, scanners, ham radios, GPS trackers, and two generators to keep it all running when electricity wasn't available. It also had a refrigerator full of water, a large coffee urn, and cabinets full of coffee, water, canned foods and snacks. He watched as a flatbed tow truck pulled out of the Kmart parking lot with the stolen/recovered Ford truck that belonged to Dusty McBride loaded on the back. Dusty had immediately spotted it when he and Lou reported to the command post to get their assignments. That discovery had caused another three hours of delay in the manhunt as they contained the area and closed down each business in the shopping center and had the occupants exit one by one. A canine was finally deployed and the search for the suspect met with negative results. Frantelli was gone. Outside the containment, most likely, and still on the run.

Sheriff Reynolds passed out posse badges to each volunteer. Yes, badges. This was small-town America, and in some ways it was lost in time. They had formed a good old-fashioned posse and they were going after a killer, armed with whatever weapon each member brought from home.

Lou and Dusty had been assigned to patrol the backroads north of the command post, from the north end of town past the Jacobson residence, just in case the suspect had doubled back or turned off a road and was waiting somewhere, biding his time while the search efforts were exhausted. Or worse yet, in the event he had invaded another home. Sheriff Reynolds had said to Lou, "You know every single family in these parts, and you'll know if something doesn't look right. That's why I'm giving this detail to you and the boy. Be safe out there."

Detective Gerardo Herrera had made wanted posters with the photograph of the outlaw Buddy Frantelli, which had been provided to him by a detective from Boise PD. Herrera, and two Explorers—teenage volunteers who hoped to someday join the ranks of law enforcement—were dispersing the posters throughout town and beyond. They posted them at every gas station, fast-food restaurant, and at all of the businesses in between. They faxed or emailed them to the highway patrol and to all of the law enforcement agencies within a hundred miles north, east, and west, and as far as two-hundred miles to the south, notifying the Kern County and Los Angeles County Sheriff's departments.

TANIKA EDWARDS AND MAURICE "TANK" SHERMAN WERE JUST WAKING up in his apartment at two o'clock in the afternoon. Her phone vibrated on the table not far from the mattress on which they slept, a mattress that was stuffed into a corner on the bedroom floor. She ignored the phone, because frankly, she was too tired to work. And that was all she had for phone calls lately, responders to her ad, men wanting special massages from the "college girl" who was just trying to pay her way through school. Though she hadn't attended school since the tenth grade.

Tank said, "Ain't you gonna answer it?" and looked at her suspiciously.

She crawled over to the table on her hands and knees, and pushed the button to make it stop, then got up and walked out of the room with her phone, naked.

As she stood in the bathroom scrolling through the missed calls, she didn't notice the girl in the reflection who appeared tired and worn, maybe haggard. She didn't look up to see the bruising around her eye, and she didn't think about the discomfort in her groin, and not from the clientele, but from the rough sex—*maybe it would be considered rape*—that she endured with Tank. Right now, all she thought about was keeping the big man happy and making her pain go away. So she retrieved her kit from beneath the kitchen sink and cooked a spoonful of heroin and pushed it into her veins through a well-used needle. She could feel the warmth rapidly spreading through her body, and she welcomed the numbness that followed.

Tanika cleaned herself with a wet cloth, paying particular attention to her crotch and underarms, and then brushed her teeth and hair. She walked out of the bathroom to see Tank sitting up in the bed, supported by pillows, eating white powdered donuts from a box. She stopped in the doorway and posed, putting a hand up high and letting her hair fall over her face and across her shoulder. Doing her best to appear sexy, though she wanted to vomit and thought she just might. She was actually starting to think about checking out of the whole fucking program—one last shot of the H, and make it a hot one.

He looked at her and said, "Damn, little girl, don't you never get tired?"

3 0

———————————

Rich and Odessa met with Jeremy the next morning under a bright morning sky outside of the diner where Rich had become a regular in his short time visiting Boise. They were there for breakfast, but hadn't yet gone inside.

After brief but pleasant morning greetings, Jeremy said, "I'm going to Bishop to help with the search for Frantelli. They think he's still in the area, according to the report I received this morning. My lieutenant has authorized it, said to take whatever time I needed since this guy is apparently good for two murders connected to Boise. We don't like murders in Boise."

"In L.A., we actually embrace them," Rich said.

Jeremy chuckled.

Rich said, "Yeah, really. One a day is all we ask. Like vitamins or almonds."

"One a week, is what they advertise. A can a week," said Odessa.

He smiled at her and said, "Yeah, but that's not nearly enough for Angelenos… we need one a day."

"Almonds?"

"Murders."

"That's demented," she said. "So you're saying you actually want that much killing in your city?"

"It's a joke, because of the number of murders we have in L.A. County. It actually averages out to more than one a day, so it could be our slogan. *One a day, it's all we ask.*"

Odessa rolled her eyes.

Rich brought his attention back to Jeremy who waited patiently, smiling at the banter.

Jeremy said, "So, what are your plans?"

"Well, do you want or need some company?" Rich asked. "I think we've done all we can do here. I wouldn't mind going with you."

Odessa cleared her throat. "*We.*"

"Okay, *we* wouldn't mind going with you, if you think we would be of any use, or at least good company."

"I think you'd be both, and I'd love to have you tag along."

AFTER PATROLLING INTO THE EARLY MORNING HOURS, COVERING A TEN-mile circumference north of where Dusty's truck had been recovered, Lou Wright dropped Dusty at his home and told him to get a few hours of sleep, he'd pick him up at about nine. That would give them each time to feed their livestock and finish morning chores. Then they'd get back to work trying to find the outlaw, probably start by checking back in at the command post to see if there had been any new developments.

But the next morning the sheriff called Lou at his home just before he left and told him there had been a pretty bad blunder on the part of his clerk back at the office. Leroy Thurman, a local retired rancher who now worked as a greeter at the Kmart, had called yesterday afternoon to report his car had been stolen. The clerk told him all the deputies were tied up on an emergency, and asked if he could wait until tomorrow to file his report. Mr. Thurman did, he waited until this morning, and at eight o'clock sharp he walked into the sheriff's office and made his report. The report stated that his car had been stolen the day before from the Kmart parking lot. Lou sighed into the phone and said he'd be over at the C.P. in a few minutes, they could discuss it more then.

SHERIFF REYNOLDS SAW LOU AND DUSTY ARRIVE IN LOU'S TRUCK, DUST coming off it as he screeched to a halt. There were two rifles in the rifle rack behind their heads. Both men were wearing long-sleeved button-up western shirts and cowboy hats. The sheriff could tell that his lifelong friend, Lou Wright, was not in a good mood when he stepped out of the truck.

"The hell's wrong with your people over there, Al?" Lou said while walking toward him, his large, muscular frame matching the square jaw that seemed tight this morning.

"Now, calm down, Lou—"

"Don't you tell me to calm down, Al. It ain't your girl who was shot and damn near killed by some lunatic who's still out there running around," he said, as he pointed to the north, back toward the crime scene.

Sheriff Reynolds was smarter than to point out that Lou's daughter hadn't actually been shot, in part because it didn't matter—it wasn't the point—and in larger part because Alfred Reynolds had been the elected sheriff of Inyo County for the past twenty-two years for a reason: he had good people skills.

"You're right, Lou," the sheriff told him, "I'm just saying we need to stay focused here. My clerk didn't know any better, and it's my fault for not leaving a deputy back at the office to handle those types of phone calls. I wanted all hands on deck, and it bit me in my ass. I take full responsibility."

With that the sheriff could see the wind come out of Lou's sails.

Lou glanced over at Dusty, then looked back at the sheriff. "I'm sorry, Al. I didn't mean to bark at you, of all people."

They shook hands and turned together to face a whiteboard tacked up against the motorhome beneath the awning. Sheriff

Reynolds motioned toward it and said, "We've got the same assignments as yesterday. You and the boy cover north of here, maybe go farther north than yesterday, say all the way up to Mesa Camp. Maybe all the way over to Swall Meadows."

Lou nodded. "It's worth a try, I suppose."

"He could be in Mammoth, Bridgeport, maybe even Reno, if he went north. Or maybe he headed back over into Nevada, but I don't think so. That wouldn't be a wise move, given that killing up on the Montgomery Pass. No, I think he went south, personally. I just don't know how he got through the barricades without being spotted, or how he has slipped through all the patrols out there on the highway—the chippies have been swarming around here."

Lou didn't respond right away.

"What do you think, Lou?"

He gave it another moment, and then said, "I think this guy is clever. Which makes me think he's gone to ground. You know the biggest buck I ever shot, I shot him right behind my barn, thirty yards from the house. He'd been holed up in a clump of brush no bigger'n this here"—he pointed from where they stood to the side of the motorhome, six feet away—"all through hunting season. I'd watched him grow up, seen him year after year in the pastures, or coming down to get my hay in the winter. One year, when he'd become a danged good trophy buck, six, seven years old and with a twenty-eight inch rack, I'd decided to hunt for him. I hunted the mountains, the tree lines, the fields and pastures around my place and over at Bill's, and even down there at old man Roundy's, but I never could find him. The last day of the season, I had given up and come back from hunting before dark. That's when I seen him step out of that pile of brush behind the barn. I checked it after, and it was hollowed out in there. He'd been bedding there all season, maybe during all the seasons before that one too. My point being, if this guy's clever like a leery old buck, he's smart enough to find a hole and go to ground for a while, wait until all the hunters have gone home."

The sheriff nodded. "What are you suggesting, Lou?"

"Keep hunting, and check all the holes. But don't get too damn far from the barn."

BUDDY WOKE UP IN THE FRONT SEAT OF THE BUICK AND LOOKED around to see what he could see now that it was light outside. He'd taken a left off the highway when he saw the sign that read *June Lake*, deciding not to take any chances by traveling farther on the main highway during daylight hours. But when he found a little campsite where he could get some rest and just hang out for a couple hours, he had decided to have another pain pill or two and washed them down with a few swigs of the Pendleton. Now here it was daytime again and it took a few minutes for Buddy to clear the cobwebs from his head and figure out where he was and what his next move would be.

Getting some food would be the priority. But he also needed medical attention for his arm and his calf, both of which were wrapped with makeshift bandaging. He got out of the car and stretched, wincing at the smell of his arm, then he began walking around to have a better look at the area. There wasn't much of a view from where he had parked, just thick stands of pine trees. But a plume of smoke rising up through the woods told him there were campers nearby. Campers who no doubt would have food and water, maybe a first-aid kit. Maybe cold beer, and even a firearm. He might end up with a new car or pickup truck, some cold hard cash to help him get by. He had some traveling to do now, and he needed to get to it.

So he straightened his *Bishop Mule Days* cap, and said, "Let's go visit some of our fellow campers, Buddy."

There was something about traveling that would cause Odessa to tell her life story. She leaned forward between the front seats of the Explorer. "When I was little, my daddy took me and my best friend at the time, Denise—who we called *Neecy* —and my big brother, Orenthal—"

"Wait, your brother's name is *Orenthal?*" Rich asked, incredulously.

"Yes, it is, *Richard...* but as I was saying—"

"No, hang on, this is important," Rich said, now twisted in the passenger's seat to face her, looking her straight in the eyes. "I just want to be clear, here... your mama—or, more likely, your daddy— named your big brother, *Orenthal,* as in *Orenthal James,* right?... *O.J.?*"

"Yes, they did, but his middle name isn't James, it's Jamal. And yes, I know who Orenthal James is, and yes, that's who my *daddy* named him after."

"And does he goes by *O.J.?*"

"Not anymore."

Rich laughed. "Now *that* is funny."

"Okay," she said, "But you need to understand, this was long before *that* O.J. went crazy and killed a bunch of white folks, and went on his little robbing spree in Las Vegas, and went to prison and got fat and ended up with diabetes and who knows what else. We're talking about back when the man was a role model, a Hall of Fame football player, an actor, and an icon in his community."

Rich chuckled. "Yeah, a real role model he turned out to be, huh?"

"Well, he was back then. At least for black people, or some of us."

"So, your brother's quite a bit older than you, I take it."

"Yes, he is. Now can I please just finish my story?"

Rich grinned. "Sure, Odessa, you go right ahead and finish your story. I'm very sorry to have interrupted."

He looked over to see if Jeremy was grinning too, but his face showed only a slight smirk, his eyes hidden behind mirrored glasses as he stared straight ahead.

Odessa said, "Now I don't even feel like telling it."

"Come on, now, I was just giving you a hard time. Tell us your story. I'm sure it was going to be really interesting. Tell us what you and your girlfriend and O.J. did one summer."

She disappeared into the back seat and said, "I'm no longer speaking to you, Mr. Farris. Neither one of you, actually."

CLIFFORD LOMELI RETIRED FROM THE POST OFFICE THREE YEARS AFTER he woke up to find his wife of twenty-nine years dead beside him. Most of the last three years had been a grind, and there were mornings he nearly hadn't gotten out of bed to face another day. But he had gotten up all of those days, more often than not hung over from a night of drinking alone and contemplating the idea of joining his wife in the afterlife. Retirement hadn't made life any easier, other than he didn't have to get up in the morning when his head hurt.

Finally, he decided that in order to save his own life, he would need to dry out, and he would need to accept the loss of his beloved wife and find a way to move forward. He had always wanted to take up golf, so he finally did, and little by little he began enjoying life again. Eventually he decided on selling the three bedroom house where he and the missus had lived their lives and raised their children, and he bought a small, two-bedroom condo that was within walking distance of a public golf course. He purchased an annual membership, and he bought a golf cart that he could drive directly from his garage to the pro shop, first tee and driving range. Then came new clubs and a wardrobe of comfortable slacks and golf shirts.

Cliff was remade.

Six months later he took his pickup and trailer out of storage, and drove it to the RV dealer. He asked the sales lady, an attractive woman nearly his age but very well preserved, what they'd give him for it.

LILLIAN MET CLIFF WHEN HE SHOWED UP WITH THE CAMP TRAILER, asking if she would help him sell it on consignment.

He told her his life story, which at first seemed quite boring, but after she realized he was widowed, pensioned, and living a comfortable life, he became much more interesting. He was mostly bald, which made him look old, and he had a beer belly and sagging shoulders, which made him look soft. He was anything but attractive, but Lillian had learned several husbands ago that there was more to a good marriage than sexual appeal. Not that any of her previous marriages would likely be considered *good*.

Besides, it had never been difficult for her to find the company of younger men—sometimes much younger—as she had two things going for her: a natural killer body that remained remarkable even as she now approached sixty, and a taste for adventure that often led her down the wrong roads and never allowed her to say no. Being married had never interfered with alternate excursions.

Lillian became bored of hearing about Cliff's wife of all those years who died and blah, blah, blah. She preferred to be the speaker in most cases, so she shut him up by telling him the sad story about her husband who had passed, and her eyes watered a bit when she mentioned it. She didn't mention the suspicious nature of the death— the cause of which the coroner had deemed to be undetermined—or that it may or may not still be under investigation. She also didn't mention the other marriages, which totaled five: four divorces and the one questionably natural death. Questionable, but timely. If he had lived another six months, they would have no doubt divorced, and then she would be left with nothing. The life insurance policy had helped her through her time of mourning, but she didn't mention that to Cliff either. Nor did she see any reason to bring up a track record that could cause someone to think poorly of her. Sometimes a girl just needed a clean slate.

He told her about his career with the post office—she couldn't imagine a more hideous job. She told him about being a nurse for many years before transitioning to sales. She enjoyed selling campers and motorhomes and meeting nice people like him, she had said. She didn't mention her jobs as a barmaid, a hostess, and in the early days, a dancer. Technically, a stripper; that would be the more accurate description of a job that had begun innocently enough. She had been a barmaid at a biker joint where tips were okay but the dancers raked in the real money. Once she started dancing, she too had made a killing. But Lillian preferred to focus on the positive, and having been a nurse garnered more positive feedback than dancing for and sleeping with bikers and outlaws. So she would only mention the nursing career, but she would avoid details rather than having to explain that she actually hadn't been a nurse at all, but had worked in the clinic at the state prison for several years filling out charts and handing out aspirin to inmates. Until she was caught having one of her several affairs, or as the termination papers read, inappropriate inmate relations.

That had forced her back into the barmaid business, since she was told she was now too old for taking off her clothes for a living. So she made do slinging liquor, and there were plenty of perks to the job since she still had quite an appetite for the company of men. Especially bad men. Outlaws. Men who were younger than she and could show a girl a good time. She enjoyed rides on Harleys and watching fistfights in the back alley or taking off her clothes for the guys at the clubhouse who couldn't believe her age.

It had been the perfect job until she was fired for stealing and nearly caught a case over the ordeal. Which would have ruined her thirty-two year streak of being crime free and avoiding jail and prison.

———————

THE SALES WOMAN WAS COMPLETELY DIFFERENT FROM HIS FIRST WIFE, but Cliff really felt something for Lillian. She was a bit forward, but, hey, she was interested—she had made that clear—and he was lonely, to say the least.

So they had a first date and then a couple more, and they shared everything about themselves with one another, or almost everything. Cliff told her about his wife, his kids, his career, his retirement. He told her how he had loved to camp and fish when he was still married, but since she passed, he hadn't done much of it, and that he had taken up golf and that was his new passion. She had said she too loved all of those things.

Three weeks later the two were hitched in Las Vegas. Lillian mentioned that if only she could quit working, they'd be able to travel and do the things he loved to do. Well, it just so happened, he said, that he had been thinking the same thing. And since he made enough in retirement to live comfortably, she could quit her job and they would do exactly that. They kept the R.V. and she moved into the new condo and the two began their new lives. That was in February, and this was their first spring together. Their first camping trip in the old R.V. with faded memories and a new lease on life.

———————

LOU AND DUSTY PATROLLED THE BACK ROADS NORTH OF BISHOP, checking known dumpsites, campsites, lakes, ponds and streams. They talked to campers and fishermen and hikers, but so far had no luck finding anyone who had seen the likes of Buddy Frantelli. Lou radioed into the command post and let them know they were headed farther north, and would likely be out of radio range and cell coverage. They'd be up near June Lake and the surrounding area.

After what seemed an eternity, Lou finally spoke to the boy. He said, "Well, son, you want to tell me what happened back there at the Jacobson place?"

Dusty's throat felt dry. He swallowed but it didn't help. He knew the time would come when Sammie Jo's dad would have questions for him. Maybe more than just questions. He'd probably have some things to say. Maybe he'd stop the truck and whip him like a man for putting his daughter in harm's way, or for spending the night with her in the loft, which would be something he'd have to tell him. He'd have to tell him the whole truth because he knew better than to not do so. He'd been raised knowing it was better to tell the truth than to be caught in a lie, and he knew he wouldn't be able to lie to the likes of Louis Wright, a weathered old cowboy with hard eyes.

He said, "We didn't do anything wrong, sir. I mean, you know, we didn't do anything."

Lou glanced over. "You start from the beginning, boy. We have nothing but time now and I want to hear the whole story from start to finish." He glanced over once more when he finished saying it. Or maybe glared would be more accurate, a warning or sorts, something to keep in mind as Dusty answered.

Dusty said, "Well, sir, you know she was taking care of Mr. and Mrs. Jacobson's place while they were out of town..."

He went on to tell him about how he'd gone over a couple of times a day, every chance he got after his own chores were done and his dad would let him cut out for a while. He said that he and Sammie Jo had talked a lot about the colts and how she had wanted to take them outside for a ride in the hills. So they took the horses out that evening before everything happened, went for a ride, and when they got back, well, it was late. They had to wash the horses and wait for them to dry before turning them out, so they built a fire and hung out, enjoying the night together. He explained that by time all was said and done, it was real late, and they were tired. And, well, they decided to just sleep up in the hay loft of the barn. But they didn't do anything, he swore to it. Dusty admitted it looked bad, and he was sure sorry, and it would never happen again, but he didn't want to lie about it, either.

He didn't mention the beer. He figured it didn't factor in, but if asked, he would be truthful.

Finally, he said, they fell asleep and were awakened the next morning to a terrible ruckus down below with Blue on the attack and the horses making a commotion. He jumped down out of the loft and saw that man trying to steal his truck, but Blue had ahold of him, had set a bite on the back of the man's leg. That's when the man started shooting at his dog. He never saw Sam after he jumped down from the loft until she fired a shot with her rifle. The man started shooting at her, and then he fired a shot at him, too. It was a real, live shootout! After the man tried to run him over, and then fled, that's when he'd seen that Sam and Blue had both been hurt. Dusty got choked up when he said, "I thought they'd both been killed."

They continued patrolling the back roads in silence. After a while, Mr. Wright said, "I'm proud of you both."

3 2

Steve Troy filed his papers for retirement. He came into the office to clean out his desk and have a final word with his partner and lieutenant. He had a few things that needed to be said. He stood staring at the desk across from his own where his partner should have been seated, then looked over at the lieutenant's office where the lieutenant should have been busy making everyone's life miserable. Neither of them was there. He grunted to himself, pissed off at the both of them yet again.

After removing the personal property from his desk and locker and loading it into his car, Troy came back in and dropped his keys on the lieutenant's desk. He considered whipping it out and having a good piss across the blotter, but decided against it.

He wouldn't turn in his badge and ID until the day he retired, which would be at least another week, according to the lady who processed the paperwork. On his way out the door he asked the few detectives who were milling about, almost intentionally ignoring him, to make sure they told Fitzpatrick to go fuck himself.

And he headed for Sheehy's.

DAVE LOOKED UP WHEN DAYLIGHT SHONE THROUGH THE DOOR AND disappeared a moment later. He wasn't surprised to see Steve Troy belly up to the bar. His arrival time seemed to be earlier every day, closer to Sheehy's ten o'clock opening. Today he was the first to arrive. It was a quarter past ten.

"Good morning, Detective."

"There ain't nothing good about it, Dave, and don't ever call me that again."

Dave watched him but Steve Troy never looked up. Dave knew Steve was a blowhard, he had always known it. He'd talk tough to those he could buffalo a little, otherwise he'd play it safe. Dave set his usual in front of him, a double Jameson, and then handed him the morning paper.

"Interesting stuff going on."

Steve glanced at it. "Fucking rag. I don't read that shit."

Dave shrugged, left the Idaho Statesman on the bar near Troy and walked away. There were dishes he could wash or maybe he could spit-shine ashtrays—anything would trump chatting with that asshole.

RICH GLANCED BACK AND SAW THAT ODESSA WAS SOUND ASLEEP IN THE back seat of the detective car. They had put the miles behind them in silence, Odessa not speaking to anyone, and Rich and Jeremy riding along taking in the views without conversation, each of them the quiet type. Rich mentioned to Jeremy that his traveling partner was out, and Jeremy glanced in the rearview mirror, raising his head slightly to see into the back seat.

After a moment, Jeremy said, "So, what's your story, Rich?"

"My story?"

He glanced in the mirror, apparently checking Odessa again. Then he glanced over at Rich. "You're pretty young to be retired."

Rich didn't answer right away, contemplating the statement. After all, it hadn't really been a question.

After a moment, Jeremy said, "Did you think I'd run around the country with someone I didn't know anything about? Working a homicide case? What kind of cop do you think I am?"

"Who else knows?"

Jeremy glanced over at him. "Nobody."

Rich looked down, and for a moment felt ashamed for lying to him. Lying to him, lying to Sheriff Walker in Louisiana, lying to Odessa... Finally, he said, "I didn't mean any harm, Jeremy. I just didn't think I'd get my foot in the door as a retired cop. It was a bit of a white lie, I'd say, but it wasn't meant to harm anyone or anything. I guess it was foolish of me."

Jeremy looked over but didn't say anything.

Rich continued, "To answer your question, I've been retired a couple years. Went out on a medical, what we call a stress retirement. I guess it would have been more honorable if I'd been shot or broke my neck, but the truth is, the job eventually broke my brain. All the years of violence, murder, and mayhem had taken its toll. All the dead kids, the dead cops, the grieving mothers and fathers, and the whole system that seemed to be against us every step of the way.

"I had a partner—" Rich began, but then stopped and turned his head to look through his window. After a moment, he continued: "I broke her in at Homicide and we stayed paired up for a few years after—"

"She still on the job, your partner?"

"She got sick, cancer, and after a while she couldn't work. I had a hard time with it, and maybe that made it to where I was less tolerant of all the other bullshit that comes with doing the job. I don't know, maybe I was just burned out; it's hard to say. It all seemed to come at once, but I honestly don't know what put me over the edge. But something sure did. I suddenly felt as if I had hit a wall or I was standing in concrete. It's the damnedest thing to try and explain."

Rich craned his neck to see into the back and make sure Odessa was still asleep. She was. He looked at Jeremy who was focused on the highway, waiting for more. "I started dreading every case, every call-out, every damn phone call. With Lizzy gone—that was my partner—I worked with different people in every rotation. They were all good partners, but it just wasn't the same as having a regular, full-time partner to work with. I missed her terribly and the job just wasn't fun anymore. At some point, I realized it never would be again.

"Something happened inside me when she passed, and it changed me even more. If I thought work was hard before that, it multiplied ten times over once she was gone. I quit going to work. Honestly, I just wouldn't go in. Nobody really ever said too much, at least not for a while. I think they knew I needed my space. It's probably a lot different where you work, with just a few guys. Our bureau has about eighty investigators, and it's not easy for anyone to keep track of anyone else. The people there are self-starters, and they don't need supervision. So when a guy checks out, like I did, it takes a while for anyone to notice.

"Of course, I'd still go on my callouts. That was the one thing you couldn't not show up for. But rarely would I go into the office or even do much work on my cases after the callouts. My partners were pretty much carrying me, probably either felt sorry for me or wrote me off as just another cop who had crawled into a bottle."

Jeremy appeared deep in thought. Rich wondered if he had said too much, but he had gone this far, so he might as well finish. He glanced back to see Odessa still asleep.

"For the first time in my career, I didn't care about the job anymore, didn't concern myself with the cases. Maybe I was just too numb to care, I don't know. But that's when it hit me, when I knew I was done. That realization that I no longer cared drove me to make the difficult call. I went and saw the department shrink and laid it all out."

Jeremy glanced over. "So when did you get better? You're obviously in a better place now. I've spent enough time with you this last week or so to know it."

Rich sat thinking about how to answer that. He watched as the young detective glanced back and forth from the road, twice. "You wouldn't believe how my day went, the day I got the call about Lacy Jane."

"I can imagine it was difficult for you."

Rich chuckled and shook his head. "Well, actually, that call saved my life."

Jeremy looked over, apparently not clear about Rich's last statement. Rich could see the question in his expression. He said, "You wouldn't believe me if I told you. Trust me."

———

ODESSA CLOSED HER EYES AGAIN AND TRIED TO MAKE SENSE OF WHAT she had heard. This wasn't the man she knew. It didn't make sense. He could never *not* care. He wasn't a drunk. She had spent day and night with him and she knew better. She had looked deep into his eyes and she had seen his soul. He was a good man. An honorable man. A kind and gentle man with an instinct for people, and a way about him that would draw you in. Who was this man he was now describing?

Well, whoever he *was,* mattered not. The man she believed she was falling in love with, was not the man in the story Rich had told to Jeremy, unaware that she was wide awake. She wouldn't worry about his past. Everyone had a past.

Odessa thought of the two of them together, picturing them in various places in the future. The beach, ballgames, fancy dinners, dances... the bedroom. And then she drifted off to sleep.

33

B uddy smelled the bacon cooking over an open fire, so he slowed his approach and measured each step, careful not to break twigs or stumble over a rock or log. When he could just see the campsite, he took refuge in the brush where he could watch without being detected. He would sit for a while so he would know exactly what he would be walking into.

Buddy was clever that way. It was no different than watching the activity on the tier before stepping out of your cell. You had to be aware of who was nearby and what was going on. Was it business as usual, or was there a heaviness that told you something was about to go down? In prison, it was more predictable, because everyone had instinct. Everyone seemed to know that something bad was about to happen, and you could feel it if you paid attention. You didn't survive in prison by not paying attention. Buddy was convinced that most people would never make it in the joint. Those people with their heads up their asses who were not aware of their surroundings, not seeing the look in a convict's eyes, not watching his hands carefully and knowing he had something behind his leg, not noticing other inmates trying to circle behind you. No, most people would be killed their first week in stir.

You survived on the streets the same way you did in the joint, only there were fewer predators to deal with outside. For the most part, the bulk of those around you would be prey. Easy town. It'd make a man lick his chops at times, like a wolf watching a pen of sheep, or a hungry outlaw watching some campers.

He would watch the camp to see how many people were there and to assess what level of threat they posed, if any. It was a head count, or sorts. The body count would come later.

CLIFF SAT ON AN OVERTURNED FIVE-GALLON BUCKET NEXT TO THE campfire, watching intensely as the bacon sizzled and popped in its grease, six slices laid out in a cast-iron pan, just so.

It drove her crazy.

He drove her crazy. Lillian shook her head silently as she peered out through the small kitchen window of their camp trailer. *His* camp trailer.

His camp trailer that was stored inside a big metal building and cost him a hundred and fifty bucks a month because his precious little trailer couldn't sit out in the weather, and there was no place to park it at the condo. And when he did take it out, it would take a full day to prepare it for departure, like it was the goddamn space shuttle or something. He'd check each of the four tires for excessive wear, signs of defect, and, of course, proper inflation. He'd check the torque of each lug nut. He'd check and recheck all lights for proper function: *Activate the right signal, now the left signal... okay, step on the brakes, now just the parking lights, okay turn on all the lights...* all according to the checklist. Oh yeah, he had a checklist, and he would follow it to the letter and check it twice: check propane bottles, check generator fluids, check RV batteries—charge *and* fluid levels—check flashlights and batteries, check the fluids of his truck, grease the hitch mechanism, inspect the hitch and its nuts, bolts, and welded joints. Check gray and black waste tank levels, fill the fresh water tank, lower the antenna, secure all items inside, check and double-check all drawers and doors to be sure they were properly secured. Close all the vents, and on and on.

She could not deal with the man.

When they arrived last evening and he began going through a second checklist, the *Setting up Camp* checklist, Lillian had taken a folding chair and found a shaded spot with a view of the distant lake. She had sat and read her book for the next hour or so and drank half a bottle of wine while the crazy man went through his stupid routine. She was starting to wonder why she could never just stay single.

Then this morning, when she began to prepare breakfast, he stopped her and said, "Oh no, I cook on an open fire, not in the camper. It isn't really camping if you don't cook outside." He told her, "I'll take care of it, I have a process."

No shit, she thought, a process. So she took her book and headed back to her view of the lake. But not her wine. Her wine would wait until close to noon. Maybe.

BUDDY ONLY SAW THE MAN SITTING ON HIS BUCKET COOKING breakfast. There would have to be others, he thought, maybe the little woman, who knows, maybe some grandkids. But where were they? Buddy could be a patient man, having learned the skills of waiting and being bored in order to do his time. Some could do time, some couldn't. Some went batshit crazy. For Buddy, this was easy time, not time in the hole where you stared at blank walls for ten hours a day and slept the other twelve or thirteen. He had all the time in the world now, and nobody to dictate otherwise. So he decided he'd watch for a while longer, just to be safe. Just to be certain of what he'd be walking into. He couldn't afford any more surprises.

JEREMY CROSS PULLED HIS CITY-OWNED, UNMARKED DETECTIVE VEHICLE into the command post, finding it with ease given the simple instructions: *Just as you pull into town, look to the left, and turn into the Kmart parking lot. You'll see us there with the motorhome.*

Rich pointed at the mobile command post but Jeremy was already steering that direction. Odessa sat quietly in the back seat.

Rich said, "This could be interesting."

"How's that," Jeremy asked, sincerely.

"Small town shit," he said. "It can be very different when it comes to law enforcement. I'm not going to lie, sometimes I get nervous when I leave the big city."

Jeremy chuckled. "That's an interesting phenomenon."

"How's that?"

"Oh, I don't know. It just seems, well, most people are more threatened—or maybe insecure, would be a better term—when they go to the big city, not when they're around small-town folks."

Rich said, "Most people aren't brothers."

Jeremy looked over to see him grin.

They stepped out of the sedan, and with the sounds of three doors closing at nearly the same time, Rich saw the heads turn to watch. There were two ladies who sat casually at a folding table beneath the awning of the motorhome. One was older, with short, gray hair and glasses. She wore jeans and a gray hooded sweatshirt with some kind of cowboy logo. The other was younger, probably in her thirties. She had long brown hair, pulled back in a ponytail. She wore tight-fitting jeans, cowboy boots, and a button-up western shirt. Both were squinting into the sun as they continued to watch the newcomers arrive.

A man stepped out of the trailer and Rich heard him say, "Who's that?"

The older of the two women said, "Well how should we know, Al, they ain't got up here to introduce themselves yet."

The man called Al walked forward, meeting the trio in between their vehicle and the command post. He said, "I'm Sheriff Reynolds, you can call me Al." Then he extended his hand to Jeremy, the first to step up.

"Jeremy Cross," he said, "we talked on the phone."

"Yes sir," the sheriff responded.

Jeremy indicated Rich with a nod. "This is Rich Farris, a detective out of L.A., I mentioned him when we spoke yesterday."

Jeremy and Rich made brief eye contact, and Jeremy smiled slightly.

Rich shook hands with the man, nodded and said, "Sheriff."

"And Odessa, who is a family friend of my victim. They've been helping out."

The sheriff tipped his hat and offered his free hand to her. He said, "Pleased to meet you, young lady."

Odessa shook his hand, smiled brightly and said, "Thank you, sir."

"Come on over. I'll get some more chairs out here and we'll sit and talk, and I'll let you know what we have going on. Maybe figure out how we can put you three to work helping out with our manhunt." Then he looked over to the younger of the two ladies and said, "Marie, do we have plenty of coffee still?"

She said, "Yes, sheriff, we do." Then she picked around the table and pushed a box of donuts toward the guests' side of the table. "Fresh donuts too, if you're hungry."

The sheriff grabbed three chairs from the back side of the motorhome and carried all three in one hand. He came back and spread them around beneath the awning. When everyone was settled, he pointed to the whiteboard and said, "So here's where we're at on this deal."

34

Tank parked in front of the trailer house that sat surrounded by weeds on a one-acre lot. He checked his phone again, first looking at the text message that held the address, and then comparing it to the Google map on his phone. He said, "This must be the place."

Tanika didn't reply. She sat staring forward with drooping eyelids half covering a dull gaze and pinpointed pupils.

The skanky whore, he thought. Yeah, sit over there like the walking dead, you worthless junkie bitch.

Sure, Tank smoked his weed, just like everyone else, but pot wasn't even illegal—or it barely was, anyway. H, on the other hand, would get your ass locked up, or at least kicked off the team. And as if the H wasn't bad enough, now the stupid bitch was into speedballs, heroin and cocaine mixed—*one-on-one, murder-one, the Belushi*—and that shit will flat kill a nigga. Now Tanika was an addict, plain and simple. Like the junkies all over the streets in Compton who'd steal or whore out their skanky bodies to support their habits. You couldn't trust them.

He would have kicked her to the curb but he discovered her scheme and saw how much money she was making selling that ass. After all, he would be taking a big cut of the action for himself now that it was out in the open what her gig was. And since that ass belonged to him, he figured his cut would be about sixty percent or so. Plus he'd take another ten percent, or maybe twenty, for rent. He also had to keep her supplied with the shit to make her not care, and to keep her going so she could keep on earning daddy a little bank. And that shit would have to come out of her cut too. Tank was a businessman.

He got out of the car and walked away, leaving her sitting in her seat zoned out and without a clue. The bitch was barely functional at this point. Yeah, it wouldn't be long, he thought, before he would be kicking her to the curb. Soon as she couldn't get the job done, soon as she stopped keeping her clients satisfied, she'd be gone. Motherfuckers expected more than just having something good to look at when they were paying for pussy. What'd she think?

Tank reached back and felt the gun tucked into his waistband at the small of his back and concealed by his BSU hoodie, just to make sure it was where he expected it to be. This was a new supplier, and according to the semi-reliable little nickel and dime dealer crackhead motherfucker who used to sell him his shit, and deliver it to him so he didn't have to get out here taking these chances, this was the only game in town at the moment. Boise had gone dry from all the goddamn junkies and not enough niggas bringing it up from the hood.

Before knocking on the door, he glanced back to see Tanika with her head laid back on the seat, her mouth open. Probably drooling on his leather seats.

He glanced up and down the street. It was quiet. Almost too quiet, he thought. No, he was getting himself all worked up for nothing, worrying about shit he didn't need to worry about. He would have noticed undercovers when he rolled up in his Tahoe. He would have noticed if there were any niggas lurking too, gangstas looking to rip off a dope dealer. He would have noticed all that when he circled twice, because Tank was no fool. He'd grown up on the streets of Compton and that made this shit in Boise seem like child's play.

He knocked on the door and stood to the side, the way cops do.

He'd heard about motherfuckers being shot through the door, and he'd seen it a few times himself. Well, it was probably in movies or something, but that shit was for real.

It only took a minute before the small slot on the door opened and a black female looked at him with one eye and said, "Yeah?"

"Chino sent me. I talked to someone on the phone."

"Two grams, right?"

Tank started peeling hundred dollar bills from a wad he kept in his pocket, saying, "Yeah, like we discussed."

She said, "Ah-ite," and opened the door.

Tank walked in, still counting the cash.

"Freeze asshole!"

Suddenly there were white guys everywhere pointing pistols and shotguns at him. Tank raised his hands, slowly, and said, "Ain't this some shit, yo."

35

Buddy walked out of the trees and brush and into the camp where the couple sat comfortably near a fire. He had watched them eat breakfast and felt confident they were alone. He had only seen the man go in and out of the camper, but finally, just a short while ago, the old broad who looked pretty well put together walked up from the other side of camp, from the woods. He figured she'd been out for a morning walk, or maybe a hike.

They both looked up as he approached, each seemingly surprised by his visit.

Buddy said, "Howdy, neighbors."

The man stood up and stepped over to meet him as he approached, offering his hand. Buddy lifted the wounded and bandaged right hand slightly, drawing the man's attention to the injured arm as he said, "Got a bad wing, rattlesnake bite."

The woman sat silent, watching.

The old man lowered his hand, staring at the bandaged arm. He frowned and said, "It looks bad, have you been to the hospital?"

"No, I haven't. My rig back there"—Buddy turned his head and nodded—"is broke down, so I've been sort of stranded. Just doctored it up the best I could, up here in camp with what I had to work with."

The woman said, "Well, we should get you to town, have it looked at."

The man said, "Honey, we can't do that today. We can't just be running into town."

She was sitting in her chair by the fire, looking at Buddy with questioning eyes. Maybe intrigue.

The old man said, "That's my wife, Lillian, and I'm Cliff... Clifford Lomeli."

Buddy was still staring at the woman. She looked good for her age, and there was something about her eyes that had drawn him in. She said, "Why can't we take the poor man into town, have him looked at? Can't you see he's in a bad way there?"

Cliff glared at her. "You remember, the kids were coming today, all the boys."

Lillian said, "The boys?"

"They'll be here shortly," he said, now frowning at her, "all four of them, coming up to go hunting."

Buddy grinned, first at her, and then at the man. He said, "Really, hunting uh? What are they hunting for, if I might ask?"

"Deer," he said quickly.

Buddy chuckled. "In the spring?"

"I don't know, or something else, maybe ducks. I just know they're coming, and they have guns with them. Should be here any time."

Buddy could see fear in the man's eyes and all over his face. The man was a coward, and Buddy was making him nervous. Buddy said, "Good, I'm glad the boys are bringing up some guns, I could stand to have one myself. Maybe I'll just wait here with y'all, have some breakfast and see when them boys get up here. Maybe see if one of them would part with one of their guns. I'd sure like to have a piece right now myself, to be real honest with you. You know, something to shoot snakes with, or whatever. You wouldn't happen to have one inside the camper, would ya, pops?"

Cliff looked back at Lillian who sat watching, one leg crossed over the other, her foot making circles in the air.

Buddy couldn't believe it. The woman hadn't shown any fear. She seemed more curious than anything else, or maybe entertained. As if she enjoyed seeing her old man cower in front of her. Buddy felt his adrenaline kicking in, and it felt good. Better than a high from coke, or crank, or uppers and bennies and shit like that. Buddy loved how he felt at times like this. It was the confrontation, the conflict, the danger, and the violence or potential for violence that gave Buddy his high. His natural high. That euphoric feel that surpassed any high he'd ever had. Every time he fought with a man, each time he had stabbed one, the time he had choked the black bitch to death, and every time he heard the sirens and never knew what would happen next, those were the biggest rushes he ever had.

Now he needed more. It was happening and he felt that charge. Buddy pulled his knife, stepped up next to Cliff and said, "How about we go inside, have a look, see about a gun for your neighbor. Maybe have a look around and see what else I might need. What do you think of that, pops?"

Lillian got out of her chair.

Cliff looked over at her.

Buddy thrust his knife into the old man's belly and quickly pulled it out.

Lillian turned and ran off toward the woods.

Cliff shouted, "No!..."

And Buddy stabbed him again.

Cliff looked down as the blood soaked through his shirt. Then he looked up, and stared into Buddy's eyes.

Buddy twisted the knife, one direction and then the other, the way it was done in prison. The way it was *taught* in prison. It didn't take much of a weapon to do some real damage, if it was utilized properly. Inmates would discuss these matters, and share their experiences with one another. Some even studied the human anatomy so they would know exactly where to strike for maximum damage and death. Buddy was pretty sure he'd just stuck the old man in his liver.

Cliff grabbed Buddy's hand that held the knife, but he had no strength. He began to wilt. As he did, he said, "Why... why would you kill me?"

Buddy pulled the knife out and watched the man crumple onto the dirt and pine needles at his feet. He grinned at the sight of him, then turned and looked toward the woods where the woman had run. She was gone.

"Shit!"

He went through Cliff's pockets and removed his wallet, took the cash and dropped the wallet onto the ground. Then he turned and headed into the woods, following the woman's trail.

SHERIFF ALFRED REYNOLDS asked RICH AND ODESSA IF THEY WOULDN'T mind staying at the command post and answering phones for a while. Someone would be there to assist them if they had any questions. Meanwhile, he said, he'd have Jeremy ride with him. There were a couple of posse members searching north of there but it was a lot of ground to cover. They would check in with Lou and Dusty to see where they had been and what remained to be checked. He had an idea they needed to get off the main roads and start looking through the campgrounds.

He said, "What I'm thinking, I can give Jeremy a quick tour and a good overview while we're riding around. Then we'll come on back here, split up, and take one of each of you back out. That'd give us more coverage, but of course I'll have to deputize each of you."

Jeremy spoke up: "Rich is a deputy, in L.A."

"Good enough," he said, "I'll just deputize you, then, since you're an out-of-state cop. You don't have any authority here in California 'less I give it to you, which I surely intend to do. And of course the pretty young lady, if she's of age."

"I'm twenty-one," she said.

He smiled at her and she returned the gesture with her sparkling eyes. They each held it there for a moment, and then the sheriff turned and walked away from the command post. Jeremy followed.

THE SHERIFF AND JEREMY RODE OFF IN THE BLACK AND WHITE SHERIFF'S patrol vehicle, a four-wheel drive Ford Bronco with a sheriff badge on each door. In addition to the markers that identified the SUV as a police vehicle, there were emergency lights in the front and back, a screen separating the front seats from the back interior, and a shotgun and AR-15 rifle mounted vertically between the two bucket seats in front.

Jeremy was looking around as they started up the highway. He indicated the two weapons and said, "How do you release the locks on these when you need to get to them?"

The sheriff pointed to a key on the keyring that dangled from the ignition and said, "This one unlocks both. I have another key in my pocket."

Jeremy wondered about something, but he hated to ask. It was a question every cop was asked by civilian friends and acquaintances, and never well received. But cop to cop, it was an acceptable inquiry. He said, "You ever had to use 'em?"

He didn't answer for a moment. Then he glanced over at Jeremy and said, "I've pulled them out more than a few times. It can be real dangerous back here in the woods where you don't have any backup and your radio and cell phone don't work. We sometimes stumble across marijuana grows or people cooking meth. There's a host of undesirables a guy can come across out here: poachers, hippies, bikers, tweakers, illegals... all sorts. When you come across these folks, they're almost always armed. There's no laws against a citizen having a gun in the woods. And that can be the dangerous part, when you come up against them, and you're alone. You know and they know too that there's nobody around to help you. They probably even know there's no way to call for help back there. It can be a little scary."

"We had two game wardens killed by a poacher in Idaho. It was before my time on the job, but I remember hearing about it. People still talk about it, and the opinions are divided into two camps."

Sheriff Reynolds glanced over at him.

Jeremy continued: "There's those who were sickened by it, and those who thought the wardens deserved it. Those who'd like to see the man who did it hanged, and those who consider him a hero."

Reynolds shook his head. "A hero?"

"Idaho can be a little different. There's a real sentiment among many of the natives, the ranchers and farmers and cowboys, all of whom are very independent, that the government should stay out of their lives. Some of these people thought the poacher should have been left alone because he was living off of the land and had a right to do so."

The sheriff shook his head. "So he can kill two wardens. He has that right?"

"That's how some see it. Some think it was self-defense, but the problem was, there was no evidence that either warden ever drew a weapon."

"Wouldn't have mattered if they had," Sheriff Reynolds said, "a lawman has a right to draw his weapon when he feels threatened, especially if he's making an arrest."

"That's right," Jeremy said, "and that's how half the people see it. It's a strange thing, because there's plenty of otherwise law-abiding, God-fearing folks who don't see it that way. Hard to wrap your brain around it. Some fancy the killer as a modern-day outlaw, a legend of sorts. There've been a couple of books written about it, and even a cowboy song from what I understand. Sort of mind-boggling, to be honest."

The sheriff glanced over from the road and said, "It's my sincerest intention to never let that happen to me."

Jeremy said, "Mine too."

TANK AND TANIKA WERE BOOKED INTO THE ADA COUNTY JAIL IN BOISE for Possession of Narcotics and Intent to Distribute. Tanika was placed under medical watch due to her level of intoxication. Tank was placed in a holding cell with three other men, all white. White guys who had been arrested for traffic warrants, possession of drugs, and domestic violence, respectively. The two who sat on the bench got up and moved without being asked to do so when he walked over to sit down. He sat for a minute, then he stretched out horizontally and went to sleep.

A short while later, two white guys—one with a shaved head and a mustache and goatee, the other with long hair pulled back into a ponytail—entered the threshold of the holding cell and yelled at him, telling him to wake up. They wore jeans and t-shirts and had badges on chains that were draped around their necks for display.

The one with the ponytail said, "Get your ass up."

The bald one said, "Mr. Sherman, what do you say we have a little chat in our office?"

Tank was rubbing the sleep from his eyes as he said, "What about?"

The guy with the ponytail said, "Hey man, this ain't fucking Compton. Get your ass up and do as you're told. Understood?"

Tank sized him up. He was solid, lean, stood in a fighter's stance and had scar tissue around his piercing eyes.

Tank said, "Ah'ight, man. Ah'ight."

BUDDY WAS HAVING A CHAT WITH HIMSELF WHILE WALKING THROUGH the woods looking for the woman and saying, "Come on now, little woman, I'm not going to hurt you..."

Saying, "You know I'm going to find you, eventually. It will be a lot easier if you just come out."

Saying, "You miserable old bitch, you better fucking come out or I will chop you up slowly when I find your tight little ass."

And between his coaxing of the runaway woman, he was saying to himself, "How the fuck do you manage to get yourself into all this shit?"

And, "Why the hell are you even looking for this bitch? Just steal their rig and leave her out here with the bears."

And, "Jesus Christ, I'd been better off if I'd just stayed in the joint. They ought to give you the option."

36

Steve Troy sat on his familiar barstool in the downtown pub where no Mormons would dare bother him, and very few people would be near enough to irritate him. Maybe other than Dave, but Dave would be serving him drinks while he did so, which made him tolerable. He could handle Dave and maybe one or two others and feel comfortable with his surroundings until late in the afternoon, at which time the bar would start to fill with blue-collar types who started work early and were finished not long after lunchtime. That would be when Troy would leave and go back to his apartment to be alone. Watch the tube or maybe have a nap and contemplate his future.

He sat sipping his Jameson and reading the classified ads, thinking if he didn't figure out something to do other than drink—once he was officially retired—he'd probably die of cirrhosis, or maybe get so fucking depressed he'd eat his gun like some cops do. Cops who had nothing to do but drink once the job was behind them. Not the Mormons. Who knew what they did—probably built a temple or went on a mission.

Dave served him another double and said, "Job shopping?"

Troy looked over the paper and asked, "Writing a fucking book?"

Dave turned back to the register where he pulled a 3x5 card from a file with Troy's name and a list of dates and charges—it was his bar tab. Steve watched him write something on it and wondered if he stuck it to him when he was being an asshole, which Troy didn't think was very often. He thought, Why piss off my bartender, about the only human I can stand? He softened his tone and said, "Just thinking, maybe I'll start a second career when my retirement comes through. I could use the extra money, plus I can only take so much of your company." He grinned a little, showing Dave he was having fun with him.

Dave didn't smile back. "Speaking of your extra money, your tab's hit three bills, and there's a week left in the month. Just a head's up."

"Jesus, you adding in tips for yourself?"

"I didn't realize you even knew what they were."

Steve Troy took a sip of his whiskey and set it down. He said, "This is a miserable goddamn place."

NANCY CROSS TOLD THE KIDS TO GET THEIR HOMEWORK DONE, THEY needed baths still and it was nearly time for bed and she didn't have the energy to fight with them about any of it. Then she said into the phone, speaking with her mother, "I have no idea when he's going to be home. He's out playing his stupid little cops and robbers game and he's gone to California. You'd think I could've picked a professional, a doctor or an attorney or whatever, someone who made enough money where I could have someone come in and clean the house and take care of the kids while I went out for coffee or to play tennis."

She cleared the table and began loading the dishwasher, saying, "I thought he would play professional ball, to be honest, and if not, go on to graduate school, make something of himself. I never imagined I'd be stuck here in Boise in a three-bedroom, married to a civil servant."

After listening for a minute she said, "Yeah, well, nice guy and good dad only go so far. Listen, Mother, I need to go now, it sounds like the kids are about to kill each other in the other room."

She disconnected, leaned against the kitchen counter and sighed. Then she tossed a hand towel aside and walked out of the kitchen just as her phone rang. She walked back in and picked it up from the kitchen counter, seeing it was her husband, Jeremy. She watched it for a moment, considering not answering it. Finally she picked it up, and huffed, "Hello."

"Hi honey, how's everything?"

"Just peachy."

There was a pause.

"Is something the matter?" he asked.

"Oh no, everything's just fine. I'm cleaning up after dinner, trying to get the kids to do their homework without fighting, trying to get them bathed, trying to get them ready for bed so I can get them up and make them breakfast and get them to school and go to work. How's the cops and robbers game going? Having lots of fun?"

He paused, then said, "Well, as you know, we're chasing a killer. He tried to kill a couple of kids here, a young boy and a girl, right here in Bishop, or just outside of town, I should say. He's a bad man who needs to be stopped."

"That's great, Jeremy. I'm really, really proud of you. Look, I've got to go. When will you be home?"

"I don't know."

"You don't know?"

"It depends. Right now we have no way to know. They have a full-blown operation going on down here, a manhunt. There's a command post and all sorts of cops from various agencies coming and going. It's a big deal."

"Your family is a big deal also."

"Honey, I realize that. I *know* that. But I also have a job to do. This is my job."

"Yeah, well…"

"What?"

"Nothing."

"What, Nancy? Just say it. I know you hate my job and wish I made more money. That's the truth of the whole thing, isn't it?"

"The truth of the whole thing is that I didn't marry a cop. I married a man I believed in, a man who had great potential, who could have gone on with his education and done anything he set his mind to do. That's the whole truth."

"Well, this is what I've set my mind to do. This is what I love doing, and I'm going to keep doing it."

"Well that's just fucking great."

She hung up the phone and immediately regretted saying it. She had never used that language around him before. She almost never used that language around anyone, other than maybe her best friend, Courtney, on occasion. Back in college, drinking, or maybe talking about boys, their occasional rebellions from the strict Mormon upbringing they both had experienced. But never in front of Jeremy before. And never *at* him.

Nancy pictured her husband, Mr. Strait-laced who never drank, cursed, cut class in school or had a single thought against his religious teachings. She saw him with a shocked look on his face, maybe staring at the phone in disbelief. The same look he had had during college when she shocked him by walking out of his dorm's bathroom naked. For Christ's sake, she had married a child.

She glanced around the kitchen, wishing she had a bottle of wine in the house.

Tank said, "Man, I barely know the bitch, and it was her that took me over there to get the dope. Honestly, I didn't even know that's what we were there for, 'til y'all started pointing guns at me and yelling crazy shit. I was just trying to help a bitch out, and next thing I know, y'all come at me ready to kill a nigga."

The bald cop—Tank had heard the other one call him *Doc*—said, "Problem with your story, Mr. Sherman, is we have a recording of the call you made to set it up." He looked over at his partner and said, "J.P., you believe this fool?"

J.P. shook his head.

Doc said, "Plus, your girl was passed out in the hoop, it ain't like she was calling the shots. And she has an entirely different story about this deal anyway. What did you think, she wasn't going to give you up? Junkies always roll over on their suppliers."

"Man, that junkie bitch be lyin'."

Doc said, "You might as well face it man, you're in the grease. But if you want to come clean and give us something to work with, we might be able to make a deal, get the DA to break the charges down to something less than Distribution. Otherwise, you're looking at a federal beef, three-year mandatory minimum."

Tank sat silent, shaking his head.

J.P. said, "You play ball at the college?"

He looked up, nodded slightly and then looked back down at the tile floor beneath his sweatpants and house shoes.

"Well, this ain't something Coach Murray is going to be very happy about, is it?"

Tank shook his head.

"I mean, the man's tried to be patient with you boys, giving you a few breaks on some of the minor shit, marijuana, booze in the dorms, shit like that, but he ain't gonna cut no slack for one of his players messing with the H. Maybe, just maybe, if we get some real cooperation here, this could go away completely. Coach wouldn't even get wind of it and you'd stay on the team, not jeopardize your future. It'd have to be something good though—something big—for the whole deal to disappear."

"Like what?"

J.P. flipped his chair around and sat down backwards in it, close to Tank. He leaned in close to him, getting in his face a little, and said, "Like you'd have to give up some of them Compton niggers that are bringing the shit up here to my otherwise nice fucking city and selling it to the stupid white kids that think all you gangsters are cool. That's like what, bro."

Tank glanced up, said, "I ain't no gangster, man."

J.P. said, "You're from Compton."

Tank didn't respond.

"Look it here, man, I'm going to give you a little education…"

Tank looked up at him again.

"I'm DEA. Doc here's a local guy. We're paired up with some other hard-charging narco coppers trying to rid beautiful Idaho of all you dope-dealing Compton transplants. In doing so, the good people of Idaho have blessed us with some serious sentencing guidelines, and the judges here aren't liberal assholes like they are in California. You following me, bro?"

He nodded.

"The deal you made on the phone, two grams, is enough to get you a three-year mandatory minimum in the federal system. All we need is that recording, which of course we have. It's called *history and hearsay,* and we use it all the time to fuck guys like you over. That's good enough in Idaho to convince a jury that you're in possession with the intent to distribute. Have you seen our juries here?"

He shook his head. "I didn't even make a buy, man."

"You were going to," Doc said. "That's good enough for us."

J.P. said, "White, bro, the juries are all fucking white. Mostly educated. Those who aren't educated, are rednecks. The educated ones are smart enough to know they didn't flee California because the weather sucked. They left because assholes like you and your homeboys made it unsafe to do their Christmas shopping at night or to send their kids to public schools. You think they want to see your ass on the streets in Boise? Fuck no, bro. And the rednecks? Fuck, bro, you're the last fucking thing they want to see in Idaho. Come on man, even you're smart enough to know that."

No response.

"Three-year mandatory minimum. Let that soak into your thick skull for a minute. You're an old fat dude by time you get done making our beautiful license plates. You seen 'em bro?"

He nodded.

"They're red, white, and blue, cause we're gun-carrying, God-fearing Americans here, bro. We got other ones too, ones with elk, steelhead, horses, even ones with fucking birds for the few liberals we've got. You're going to enjoy making 'em. Plus I think they pay you like a quarter a day or something, so you'll be earning a living, not just doing time.

"The bad part is, you'll be too fat to play ball again by the time you get out. Old and fat. And that's if the white boys don't kill you first. This ain't California, bro. The white boys run the yards around these parts. Big white boys with some racist shit tattooed all over their bodies. Nazi shit. You dig what I'm saying, bro?"

Tank said, "Man, what is it you want from me?"—nearly in tears —"I swear to God, man, I don't need to be wrapped up in all this bull-shit. I ain't tryin' to catch a case, man. What is it you want from me?"

"Just what I told you, the suppliers. You'll make a buy from them, same type of deal you got busted for today, only you'll be working for us and wearing a wire. Order up a pound of heroin and make it happen."

"A pound?"

"Yeah, bro, a pound. We give you 20K of marked bills and you make a big buy from your old homies from the hood. Then you walk. How's that sound, bro?"

Tank looked up, frowning, and said, "Man, you think I'm stupid?"

"It crossed my mind."

37

Buddy had finished moving Cliff's body the thirty feet into the brush and woods just before hearing a vehicle coming up the road. He squatted and watched as it passed, and his heart had skipped a beat when he saw it was a sheriff's patrol vehicle. He waited until it was long gone, the engine noise no longer audible. Then he started working fast.

He checked the truck but of course the keys were not in it. He ran back to the dead man and rifled through his pockets again, but there were no keys there either. He walked briskly back to the camper, went inside and began searching through the cabinets and drawers and looking on countertops and tables. He no longer cared about the woman, he just wanted to get out of there.

LILLIAN LOMELI HAD RUN OUT OF THE WOODS AND STOPPED IN THE middle of the dirt road, waving her arms at the sheriff's vehicle that passed by and left a cloud of dust. She lowered her arms and watched as the vehicle grew smaller and finally disappeared through the forest as it continued up the winding road.

She looked back at their camp, just a couple hundred yards away, but she didn't see any movement. She couldn't imagine that he had stayed, not after stabbing her husband. Especially not after the cops came by. But she didn't know for sure.

Lillian stepped back into the woods, and using the cover of the trees and brush, she slowly worked her way back toward camp. She wasn't going to be stranded out here overnight, that was for sure.

HE COULDN'T FIND THE KEYS. BUDDY STOOD NEAR THE ENTRYWAY, looking around, pissed off now, trying to think of his next move. He needed to get out of there, and at this point, the Buick had probably been reported stolen. The old man's truck would be perfect, if he could only find the keys.

And what the hell were the cops doing around here anyway? Were they looking for him, or was it a coincidence? He didn't know. But it would be just his luck to have cops drive past a campsite in the middle of nowhere right after he gutted an old man and dragged his dead ass into the bushes. For fuck's sake.

Buddy caught movement in the trees, fifty yards from the camper. He watched for a moment and saw it again. Someone was in the woods, sneaking around, as if anyone would be able to sneak up on him. Buddy smiled and said, "The little woman."

JEREMY WAS ASKING THE SHERIFF HOW MUCH GROUND DID HE THINK they'd need to cover, how far into the woods did he think they should canvass.

"The problem is, these roads go all over. This one we just came up, it forks two or three times and comes out in a couple different spots. There's camping all through here, but not many people take up these first camping areas we're going by now until the ones farther up are full. Most of the preferred camping is on up the road, up there near the lake where there're better spots, places with hookups for the RVs, restrooms, and showers."

"That truck and camper back a ways, you didn't think that was worth checking out?"

"I didn't see anyone out there, and there weren't any cars around. This guy's either in that stolen Buick or he's stole something else. He didn't walk up here, and he didn't drive a camper up here either."

Jeremy paused a moment, thinking the sheriff missed his point. He had pointed it out when they passed by, and the sheriff had looked over but continued driving. Now he seemed to be having none of it, still dismissing it.

Jeremy thought he'd try another direction. He said, "But maybe they've seen something if they've been up here a couple a days. Maybe someone's come by that they noticed... maybe the Buick."

Sheriff Reynolds looked over at him and said, "We don't have time to talk to everyone out in these woods. I'll know what's good when I see it. It'll be obvious to me, something that don't seem right, out of place so to speak. It's different in these parts, son. You need to trust me on that. I know these woods like the back of my hand, and I know these campers and I think I'd know if something didn't seem right."

Careful to not offend him, Jeremy said, "I don't doubt that at all, sir. Not one bit."

———

ODESSA SAID TO RICH—OUT OF NOWHERE—THE TWO OF THEM SEATED beneath the canopy at the command post, "I expect honesty in my relationships."

Rich looked over, surprised. "What the hell are you talking about, girl?"

"First, don't you *ever* call me *girl*. That's ghetto. Second, I heard the conversation between you and Jeremy on the drive here."

"I thought you were sleeping. Pissed off and sleeping."

"Just pissed off. And maybe I had a nap. But I'm pretty sure I was awake for the good stuff, about how you're retired from the job, and why."

Rich didn't say anything. He didn't show any emotion either. He just looked at her and waited for more.

She said, "Stress retirement, or something like that, is what I heard. I don't even know what to believe any more."

He waited.

She said, "Well, don't you have anything to say for yourself?"

"What do you want me to say, Odessa?"

"I don't *want* you to say anything. I just thought maybe you could explain to me what's going on, and help me to understand why you would lie about being a cop."

"First," he said, defensively, "I didn't *lie* to anyone. I may have misled a few people, but I wouldn't call that a lie. I said I was with the sheriff's department. I remember what I said, because I wanted to leave myself some wiggle room. But I only did so for Lacy Jane. I didn't imagine there was any way the sheriff down there in your neck of the woods, or these fellas over there in Boise, were going to let me anywhere near any of this if I told them I was retired. So I said I was *with* the sheriff's department. Which is true. I'm retired *with* them. I carry a badge and ID card that say I am honorably retired *with* them. When Cherie called me looking for help, well—you know what, never mind."

"What? Tell me what happened when she called."

He paused. Then he looked her in the eyes and said, "What was I supposed to do, Odessa, not help family? Turn my back on her, give her a reason to believe all the bullshit my ex probably told her over the years? She asked for my help, and told me the situation. I wasn't going to shut her out. That's not who I am."

"But it's still lying, Rich, no matter how you justify it."

"It wasn't my intention, Odessa. But wait a minute, I have something more important to address here. What exactly do you mean by *relationship*."

"What do you mean?"

"No, what do you mean?"

"You said it, not me."

Rich said, "No, you started this whole damn conversation by telling me about what you expect in your *relationships*. So explain that to me."

"Well, first off, don't swear at me."

"I didn't swear *at* you."

"Secondly, I'm pretty sure you know what I mean when I say *relationship*."

Rich watched her the way he had studied a thousand eyes over the years and found truth and answers on some occasions or deceit and denial on others. But this young woman had both power and mystery in her eyes that made him uncomfortable and caused him to doubt his strength and resolve. Sometimes he didn't know how to read her, which left him puzzled. Other times, he was certain he read her correctly, which left him bewildered.

She was too young for him, yet he felt the connection that she now openly referenced. It seemed unfair. Maybe the perfect woman, but too late. A perfect match, someone who captivated him while also equaling if not overpowering him intellectually. Did she know she did those things to him? Did she realize she was in complete control? Probably, he thought. And here he was on the other side of the table, a suspect who didn't know the evidence stacked against him and trying to lie his way out of a crime.

But this wasn't a crime.

Or was it?

Jesus, his life could be such a mess at times.

He thought back to the day Cherie Lewis had called and asked for his help in finding Lacy Jane. It had been just moments before his exit from the complicated world of which he'd grown weary, the world from which he felt detached. It turned out to be the call that had saved his life—at least for the time being—and it had ultimately been the call that introduced Odessa into his esoteric world.

Was that an accident?

Or more divinity?

He finally said, "By relationship, you do mean *friendship*, right?"

She said, "You know *exactly* what I mean, Richard James Farris."

3 8

B uddy Frantelli charged through the trailer door headed directly toward the tree line where he had detected movement moments before. The woman popped up and screamed, then turned and ran farther into the woods. He caught up to her, tackled her, and the two of them went down hard on the layers of pine needles that did little to cushion their fall.

"Let go of me, you bastard!"

He slapped her across the side of her head, her face down in the dirt. He said, "Watch that mouth, you old hag."

"I oughta—"

"You oughta what? Tell me what you oughta do, grandma."

She twisted and tried to turn but couldn't move under his weight. Finally, Lillian Lomeli relaxed, her body melting into the ground, and she whimpered.

Buddy yanked her up by the arm. "Let's you and me go have a look around in your camper, see where the old man put the keys for that pickup."

She didn't resist him as they made their way to the camper and climbed up the two steps to walk into a living area with a kitchenette. The bedroom was in the back. Buddy guided her toward a small dining table and shoved her onto a seat. He then began looking around the camper.

After a few moments, Lillian said, "You just get out of prison?"

He looked over and saw her push her graying hair behind an ear.

He said, "The fuck business is it of yours?"

"Just wondered."

She shamelessly looked him over, head to toe.

He said, "Lookit, lady, I don't have time for your games. I don't have time for answering your stupid questions or telling you my life story, as interesting as it is. But I do have a minute to give you a little warning, something you might want to keep in that pretty little head of yours. You just mind your manners, help me find the keys to that truck, and you'll make it out alive. You don't, well…"

"I'll do better than mind my manners, honey. I can imagine you've been lonely for some company, a good little while now. Am I wrong?"

He chuckled. "Well I can see you're just all broke up over the unexpected passing of your husband, uh?"

"We've only been married a little while. I barely knew the man, to be honest. Haven't even consummated the marriage, if you must know. So it turns out that marriage thing was probably just another mistake to begin with. I'll be honest, I've had terrible luck with men, it seems, my whole goddamn life."

SHERIFF REYNOLDS AND JEREMY FINISHED DRIVING AROUND THE LAKE. The sheriff said, "I think we'll head back down the way we came in. I've been thinking about what you said, as far as that camper. You're probably right, it wouldn't have hurt to have stopped in and had a little chat, find out if they've seen anything. I thought there'd be more people to check up here, more people to talk to. I'm kind of surprised there aren't more campers up here this week. It may be a little soon in the season yet."

It was noon in Bishop, one o'clock in Boise, when Federal Drug Enforcement Agent J.P. Long finished up the paperwork with Tank. He said, "You've made the right decision, bro. I'm glad you saw the light."

Tank grunted.

His attorney said, "When it's filed, and official, my client will provide the information per the agreement. But not until there's a supervising prosecutor's signature."

J.P. ignored the attorney. He had nothing but contempt for these two-bit lawyers. He said to Tank, "Signatures or no signatures, you fuck me on this in any way, shape, or form, you're doing the time."

"Detective!" exclaimed counsel. "That's a threat, and I won't tolerate it."

J.P. stood and smiled at the attorney, then pointed his finger at Tank and said, "It has been a real pleasure doing business with you, bro. We'll be in touch."

———

At the command post Rich was restless. He glanced at his watch every few minutes and paced under the canopy, in and out of the motorhome, and around in the parking lot in the immediate vicinity. He would look up toward the mountains north and west, and then back to the map that hung on the wall of the motorhome next to a whiteboard with assignments and call signs and phone numbers written in black or red marker. He finished a bottle of water and tossed it six feet away into a trash can.

Odessa said, "Rich, have a seat and relax."

"I'm not good at waiting; I'm good at doing. We should be out there too, not sitting here wasting our talent."

"Yours."

"What's that, hon?"

"*Your* talent," she said. And then she winked and said, "Honey."

He looked at her a moment, then turned back to the mountains.

He needed an assignment. Or a drink. He said, "They've been gone a long time and I'm starting to get concerned."

"You like him, don't you?"

"Jeremy?"

She nodded.

He sat down. "Yes, I do. He's a good guy, and he's a good cop. The guy has a lot of potential."

"He's cute, too."

Rich smiled. "I suppose."

"You'll never get it out of your system, will you?"

"What's that?"

"Being a cop."

He looked away. A long way away—beyond the nearby mountains and beyond the faraway mountaintops and into the deep blue skies that hung over Northern California and Nevada. He said, "I was almost cured of it, until this happened."

"Yeah, how's that? Were you seeing a psychiatrist?"

He chuckled. "Yeah, Odessa, I saw a shrink. Quite a bit, as a matter of fact. Didn't help much though."

"So how were you almost cured?"

Their eyes met and Rich did not look away. After a moment, he said, "You wouldn't believe me if I told you."

"Try me."

He shook his head.

"Richard?"

"I prefer *Rich*."

"Okay, *Rich*, try me."

He looked off again, but only for a brief moment. He didn't make eye contact with her when he said, "I have absolutely no intention of ever telling you that story. Ever."

She said, "You'll tell me, eventually."

BUDDY PULLED HER HEAD AWAY FROM HIS LAP BY GRABBING A HANDFUL of her hair. He said, "Shhh!"

She turned her head toward the door and listened, Buddy still holding a lock of hair. He pushed her to the side and stood up, pulled his pants up and zipped them as he hurried to peek through the small window above the sink. He looked over at her and said, "You're going to get in the back and keep your mouth shut, or never make it out alive. Got it?"

She smiled at him and said, "What makes you think I want out?"

He frowned.

She said, "Is it the sheriff coming back?"

He nodded, still watching through the window.

She said, "You'd have a much better chance if I go talk to them, you know. I could handle it pretty easily, just tell them everything's okay and we haven't seen a thing. Send them along on their merry way."

"Do as I say. Just get in the back and shut-up."

"Give me five minutes, we'll be fine. Trust me."

"You think I'm going to trust you?"

She stood and began walking toward the bedroom. He grabbed her arm and yanked her back. She grabbed the forearm of the hand he held her with and said, "Get your hand off me, convict. I'll show you how much you can trust me."

She jerked away and walked into the room. She opened a cabinet above the bed and retrieved Cliff's pistol. She turned to show Buddy, who was more interested in what was happening outside until he saw the business end of the revolver coming at him. He took a deep breath as she approached him holding the pistol pointed straight at his face. Then she lowered the gun, reversed it in her hand and handed it to him, butt first.

She said, "Now you just sit tight, Billy Bob, or whatever the hell your name is, and I'll send them along." She brushed past him and was out the door before he could object.

Lillian stopped near the smoldering campfire and stood with her hands on her hips as the lawmen arrived.

"Good afternoon," she said.

Both men got out of the sheriff's vehicle. The driver tipped his cowboy hat and said, "Ma'am."

The other nodded, and then proceeded to look around though he stood still near the front of the vehicle.

"May I help you?"

"We're looking for a man..."

"Aren't we all, honey?" she said, and smiled widely. "I'm just kidding, don't you dare tell my husband I said that."

He looked around and asked, "Your husband inside?"

"Nope, he's out for a hike. Well, he left with a pole and said he was going for a hike. If I know him, he'll hike about half a mile to the nearest fishing hole, plop his fat butt down and wet a line for the afternoon. I'd say he's probably snoring about now, missing all the nibbles."

The man in the hat chuckled and said, "That actually sounds like a good way to spend the day. Listen, you folks haven't seen any rough-looking characters around here, have you? Guy about forty, lot of tattoos, looks like he's fresh out of prison?"

She opened her eyes wide, a look of surprise. "Oh my Lord, no. Should we be concerned about something?"

"You'll want to avoid him if you see him, that's for sure, and give us a call right away."

She shook her head, put her hand to her mouth and held it there for a moment. She finally said, "Well, when Cliff gets back from fishin', I think we'll pack up and move on out. We sure don't need any trouble."

"Probably not a bad idea."

She stayed outside and watched and waved as the two drove off. Then she turned back and walked into the trailer with a smile on her face, proud of her performance.

Buddy was smiling too. He backed away from the door as she walked in, and lowered himself onto the couch, watching her.

She said, "Well, how was that, outlaw?"

He said, "You know, I always did have a thing for older women."

LATER THAT AFTERNOON, AS THE SUN BEGAN TO SETTLE BEYOND THE high mountaintops to the west and the temperature cooled, Sheriff Reynolds and Jeremy Cross pulled into the lot and parked near the mobile command post. Another pickup arrived at the same time and a man and a boy stepped out. The man said, "Well, Al, you guys have any luck?"

"No, Lou, we didn't," he said. "What about you?"

The man shook his head. The boy now stood next to him. He shook his head also.

The sheriff said, "This's Jeremy Cross, a detective from Boise, Idaho. They're hunting the same man we are, this Frantelli character."

Lou stepped up and shook his hand. The boy followed suit. He said, "Dusty McBride."

When they finished, Al said to Lou and Dusty, "Come on over, let me introduce you to some of his friends."

After all the introductions were made, the sheriff told them about the few people they had spoken with up toward the lake. He said he'd been surprised by the low number of campers, but he expected more would be coming in tomorrow, as was usual for Thursdays. Maybe they would split up a little more and hit it hard then. He said, "Lou, you have any thoughts on that?"

"It sounds okay to me," he said.

But Lou sounded a bit deflated.

The sheriff said, "How's Sam?"

"She'll be fine, Al. I talked to her mom a little bit ago, and she said they'll be releasing her from the hospital this evening. It's not how she is that has me bothered, it's how she could have been, what could have happened to her. How does something like that happen around here?"

Rich and Odessa stood quietly listening. The boy, Dusty, stood at Lou's side.

Jeremy chimed in: "We don't expect much of this to happen in my neck of the woods either, and it's always a surprise when it does."

Detective Gerardo Herrera stepped out of the motorhome. Sheriff Reynolds nodded his head toward him and said, "Afternoon, Gerry."

"Sheriff."

"Anything new on your end?"

"No. We broke down the barricade for traffic headed south. No point in it now. CHP are well aware of what we're looking for and they'll have a close look at everything leaving town. I think we missed him, to be honest. I think he was south of here before we had it set up."

Sheriff Reynolds nodded his head, but just slightly, more like he was considering the possibility than agreeing. He said, "We're going to change it up a bit for tonight. I think there'll be a few campers coming in, and they can be our eyes and ears. I want to set up on the three main roads going up toward the lake. We can pass out fliers, tell people to keep their eyes open. It might help us find him, and it might save a camper's life if he comes across him. If nothing else, it will cover our asses a bit. Rather, my ass.

"Gerry, I'm going to have you team up with Jeremy, and the two of you can cover the south fork. Lou, you and Dusty cover the middle fork. I'll take Rich and Odessa with me, and we'll set up on the north fork. I expect that road to have the least amount of traffic, so if we have to break away, I won't feel too bad leaving it open.

"Any questions?"

No one spoke.

"Okay, let's get at it."

39

Steve Troy had become accustomed to reading that rag, The Idaho Statesman, but only because he wanted to look at the classified ads and see if anything interested him, job-wise. This afternoon he sat at the bar reading about the manhunt for Buddy Frantelli, the parolee at large suspected of killing Lacy Jane Lewis outside of the Lucky Seven nightclub. He was also implicated in a kidnap and hijacking of a local trucker named Elwood Johnston. The trucker was found dead on the Montgomery Pass in Nevada, not far from California. Boise Police Detective Jeremy Cross was leading the investigation, and was now teamed up with California law enforcement officials who were actively hunting the fugitive after an attempted murder occurred outside Bishop, California.

He couldn't believe it. The Mormon mafia detective *leading the investigation*, as if he had any fucking clue about police work or being an investigator. Troy shook his head, tossed the paper onto the bar and then gave it a shove, sliding it a couple of empty stools down. He looked over at Dave, who busied himself arranging glasses behind the bar, and said, "What's a guy got to do to get a fucking drink around this place?"

BUDDY TOLD LILLIAN THEY DIDN'T HAVE TIME FOR ANY MORE FOOLING around, they needed to get clear of this place before the pigs came back around and found her dead husband in the bushes. She said, "Not until we do something with that arm of yours," and told him she had been a nurse.

When she began to unwrap the bandaging she stopped, pulled back with her nose wrinkled and said, "You're a damn mess. You're gonna lose that arm, mister."

"The hell you mean, lose my arm?"

"It's dead. Rotted flesh and bone. That's why it stinks so bad. You can't tie a tourniquet around a limb and leave it for days on end. That's meant to be a very temporary fix to stop massive bleeding, or in your case, to keep the poison from getting to your heart until you can get to a doctor. That's it. You don't leave it on there, you big dummy."

He glared at her and said, "You best watch how you talk to me, woman."

She forced a smile, then put her hand on his shoulder and said, "We need to get you to a medical facility, Buddy, and get done what has to be done."

"They'll amputate it?"

She nodded. "I don't see they'll have a choice."

"Jesus Christ," he said, "that's just my luck. Can you believe it? I'd been better off if they'd kept me in prison. It's been one goddamn thing after another out here."

She listened.

After a moment, he said, "You know how to drive this rig, lady?"

She frowned a little. "Well, no, I never pulled a trailer."

He sat silent, thinking about how they'd get down the road, neither of them knowing how to pull a trailer. Him with his one arm and his new girlfriend who never had to drive with her late husband around, probably just sat over in the passenger's seat grinning like an idiot and knitting or maybe reading a book about making love to an outlaw.

She said, "Why do we need the trailer?"

He cocked his head. "Leave it here?"

"Why not?"

"You know how to unhook it?"

"The asshole made a list. Shouldn't be too hard to figure it out."

Buddy smiled and said, "You know what woman, I sorta like the way you think."

She smiled and said, "We can start working on it in about twenty minutes. What do you say?"

"I figured I'd keep you two together, since Odessa's a civilian," Sheriff Reynolds explained as they approached the Bronco. "Besides, there's plenty of room in this rig, once I move some of my crap out of the back seat."

He moved a large black nylon bag with a shoulder strap, a rubber tote, a jacket and a pair of pull-over muck boots from directly behind the passenger's seat, shoving it all to the other side. He collected a few empty cups and water bottles and stuffed them into a fast food bag, and crumpled it up. Then he stepped out of the way and gestured for Odessa, offering a hand to assist her in stepping up.

As she did, he said, "Let me know if you're not comfortable back there, young lady."

"I'll be fine," she assured him.

Rich stood watching. Their eyes met briefly, but he looked away and climbed into the front passenger's seat. He wondered what she was thinking, seeing the thoughtful expression in her eyes.

He was thinking about tomorrow. Tomorrow and the day after tomorrow and all the days after that. And he wondered when he would be alone again. Soon there would be no case to work, which meant there would be no Jeremy and no Odessa. His friends. Maybe more than friends, as far as Odessa went. He'd return to his lonely home and and resume his lonely life. He might have to get a pet, but a real one, a dog he could walk to the park and play fetch with. Otherwise, it would be just him and the neighbors he didn't know. Like the flight attendant from 103 whose name he hadn't learned, but who he guessed was thirty-five and a size seven. And single. But probably out of his league.

Sheriff Reynolds broke the silence as they drove north. He said, "I'm afraid this fella isn't done killing, and he won't be done until we catch him, or kill him, one or the other."

"He's as dangerous as any I've seen," Rich said, "that's for sure. But we'll catch him. I'm certain of it. He's reckless. He'll miss a step, and when he does, we'll be right there."

The sheriff glanced over but didn't respond. Odessa sat quietly in the back seat. The silence continued until they passed the south fork where Detectives Gerardo Herrera and Jeremy Cross were posted, parked on the dirt shoulder at the turnoff in their unmarked Chevy Caprice with its red light on the dash and blue and amber lights on the rear deck. Sheriff Reynolds pulled his vehicle over and stopped alongside them, facing the opposite direction so that the drivers' doors were adjacent to one another.

"You boys need anything before we head on up to the north fork?" Reynolds asked.

Herrera looked up through mirrored sunglasses beneath a ball cap with a sheriff's star on the front. He said, "We're good here, boss. How long do you want us to take it this evening?"

Sheriff Reynolds checked his watch. "Maybe till ten. I don't think anyone will be coming in past that, not many if they do. Most people like to be set up and settled in long before that."

Herrera nodded.

"Listen, Gerry, I don't want you taking any chances. You see something you don't like, get some backup."

"Will do, boss."

The sheriff tilted his head down to see past Detective Herrera. "Jeremy, you are armed, aren't you?"

"Yes sir."

"Okay. Gerry has a long gun in the trunk too. You guys should go over that real quick before you get too comfortable. I want everyone prepared for the worst, and we'll hope for the best."

Gerardo began to speak but stopped to study the pickup truck coming down the dirt road toward the highway. The sheriff followed his gaze.

A woman drove. Her man appeared to be asleep in the passenger's seat, his head tucked into the corner of the seat and door with his hat pulled low. It was an older couple, probably in their sixties. It pulled onto the highway headed north.

Sheriff Reynolds said, "We talked to her earlier. Nice gal, but she hadn't seen a thing. Looks like they decided to leave the camper, maybe come back after the search is off. I guess my warning scared her a bit."

"Warning?" his detective asked.

"We told her about the convict running around, told her to keep her eyes peeled and to be careful."

The truck accelerated north on the highway and Rich watched it grow smaller as the sheriff finished the conversation with his detective. Then they pulled away too, driving in the same direction, north. Rich could see the truck ahead of them, but only on the straightaways. It was barely in sight.

After a short distance, Rich said, "So you talked to that couple, you say?"

"Back at the campground, up that south fork road a ways."

"Everything seemed okay with them?"

The sheriff glanced over. "Well, yeah. Why?"

Rich paused for a moment, looking straight ahead, still catching glimpses of the truck. "I don't know, just something about the way that passenger rode in the front I didn't like."

"Looked to me like the old man was sacked out."

"That's what bothers me a little," Rich said.

"Oh?"

Rich glanced in the back seat to see Odessa listening too. He then directed his attention to the sheriff, who continued glancing over at him, apparently waiting for more. Rich said, "It's not always the way a crook looks at you that gives you the feeling he's up to something. Sometimes it's the way he doesn't look at you, the way he *won't* look at you. You know what I mean?"

The sheriff nodded.

Rich continued, "I mean, sometimes, you'd be the only two cars on the road, maybe passing right by each other, or sitting next to one another at a stop light. You could look over and see the crooks sitting up straight and proper, staring ahead like they were in Sunday school, and you just got a feeling they were up to no good. We used to joke that they'd think if they didn't look at you, you didn't see them. But when they did that, it was as telling as when they'd look over and panic, seeing the cops watching them. Either way though, you felt something. You knew they were dirty. You had that gut instinct that you'd better stop their car and see what they were up to. I really learned to trust my gut on those deals."

"Okay, I get that. But what is it about the old couple camping you don't like?"

"That passenger looked to me like he was hiding."

"You think?"

"I think most of the time, the man drives."

Odessa said, "Oh brother."

"Especially a big truck like that, those dual wheels in the back. Just seems more like a man's truck. I also think most people wait until they're out on the smooth highway to lay their heads back and take a nap, rather than trying to nap coming down a bumpy dirt road. Another thing I didn't like, most people have a tendency to gawk at the cops, sit up and look around and pay attention to see what's going on. Not only did the passenger of that truck not do that, but the woman driving never glanced over either."

The sheriff was picking up speed now, trying to close the distance but not being overly obvious about it.

"I'm just saying, I have a bad feeling about it. That's all. I could be wrong."

They were closing in now and the sheriff reached down and activated his emergency lights. He said, "Well, let's have a look then, just to be safe."

Rich nodded. Then he glanced back at Odessa. She sat silent and wide-eyed. He said to her, "When we stop them, I want you to stay in here, keep a low profile and be careful. If anything happens, flatten out on the floorboard and don't move or make a sound until I come back for you."

Then he said to the sheriff, "I'm carrying a Glock nine on my right hip, an extra magazine on my left."

"I noticed."

"You might want to unlock that shotgun."

4 0

Buddy said to Lillian, "Don't pull over."

She said, "What are we going to do?"

"I don't know. I need time to think. Turn your blinker on, start slowing down more, make it look like you're trying to find a good spot to pull off."

Lillian watched the mirrors and slowed down. She moved over but continued driving, the sheriff's vehicle now right behind them. "I better stop."

Buddy watched in his side-view mirror. He slowly reached beneath the seat, trying to not show any movement in the cab of the truck, and he retrieved the .44 Magnum revolver belonging to the late Mr. Lomeli.

Lillian glanced over. "What, you're going to shoot it out?"

"I don't know yet."

"Great, we'll both die out here, gunned down by the fuzz."

"The fuzz?"

She looked over. "It's what we used to call them."

"Back in the forties?"

She frowned.

An announcement crackled over a loudspeaker: "Pull the truck over and stop!"

She looked over again. Buddy said, "Well, here we go."

"I HAVE A BAD FEELING NOW MYSELF," SHERIFF REYNOLDS SAID AS THEY eased in behind the truck that was now coming to a stop on the soft dirt shoulder with a cloud of dust bellowing up behind it. "You may have been right about these two."

"Can you radio it in, maybe get another unit rolling out here to back us up?"

"I can try. It's a long roll."

The sheriff picked up the radio, but before he keyed the mic, a string of broken and garbled words sputtered over the airwaves. They were stopped now, and the two occupants of the pickup sat still, waiting.

Sheriff Reynolds said it was the voice of his detective, and he keyed the mic. "Gerry, come again, can't copy."

Another transmission came across as a melody of static, but then as clear as a bell the words "he's dead" came across.

The sheriff shot a look at Rich. "Did I hear that right?"

Rich said, "Something about someone being dead."

Odessa agreed: "That's what I heard too."

The sheriff shifted the truck back into Drive and flipped a U-turn across the street, onto the opposite shoulder, through the dirt, and back onto the pavement, the tires squealing and dust and smoke rising up behind them. He hit the siren and stomped on the gas, and the sheriff's vehicle headed south at a high rate of speed, the engine growling against the siren.

Rich glanced back to see the pickup driving off, headed north, and he had a bad feeling. That feeling he would get in his gut. The feeling that helped him survive twenty-plus years of being a cop in Los Angeles.

He didn't mention it to the sheriff.

"JESUS CHRIST, LOOK AT THAT!" BUDDY SAID, TURNED IN HIS SEAT AND watching through the rear window. There was a wall of dust and gray smoke, and the dumb cops were headed south with their lights on. "I think my luck has finally changed."

"Maybe all you needed was a good luck charm," Lillian said.

He looked over to see a big grin on her face and thought, Jesus, this goofy fucking broad.

41

Sheriff Reynolds arrived at the campground with Rich and Odessa. His detective and several patrol vehicles were scattered about the premises, and deputies were putting up yellow tape. He realized that this was where he and Jeremy had briefly visited with the woman. Her trailer was still here, but the pickup truck that had been attached to it was gone. The sheriff felt a sickness in his stomach.

As he exited his patrol vehicle, he smelled the engine's heat and heard ticking sounds from under the hood. He called out to his detective, "Gerry, what do you have?"

The detective walked away from the tree line, back toward Sheriff Reynolds where he had parked next to the vacated camp trailer. He said, "Elderly man, looks like he was stabbed."

"Damnit!" Sheriff Reynolds shouted. Then he removed his cowboy hat and smacked his leg with it and said, "Goddamnit!"

Jeremy Cross had stepped alongside the detective.

Gerardo continued, "Right after you guys left us sitting down there on the highway, we had another camper coming out. They stopped and told us there was a dead man in the brush up here, near a camper. They had just come in a couple hours ago and set up camp not far from here, just up the road. The wife went walking the dog, and the dog ended up running over to the brush over there, probably on a scent. He started barking and she tried to call him back, but he wouldn't come. She walked over and saw the man. She saw the blood and knew he was dead. They drove down to the highway with the intent of finding a cell signal, and saw us sitting there."

Sheriff Reynolds wiped the sweat from his forehead and put his hat back on. His face was bright red. He said, "Damn it, Gerry, had I known..."

"What's wrong, boss?"

"The truck that goes with this camper, we had it stopped right when you put out something about someone being dead. It was the truck that pulled onto the highway when we were parked next to you down there, the one with the woman driving."

Gerardo grimaced.

"Your radio was breaking so damn bad, we had no idea what you were saying. All we heard was 'He's dead,' and then garbled transmission. The first thing I thought was you guys had caught and maybe killed our suspect. We just couldn't hear anything."

Gerardo waited a minute, then said, "I guess maybe we should've radioed in what we were going to go check, what the campers had told us. I'm sorry, boss."

Jeremy asked, "Who was in the truck, Sheriff?"

Sheriff Reynolds looked at him, glanced at Rich and Odessa, then came back to Jeremy. His voice was low and the tone soft when he said, "Probably our suspect, that's who."

Nobody said anything.

After a moment, the sheriff asked, "Who's the dead guy?"

"We have to assume it's the owner of that camp trailer, but we have no way to run the license until we get into range. Trailer's clear, nothing inside of immediate interest. No additional victims, anyway. But we backed out of it after a cursory search, figuring it's going to be part of the crime scene. I'm sorry, boss, really."

"It's not your fault, Gerry. Not at all. This kind of shit just happens." Then he looked at Rich and said, "I should have stayed with my gut."

Rich held the sheriff's gaze but didn't reply.

"It'll be dark soon," Gerardo said, "so I've sent one of our deputies back for lights and a generator, and when he gets into cell range, he'll get the coroner rolling too. It's going to be a long night."

EARLY THE NEXT MORNING WHILE THE SHERIFF AND HIS DEPUTIES AND the civilian volunteers were finishing up the homicide investigation in the mountains north of Bishop, California, there were heavily armed and highly energetic cops assembling five-hundred miles away in Idaho.

The Boise Area Narcotics Drug Interdiction Team, *BANDIT,* consisting of narcotics officers from the cities of Boise, Nampa, Caldwell and Meridian, as well as agents from the DEA and FBI, gathered in a room at city hall in Greenleaf, Idaho. The town of about eight-hundred residents, located thirty miles west of Boise, was best known for its ordinance requiring residents to each own and maintain a firearm in their home. It had been unanimously passed by city council with the intent to protect against being overrun by refugees from the Gulf Coast. Thus far, it seemed to have been an effective law; the residents went about their daily routines and travels without confrontation or fear of takeover.

The men and women who gathered there this morning were dressed in jeans or tactical pants, and they wore jackets or vests with various police insignia printed boldly on the fronts and backs. They referred to this outerwear as raid jackets, or raid vests, and they would be worn in conjunction with body armor. Although they were about to place their lives in imminent danger, they milled about casually, drinking coffee and eating donuts and visiting or joking around with one another.

In addition to the narcotics officers, there were uniformed officers from the Idaho State Police and the Canyon County Sheriff's Office, there to provide a uniformed presence and assist with the operation.

J.P. Long positioned himself at the podium in the front of the room and called for everyone's attention. He had to make several requests before the chatter quieted, and a voice from the crowd said, "Nice ponytail, sweetheart."

Everyone laughed and J.P. said, "Yeah, well, fuck you too. Okay, moving right along... Good morning, ladies. If you don't already know me, I'm J.P. Long with the DEA, currently assigned to BANDIT. Before we execute our search warrant this morning, I'm going to fill you in on some background of the case, and then Doc here will go over the operations plan.

"We've been working with some informants and making a few smalltime busts of heroin coming out of Southern California, mostly the Compton area. Crip gang members and associates are bringing it in, transporting it in small quantities to avoid losing large loads if they get popped, usually a pound or two per vehicle. For the most part, they drive rental cars, usually sedans, never anything fancy. Our information is that these assholes have deliveries just about daily, and the drivers come in using various routes. They're not stupid when it comes to moving dope.

"Last week we busted a guy who plays for BSU, some dude out of Compton who was scoring a couple grams of H. Apparently, he didn't want to go to the joint, and he doesn't want to mess up his future career with the National Felony League"—he paused to appreciate the laughter for a moment—"so he decided to work off his case.

"Being a former upstanding resident of the fine City of Compton, a quaint little town south of Los Angeles at which I have been privileged to spend a few years of my illustrious career"—he waited for the jeers to subside— "Mr. Sherman, or *Tank* as the *fellas* call him, had no problem stepping up his game and ordering a pound of H and having it delivered straight to his apartment in Boise. These guys didn't even blink at the request, knowing our star football player by name and reputation. We paid 20K of your hard-earned tax dollars for the pound of shit, and we let them walk with the duffle bag full of cash.

The bag has a GPS tracking device sewn into the seam, which has been steadily recording its location as the trailer house in question, out here to our south, in the middle of East Jesus. This, of course, will present a myriad of problems, all of which my partner in crime fighting, Doc, will address with you in just a moment.

"When we hit the place, we expect to find a lot more dope and money. And, of course, a shitload of guns and ammunition. From what we've been able to figure out, with a couple days of surveillance and through talking to our informants, this place out here in the desert is their main headquarters for the dope operation, the place where the dope lands when it gets to Idaho. Safe and sound out in the desert where they can see the cops coming from a mile away, when they're awake.

"Our money is marked, but there will be a lot more than just ours, I'm sure. Everything will be secured in place after all suspects are detained. At that time, our Special Agent in Charge—and I believe either a SAC from the bureau or a supervisor from Boise PD—will team up to inventory and record all the money and dope.

"So that, ladies, is why we're all gathered here on this fine spring morning rather than sleeping in late and having a big breakfast like the firemen do. We think this has the potential to be big, maybe the biggest bust of the year, and with that we expect it to be well-guarded. There could definitely be some resistance from these Compton gangsters. They don't hesitate to shoot down there, so be sure to double-check your chambers and magazines. If it goes hot, no contagious fire —please! Only shoot if you have an immediate threat in front of you."

He waited a minute, his gaze wandering the room. He pointed toward the side where a table held several boxes of donuts and an urn of coffee. "The coffee and donuts are on the federal government, so feel free to load up before heading out. Any questions?"

A hand went up in the back of the room.

"Go ahead, in the back there, sir."

"Any friendlies in the loc?"

"None that we know of. If you come across a black man about six-five, three-fifty or better, that would most likely be our informant,

Tank. But I don't expect him to be there. He isn't real bright but I think he's smarter than to be hanging with those Compton fools after making that buy for us.

"Anything else?… Okay, Doc, they're all yours."

AFTER THE BRIEFING, THE TASK FORCE AND THEIR ASSISTING PERSONNEL deployed from the auditorium and caravanned to a remote location ten miles south of Greenleaf, Idaho. At exactly seven o'clock in the morning, flashbang grenades were tossed through windows on the east and south sides of the doublewide mobile home. Blinding flashes of light and deafening blasts shattered the morning silence. Fractions of a second later, detectives pulled the front door off its hinges with a pry bar tool and brute strength, and an entry team swept through the residence with automatic weapons, the beams of headlamps affixed to their helmets leading the way. They yelled vigorously and repeatedly, announcing their presence as police officers entering the home, and demanding all occupants put their hands up.

When the smoke cleared and the occupants were detained, J.P. declared it a success. At a glance he saw there were weapons, piles of cash, and packages of dope to be seized. But most importantly, there hadn't been a single shot fired. J.P. had been involved in enough shooting incidents to appreciate each and every time they were avoided. He was no youngster.

TANK AND TANIKA HAD JUST PASSED OUT IN THEIR APARTMENT THIRTY miles from the drug bust. A fan twirled lazily above their mattress that lay on the carpeted floor among ashtrays full of cigarettes and roaches, discarded alcohol containers, and dirty laundry. Tank had no idea that his homeboys were being detained at gunpoint, or that in the coming weeks he would be asked to testify at a Grand Jury hearing at which point he would be considered a snitch, a punk, and a dead man.

Tanika had no idea that the heroin in Boise was about to dry up, which would have an immediate effect on the price of the product. This would have an immediate effect on how many clients she would need to see each day to support her increasingly demanding habit.

BUDDY FRANTELLI AND HIS NEW LADY FRIEND, LILLIAN LOMELI, PULLED into the Renown Regional Emergency Room in Reno, Nevada, and parked the truck at the back of the hospital, out of view. Buddy had told her where to park, and told her if shit went bad, they'd meet there and haul ass together. But, he said, he'd better keep the keys, until he knew for sure he could trust her. They entered through the emergency entrance which allowed access twenty-four hours a day. It was just past seven, and the main hospital hadn't yet opened.

Buddy said, "Remember, you're my mother—"

"Do I look old enough to be your mother?"

He didn't answer.

After a brief pause, he continued, "The story is, I was lost in the woods for several days. I don't have any ID or anything else, because I lost my backpack when I tumbled off a cliff. That's why I look like shit, and smell bad too. Also, tell them I'm a full-time student, and I'm still on your insurance. *That's* why I want you to say you're my mom. They won't be able to check that out before we're gone. Give them your ID, your insurance card or whatever, and complete all the forms. I'm going to act like I'm out of it so I don't have to talk to anyone. You know, delirious or dazed or whatever you want to call it. Use all of your information, you and the old man. Your address, phone, et cetera. Just tell them my name is Buddy, and whatever the fuck your last name is, and whatever birthday you want that makes me about thirty."

"You don't look thirty."

"I've had a rough life."

"Lomeli."

"Huh?"

"My last name… it's Lomeli."

"*Lomeli,* huh? Is that eye-tallion?"

"How the hell should I know? I've only had the name a couple of months."

"Mine's eye-tallion, but I'm not going to tell you what it is. Not until I get to know you better."

"So you're a wop?"

Buddy frowned. "You say some weird shit sometimes, you know it?"

They paused just before entering, Buddy halting their movement with his hand in front of her. He said, "No funny shit, you hear me? I know I can trust you, but I'm not sure about it."

"That doesn't even make sense."

"Look, woman… they're going to have to put me under. I don't want to wake up wearing handcuffs."

Lillian smiled and said, "Well if you do, I'll have the key."

"I'm serious."

She said, "Quit being such a pussy. Come on, let's get this over with and get the hell out of here before the fuzz catches up to us."

42

More than half a million in cash and at least twenty pounds of uncut heroin were recovered from the mobile home in the desert south of Greenleaf, Idaho. Six people were arrested. All males. All residents of Compton, California. All members of the street gang known as Southside Crips. All convicted felons. There were plenty of guns in the house to go around, one for each. Which meant additional charges and enhancements for the convicted felons possessing firearms, and for possession of Schedule I narcotics while in possession of firearms. All heavyweight charges with mandatory minimum sentences beginning at twenty years. Their balls were on the chopping block now, J.P. had assured them, each and every one of them.

But there would be negotiations. Each would be offered a deal. Each would have the choice—the opportunity—to give up bigger fish or spend the next twenty-some years of their lives in prison. In Idaho. With all the white boys. Or die trying.

J.P. and Doc high-fived each other at the trunk of their car while removing the cumbersome body armor that made them sweat against the cool morning air. It had been a success. All of their hard work had paid off. These operations required long, hard hours of planning and reams of paperwork that passed through the hands of supervisors and district attorneys and judges. There was nothing more gratifying to hard-working cops than when there was a big payoff at the end.

Later, when the long day ahead of them was over, the last entry logged in the evidence ledger, the last booking slip approved by the watch sergeant, and the last report tossed into the SACs in-tray, the team would consume large quantities of alcohol in traditional celebratory fashion.

NOBODY WAS CELEBRATING IN BISHOP. DONUTS SAT MOSTLY untouched by the tired detectives, deputies, and civilians who had gathered. The coroner and Sheriff Reynolds stood to the side, discussing final details while the others waited to be debriefed on the situation so they could call it quits for a few hours. Each had been up all night.

Sheriff Reynolds finished his private conversation and then addressed the group.

He said, "I appreciate everyone's help. I feel horrible about that truck getting away—"

He waited while several people spoke up, telling him he did what he thought was best, working on the information he had, he didn't owe any apologies...

"We're going to all go get some sleep for a few hours, and then I'd like to meet one more time, here at the command post, and have a formal debriefing. I'll need a report from each team, and I'll need any badges turned back in from you posse members. We're going to wrap it up, because there's no doubt in my mind he's gone from my jurisdiction, probably for good. I doubt he'd even think about heading south after what transpired last evening.

"I want to thank each of you, more than anything else, for being there with me throughout this ordeal. Some of you are with me each and every time I need you, and that's been the case for a lot of years.

"Finally," he said, and looked directly into the eyes of Rich Farris, "when we get back together this afternoon to break this down, I'm going to ask the media to be here. When we're all done with business, I'm going to announce my retirement."

There were gasps and sighs and mumbles.

Lou Wright said, "Al, let's take some time to let this all calm down before making any rash decisions. We're all a little tired, and I think I speak for everyone here when I say we appreciate your work and dedication to our community. Mistakes happen, and you acted on the best information you had at the time."

He nodded, and said, "I appreciate it, Lou, but I've lost a few steps. I could have gotten some people killed here this time. I've let a dangerous fugitive escape, and it happened because I stopped trusting my gut. It's time to do some fishin'."

There was silence.

Rich didn't have anything to say. He watched and listened, and as he absorbed the words, he wondered if the sheriff drank. He imagined that in the near future, the veteran lawman would be having a drink in the privacy of his office, or maybe at home. Maybe while sitting at the breakfast nook or outside on the porch, alone or with a wife of forty years—Rich didn't know. But he did know all too well how it felt to be at the end of a career, which for law enforcement, all too often, meant the end of a life. Mostly figuratively, but sometimes, literally.

Rich knew that when a lawman reaches that place where he knows it's time to hang up the badge and gun, there is a terrible emptiness inside that rivals the loss of a loved one. He had felt it firsthand himself, of course, and he was all too aware of the toll it could take on a person. He knew how it felt to realize you had given all you had to give, and the tank was now empty. Rich remembered having felt guilty; though he had given much more than many others, he felt he hadn't given enough. The shrink had told him it was common to feel that way, that many dedicated cops had the same repentance. Rich also knew that the sheriff was most likely making the correct decision. Because nobody ever knew when the time would come, but when it came, there was no mistake about it. When you were done, you were done.

There was a number, Rich had often said, and it differed for every law enforcement officer. For some, it was the number of years. For others, maybe the number of chases, fights, or shootings. There were only so many a person had in them. Or, it was the number of bodies. Everyone had a breaking point when it came to dealing with the death and mayhem. And everyone's number was different, so it often took them by surprise when the time arrived. Like coming home and finding a spouse gone or a loved one dead—you never expected it. Nobody ever seemed to handle it well. Some appeared to handle it better than others, but nobody handled it well. Ever.

Rich turned and walked away with a cup of coffee in his hand and moisture in his eyes.

THE EMERGENCY ROOM DOCTOR TOLD HIS STAFF THEY'D WORRY ABOUT the paperwork later, this was an emergency. The arm would have to be amputated, and because he feared there would be infection, he needed to get to it right away. They would then pump the patient with antibiotics to fight against infection, and narcotics to manage the pain.

Buddy cringed at the thought, but he had prepared himself for it the best he could mentally and accepted the news without comment. He did look forward to the narcotics part, and wondered what he would be given, and how much. Within a half hour, Buddy saw the bright lights over his head begin to fade. Shortly thereafter his eyes became heavy and he fell asleep.

He dreamed of prison, as he all too often did, but this time it was about the man he repeatedly stabbed until he lost the shank and calmly walked away. But in his dream, Buddy went straight to the room of Big John Wilson, who sat in an oversized, red velvet chair smoking a pipe and reading a magazine. The big convict looked down on Buddy and smiled, and asked if the deed had been done. He told him it had, and the shot-caller stood from his chair and took Buddy by the hand. He led him down a dark hallway that seemed to go on and on with twists and turns and doorways on both sides. The doors glowed red from heat, and smoke drifted from the bottoms and edges, and Buddy could hear crying and screaming beyond the barriers. Finally they reached the end of the hallway where Big John shoved the last door open and stepped aside. A bright light blasted through the opening, nearly blinding Buddy, and there were more screams. Big John Wilson laughed, wickedly. Buddy jumped at the sudden blast of a train whistle and felt himself falling through the doorway. He landed on his back and looked up at the light as he waited for death. But the train went by and now people spoke in soft tones and low voices around him.

Buddy opened his eyes and blinked at the light that hung above his bed. Then he turned his head and saw Lillian sitting at his side. His right arm itched terribly, but when he reached to scratch it, there was nothing there. He looked around for his arm but it was nowhere to be found. He again looked at Lillian, with questions for her, but he was unable to speak. She sat smiling, and then she stood over him and began rubbing his forehead and talking to him.

Again with that stupid grin on her face. She was making him crazy.

He closed his eyes and fell back to sleep.

Steve Troy awakened to the morning news following the story that had begun with a convict named Buddy Frantelli, who, shortly after being released from prison, *allegedly* committed a murder, and then kidnapped a trucker, and had been on the run ever since. Lt. Ryan Fitzpatrick told the reporter—on live TV—that his detective was currently in California, directly involved in the manhunt for the dangerous fugitive.

Troy turned the channel to a sports program, cranked it up so he could hear it from the other room, and then stumbled into the bathroom cursing the Mormons and the convicts and the aches in his head. He stopped at the sink, turned the hot water on and looked in the mirror as he waited for it to warm up. He stared at the unshaven, graying, bloated, miserable son of a bitch in the reflection, and said to him, "You have got to dry out."

SHERIFF ALFRED REYNOLDS DID CALL A MEETING ONE LAST TIME THAT afternoon beneath the canopy of the mobile command post in the parking lot of the Kmart shopping center. All who had been involved in the operation were present but subdued as they waited for the sheriff to speak. A reporter from the local paper, The Mountaintop News, stood away from the others with a notebook and a pen and an attentive expression on her young face.

Sheriff Reynolds said, "I appreciate you all gathering one last time here this afternoon as we close out this operation, the hunt for the fugitive Buddy Frantelli. It is my understanding that all reports are submitted, the IDs and badges have been accounted for, and all additional personnel, agencies, and interested parties have been notified that we are shutting down the operation.

"Again, I want to thank you all for your hard work, your dedication, and your commitment to assisting me in keeping your community safe from villains like this Frantelli character. I have failed you, and I have failed the community."

Lou Wright began to speak, but the sheriff stopped him with a hand held up toward him and a subtle shaking of his head.

He continued, "Detective Gerry Herrera has been by my side for more than a decade. He is as competent a law enforcement officer as I have ever seen. He is young enough to bring energy and fresh approaches to law enforcement, and seasoned enough to do it well with a lot of experience as his foundation. I am stepping down, as of this afternoon, and appointing Gerry to be my successor. He will be the sheriff of Inyo County until the election next fall, and then the people will decide from there. I intend to fully support him now and as long as he is sheriff and I am alive and able.

"I wish you all the very best. You all know where my place is, don't be strangers."

And he walked away.

43

Tank awoke that afternoon to the sounds of Tanika vomiting violently in the bathroom adjacent to their room in the small apartment. He said, "The hell's wrong with you now, girl?"

She didn't answer.

He said, "I coulda tole you, you keep fucking around with that smack, you gonna be sick. That shit'll kill you."

He listened as she heaved again.

"Goddamnit, bitch, you need to get yo'self some medicine, or some methadone, or whatever... something to keep yo skinny little ass from dying in my motherfuckin' house."

That would be all he needed.

She stepped out of the bathroom, wiping her mouth with a dirty hand towel. She was naked, and her body was shaking. Tank looked at her messy hair, her dark eyes, her dirty, skinny-assed arms with tracks all up and down both sides, scabs and scars from intravenous drug use. She looked like she'd just arrived from Ethiopia or some goddamn place where people didn't eat, they sat around patting mud together and drinking dirty water and not even crying because they didn't know how fucked up their lives were. He saw tears rolling down her cheeks as she looked at him with pleading eyes.

She said, "Tank... Baby... I need you to help me."

He shook his head in disgust.

She sobbed, saying, "Baby, please..."

Tank said, "Bitch, I need you to go on and get the fuck out. That's what the fuck I need. That's how *you* can help *me*, if you're wondering about that.

"See, I tried to warn you about this shit, but you wouldn't listen. Now look at your dumb ass. You done turned yo'self into a skanky-ass ho and you prolly gots the aids now, fuckin' around with needles and all them niggas. It's time for you to kick gravel, bitch, and just head on down the road. Say goodbye to Tank and get the fuck on."

She stared at him but didn't say anything. Her tears dried up and her expression turned dark. She walked out of the room and into the kitchen, only to return a moment later with a butcher's knife in her hand. She stopped in the doorway and watched him.

Tank said, "Now, little girl, what the hell you think you gonna do?"

She raised it above her head and screamed as she ran at him with faraway, crazy eyes.

Tank rolled to the side, the college athlete moving much faster than most people his size. She threw herself onto the mattress and thrust the knife through the pillow where his head had rested just an instant before. He came up to his knees, now behind her as she started to push herself up from the mattress, and he punched her in the back of her head. She dropped instantly and was out cold. Tank waited, but she didn't move. Not then, not after a little time had passed, and not after a lot of time had passed.

The bitch never moved again.

Ever.

Not on her own.

ODESSA BROWN RETURNED FROM THE OFFICE WITH A KEY AND TOLD Rich they only had one room left, but not to worry, it was a double queen. He looked at her suspiciously. Then he looked around the near-empty parking lot, and said, "They only have one room, huh?"

She said, "Isn't that what I just told you?"

"Yes, but it seems—"

"Don't worry, Mr. Farris, I don't have any intention of allowing you to misbehave with me."

He looked over at Jeremy who stood to the side near the two parked vehicles, his city-owned SUV and the rental car they had just picked up for Rich and Odessa. Jeremy was grinning. He said, "I don't know about you two."

Rich said, "Her, not me."

Odessa nudged him with her elbow. "You'll think, *her*."

Jeremy said, "Okay, you guys are all set, right?"

"Yes," answered Rich, "we're good. We've got wheels and a room. Tomorrow we'll head to L.A., and I'll put little miss pain-in-the-pajamas here on a plane, send her back home before she gets into any more trouble."

"You're going to miss me," she said.

"That's probably true," Rich said, and thought, *you have no idea.*

The two men shook hands. Jeremy turned to shake Odessa's hand, but she stepped into him and wrapped her arms around his neck. She said, "You be careful, Detective Cross."

"Jeremy."

"Okay, Jeremy, you be careful."

"I will," he said. Then he smiled at each and turned toward his car.

As Jeremy opened the driver's door, Rich said, "Hey, Jeremy..."

He looked over.

"You're good at this. You know that, right?"

He smiled, then folded his tall, lean frame into the sedan and closed the door behind him.

The next day, Buddy Frantelli sat up in his bed, groggy from the pain meds. He was hungry. He looked at the tray next to him that held several containers of food—applesauce, pudding, some type of sandwich—and started to reach for the sandwich with his right hand. But his arm wasn't there, just as it hadn't been the last time he had awakened, but this time, he remembered why it was gone. He remembered the snakebite and the tourniquet he had tied around his arm and left there until his arm had died and the flesh had rotted.

The old woman, Lillian, was fast asleep in a chair just a few feet from his bed. Still with him, the goofy old broad. The goofy old broad with her silver hair that Buddy had started to think was kind of sexy, and her body that looked like it was forty—*tops*—and her real cool attitude. She had stuck with him.

Buddy thought about that as he watched her sleep. He hadn't had the company of a woman for a lot of years. The young broads were into shit that didn't make any sense to him, which he had discovered the hard way. Maybe this was just what he needed, an older broad who'd been around a bit and knew how to take care of a man—in more ways than one, too. This crazy broad with her thing for outlaws. She also seemed to have a bit of outlaw in her, herself. There was something about the old broad that made Buddy think she would do some scandalous shit, if needed. Well, she already had, getting the cops away from the camper, then getting the two of them off that mountain and out of there. Now helping him get the medical attention he badly needed, and sticking with him when she could have easily left. As he pondered it, he'd never known any woman that loyal. Not even his mother, that crazy old bitch.

Maybe his luck had finally changed. Buddy laid his head back on the pillow and went to sleep.

Jeremy Cross walked into the kitchen to find his wife making lunches. The kids were in various stages of finishing their breakfasts and putting their backpacks together, ready to leave for school.

He walked over and kissed Nancy on her head, because she didn't make herself any more available than that. The kids were telling him about school and sports and the neighbor kid who got in trouble for bringing a knife to school, and then they wanted to know all about the bad guy he had been chasing. Before he could respond, Nancy interjected that there was no time for storytelling, and then she gathered jackets and packs and lunches and ushered the kids out the door.

She looked back at Jeremy before closing the door behind her and said, "I'm taking the kids to see my mom this weekend. We'll leave after school Friday."

"Oh?"

"Just letting you know, in case I don't see you again this week."

She slammed the door behind her.

Jeremy looked through the window as the minivan pulled out of the driveway, vapor rising from its exhaust pipe. He turned and leaned against the kitchen counter, and looked around the empty room. He listened to the silence, and considered life without his children. He let out a long breath and sighed. Jeremy knew his marriage was not a healthy one, to say the least. But he was in for the long haul. The question was, was she?

ODESSA RODE ALONG IN SILENCE, WATCHING THE LANDSCAPE CHANGE from steep rugged mountains with jagged tops still covered with snow, to open valleys with purple mountains in the distance and red and yellow and orange hills close by. She thought about the song, America the Beautiful, and its reference to purple mountains, and she realized she'd never actually thought about that description before. Maybe she'd never seen mountains that looked purple before. Then she wondered if there were purple mountains elsewhere, places other than California. She had never seen any in Texas or Louisiana, she knew that.

She also thought about her next move, how she would tell Rich that she had changed her mind, that she wasn't going home. At least not yet. Put it to him that way, and make it sound like just a temporary change of plans, so as to not scare him away.

But should she ask to stay with him, or suggest she could get her own place? Maybe the latter, and wait for him to offer. Or would he insist she go home? Would he give her the spiel about their age differences again and continue to deny what surely they both felt between them? Maybe she'd tell him she loved him. Put that out there and see what he came back with. Let him deal with it, see how Mr. Poker Face handled a little bit of southern sweetness. Or she could seduce him. Because Richard Farris was the man to whom she would give herself; she was sure of that. That she had decided in Boise, while sitting in her room looking at the doors that adjoined hers with his and wishing he would knock. Practically dreaming he would knock. Fighting off the temptation to be the one to knock, to make that move. She didn't want to throw herself at him, but she was close to doing so.

And then last night. Oh, Dear Lord, how that temptation had put her to the test. The next bed over in the same room. She knew he had to have been thinking the same things. She had seen the way he looked at her at times, and she knew he wanted to be with her but for some reason was holding back. Being a gentleman. But Odessa had had about all the gentleness she could stand from this man. Now she wanted him to take her in his arms and ravish her.

This was the man she had always longed for, she knew that without question. She had never had much interest in the little boys who chased and begged and tried to make their moves on her; she had disregarded all of them. She had been patient, saving herself for someone special. She knew the right man would feel a certain way to her when he came into her life.

Rich was that man.

RICH THOUGHT ABOUT THE LONG NIGHT OF TOSSING AND TURNING, trying to sleep but restless from start to finish. Maybe because of the beautiful woman sleeping soundly in the adjacent bed, or maybe because their journey together was coming to an end. He watched a slide show in his head of the memories he had unwittingly stored away for just this occasion, and future occasions too. He pictured her at the hotel when they first met. He saw her barge into his room and tell him she was going with him. He saw her at the diner, at the dinner table, walking on the sidewalk next to him. He saw her smile and bat her sparkling eyes and he saw the various rooms and other settings come to light as she brought joy to all who had the pleasure of interacting with her.

Then he saw the story end, as all stories must. He saw her boarding the plane and waving goodbye, maybe blowing a kiss but not seeing the moisture in his eyes or knowing the thoughts that were in his head. The inappropriate thoughts, perhaps. The thoughts of a man twenty years her senior fooling himself into thinking that age wouldn't matter.

And as he had lain alone staring into the darkness, listening to her breathe, imagining himself holding her tight and telling her he loved her, he felt the tears well up in his eyes. He realized the end was near. It had to be. Maybe not just the end of this friendship, or *relationship*, as she had called it, but maybe the true end. He couldn't deny his past, the thoughts, feelings, and actions that came from that tremendous emptiness he felt inside before meeting her. Those things could easily sneak back into his world, and where would it lead him? Back to the dark side, he feared. The very dark side where he had often found himself at the edge and slipping, on more occasions than he cared to remember. Because sooner or later, he had to admit, he would likely fall.

TANK AND HIS BUDDY AND TEAMMATE LADARIUS LOVE STOPPED FOR A burger at the bottom of Bogus Basin where they had driven during the predawn hours to get rid of some trash. That's how he had put it when he called Ladarius on his cell, told him he needed help getting rid of some trash. So they had wrapped Tanika Edwards in the bedding and hauled her out of the apartment in the middle of the night when none of the neighbors would be outside or looking through windows. They had taken her up to the top of the ski resort not far from town, and rolled her off an embankment. Tank had told Ladarius that the bears and deer would eat her before the next ski season, so they had nothing to worry about. Besides, who would miss the bitch anyway?

At about the time he bit into a burger—the patrons around him all eating breakfasts—the phone in his pocket vibrated. Tanika's phone. He pulled it out and looked at it, but the caller ID read *Private Number*. He turned the phone off.

Ladarius said, "Who dat, cuz?"

"Man, I don't know. Dat the bitch's phone."

"You keepin' it, bruh?"

"I put the minutes on it, I might as well use 'em. I just ain't gonna answer no calls. I ain't trying to hook up with no niggas."

They both burst out in laughter, and Ladarius spit part of his burger on Tank.

Tank looked down at the food on his arm and said, "Nigga, you worse'n dat skanky-ass ho."

Ladarius said he was sorry, and reached over with a napkin. Tank knocked his hand away and told him not to stress. He looked around but nobody seemed to be paying attention to them, all white folk probably afraid to look at them. He lowered his voice and said, "When a brutha help you get rid of some trash, you don't sweat the small shit. Ya feel me?"

Ladarius nodded and grinned.

They bumped fists and went to work on the burgers and onion rings that were drowned in ketchup.

STEVE TROY TURNED IN HIS CREDENTIALS AT THE POLICE headquarters, signed the final documents, and collected his retirement badge and identification card. It would be his final transaction with the Boise Police Department. He walked out feeling a mixture of relief and regret. The retirement hadn't really been on his terms, but when it was time to go, it was time to go. That he understood, and he recognized his departure as a tactical move to avoid tarnishing his career, or worse yet, jeopardizing his pension.

Then he drove to the Idaho Department of Corrections and completed an application for employment. He had seen the ad in The Statesman, that filthy rag full of lies and liberal propaganda.

While the sergeant at the front desk fished around for the paperwork, Troy mentioned to him that he knew a few of the guards who worked there. Making small-talk, he told him he had heard it wasn't a bad job for a retired cop, being a guard at the prison. He smiled to show his friendly personality.

But Steve Troy's smile faded when the sergeant told him—he might even say he *scolded* him—that they too, are law enforcement officers, just as he had been. He went on to tell him they preferred not to be called *guards*, and then said, in a sarcastic tone, "Good luck with the application."

Troy walked away thinking the guy looked and acted like a goddamn Mormon, and he should have caught on to that when he first went in. Then he thought, that's exactly what he got for being friendly. He should know better.

He left in a huff and headed over to Sheehy's for a much-needed adult beverage.

44

Odessa drove like an old lady, scrunched up to the steering wheel which she gripped with both hands as she peered over the top of it. She was killing him. She had insisted on driving, telling Rich he should take a break, relax and enjoy the ride. But how could he?

He said, "Look, it's fifty-five through here. You can do sixty. This is California, nobody does the speed limit. You go the speed limit, you get run over. Or at least flipped off. The chippies don't write anyone doing less than ten over. Most of the time."

"Do you want to drive, Mr. Farris?"

"Yes."

"Well, too bad. I'm tired of riding shotgun."

He laughed. "Riding shotgun, huh?"

"Besides, I need you to sit over there and focus for a minute. Not say anything, just listen. I have something to discuss with you, and I don't want you saying anything until I'm ready to hear from you. Got it?"

"Sounds like a lecture, not a conversation."

"It's not a lecture, but I don't want to be interrupted until I finish saying what I need to say."

"Okay, Odessa, I'm all ears. Lay it on me."

She looked over, and the car swerved.

He gasped. "Hey!"

"What!" She eased back into her lane. "Don't yell at me. You scared me."

"*I* scared *you*? Do me a favor and just keep your eyes on the road while you talk, would ya?"

She stared straight ahead, both hands on the wheel.

Rich had turned in his seat to face her. He noticed the smooth shape of her profile, her perfect nose and pouty lips. Her small chin, the skin tucked tightly beneath it. Her arms and legs seemed stretched to reach the controls, the young lady appearing small behind the wheel.

He said, "Well?..."

Odessa took in a breath and let it out slowly. She said, "Okay, so here are my thoughts. Or maybe you could call it my proposition. I've put school on hold, dropped my classes for the semester—"

"When did you do that?"

"Can I finish? I told you to just sit there and shut it, right?"

"Okay, go ahead then."

"Thank you. I did it last week. I was beginning to fall behind, so I had to either go home and hit the books hard to bring my grades up, or drop the classes before they counted. So I dropped the classes. It was the smart thing to do."

He fought the urge to interject his thoughts.

"I told my boss that I would need an extended leave of absence from my job. He understood. He said they were going to need to replace me, but I would always be welcome to return if there were any openings. He also said they would give me a good reference.

"So basically, I'm free. Free to stay a while and see what happens with this wild man on the run. Hang out with you, and see what you do, and how you do it. I am very intrigued by all of it, you know. In fact, I've thought about changing majors again. That's another reason I dropped my classes. I may move schools and look at Criminal Justice."

He opened his mouth, and she must have seen it in her peripheral vision or just sensed it was coming. Either way, before he could opine, she held a hand out to silence him, and then quickly returned it to the steering wheel.

She said, "Besides, I've never been to L.A. and I'd really like to see it, spend some time there. I've sort of been sheltered my whole life. You're retired and have nothing else to do, so you can show me the sights. I'd like to see Hollywood and the Walk of Fame, maybe meet some movie stars. I want to go to Universal Studios and Disneyland. Maybe even Sea World. I want to go to the beach. Any of them. Maybe all of them. I'd like to see a Dodgers game."

"A Dodgers game?"

"Yes, I like baseball, and all we have is minor leagues down home. I've never been to a professional game—a big-league game—and I would like to go. Now, you just keep listening because I have more to say. Got it?"

He didn't say anything.

She said, "Oh, so you're being a smartypants."

Nothing.

"Good, so here's the rest. I can stay with you, or we can find me a place close by. Either way, whatever you're comfortable with. I have money. I have a nice little savings which would last me a while, or I might even find a job. I'm not asking for you to support me. I wouldn't have that.

"Also—and I'm just going to put this out there, so you best be ready—I think... no, I know... wait... okay, so what I was also going to say is this..."

She glanced over.

The car swerved. The tires ran over the warning bumps in the asphalt and a loud, horrible noise filled the inside of the car. She screamed, "Yikes!"

He said, "Jesus!"

She straightened the car, and said, "Richard James Farris, you will quit taking the Lord's name in vain before me. Got it?"

He laughed. "Before you? You sound like you're quoting scripture."

She jerked the car to the side of the road and slammed on the brakes.

"You can't just stop on the side of the highway—not unless you have an emergency!"

"You're going to have an emergency in about one second, mister. Now you listen to me—"

Rich looked through the back window, scanning for cops—the chippies. Traffic cops took these types of violations seriously, more so than exceeding the speed limit. His badge wouldn't help in this situation. He said, "You need to keep driving."

She said, "You need to shut your mouth and listen for one damn second. I love you, Richard Farris, and I have no intention of leaving you to go back to Louisiana. Not unless you can look me straight in the eyes and tell me you don't love me and you want me to go home."

Odessa didn't wait for a response. She glanced in her side-view mirror and floored it, merging back onto the highway with tires spinning and rubber squealing and gravel flying. She watched her speedometer and when it approached fifty-five, she eased off of the pedal, let out a breath, and settled in as if nothing had happened. Eyes forward, two hands on the wheel.

Rich sat speechless.

THE NEXT TIME BUDDY WOKE UP, THE DOCTOR WHO HAD AMPUTATED HIS arm stood in his room alongside one of the nurses. They were speaking with Lillian about Buddy's injuries. Buddy quickly closed his eyes and listened.

The doctor asked, "What happened to the back of his leg, down there on his calf?"

Lillian said she had no idea.

He said, "There was a lot of damage down there, but a little hard to figure. He had obviously been bitten by a canine, and there was a fair amount of damage to the muscle. He'll be okay, but he might have trouble walking on it for a while. Then there was another injury in the same area that appeared to be a gunshot wound."

She shrugged and shook her head.

He said, "I can't be sure it was a gunshot wound, because it was mostly superficial, just took some skin and a little flesh. Nothing worse than a graze. It had been wrapped up with strips of what looked to be a t-shirt, cut or torn and used for bandaging. He didn't mention the injured leg when you brought him in. That makes me a bit curious as to how that might have happened."

Lillian said, "Your guess is as good as mine, Doc. When I found him, he was a mess, and had been through an ordeal. Who knows what all happened to him. I haven't even gotten the whole story yet."

The doctor was silent for a long moment. Buddy squinted and saw he was looking at him, so he closed his eyes tight. The doctor said, "I'll check in again after a while, see if he's awake. I'll need to have some information about those injuries for my report. Basically I'll need to know for sure whether or not that was a gunshot wound. If it was, we're obligated to report it to the police. That's the law."

Lillian said, "Well, I can't imagine it would have been. Probably got poked by a stick or something. He had a terrible go out there, lost in the woods."

"If it was a gunshot wound, it may have been self-inflicted," the doctor said, "judging by the direction and angle of the wound. Do you know if he had a gun with him?"

Buddy listened, thinking, yeah, it was self-inflicted you asshole... self-inflicted while trying to shoot a rabid wolf off of my leg.

He heard Lillian say, "I don't think he had a gun. I just can't imagine how that could've happened, honestly."

Buddy heard the doctor and his nurse leave, each saying they would see her later. He peeked through one squinted eye to be certain. They were gone. He opened both eyes and said to Lillian, "We've got to get the hell out of here."

JEREMY RETURNED FROM A THREE-MILE RUN WITH AN AGENDA FOR THE day. He liked to think about his cases and work in general while running, because there were no interruptions or distractions and it was then he seemed to be sharp and focused as the endorphins flowed through him.

As he had jogged the streets of North Boise this morning, he had decided that his first order of business at the office today would be taking care of the due diligence on the Lacy Jane Lewis case. Which meant he would contact each of the agencies who were on the hunt for Frantelli to see what progress had been made. Then he would check with the state's crime lab to see if there were any results on the forensic testing of evidence in the case, the focus of which would primarily be DNA. Was there trace evidence recovered from her body or clothing that might have provided DNA other than hers? DNA that would hopefully be matched to Frantelli. Lastly, he would update his reports, brief his lieutenant, and, he thought, maybe call Rich and check in with him, see how things went with Odessa.

But while cooling off in the quiet kitchen before hitting the shower, he looked at his phone and saw that he had missed two calls from his office, and another from the lieutenant's cell phone. This was unusual, which made him wonder if there had been a break in the case. Maybe Frantelli had been captured or killed.

He pushed the dial button for the lieutenant's cell. Fitzpatrick answered on the first ring and forewent the greeting: "Jeremy, I need you to head toward Bogus Basin. There's a body dump up there being handled by the sheriff's office."

"Oh?"

"Yeah, a black female."

He thought of Lacy Jane Lewis, seeing that crime scene in his mind. He said, "What are the circs?"

"Don't know much yet. Black female, naked, thirty feet from the top of the road, up near the lodge. The body was spotted by a moun-tain biker, apparently. That's all I know at this time. The SO has their Search and Rescue team up there to retrieve the body. I guess it's down a steep hillside, and it's going to require rappelling to get to her and get her out."

Jeremy said, "What's my role in this?"

"Lieutenant Parker is overseeing the investigation," he said. "I told him about the Lewis murder and gave him a Reader's Digest on Frantelli and the manhunt."

"I can't imagine he's back."

"You never know. Anyway, have a look. It may be nothing, but I want you to stay with it until we know for sure one way or the other if it could be related."

Jeremy glanced at his watch. He said, "Okay, Lieutenant, I'll be en route in about fifteen. Just need to grab a shower."

"Keep me posted."

<hr />

ODESSA SAT COMFORTABLY IN AN OVERSTUFFED CHAIR NEAR THE PATIO, which offered a view of other patios and sliding glass doors on the adjacent building. Rich had placed her luggage in the entryway, not yet entirely sure how to proceed with the sleeping arrangements. He stood near her on the couch, and was just about to broach the subject when he was saved by Jeremy's call.

"Jeremy, how are you?" he said into the phone while smiling at Odessa.

She returned the smile. She had made herself at home and appeared comfortable and happy. Man, she was beautiful. He liked seeing her in his home, breathing life into the organized and well-furnished yet dreary condo.

Jeremy said, "Rich, I'm on my way up the hill to Bogus Basin, the ski resort I told you guys about..."

"Yeah?"

"The SO is handling a body dump."

Rich's smile faded. He lowered himself to the edge of the couch, and looked over at Odessa. She must have read something in his demeanor as her smile faded and her face contorted with question.

"Go on," Rich said into the phone.

"Black female. Nude. That's all we know."

Rich thought for a moment.

"It's not Tanika, is it?"

There was a moment of silence. Jeremy then said, in a soft voice, "I hadn't even considered that."

"Just a thought."

"Yeah, an interesting one. From what I understand, they have no idea. She's off the side of a mountain, and they haven't brought her up yet."

He said, "Okay. Well, what are you thinking, Jeremy?"

"I don't know what to think yet, Rich. My lieutenant is thinking I need to monitor the case in the event it's related to ours."

"Uh-huh."

"It seems a stretch to think he could be back, don't you think?"

"My first instinct would be to say yes, that it would seem a stretch to think Frantelli was back in Boise. But my rule is to never disregard a possibility until you can positively eliminate it."

"Okay, that makes sense."

"Listen, Jeremy, you probably know all this, but just some thoughts I'm going to throw out there—"

"Please do, that's why I called."

"A naked woman tossed off a mountain has usually come from the city. There's a good chance this case will end up being yours or someone else's there in your bureau, and not the sheriff's. At least I assume that's how it works there. Here, wherever the crime occurred, that's who has jurisdiction. It doesn't matter where the body is recovered. Is that the way it is there?"

"I have no idea, to be honest. I've never even considered such a thing."

"Okay, well my point is, this is what we consider a secondary crime scene, and it needs to be processed as such. Tire impressions, shoe impressions, check for video surveillance at the site and along the routes to and from that location, traffic cameras, security cams, everything. When they go to bring the body up, encourage them to consider trace evidence. Ask them to be mindful of that—"

"How would I do that, Rich? It's not my case."

"Diplomatically. Just suggest it. Mention it. You'll do the right thing."

"What else?"

"Well, obviously, you need to get her identified. That's the first step in finding the actual crime scene. Which is your second step, and the most important step overall. Find out where she was killed. All of the answers will be there, waiting for you."

"This's crazy."

Rich said, "Jeremy, I have a feeling about this, and it's not good."

"Me too."

"But I hope I'm wrong."

"I doubt you are," Jeremy said.

"Listen, a lot of body dumps aren't murders. There's a chance I'm wrong."

"Really?"

"Really what?"

"That a lot of body dumps aren't murders."

"Yes, really. Junkies dump their buddies all the time. One junkie dies in another's living room, they don't want to call the cops. They don't know what else to do, so they get rid of the body."

"Interesting."

"I had a case not long ago where they took the junkie, put him in his own trunk, and drove him to the nearest parking lot. Parked the car and walked away. What else are you going to do? Nobody likes to have dead people in their houses, and they like even less to tell the cops about it."

"Makes sense. But what about being nude?"

"People die naked, Jeremy. It happens. She could have died in her sleep, or after making love. Who knows? That or it could be a sexual murder. You'll find out soon enough."

"That I will," Jeremy said. "Listen, I'm going up the mountain now and I'm not sure my signal will carry. I'll check in when I can."

"Keep me posted, Jeremy. I'll be waiting to hear from you. Don't worry about the time of day or night and call me if you have any questions, or information, or if you need anything at all."

Jeremy assured him he would and disconnected.

Rich looked over to see Odessa watching him closely, measuring every word. She said, "Tanika?"

He shrugged. "Maybe. I hope not."

45

The good news, she said, was that they hadn't unpacked.

"Why's that?" Rich asked.

"I'm just saying, if we have to go back."

Rich frowned. "You want to go back to Boise?"

"I wouldn't mind. I like it there. Plus, if it's Tanika, I feel like I should be there. I want to know what happened, firsthand."

"Why?"

She paused, her eyes shifting around the room. She appeared to be scrambling for an answer. Finally, she said, "Because I hold her responsible for Lacy Jane being killed. Also, it just seems like someone who knows her, someone from home, should be there. If nothing else to liaise with the family."

Rich said, "Why don't we just sit tight, see what shakes out. This might not have anything to do with Tanika. Or Frantelli, or Lacy Jane, or anything else we'd have an interest in."

"Fine, Richard. We'll wait. In the meantime, what's the plan?"

"The plan?"

"Yes, the plan. Here we are, together in your home, and the luggage is stacked there in the hallway, unsure of where it belongs. Is it all going into the master bedroom, or just half of it? Will mine go in the guest room? I assume you have a guest room."

Rich thought about it for a moment. His eyes drifted to the condos across the way, outside his sliding glass door and patio. There were three levels of small patios, some with tables, some with chairs. Some had bicycles or other sports equipment, others had plants and hanging flower pots. Several had barbecues. Nobody was outside at the moment—not anyone he could see—and he wondered if the people in those buildings were burdened with such conflict in their own lives. Rich slid back, nestling into the back of the couch, still avoiding eye contact with this young woman who easily read his thoughts. She had turned the tables on him—again. He was now the one who would be read like a book, and *anything he said could be used against him.*

Finally, he looked over and said, "I have no choice with you but to just put it out there. Confess. Give it all up. Tell you the truth and level with you and throw myself on the mercy of the court. Odessa's court. The Honorable Odessa Brown."

She waited patiently, sitting with one leg folded over the other, her foot drawing invisible circles in the air.

Rich rubbed his forehead at the first sign of a headache coming on, likely from the stress, something he was no longer accustomed to in his life. Depression, sure. Stress, not so much. There were no misunderstandings about his feelings toward her, just an internal battle over whether it was right or wrong. He thought of a line to a song, *If loving you is wrong, I don't want to be right.* But that was just a song; that wasn't facing life and society and all of its critics and judges. *His* daughter. *Her* parents. He said, "I need a shower."

"Richard Farris!"

"Listen, I'm not trying to avoid the conversation, I just need time to put the words together in my head. You have to allow that."

Her eyes narrowed at him.

"How about a nice dinner tonight?"

She cocked her head, slightly, one eye still squinted. Skeptical.

"I'll grab a shower and then take a short nap while you get ready. Then my headache will be gone and we can go out for a nice dinner and a cocktail. And we will discuss whatever you want to discuss, to your satisfaction. Deal?"

"Fine," she said. "But I take this as a promise."

"I promise. We'll go out and have a nice evening. It will be good. It'll be a much better time and environment than here and now to have this conversation."

She said, "Okay, fine. So in the meantime, where shall I take my bags?"

"I'll get them for you," he said. "And for now, I'll just put them in the spare room. You'll have your privacy."

Lillian said to Buddy, "How do you plan to do that? We gonna just get you out of bed and walk out of here? Wave bye-bye to the nurses and thank them for the help? They'll have the cops here so fast it'll make our heads spin."

"Lemme think."

"You do that, Buddy-boy... you think. But you best not come up with some harebrained idea that'll get the both of us killed or locked up for the rest of our lives. We need to be able to leave here without being noticed and head straight for Canada."

"Canada?"

"That or Mexico."

He considered it a moment. "Too many damn Mexicans."

"Well then, north it is. How are we going to do it? How are we going to get you out of here without creating a stir?"

"I said lemme think, woman."

"Well you just take your sweet time, buttercup, and you'll be doing all your thinking from the pokey."

Two hours later, Odessa walked from the guest room into the living room to find Rich waiting on the couch. He was dressed in slacks and a pullover sweater, what she might call *business casual*. He was handsome. Sitting patiently in his chair with a book, reading glasses at the end of his nose.

She said, "You look nice. Distinguished in your specs. I haven't seen you wear glasses before."

He closed the book on a marker, looked over the small, rectangular-shaped specs and smiled. He removed his glasses and studied them as if he had never noticed them before. "I didn't have them with me on our little cross-country excursion. forgot them at home. I can read with or without them, but it's easier with them on because I don't have to hold the book three feet away."

"We could have picked up some readers, cheap ones at the drugstore."

Rich nodded.

"What are you reading?"

He looked at the book, "A Drink before the War, by Dennis Lehane."

"Is it good?"

"Very. Do you like him?"

"Never heard of him."

He chuckled. "You don't read much?"

"Oh, I do, but a very different genre than you, I'm sure. What's it about?"

"It's about a P.I. in Boston who gets himself into some deep shit. Kind of has a noir feel to it, which I like."

"Noir?"

"Like a Raymond Chandler novel, sort of hard-boiled and before everything started being influenced by political correctness. Do you like crime fiction?"

"I mostly read romance, but not the filthy stuff. There's actually quite a bit of Christian romance, which gives a girl what she needs without feeling like she has to shower afterwards. That and I read the Bible every morning, sometimes again at night. Every once in a while, I'll read an autobiography of someone interesting."

"Like?"

"Oh, I don't know. Oprah."

Rich rolled his eyes.

She pointed a finger at him and said, "Just stop."

He held his hands up as if to surrender.

Odessa said, "Maybe I'll try one of your books, this Lehane guy and something else you'd recommend. I'm really starting to get into this detective thing."

He chuckled.

Disregarding his reaction, Odessa proffered a polite smile. "You ready?"

He set the book down on a table next to his chair and stood up. "I'm like lunch meat, always ready."

JEREMY WALKED AWAY FROM THE ACTION TAKING PLACE OFF THE SIDE OF the mountain near Bogus Basin, watching his phone for a signal. When he got one, he held his ground and made the call. When Rich answered, Jeremy said, "It's her. Tanika."

There was a pause. Jeremy could hear Odessa in the background, asking was something wrong. He could also hear the sounds of people talking and faraway music.

Rich said, "Are you sure?"

"Yeah, there's no doubt about it. She hasn't been here long at all, so it's an easy ID. Remember, I met with her when she came in to report Lacy Jane as a missing person."

"I do remember that."

"Well, it's her, though she looks like she's been through heck the last couple of weeks."

"Any obvious signs of trauma?"

"No, nothing obvious. I mean, no gunshot wounds or stab wounds. Maybe it's the junkie thing, like you said, she OD'd and someone needed to get rid of her body. She has tracks on both arms, so that could be the case."

"Maybe," Rich said.

Neither spoke for a moment.

Jeremy said, "You think you'll come back up?"

"It's what I'm thinking, Jeremy. I'll talk to Odessa and let you know."

"Listen, the wife and kids are gone to Utah this weekend, so you have a place to stay, if that helps. Both of you. It'd save you some money."

Rich said, "I'll let you know."

Jeremy slid the phone back into his pocket and meandered back to the action. The sheriff's Search and Rescue team was disconnecting ropes and releasing the buckles and latches of a titanium rescue litter that had secured Tanika for a ride back up the mountain. The coroner's investigators were readying a gurney for the exchange. Red, blue and amber-colored lights flashed against the mountainside in the twilight hour as men in harnesses and safety gear and helmets worked in relative silence, only the sounds of engines idling and radio transmissions filling the mountain air. There was no sense of accomplishment, and no congratulations for a job well done. It had been a dangerous task, but unlike a rescue, there was no happy ending. Just the naked remains of a young woman who had been discarded as trash. It had been all business. A necessary but unpleasant business.

THE BULK OF FOOT TRAFFIC AT THE RENOWN REGIONAL HOSPITAL IN Reno came through the front of the hospital which opened onto a large parking area. The emergency room parking area at the back was limited and discouraged long-term parking. There was a guard who sat at a desk just inside that entrance, directing pedestrian traffic. Which in most cases meant he would send would-be patients and their companions to the left where they would be met by clerical workers before being admitted. The patients who had truly life-threatening emergencies, most of whom arrived by ambulance and were accompanied by first responders, would go to the right, unimpeded by security. The front entrance had no security, only a greeter.

Lillian sized him up as the equivalent of Walmart greeters: old, retired, friendly, and of very little use otherwise.

She returned to the room and described the layout to Buddy in full detail. She said, "All I need are some scrubs and a wheelchair, and we'll walk right out the front in broad daylight."

Buddy nodded slowly, his groggy eyes shutting and bouncing open again like a baby fighting sleep.

She said, "Get some rest, I have some shopping to do. I'll be back in a couple hours and we'll bust out of this joint."

ODESSA ASKED RICH WHAT THE CALL FROM JEREMY HAD BEEN ABOUT.

Rich said, "It's Tanika."

She just watched him.

He said, "You okay?"

There was no reaction. She appeared to be deep in thought. Her eyes were locked onto his, but she appeared to be faraway, not there. Finally, she seemed to come back, her eyes now engaged. She said, "We need to go back."

He nodded. "I think it would be a good idea."

"You think it's him?"

"It just doesn't make sense." Farris thought about it a moment and shook his head. "No, I don't think it was him. It's not his style, and I can't see the reason for him killing her. I don't see him taking the risk, either."

"How do they both get themselves killed in Boise? It's not like they went to Chicago for vacation, or Detroit. My goodness."

Rich shrugged and took a sip of beer from a frosted mug. "I don't know. Bad choices maybe. But let's not get ahead of ourselves; she might not have been killed."

Odessa had a sip of her wine. She didn't drink often, but when she did, she liked a simple chardonnay, she had told him. Rich watched as she set her glass on the table. She seemed older tonight, more mature. Or maybe he was seeing her in a different light in her evening wear, black slacks and a blue blouse, simple and elegant, offset with pearl earrings and a necklace to match, both of which stood in stark contrast to her dark brown skin.

She prompted, *"What?"*

"Nothing."

"You're looking at me and you're deep in thought."

He said, "Just thinking about Boise. About Tanika and Lacy Jane and this Frantelli asshole who's responsible for all of it. Regardless of how she died, it all started with Lacy Jane. Two young, innocent girls."

"Well, one innocent one."

"Neither one of them deserved to die."

"I agree with that. Same goes for the poor trucker," she said. After taking another sip, she said, "Well, are we going?"

"My gut tells me we should go."

Odessa said, "That's good enough for me. Should we leave tonight, or tomorrow morning?"

Rich thought it would be better to go tonight, avoid the awkward part of her staying with him at his home. Which room? He hadn't dealt with that yet. He didn't want to yet. Traveling would be a way to avoid it. Maybe that's why he wanted to return to Boise. But there wouldn't be time to catch a flight to Boise now. Not unless they abandoned the dinner idea, left the restaurant this very minute and raced back to get their luggage and go. Plus, what would they accomplish by doing so? It would be better to get a good night's sleep and start fresh the next day.

Rich said, "I think tomorrow works best. Let's enjoy a nice dinner and a relaxing evening. Get a good night's sleep and head out tomorrow. We can book the flight tonight when we get back to my place, as long as I can still get on the Wi-Fi."

She giggled. "You steal your neighbor's, don't you?"

"It's not really stealing."

"Look, Rich, let me help you out here... if you take something that isn't yours, without permission, it's stealing. We non-heathen types learned that in Sunday School."

"It's sharing."

"Oh, so they said you're welcome to use it?"

"Yes."

She narrowed her eyes. It told him she knew he was full of it. It drove him crazy that she was this way. There was no way a man could ever cheat on this girl, not that any sane man would.

He added, "If I wasn't welcome to use it, they'd have it secured."

She shook her head. "I can book us a flight on my phone. I'll do it on the way home."

Home.

He nodded. "Whatever works, dear. I don't get all that stuff on my phone, but if you do, have at it."

She offered a toast. He raised his beer and saluted her. She said, "To traveling the world with the world's greatest detective."

Rich smiled.

46

Early the next morning, Rich was awakened by a knock on his door. He looked at the clock and frowned. 7:33. This couldn't be good—nobody ever knocked on his door. He never had visitors. He glanced at the other side of his bed; it was empty. Of course it was. That's how it had been settled last night, and the conversation had been awkward. What did he think, she'd just come in during the night and crawl into his bed?

He stepped into a pair of shorts that lay crumpled on the floor, then grabbed a t-shirt from his drawer and pulled it over his head as he made his way to the door. Just before he opened it, he wondered if Odessa had gotten up early and gone for a walk or a jog, and locked herself out. That was the only possibility he could think of, other than maybe the HOA Nazi, the little dweeb having manufactured something to complain about. If so, Rich would shut the door on him, maybe tell him don't ever knock on his door this early again, or else.

He opened the door and saw that it wasn't the Nazi and it wasn't Odessa. He was speechless.

ODESSA HEARD THE KNOCK AND OPENED HER EYES BUT DIDN'T MOVE. She waited and listened. Was it the front door, or had Rich knocked on her bedroom door? That was a nice thought. Maybe he was bringing her breakfast in bed. Maybe he was just going to say good morning, tell her they needed to get going, they had a flight to catch in a couple of hours. She glanced at the nightstand clock; the display read 9:04. She shot up out of bed and grabbed her phone, relieved to see it was actually 7:34.

Now she was wide awake.

She heard footsteps going past her door and into the hallway toward the front door. The hallway ran along the north wall of the room she slept in, and the front door was only a few feet from her bed, on the other side of that wall. She listened as the door was opened and a woman's voice said, "Hi, I'm Vanessa."

———

"I'M YOUR NEIGHBOR," SHE SAID, AND TURNED TO LOOK IN THE direction of her unit, "from one-oh-three."

He smiled. "The stewardess."

"Flight attendant," she said with a wink.

"Sorry, flight attendant."

"How did you know?"

After a slight pause, he said, "I've noticed you a few times, coming and going in uniform."

She nodded.

Rich thought about how that might have sounded, and hoped she hadn't thought him a stalker, a pervert who watched women come and go from their units. He shouldn't have let on that he knew who she was. He thought of Odessa in her room, just on the other side of the wall, and wondered if she were awake, if she were listening.

"Nice to meet you. I'm Rich. Rich Farris."

She smiled and shook the hand he offered.

"Anyway," she said, "the reason I stopped by this morning, I saw you come in last night, you and a young lady..."

He didn't offer any information, careful now in choosing his words. "Uh-huh."

"The reason I noticed, I had been at the pool a few days ago, and I was speaking with Allison, from over on the other side—I don't know if you've met her, I think she lives in Building B—but she knows who you are and she told me that you're a cop."

Rich shook his head. "I don't think I know her."

"Oh, well, but you are a cop?"

"I'm retired," he said.

"Oh."

"Is there something—"

"My ex is stalking me, and I'm not sure what to do about it."

He looked over his shoulder, thought about inviting her in and then decided against it. Of all the mornings for her to come over. For a year he had noticed her and never made an effort to meet her. Now here she stood at his doorstep, needing help, and announcing—essentially—that she was available, having referenced the *ex-boyfriend*. Or maybe it was an ex-husband. Either way, Odessa was in the other room, making her timing nearly impossible.

At least he thought she was in the next room. But then he felt Odessa squeeze in alongside him. She took his arm, coupling them together, as she smiled charmingly and said—with her southern accent prominently displayed, "Do we have company, hon?"

Rich felt the overdone smile and southern charm was designed to send a signal to this other woman standing at his door that she wasn't welcome. The woman—*Vanessa*—must have received whatever female signals were transmitted, which were apparently beyond his tone capacity, like a dog whistle. Because Vanessa smiled back, but it was more of a smirk, a different smile than the one which she had worn while greeting him just moments earlier. She said, "I'll leave you be, sorry to bother you."

Rich was saying, "No, it's no bother—"

As Odessa said, "Bye," and reached to close the door. Once closed, she said, "*Felicia.*"

Rich stood staring at her.

She tapped his chin with her finger and said, "We don't need to be taking in any strays, darling."

Then she walked away and Rich took in the view, a t-shirt that barely hung past her shapely backside and revealed a hint of panties beneath it. She rounded the corner and Rich heard the bedroom door closing behind her. He stood staring at the empty hall, the image of her walking away burnt into his brain, shook his head and started for his room.

———

LILLIAN CAME INTO BUDDY'S HOSPITAL ROOM WEARING BLUE SCRUBS and sunglasses and pushing an empty wheelchair. When Buddy opened his eyes, she said, "Let's go, we don't have much time."

He sat up and began unhooking the tubes and wires that connected him to a machine. An alarm sounded.

Lillian said, "Shit. Hurry up."

He slid into the chair and she steadied him as he did. Then she pulled a blanket off the bed and covered his lap, set a bag containing his clothes on top of it. She wheeled him around the bed and headed for the doorway. As they turned into the hall and started in the direction of the main entrance, a nurse called out to them from behind. She said, "Hey."

Lillian sped up.

The nurse, now walking briskly, said, "Hey, lady!"

Lillian started jogging.

The nurse was now running after them, saying, "Hey, hey, where are you going? You can't take him out of here." And, "Someone call security!"

As they reached the front, an elderly man wearing a vest with the hospital logo and various pens on its lapel got up from his stool, slowly, and moved toward them. The nurse was still yelling from behind. Lillian saw the greeter walk into the path with his hand held out, the universal traffic cop signal to stop. She ran straight at him and plowed into him with the wheelchair.

Buddy raised his one arm to shield him from the collision, yelling, "The fuck?"

The man stumbled backward, lost his balance, and tumbled onto the floor like a toddler.

The nurse yelled, "Someone call the cops!"

The automatic doors slid open and Lillian was now running as she pushed the wheelchair toward the pickup which was parked at the curb, waiting. Buddy began lifting himself from the chair and reached for the door when they arrived at its side. Lillian felt the nurse grab her by the hair. She turned and punched the woman in the face, sending her backward.

Buddy yelled, "Let's go!"

Lillian stepped into the nurse and shoved her. The nurse stumbled over the curb and fell into a planter. Lillian kicked the woman in her side, a heavy thud followed by a shriek, and then she ran around to the driver's side of the truck. She fired the motor and yanked the gearshift into Drive, then floored it. Her tires spun against the blacktop as she pointed the pickup toward the street. She glanced once in the mirror to see a small crowd gathering where they had left the nurse lying on the ground. Lillian said, "Stupid bitch."

Buddy watched it all in his sideview mirror, grinning.

Lillian said, "How do you like me now, Outlaw?"

47

Rich and Odessa picked up a rental at the airport and met Jeremy at the coroner's office in Boise. They had spotted him parked beneath a tree at the far side of the lot, away from all the other cars. In cop fashion, Rich pulled alongside him, driver's door to driver's door, and greeted him through their open windows.

"Did you miss us?"

He chuckled. "Were you away?"

Rich nodded, "Just long enough to grab some fresh *chonies* and get into some trouble."

"Oh?"

"Oh yeah," Rich said, and glanced at Odessa. "My houseguest is a handful."

"Hi Jeremy," she said, speaking across Rich as she leaned forward and toward the driver's window.

"Hi Odessa. Are you misbehaving?"

"No, it's not me. It's Mr. Player here, with all the girls in his condominium complex knocking on his door all hours of the day and night, needing a little favor." She put some serious southern drawl on the last part.

Rich smiled at him.

Jeremy said, "Must be rough, being single in L.A., all those beautiful women."

He shook his head. "She's exaggerating, to say the least. A neighbor asked for some help."

"Yeah, a hot neighbor who happens to be a single flight attendant who's got a thing for cops."

Rich still shaking his head, "I plead the fifth."

"You're going to think *the fifth*," she said.

Jeremy's smile faded and he said, "Well, she was in fact murdered."

Rich took a breath and let it out slowly. "What's the cause of death?"

"Blunt force trauma to the back of the head. Something large and heavy."

"Any ideas on what it could have been?"

Jeremy shook his head. "None. One blow that caused a small fracture to her skull. Her brain swelled and bled but she likely would have been knocked unconscious and wouldn't have suffered, even though it took her a while to die."

Rich looked over at Odessa and saw angst in her eyes. He said, "You okay?"

She nodded.

Jeremy said, "She was picked up last week; she and some dude from the college walked into a sting trying to buy some heroin."

He raised his brows. "Oh?"

"Neither was charged, so that might be an angle. Maybe she rolled on someone to get out from under the charges, and it got her killed."

"Who's the dude?"

Jeremy reached across to the passenger seat of his car and pulled a file from his briefcase. He thumbed through the papers inside, stopped and began scanning a page. Without looking up he said, "Maurice Sherman, AKA Tank. Plays football at the university."

"Anyone talk to him yet?"

"I don't think so," Jeremy said. "I don't know if anyone else knows about it yet. The lead detective from the SO didn't even attend the autopsy. I'm not sure what's going on."

"That's odd."

"You know," Jeremy said, "when we spoke with Tanika, she mentioned meeting some guy from the team that night at the bar, the night Lacy Jane was killed. I would bet this is the same guy."

"Or one of his friends."

"But he wasn't charged in that sting bust either, so it's not like she rolled on him. They both probably rolled."

"Who handled the dope case?"

"BANDIT. It's a local task force made up of cops from several agencies and some feds—Boise Area Narcotics something or other."

"We need to talk to them, preferably before the SO does. Then we should get together with this sheriff's detective and see what he plans to do with the case, fill him in on what we know. If it were my case, I'd talk to the guys from Narco first, and then I'd be looking for her buddy, the Sherman Tank."

Jeremy smiled.

"What?"

"*Sherman Tank.* I hadn't even put that together. I figured the moniker came from his stature."

"Probably both," Rich said, "Since he plays football, I'd bet he's been called that his whole life. He's probably from my neck of the woods, too, South L.A. or Compton."

Jeremy nodded, "It wouldn't surprise me."

BUDDY TOLD LILLIAN TO PULL INTO THE PARKING LOT OF THE GROCERY store they just passed. He said, "I hope you don't have any personal attachments to your husband's truck."

She rolled her eyes. "Please."

"Park out here and walk the aisles until you find something with keys."

"What are the odds?"

"You'd be surprised. These small towns, I can almost guarantee someone's left their keys in the ignition. Look closely at anything with its windows down, that'll be the same dipshit who didn't take his keys out."

"Okay," she said, her doubt coming through with her tone.

"Trust me, Miss Lilly."

She snapped her head around to look at him. "*Lilly?* Nobody's called me that since grade school."

He smiled. "I might just call you Miss Kitty instead."

She frowned.

"You know, since you're a cougar and all."

She rolled her eyes again and turned off the truck. She said, "I'll be back, you sit tight."

"Hurry up, Miss Kitty."

Buddy watched her walk away, thinking maybe after they picked up a new ride and got a little ways from town, he'd have to get her to pull over and fool around with him. He was feeling the urge again, because there was something about Miss Kitty that made him horny. She was a sexy old thing, but that wasn't all. This bitch was straight outlaw when it came down to it, and that was just what he liked in a woman, and what he needed.

Thinking about it like that made him feel guilty that he'd have to kill her later. But then again, maybe he wouldn't. He had no idea how it'd play out now, crazy as shit had been.

STEVE TROY, ONLY RECENTLY OUT OF BED, ATE A STACK OF FROZEN waffles while watching the noon news. He was thinking about heading to Sheehy's when the phone rang. He answered it, and the lady on the other end said she was from Personnel at the Department of Corrections and that they were prepared to hire him. When could he come in to process the paperwork?

He said he could come in this afternoon, he didn't have anything else going on. She said that would be perfect, and told him to ask for her by name, Mrs. Harris. He glanced at his watch. If the shit didn't take too long, he'd be throwing a few back by three. He turned off the TV and walked into the bathroom, started the shower and glanced at the mirror. "Fucking prison guard."

JEREMY LEARNED THE NAME OF THE DETECTIVE WHO HAD HANDLED THE case involving the arrests of Tanika Edwards and Maurice Sherman, and he called the DEA headquarters to reach him, but it was a day off for agent J.P. Long. He asked if they'd page him, have him call, saying it was an urgent matter regarding a murder investigation, and they agreed to do so. Several minutes later, Jeremy's phone rang. He glanced at Rich and then Odessa as he said, "Detective Cross."

It was Long.

Jeremy briefed him on Tanika's death, and said it was just a hunch, but thought maybe the drug arrest could have something to do with the murder, especially if she had turned informant. He then said, "Uh-huh... Uh-huh... okay... yeah, thanks. You bet." And then, "Yes, Jeremy Cross, Boise PD."

He ended the phone call and looked at Rich, his lips pulled in tightly and a breath held in his cheeks. After releasing the breath, he said, "He doesn't think the murder could have anything to do with his case."

"That's all he said?" asked Odessa.

"No, he actually said there was no freaking way it could have anything to do with it, so he didn't know why he was being bothered on a day off, and who freaking was I again."

Rich said, "I couldn't make out much of what he was saying, but I did hear enough to know he didn't say 'freaking.'"

Jeremy said, "You're right about that."

"So what's next?" asked Odessa.

They both looked at her.

She said, "Well?"

Rich looked at Jeremy and said, "What do you say we have a chat with Tank?"

He shrugged. "I guess that's our next play, right?"

Rich said, "I guess."

———

TANK AND HIS BUDDY AND TEAMMATE LADARIUS LOVE WERE SMOKING A J and sipping on two forties of Old English 800 when someone knocked on their door. The two looked at each other. Tank frowned and Ladarius shrugged.

Tank said, "You invite any niggas over?"

"Not me, man."

He sighed, then hoisted his large body from the sunken couch cushion and went to the door. When he opened it, he said, "The fuck, nigga? You mus' be out yo' muthafuckin' mind, comin' over here."

Ladarius said, "Who dat?"

Tank looked over. "Little snitch-ass nigga name Chino is who dat is."

The small man with blinking eyes kept looking left and right. He said, "Tank, lemme in, man, I can't be standing out here."

Tank stepped back. "You ain't gonna be standin' in here neither, man, not fo' very long. I'm gonna hear what y'all got to say 'bout snitchin' me off and settin' me up on that bust, then I'm gonna beat yo' little ass, maybe throw you off the goddamn mountain."

Ladarius laughed loudly. He said, "We can roll some niggas off a mountain, huh, Tank?"

Tank glared at him. "Really, man? You gonna say that kinda shit in front of a snitch-ass nigga?"

He stopped laughing. He didn't even smile. He went back to hitting the J, inhaling hard and holding his breath like he was under water.

Chino said, "Look, Tank, they had me by the balls, man. They had you, too. They saw me deliver to that bitch that stays here—what's her name?—and they was comin' for you either way. I just helped them bring you out. They say it's better that way. Man, I knew they'd make you a deal. You gots to believe it, brutha."

"Don't you be brotherin' me, you sketchy little snitch-ass punk. You lucky I don't kill you right here."

"Where's homegirl?" Chino asked, blinking as his shifty gaze bounced around the room.

"Nunya bidness."

Chino looked over at Ladarius, who quickly looked down. He said to Tank, "Something happen to her?"

"You askin' a lot of questions, man… you wearing a wire or somethin'? Still working for that ponytail-wearing redneck cop?"

"Nah, man, I's jus' wonderin', cause I got a fresh supply. Hadn't heard from the bitch, thought maybe she found a new supplier. Chino's back in bidness, bruh."

"Yeah, well, she ain't gonna be buyin' no mo shit, yo."

Ladarius chuckled.

Chino looked over at him, and then back at Tank. He said, "Damn, man, I gots a bad feelin' 'bout homegirl."

"You just never mind all that bullshit. You gots any weed for sale?"

"I know where to get some," Chino said. "Best shit in town, my brutha."

Tank said, "Betta kick it down, bitch, you at least owe me a dime or two."

LILLIAN ARRIVED BACK AT THE PICKUP DRIVING AN OLDER MODEL BLUE Toyota Corolla, the first car she had spotted in the lot with its keys hanging from the ignition. Buddy smiled and came out of the truck as soon as he could, having struggled for a minute trying to open the door with his left hand. He brought the pistol with him but nothing else. He had changed into the jeans and shirt he'd gotten from the house outside of bishop, and he left his hospital gown on the floorboard. She came back to the truck for her purse. They left the keys in the pickup as a manner of exchange, or so he had joked, and then drove their new car a short distance out of town. Buddy directed her to turn down a gravel road that headed off toward the woods. They found a little place to pull over, and it didn't take much to get busy with Miss Kitty. Afterwards, he told her something he'd been thinking about.

"My ol' lady—"

"You're married?"

"No, I'm not married… my mother, for Christ's sake."

"Oh."

"Anyway, that crazy old bitch tried to kill me right after I got out of the joint."

"Yeah?"

"I went by to see her—something she never bothered to do for me while I was inside—and she was downright inhospitable. I'd asked her about some cash, you know, to help me get by for a while, and she said she didn't have none to spare. I got to looking around, and she pulled a goddamn shotgun on me and took a shot."

"Jesus."

"Yeah. Damn near blew my balls off."

"Now *that* would be a shame."

"So I been thinking about it, and I been wondering what the hell she was protecting. She ain't gonna kill me over no twenny bucks, or even a hunnert. I think that scandalous bitch has somehow gotten herself some money."

Lillian sat up. They were lying on a patch of grass beneath a stand of trees, both relaxed after fooling around. But now she wasn't so relaxed, or maybe she was just a little excited. She stared Buddy in the eyes and said, "What do you mean, she has some money?"

Buddy sat up now too, and he began rubbing the stump on his right arm with his left hand. He said, "See, I been thinking about it, but I didn't want to say anything till I knew I could trust you. Now I'm thinking I'll keep you around, since you come in pretty handy at times, for different things." He smiled, showing her his crooked teeth.

She said, "You ain't seen the half of it."

"I was wondering if maybe after the old man died, she didn't get some money and she's been hoarding it. She don't owe nobody nothin' and the house is paid for. She gets her social security, and if he had an insurance policy or somethin' else, she's probably been stashing it away the whole time. She ain't got nothin' to spend it on, and she's a goddamn hoarder like that. Crazy bat thinks she'll get to take it with her."

"Where would she have it?"

"Well, that's the other thing I been thinkin'. Maybe it's under the house, or up in the attic. Maybe just under a mattress, or in the freezer. I don't know, but I plan on having a look-see. But I'll have to catch her by surprise, get that shotgun away from her first. That's where you'll come in handy again."

"Wait a minute," she said, "this is where you ain't even thinking straight. Cash or no cash, she owns the house, right?"

"Yeah?"

Lillian chuckled. "Well, hell, Buddy-boy, how much do you think that's worth? Gotta be a hundred-K even if it's a piece of shit."

He nodded.

"Get her to sign it over, and we'll sell it."

"She wouldn't do it."

"Even at gunpoint?"

"Nope."

"What if you tortured her?"

"My mother? Jesus, lady, what kind of monster do you think I am?"

She thought about it a minute. "I got it. What if she had a little accident, you know, something she didn't make it through?"

"Now you want me to kill her."

"I'm just saying, if she weren't around, we'd own the house."

"Did you forget I'm on the run? Ain't no way I could stay in Boise."

"Maybe not, but if she's gone, the house is yours. We sell it, go live on the beach in Mexico. We'd be set for the rest of our lives."

"I tole you I don't know about Mexico. What about Canada?"

"Too cold. You'd freeze your stump off nine months out of the year."

Buddy sat and thought about it for a moment as Lillian pushed herself up and stood naked before him, watching. She offered a hand and pulled him up. When she turned around and reached for her pants, Buddy slapped her on the ass, and said, "You gonna trust me around those little señoritas?"

She looked back and said, "What makes you think I trust you at all?"

He chuckled. "Take me to Boise, woman. I wanna go see my mama."

4 8

Ladarius drove and Tank rode shotgun as they sped away from his apartment, Chino in the back seat directing them to where they could score more weed.

Tank saying, "It better not be another one of them stings, where a nigga gets all sorts of guns pointed at his fat head by a buncha nigga-hatin' redneck cops."

Chino said, "This is legit, bruh, the best shit in town."

"If not, we can take a nigga up to the mountains," Ladarius said and laughed.

Tank shot him a look. He was thinking maybe he'd have to kill both these niggas, Chino for ratting him out the first time, and Ladarius for not knowing how to shut the fuck up. He needed a gat. Nothing fancy, maybe a nine or even just a little twenty-five auto. Something to put behind a nigga's ear and say goodbye. The both of 'em, right here in Ladarius's car but outside of town somewhere. But not all the way up on the mountain where he had rolled the bitch off the side, somewhere closer where he could Uber back to his apartment. He'd have to give it some more thought after they scored the weed.

He said, "How much money all y'all niggas got witchya, anyway?"

JEREMY PULLED HIS SEDAN TO THE CURB IN FRONT OF THE APARTMENTS, looked at the rap sheet in his hand that listed the address for Maurice Sherman. He looked at the numbers on the wall ahead of him, and then leaned down to look through his windshield at the numbers on the second level.

He said, "This is it, upstairs there, looks like the second door over from the stairs."

Rich turned to look at Odessa in the back seat. "Would you be offended if I asked you to wait in the car?"

She shrugged. "I don't know. Why would you though?"

He turned to study the apartment building again, then looked over at Jeremy behind the wheel. "I just have a gut feeling on this, worried this guy might be bad news."

Jeremy nodded in agreement.

After a moment of silence, Rich looked into the back seat again to see Odessa sitting quietly, her arms crossed. He said, "Well?"

"Fine."

Rich and Jeremy stepped out of the car and met in front of it, pausing briefly to talk it over. Rich said, "Well at least we don't have to worry about covering the back."

"Why's that?"

"Two-story. Bruthas from the hood don't like heights—he ain't gonna jump out a window."

Jeremy smiled.

Rich said, "I'm serious."

ODESSA WATCHED FROM THE BACK SEAT AS THE TWO DETECTIVES approached the apartment and stood on either side of the door. She saw Jeremy knock but didn't hear it. After a minute passed, Rich reached over and knocked. It must have been more forceful, because she could hear it from where she sat. Then they stood waiting. After another minute or so, Rich and Jeremy looked at each other, and Jeremy shrugged. The two returned to the car.

"Nobody home?"

"Nobody answered," Rich said.

With that, Jeremy turned the car and headed back the way they had come.

"Now what?" she asked.

Rich chuckled. "You seem anxious."

"Just curious is all."

Jeremy said, "I say we call it a day, start off tomorrow with a knock on the dope guy's door, Mr. J.P. Long. Talk to him and then try to get together with Clark."

"Who's Clark," Rich asked.

"Oh, sorry... that's the detective from Boise County Sheriff's Office who's handling Tanika's case. I thought I'd mentioned it."

"Not by name. Boise County, huh? The city of Boise in Boise County."

"Nope. Actually, Boise is in Ada County. Boise County is next door, covers about two thousand square miles but it's mostly rural. Bogus Basin is in their county."

Rich said, "Okay, well, that's probably a good plan. Then we can try the ballplayer again, see if we have any better luck."

Odessa said, "Sounds good, men."

They both chuckled.

When Chino Introduced Tank to his connection, a dark skinned, tattooed Hispanic man with hard eyes, Tank said, "My boy, Chino, says you've got the best stuff around."

The man looked at Chino and said, "Wait outside."

Tank didn't like it, it gave him a bad vibe. He thought about Ladarius who waited in the car, and wished he were inside with him. Not that he couldn't whip this hardcore gangster—if it were a fair fight—but he knew a killer's eyes when he saw them, and he knew these Mexicans didn't mess around. The man no doubt had a weapon under his baggy button-up shirt.

Chino closed the door behind him.

After he did, the Mexican looked Tank in the eyes and said, "Call me Lil' Chongo."

Tank relaxed somewhat after the introduction, and thought he'd break the ice a little more. He said, "You ain't so little, man, how'd you get a name like that?"

"By being Big Chongo's little homie."

Tank nodded. "Ah."

Then he said, "And Chongo due to my dark skin. Big Chongo was even darker."

"Chongo mean dark, in Spanish?"

He smiled. "It means monkey. It's what Mexicans call black people behind their backs."

Tank didn't smile.

Chongo, grinning wide now, said, "You got a problem with that, Chongo?"

Tank held his hands out wide, as if to surrender, grinned and said, "Nah, man, I got no problem with it, my brutha," and in an instant brought his right fist crashing down on the side of the man's head.

The man dropped, but Tank wasn't done. He kicked him in the torso and then the head. He kept stomping on that melon until it caved like a pumpkin. Blood flowed freely from the back of Lil' Chongo's head, from his ear, his nose, and his mouth. It was everywhere, pooling up on the tile floor beneath him.

Tank said, "Well, motherfucker, who's the stupid monkey now?"

He quickly reached down and searched him for a weapon, removing a Glock 9mm from the small of his back. Tank pulled a wad of bills from the man's front pocket and stuffed it in his own. He kept the gun in his hand and quickly searched the house. Nobody was there. He tucked the gun into his pants and kept searching until he found the stash. Four one-gallon Ziploc bags full of marijuana. Tank stepped over the dead man on his way out, careful not to step in the blood, and glanced back at him before walking out the door. The

Mexican looked back at him, but only with one eye because the other one was gone. Tank looked around near the man's head but didn't see the other eye anywhere. He had never killed anyone before, other than when he had accidentally killed the bitch who tried to kill him first, and maybe one other time when he was fourteen and shot from a car into a group of boys from another neighborhood. But he didn't know what happened that night because they didn't wait to find out. Now, though, this was no accident, and there was no question that he had killed the man. And it didn't bother him at all.

Tank closed the door behind him, and smiled on his way to the car where two brothas who knew way too much now were waiting for him to return.

They both stared, focusing on the bags he carried. Ladarius said, "Bruh, what'd ya do?" and then he smiled.

Chino said, "Ah, hell no... Man, don't even tell me what kind of shit just happened."

Tank indicated Ladarius with his chin. He said, "You drive. Chino, you ride up front wit' my boy. I'll be in the back."

<hr />

A FEW BLOCKS FROM THE MEXICAN'S HOUSE TANK TOLD LADARIUS TO pull behind the market, and pointed to an alley that took them out of view. He said, "Over by the dumpsters, so I can get rid of some trash."

When Ladarius put the car in park, Tank shot Chino in the back of the head. Blood and brain matter exploded from the exit wound where his face used to be.

Ladarius shouted, "What the fuck!"

Tank said, "Damn, nigga," and smiled.

"What the fuck, man? Seriously, what the fuck? In my hoop! Couldn't you have got the nigga outside and did it there? Goddamn, man!"

"Sorry, bruh."

Ladarius started saying, "Sorry my—" when Tank raised the gun and shot him in his face.

Tank's ears rang from the gunshots as he sat still for a moment, looking through gun smoke at the two dead men in the front seat. Blood was everywhere. Parts of brain and skull and other unknown matter was spattered all over the windows, the windshield, the dash and steering wheel, and the front seat. Ladarius was leaned against the driver's door, looking up with the part of his face that was still intact. It seemed he had died instantly, and Tank was thankful for that. He didn't want to hear any shit from him, and didn't want to explain anything to him either. The snitch was slumped forward like he was tying his shoes. His arms hung down to the floor. Tank shook his head, amazed at how much of a mess it had made, and glad it wasn't his car.

He stepped out of the car and saw there was nobody around. No witnesses. Nobody else to put a bullet in. He went to the dumpster and opened the lid and started digging through the trash. He found two plastic shopping bags that were clean so he stuffed the four bags of dope inside them. He began to walk away, and stopped, went back to the dumpster and tossed Chongo's pistol inside.

Tank turned and walked casually down the alley, and the thought occurred to him that maybe Chongo would take the rap for killing Ladarius and Chino. Then he realized that doesn't work, since Chongo had his melon crushed. Shit. Well, maybe if the cops don't know who died first, he thought... Yeah, if the cops think Chongo killed Ladarius and Chino, and then he went home and got his melon crushed, then Tank could chill in Boise and keep playing ball. As long as the skanky bitch didn't come back on him, but that had been an accident.

He decided he'd walk a couple blocks and then pick up an Uber or maybe a cab. Head home and get his shit and get on down the road for a bit, let things cool down in B-town. Go back to Compton where he could find a little peace and quiet.

49

uddy had Lillian pull over at the first used car lot they saw when they pulled into Winnemucca, Nevada. His plan was to get some fresh license plates for the stolen car they were driving. He told her, "This is how you avoid going to jail for riding in a G."

"A 'G'?"

"G-ride, grand theft auto. I forget how old you are sometimes. Anyway, you steal plates off just any car, that gets reported when someone notices them missing, and then the plates are hot now too. The douchebags that run these used car lots will never notice plates missing off one of the cars on the lot, or at least not very soon."

Then he told her she'd have to do the work because he didn't think he could do it with his left hand, or if he did, it would take too long. She did as directed and in five minutes they were back on the road with clean plates and a cooler car. They found a cheap motel off the main drag and paid cash for a room. Buddy had said they'd better not push their luck and try to make the drive at night. Get out of there tomorrow in the daytime when there's more traffic to blend with and they can see what's up ahead. He told her, "You'll learn a lot about being an outlaw if you pay attention to what I tell you."

She said, "Buddy-boy, you'll learn a lot about having a good old lady, if you get showered and cleaned up while I walk down the road to that liquor store and get us a bottle."

He smiled and said, "I'll be ready for you, Miss Kitty."

TANK ARRIVED BACK AT HIS APARTMENT IN AN UBER, AND HE TIPPED THE driver fifty bucks and a dime bag of weed to mark the service call as canceled and to have a bad memory. He had plenty of both now, money and weed, which helped him reconcile the fact he had just shot his friend in the face. The snitch was no big deal, plus he never saw it coming. Ladarius, on the other hand, took it to the grave. He had seen Tank point the pistol at him and he had likely seen a flash of light and then nothing at all. If he hadn't talked so goddamn much, it wouldn't have had to happen. But one murder or three, what's the difference? And once the killing starts, it's hard to get off that train.

As he fumbled for his keys, his next-door neighbor opened her door just a crack and poked her nose through it. She said, "You had company earlier."

Tank turned his head to see her grinning. She reminded him of his grandmother—"Na-na"—who had nothing else to do but poke her nose in everyone's business. He didn't even know the neighbor's name, and had never seen any more of her than one eye and the nose, maybe part of her mouth every time she had something to say through the crack of her door. Always something smart, like, "I can smell that dope, boy." Or, "I see that whore you're keeping now." And the last time, the one that nearly got her killed: "Was that the whore you and that other nigga carried outta here in the middle of the night?"

He said to her, "Lady, why don't you mind yo' bidness?"

She laughed.

He began to step inside his apartment when he heard her say, "You gonna wanna know about the cops that was here."

Tank eased back out, looked over the other shoulder, then back to the eyeball and nose in the crack of his neighbor's door. He said, "What's that, grandma?"

"Two of 'em, one black, one white. Detectives. Probably the FBI, that's what they looked like to me."

"When was that?"

"Just a few hours ago, boy. What'd you do now, anyway? Is it about the body you boys moved outta here the other night?"

He stepped toward her and she quickly closed the door. He could hear her locking bolts and chains, and for a moment he considered kicking it open. But damn, where does it end? Tank knew he had to stop. He'd seen it happen to others from the neighborhood where he grew up. Regular kids who grew up to be gangsters and drug dealers and before long it seemed normal to kill or be killed. Football had saved him from it. There had been a few times where he had let peer pressure drive him the wrong direction, off of the good path he was on. Usually it happened in the off-season, like now, when there was time to get into trouble. Sometimes he wished football lasted all year so he wouldn't get caught up in all this bullshit.

He retreated into his apartment and stood in the dark and quiet living room holding his bags of marijuana. He didn't need all of it, just a small portion. He thought maybe, before heading out, he'd sell the dope. He could get more for it here than back in Compton or over in Long Beach. Plus then he wouldn't have to travel with it and take an extra chance of ending up in the slam. He'd been pushing his luck enough lately.

After making a couple calls, he found a buyer for the lot of it, minus what he would keep for personal use. They would meet later tonight, and he would leave for California in the morning.

EARLY THE NEXT MORNING RICH, ODESSA AND JEREMY MET AT THE police station and were ushered into the back where they were introduced to a broad-shouldered man with skeptical eyes and long blond hair pulled into a ponytail, a DEA badge draped around his neck on a chain. Rich had learned to trust his instincts when it came to people, and he didn't like this guy from their first meeting. Though at times he would be wrong, there was never any harm in keeping one at arm's length when he had a bad feeling about them. This wasn't a court of law, and Rich had no problem considering someone guilty until proven innocent when it came to character.

After the introductions, they all had a seat. Rich noticed that the fed, the man with the ponytail named J.P. Long, seemed to watch Odessa closely. This only strengthened Rich's preconceived feeling of the man. Now he not only didn't like him, he didn't trust him. There was something about the man that rubbed him wrong.

Jeremy said, "Can you tell us about the arrest of Tanika Edwards, and her friend, Maurice Sherman?"

He smirked. "What do you want to know about old Tank and his skank?"

Rich glanced at Odessa. He could tell she didn't like him either. Her face was solemn; there wouldn't be any room-lighting smiles this morning. Not in the company of this fed.

Jeremy said, "Well, she ended up dead, and we don't know why. Maybe tell us the whole thing, how you came onto them, what happened with the arrest, why neither was charged, whatever else you know that might help us out."

J.P. grunted with a half-grin. He said, "I'll have to review my files, I don't recall much about it."

Rich said, "Really, man?..."

J.P. glared at him and Rich held his stare. He said, "You don't remember much but you call him by his nickname and refer to our victim as a skank. That seems odd to me."

J.P. said, "Excuse me, but could you explain your interest in the case? As I recall, you're from L.A., right?"

"Right."

Jeremy said, "It's a long story, but he's assisting us in an official capacity."

"He has no jurisdiction."

Rich said, "We going to measure dicks here or investigate a murder case?"

Odessa flinched and looked over at Rich.

J.P. pushed out of his chair and picked up his cup of coffee. He looked at Jeremy and said, "I'll have a look at my file and give you a call." Then he walked out.

Rich shook his head. "I didn't like that guy from the moment I laid eyes on him. Typical cocky fed."

IN BOISE, BUDDY DIRECTED LILLIAN PAST HIS MOTHER'S HOUSE AND told her to slow down, let him have a look. They crept along past the small ramshackle home, both of them craning their necks to look through the driver's window.

Lillian said, "Geez, looks like a junkyard."

Buddy frowned. It was his home, the place he grew up. It might not have been much, and his parents might not have been the best, but it was home and his old man and the crazy old bat he called Mom raised him up here. They fed him and clothed him and beat his ass sometimes too.

She glanced over at him. "Well?"

His anger welled up inside him. This goofy bitch was going to call his home a junkyard? He'd had about all he could take with her. Did he even need her anymore? Maybe. He was still adjusting to being a one-armed bandit. Right now, he couldn't even steal license plates, for Christ's sake, and needed her to do it for him. But that was okay, he was the brains of the operation, and for now, he'd keep her around. At least until he adjusted to his handicap. But maybe be a little meaner to her, especially during sex. Keep her in her place.

"Well, what? What the fuck, you want me to hire a gardener?"

She pulled to the curb and parked. They were both looking over their shoulders now at the little house behind them on the other side of the street. Rusted and dilapidated vehicles with rotted rubber tires littered the front yard and driveway, and weeds grew up through the broken sidewalk.

Lillian's gaze still set on the home, she said, "I mean, it could be a nice place, with a little work."

She wanted to play house, the stupid bitch. That's what this was all about, it occurred to him. He said, "Look, we ain't staying here. If there's a way to get money out of her, or out of this place, that's what we'll do. Then we move on. Got it? For fuck's sake, woman, do you not realize I'm a wanted fugitive? I'm famous around here, like Billy the Kid or Jesse James. Only I'm still alive, and I plan to keep it that way."

She turned her head and looked him in the eyes. "We're all going sooner or later, Buddy-boy... you might as well go out in a blaze of glory and make a name for yourself. Don't be a bitch."

He slapped her face.

She raised a hand and ducked away to fend off any other blows, but none came. She watched him, her eyes unblinking and without any tears.

He said, "You watch your mouth."

She snapped back, "You watch your back."

Buddy reached across his body with his only arm and fumbled with the door handle. When it opened, he paused and looked back at her. "Are you going to sit there pouting or come with me?"

She didn't say anything. He reached over and pulled the keys from the ignition, and stepped out of the car. If she was there when he got back, fine. If not, that's okay too—he'd had enough of her shit. Either way, you had to slap them around sometimes to keep them in line. He knew that from his childhood.

50

Jeremy pulled to the curb before reaching the apartment complex where Tank lived, not making the mistake of pulling up out front as he had at Mrs. Frantelli's house. Rich liked that Jeremy learned quickly and never seemed to forget anything he was told. The man was a great cop in the making, and Rich yearned for the days of breaking in new guys and being proud of how they turned out.

Before getting out, Rich turned his head, but not enough to look into Odessa's eyes.

She let out a huffy breath before he could say anything, and said, "Yes, I will wait in the car—again."

Rich said, "I'm sorry, but—"

She said, "What are *they* doing here?"

"Huh?"

Odessa indicated beyond his shoulder with a slight nod, and he followed her gaze.

Rich said, "That's a good question."

Jeremy opened his door. "Let's go find out."

"Stay here, Odessa," Rich reiterated as he stepped out of the car.

Jeremy was out ahead of him, but Rich could hear him say, "J.P., what brings you here?"

J.P. Long snapped his head around in their direction, flinging his ponytail in an arc behind his head. He pushed his sunglasses up into his blond hair and nodded. "Same as you, probably, came to have a little chat with our boy."

"What about?"

He smiled and held up a piece of paper. "We have a warrant for his arrest."

The three of them stood facing each other. A bald, quiet man stood behind Long. Jeremy nodded to greet him. "Doc."

The bald man nodded back but remained silent.

J.P. handed the paper to Jeremy. "He sold two pounds of marijuana to an informant of ours last night."

Jeremy looked up from the papers.

Rich shrugged and said, "Good, lock him up. Doesn't matter to me where we talk to him."

Jeremy nodded in agreement. He looked to J.P. and said, "You want some help here, maybe someone to cover the back?"

Rich chuckled and Jeremy smiled.

J.P. Long frowned, clearly not tracking.

Jeremy explained, "Last time we were here, Rich said there's no reason to cover the back because the dude wasn't going to jump from the second story window, that brothers are afraid of heights."

J.P. looked at Rich. "That a fact?"

Rich shrugged. "How the hell should I know?"

Doc's voice surprised everyone. "There he is."

They turned to see Tank crossing the parking lot. He had a duffle bag slung over his shoulder and a suitcase in the opposite hand.

J.P. started toward him, first at a fast walk, and then he broke into a jog. Tank dropped the duffle and the suitcase and turned to face them while reaching under his jacket.

J.P. yelled, "No!" as he pulled his gun from beneath his flannel shirt.

Rich nudged Jeremy and began moving fast toward the cover of parked cars that were not in the direct line of J.P. and Tank. His gun was now in his hand, and he saw that Jeremy had drawn his also. He glanced back but didn't see Odessa in the car. He hoped she was prone on the floorboard as he quickly scanned the area outside of their car but didn't see her anywhere.

J.P. yelled, "Freeze, asshole," just as the shooting started.

Rich and Jeremy, side by side, leaned across the hood of a sedan in the parking lot. Rich saw muzzle flashes from Tank's gun, and everything slowed to nearly a stop. He was looking over his front sight at the big man across the parking lot who stood with one arm extended in the direction of J.P., or where Rich had last seen him. Rich pulled his trigger. Once, then again, and again and again, but slowly and steadily, almost as if he were at the firing range. He was aware of muzzle flashes to his side, though he didn't hear the gunshots. Jeremy was firing too.

Rich could tell that their bullets were striking Tank, who flinched and buckled, but remained on his feet, continuing to shoot in the direction where J.P. Long had been. Rich's slide locked back and he reached for his second magazine just as the big man collapsed, his head striking the pavement with the sound of a dropped melon. Rich reloaded and waited, his gun trained on the man down on the ground. He watched for a long moment before he stood up from behind his cover and looked over to where he expected to find J.P. and his companion, Doc. At first, Rich didn't see either of them. He moved from behind the car and started in the direction of where they had been. Then he saw Doc on his knees, and on the ground next to him was the big, blond-haired narcotics cop. Doc pulled J.P. into his arms and cradled him while yelling for help.

Rich looked back to where Tank had fallen and saw that Jeremy had approached him with his gun trained on the man, and then kicked Tank's gun several feet away from his reach. Rich jogged toward him and said, "I've got you covered."

Jeremy holstered his gun and handcuffed Tank. Rich could see he was still alive, writhing as he labored to breathe. His clothes were soaked and a pool of blood was spreading on the pavement beneath him.

Jeremy got on his cell phone and made a call. His voice remained calm but urgent as he reported that there had been an officer-involved shooting, and that an officer and a suspect were down.

Rich could hear Doc sobbing behind him, begging his partner to hang on, telling him to not give up, telling him he would be okay. But Rich had seen J.P.'s eyes, and he had seen hundreds of eyes just like them—dead man's eyes. And he knew the young fed was gone.

WHILE THE PATROL OFFICERS AND AMBULANCES AND PARAMEDICS WERE racing to the scene of a shootout where an officer and a suspect were down, coming from all points of the city and the county and adjacent jurisdictions in response to the radio traffic the dispatch center had put out over all of the airways with urgency in their voices, the 9-1-1 board was flashing and blinking with calls on every available line. There were more calls coming in than the dispatchers could handle. All of the calls had similar messages: there had been a shootout and several people had been shot. The phone calls were handled quickly: *Thank you, we have units responding. Thank you, we're on our way. Stay in your house, we've got units coming...*

Until one caller calmly said, "She's shooting again, and I don't think it's at possums this time."

The dispatcher had started to say they were on their way until it struck her that the address displayed on her computer screen was that of a home on the other side of the city. She said, "Who's shooting, sir?"

"That crazy old Frantelli woman who lives next door in the junkyard."

"Can you see anyone out there? Can you tell what's going on?"

"No. Normally she fires one or two shots to kill a possum or a skunk or whatever, something that's getting after her chickens. But she's been shooting for ten minutes now and it sounds like a war zone."

The dispatcher heard gunshots in the background, loud booms of a shotgun. One shot and then another, a pause, and then another. But there was nobody available to respond, no units left to handle the call. A cop was down, for Christ's sake. She said, "We'll have someone there as soon as we can. Stay in your house."

She disconnected and yanked the headset off her head. "Jesus Christ, all hell's broke loose!"

THERE WERE COPS FROM EVERYWHERE, IN ALL TYPES OF UNIFORMS AND in marked cars and SUV's and unmarked sedans, the vehicles left unattended throughout the street and in parking lots and in some cases parked on lawns. Men and women were running around in the chaos. Firetrucks and ambulances were fewer in numbers but similarly contributing to the congestion and pandemonium at the scene. Radio traffic was blaring from a handheld radio as a man with stripes on his uniform was yelling, "Get that fucking truck out of the way so the ambulance can get through."

Rich watched and listened and tried to stay out of the way. This was not his show. He needed to remember where he was, and *what* he was. And then he heard the call come over the sergeant's handheld radio: *We have another report of shots fired, 3224 Maple, neighbor reports Mrs. Frantelli is shooting again.*

He ran over to where Jeremy and Odessa stood watching emergency personnel working on J.P.

"We've got to go, it's Frantelli!"

Jeremy squinted at him.

Odessa said, "What?"

Rich turned and started toward Jeremy's car. "Let's go, he's back at his mom's. Hurry up!"

The two followed, first at a fast walk but both broke into a jog as they hurried for the car.

Before all three doors had slammed shut, Jeremy had the car started. With everyone in, he began inching forward, then backward, and then forward again, turning and jockeying the car that had been blocked by police cars and fire trucks. When he finally got into a position where he could squeeze past a firetruck and a squad car with its door left open, he accelerated through it, hitting the door with his bumper and slamming it shut. The engine roared and the tires of the detective's car squealed against the black top.

"Okay, what the heck is going on, Rich?"

"I heard it over the radio. Shots fired at Frantelli's. I can't imagine you have more than one Frantelli home in your city where a shooting would take place."

"Probably not. Did you catch the address?"

"Maple is all I got."

"That's it, no doubt about it."

"It's what I thought, though I didn't remember for sure what street she lived on. Maple sounded familiar."

Odessa said, "Oh my gosh, this is insane."

Jeremy picked up the radio and told Dispatch he was responding to the shots-fired call on Maple. He asked for a tactical frequency, and told the dispatcher to have all responding units switch over. He changed frequencies and immediately began coordinating the response, something usually handled by patrol officers. Jeremy said into the mic, "All units responding, there's a real good chance this has something to do with the wanted killer, Buddy Frantelli. Keep your heads up and let's seal off the block. I don't want him escaping again if he's there."

But nobody responded to his message.

He then requested a K-9 unit if any were available, and suggested that the SWAT team be notified and prepared to respond.

The dispatcher, sounding defeated, said, "I'll see what we can do."

Buddy lay prone beneath a rusted 1971 GMC pickup that sat low on rotted tires in the front yard of his childhood home. Shotgun pellets blasted against the metal that surrounded him, and dust flew up from the ground near him. The sonic crack of bullets passing over his head told him that Lillian was firing her gun too. He was surrounded by two crazy bitches, each trying to kill him.

"You won't ever lay a hand on me, you son of a bitch!" Lillian yelled from one direction.

From the other: "I told you never step foot on my property again, you good-for-nothing bastard."

His face was pressed against the rusted steel frame above him. Every time a bullet or shotgun pellet would hit the truck, dirt and debris would fall onto his face and into his eyes. His gaze darted around the yard but he could only see weeds and the flat tires and rusted bodies and frames of the other vehicles in the yard. He had nowhere to go, and decided it wouldn't do him any good to try to move until the crazy bitches quit shooting. Maybe they'd run out of ammunition, and then he'd get the hell out of there.

But where would he go? To the house, or would it be better to just get away? He could run into the house and knock his mother on the head with something, maybe pick up a stick or a rock along the way. Maybe a car part, some type of steel junk he'd find out here in the yard. He'd have to have a quick look around. He could knock her out or do her in, either one, then he'd have her shotgun and he could march out onto the street and kill the other crazy bitch. Finish the job he had started back in California, up in the mountains.

The plan was coming together and he could see it all play out and was starting to feel good again about his chances of getting through this. Then he heard sirens, and moments later he heard the sounds of tires squealing and doors slamming and people yelling cop shit like freeze and put the gun down and—Jesus Christ, more shooting.

It only lasted a moment, a single gunshot followed by two short volleys of more shooting, different guns than the first. Semi-automatic pistols, based on the number of shots and the speed and pace at which they were fired. Silence followed, but only for a long moment.

Buddy strained to hear what he could only picture in his mind, and he had a bad feeling about Lillian. Little Miss Kitty. The crazy wannabe outlaw broad with the gray hair and hard body who wanted to go out in a blaze of glory. The fool.

His thoughts were disrupted by voices and footsteps. He heard someone say something about calling Rescue, then there was talk about checking for someone inside the house. He froze and held his breath as two sets of dress shoes walked quickly past him, followed by two sets of dark blue pants and polished boots. Cops. Detectives followed by cops, headed for the house.

This was his chance. Maybe his only chance. His last chance. He shimmied from beneath the rusted pile of metal and rotted rubber and, when he saw daylight, pushed himself up with his only arm and took off. He ran away from the house until he heard more gunshots that sounded distant, but he knew they were at the back of his mother's house, or maybe inside. As he glanced over his shoulder, instinctively looking toward the sound of the gunfire, his legs tangled up in something and he hit the ground. Someone jumped on his back and began hitting him on the back of his head.

OLD LADY FRANTELLI YELLED, "WHY THE HELL ARE YOU SHOOTING at me?"

Rich was saying, "Hold your fire!"

Jeremy looked around to see if anyone had been hit. Rich stood next to him at the side of a chicken coop that offered concealment, though he had no confidence in its ability to stop bullets. He saw one officer behind a junked car on the other side of the backyard, and the other peeking around the corner on the other side of the house, looking toward the back door.

The woman said, "I'm coming out. I don't know why in hell you're shooting at me."

Rich called back to her, "You leave that shotgun inside, now."

"I know... I know. What do you think, I'm an idiot?"

She stepped out in her nightgown, the same she had worn the last time Jeremy saw her. No gun, but her hands were at her sides, held low.

Jeremy said, "Raise those hands, ma'am."

She raised them up and said, "Oh, piss off, you sorry bastards. Goddamn cops hassling an old woman."

"Where is he?" Rich asked.

"Who? Where's who?"

"Your boy."

"Oh," she clucked. "Hopefully he's out there under that old pickup in the front yard, bleeding out or maybe dead. I warned him last time he was here, and he didn't listen. So he got what he deserved."

Rich glanced at Jeremy. "Shit."

Jeremy nodded. "Let's go," and then to the uniformed patrol officers, "Watch her, she's all yours."

Rich and Jeremy ran from their positions near the chicken coop in the backyard, down the side of the house, and into the front yard. They each slowed and followed the sights of their pistols, checking beneath the various abandoned vehicles.

Jeremy saw the GMC truck, and he remembered her words, *That old pickup.* He glanced at Rich, who nodded. They separated, Jeremy to the left and Rich to the right, and moved cautiously toward it. When they were within twenty feet, they checked each other again, and then both stooped down quickly and pointed their guns beneath it.

Jeremy stood up and looked around, disappointed but also concerned about the whereabouts of Frantelli, the evasive murderer who had left a trail of death and destruction throughout the west. The man believed to be responsible for his first murder case, the murder of Lacy Jane Lewis. Jeremy wanted him badly, and this seemed to have been their best chance. Yet the outlaw had vanished again, right beneath their noses this time. Jeremy stared at the truck and wondered if they had walked right by him on their way in.

"Shit!"

Jeremy looked over. "What?"

Rich said, "Odessa!" as he turned and began running toward the street.

Jeremy followed, and as they rounded the corner onto the sidewalk, he sprinted past Rich like the college athlete he had been. Only this time he ran with fear and trepidation on his mind, not second base. He had a horrible feeling in his gut.

51

Rich could see a commotion on the ground outside of Jeremy's sedan where they had left Odessa. He bobbed his head as he ran, stealing glances around the back of Jeremy who had pulled away from him and sprinted toward what appeared to be a fight.

Frantelli and Odessa?

Rich pushed himself to run faster. Jeremy was nearly there. Rich was close enough now to see that yes, it was a fight, and that it did appear to be Odessa and a man rolling in the street. Frantelli rose from the ground and stood over her, raised his leg above her head, and stomped down. She moved just enough that he missed. He cocked his leg again just as Jeremy reached them.

Jeremy left the ground, using the speed of his sprint and the strength of his legs to launch himself like a human missile into the body of Buddy Frantelli.

Rich saw it, and he heard the collision. He would later describe the collision as being similar to a linebacker having a free shot at the blind side of a quarterback, and cashing in all his chips. Rich was just coming up on them, and he could hear Buddy gasp as he was hit, and he heard the thud when Buddy's body hit the ground. Jeremy raised up to separate himself slightly from the man beneath him, then cocked his arm and drove an elbow into Buddy's face. He raised back and cocked his arm again, and Rich yelled, "No!"

Jeremy froze there, hovered over Frantelli, ready to strike him again.

Rich settled next to them and saw that Buddy was motionless, out cold. Rich touched Jeremy and said, "We're good here, partner. You've got your man."

Jeremy lowered his arm, rolled the convict over and stuck his knee in the small of Buddy's back. He glanced back at Rich, and smiled while panting to catch his breath.

Rich said, "Nice work, but I'm not sure what we do now."

"How's that?" Jeremy asked.

"I've never had to handcuff a man with only one arm."

ODESSA STOOD AND BRUSHED HER ARMS AND HER LEGS, THEN MOVED her scraped and bleeding hands to her head and pushed her hair around, shaping up the cloud-like puff that had lost its dome shape. Rich reached over, his hand gently touching the side of her face where dirt and blood covered scrapes and road rash. He left it there. Her eyes began to tear.

"What the hell happened to you?" he said, softly.

Her lip quivered and tears slowly rolled from the corners of her eyes and down her cheeks. Rich kept his hand on her face, catching the tears, then took her face in both hands. She pushed through his hands, wrapped her arms around his neck, and nestled her face into his chest. He felt her convulsing as she wept. He wrapped his arms around her and held her tight, tucking his chin into her hair.

After a few moments, once she had calmed and gained control of her emotions, Odessa pulled back and looked at Rich. "That was my first fight."

He smiled. "Hopefully, your last fight."

She nodded and nestled back into the comfort of his chest.

JEREMY STOOD LOOKING FROM RICH AND ODESSA BACK TO BUDDY, WHO lay still on the ground beneath him. He glanced behind him when he heard voices, and he saw the two officers walking toward them with Mrs. Frantelli between them. Her hands were cuffed behind her and a cigarette dangled from her mouth, and she squinted against the smoke as she said, "He dead?"

Jeremy shook his head. "I don't think so."

The cigarette danced from her lips as she spoke. "Well that's too bad, the rotten son of a bitch."

Frantelli moaned, giving the first indication that he was coming around. Jeremy crouched down next to him and took his one arm and pulled it behind him, handcuffing his one arm to a belt loop at the back of his pants.

"How'd he lose that arm?" his mother asked.

Jeremy looked at her and shrugged. "No idea."

"Well, serves him right, the way he treats his mother. I'd call that karma."

Jeremy said to the officers, "Can someone call for an ambulance for him?"

One of the two nodded and stepped away while the other kept hold of Mrs. Frantelli.

"And a transport," Jeremy called to the officer's back. He looked over at Rich, then looked across the street at the blue Toyota that sat riddled with bullets, a woman slumped over in the driver's seat. He said, "We're going to be out here a while."

Rich nodded. "It's going to be a long night."

"For everyone," Jeremy said, "the city went completely mad today."

52

Back at the Boise police station, Rich sat isolated in a small, quiet interview room waiting to give his statement to detectives. It would be a reversal of the roles he was accustomed to playing, and his mind replayed the scenario as he prepared for it. So much had happened in such a short span of time—but didn't it always? How many times had he heard that from other cops who were involved in shootings. Looking back at it, the details were sharp, crystal clear, images of the gray-haired woman who sat in the blue Toyota watching as they had started toward the Frantelli house. Many cops described their thoughts during shooting scenarios as surreal, that they couldn't believe it was happening, yet there they were, suddenly in a gunfight. Now Rich knew that feeling himself, firsthand, because nothing could have surprised him more than when the woman raised a pistol and fired a shot at him and Jeremy.

He was now certain that this woman was the one with whom Frantelli had left Bishop, the widow of one of his victims—adding to the insanity of this entire case. Rich was accustomed to craziness in Los Angeles, but he hadn't expected to find it here in Idaho, too. It reinforced his being more comfortable in the city where the criminal element was more predictable, and a lot less bizarre.

Rich pictured Odessa sitting in another room, and he worried about how she was handling the situation. He knew he could handle everything that would be coming his way, but it would be a lot for her to process.

He recalled the brief conversation the two of them had had just before leaving the scene. Odessa described sitting in the car when the woman fired a shot from the window of her sedan. She saw it happening in slow motion, yet she was frozen. She said she didn't remember getting down in the car, but she had, and she had just started to sit up when the shooting began again. This time, the gunfire was farther away. She ducked back down, and the next time she looked up, Buddy Frantelli was running toward her. Rich recalled her smiling as she told this part of the story: she said he ran with his one arm swinging far and wide to compensate for the lack of balance he must've experienced with only the one arm. It struck her funny at first, and then it occurred to her that he was running from where she had heard the shooting.

Rich pictured her moist eyes as she had told him that all she could think of was that he and Jeremy and everyone else had been killed back there. Why else would this man be running from the house after all that shooting, and with nobody chasing him?

That's when she'd decided she hadn't spent all these days tagging along with the two best cops in the country—those were her words—to sit like a coward in the back seat while this killer got away. She would do something, no matter if the cost of doing so would be her life. She sat low and waited as he ran directly toward their vehicle. As he started to pass by, he glanced over his shoulder. That was when she opened the door and stepped out, thrusting her leg across his path. He tripped and fell, and she jumped on top of him.

Odessa said though she had never been in a fight, she used to watch the UFC with her brother and their dad, and she had an idea of what to do. She jumped on his back before he could get up, and began punching him in the head. Her anger grew and she punched faster and harder with every swing of her fists. Just when she thought she was kicking his ass, he flipped her over. She couldn't believe it.

Rich had smiled, picturing her in a fight. He could hardly see it.

She didn't remember much after that, she had said, until Jeremy tackled him. It was the second best sight she had ever seen, topped only by looking to see Rich coming too. She had smiled and said, "You were pretty slow, compared to Jeremy."

Rich's smile faded as he thought about the woman in the car. He just couldn't understand it. What had been her motive? Why had she turned into an accomplice? He shook his head as he stared at the mirrored glass window across from him, then lost his train of thought. Who would be watching him, and what were they thinking? Would the brass here in Boise be pleased with the outcome, or pissed off that this cop from L.A. was in the middle of it all? He wondered if they would blame him, believing it might have all worked out differently had the L.A. cop not been involved. It wouldn't surprise him if that's how it played out.

He thought of the woman again and saw his bullets striking her, saw her convulsing and then slumping over, lifelessly. He questioned if there could have been another way to take her down, if there had been any other options. Had they really needed to kill her? He knew in his heart that she had left them no choice, and now he only needed to figure out how he would live with it.

In all of his years as a cop in L.A., he'd only been in two shootings, and he had never killed anyone. He never dreamed of having to shoot a woman, and yet now he had. In Boise, Idaho, of all places.

JEREMY WAS IN AN ADJACENT ROOM FINISHING HIS STATEMENT TO THE detectives from Nampa PD, a tall slender woman and a shorter, stocky man, clean-shaven with an army-style haircut and a boyish face. It was a common practice for the various agencies in the Treasure Valley to assist one another in officer-involved shooting investigations—it gave a more unbiased appearance, or so the administrators believed.

Jeremy covered details of the original case, the murder of Lacy

Jane, since these two investigators likely knew little or nothing about it. He told them about the truck driver who was kidnapped and murdered in Nevada, the manhunt, and finally, after all else was covered, he explained his actions during the two shootouts that day—the first one with Tank and the second with the woman Buddy Frantelli had run off with. Then he had to explain Rich's involvement with all of it. As he looked each investigator in the eye—the slender woman and the man who looked like a wrestler—he told them Rich was an L.A. cop with family ties to the first victim, Lacy Jane Lewis. That was mostly true. He said Rich had come out with another family friend, Odessa, who was here as a liaison for the family—another blurred fact, though fairly accurate. Then he told them, "Detective Farris really helped a lot with this investigation. What neither of you would know is that I've been on my own throughout this case, my first homicide. My training officer unexpectedly retired during the middle of it."

He waited as the two detectives let that sink in. The wrestler jotted a note and the lady cop just nodded.

"Honestly, I'm not sure I could have put this case together without his help," Jeremy concluded.

Odessa waited in the lobby, sipping a Dr. Pepper. She had gone first, telling about the shooting of the woman and her fight with Buddy, and how Jeremy had saved her life. She had added, "He should get a medal."

But as she waited, her mind replayed the violence on a loop. There was something that bothered her about the shooting. Yes, it was true what she had told them, that the woman had fired her gun first. But that was it, one shot. In her mind, she could see the woman pointing a gun from the window of the car, and she heard the shot as flames erupted from the barrel. There had only been one shot, and for the first time, she wondered why Rich and Jeremy had fired so many shots in return.

Had they intended to kill her?

It seemed an overwhelming response. One shot, answered by many. Maybe ten or more, she couldn't be sure. Both of them, stooping low and firing away. She saw it. She had looked back and forth as if watching a tennis match. She saw their pistols erupt in answer to the single gunshot that had been fired at them. She saw the woman hit by gunfire, her body flinching, almost jumping at times, her head finally slumping as if she had nodded off to sleep. Odessa knew she had passed.

Did they stop shooting then?

She couldn't remember. She replayed it in her mind, but the sequence wasn't clear. She didn't think there was shooting after the woman's head had slumped to the side, and she hoped that there hadn't been. It should have been obvious to everyone that she was dead.

The gun... the gun had fallen to the ground outside of the car. She remembered it now. Was it before or after they quit shooting? Had she told the investigators that? She didn't know.

As she sipped her soda and reflected, it struck her that she had been mistaken in her statement. She had told them that she ducked down when the shooting started, but clearly, now that the events played out again in her mind, she realized that she hadn't; she had watched in horror as it all unfolded. How long had it taken? Maybe just seconds, she realized for the first time. Was she unfairly questioning the actions of Rich and Jeremy, their instant responses to being shot at and the actions they took in the flash of a moment? Odessa drew in a deep breath and let it out slowly, considering for a moment that all of this might just be a bad dream.

But she knew it wasn't. There were people talking all around her from the various offices and cubicles nearby, real conversations involving real people. There was chatter from the voices on the police radio and a lot of activity, a heightened sense of urgency everywhere. But she tuned it out and replayed the scene, over and over. While doing so, she'd interrupt her thoughts to say a silent prayer. She prayed for the soul of the woman she had seen killed. She prayed for

Rich and Jeremy, for whatever they would now endure. She prayed that what she had witnessed was necessary and justified, though she didn't know if she would ever be able to reconcile such violence in her own mind. It was the worst thing she had ever seen, and she prayed she'd never see anything like it again.

THE THREE OF THEM WERE REUNITED IN THE FRONT LOBBY OF THE station after what seemed to have been hours of waiting. Maybe it was. Nobody spoke. They stood in a circle and looked at one another with solemn faces. Finally, Odessa began choking back tears.

Rich reached an arm around her shoulder and said, "What do you say we go have a drink?"

Jeremy grimaced. "You know I don't drink."

"Well, if you ever were going to start, this would be the right day for it."

Odessa shrugged Rich's arm off and started for the lobby doors. Rich called out to her, but she didn't stop. He watched her hurry through the doors and down the steps outside. He looked over at Jeremy.

"Go catch up with her, she needs you. I'm going home, Rich. We'll be in touch."

Rich nodded. The two men started to shake hands when Jeremy stepped in and hugged him.

"Thanks, for everything," Jeremy said. "I mean it." He turned and walked back in the direction of the door that would take him toward his office.

Rich watched the door close behind him, then turned and looked at the front doors again. It was dark outside, but he could see Odessa waiting just below the steps. When he walked outside, she turned and looked him in the eyes.

"Odessa," he began.

She interrupted his thought. "I want to go home."

53

S teve Troy sat on his usual barstool with his usual scowl, reading that rag of a newspaper. Dave walked over from the other end of the bar with the Jameson and held it up as a gesture. Steve nodded. As Dave poured his drink, Troy kept his nose in the paper, saying, "Can you believe it? All the goddamn shootouts around here?" He lowered it and looked at Dave. "You'd think we were living in Detroit, for Christ's sake."

"You're just pissed off that you missed all the action," Dave said with a grin, then turned to walk away.

Troy said to his back, "Yeah, I missed it all right, which is why it's so fucked up. They should have nailed this bastard two weeks ago. Then the black dude, the ballplayer who killed that broad who was living with him—*which we knew a week ago*—how come he wasn't hauled in before he killed three more people, including a cop?"

Dave wiped the bar with a wet towel in his slow, methodical way. "Beats me."

"Well, let me tell you why. Because the fucking Mormon mafia would rather have incompetent investigators than to put up with a Catholic Irishman like myself, someone who might say a bad word once in a great while and occasionally enjoys a cocktail. It serves them fucking right," he said, and downed his Jameson.

Dave smiled.

"I'll tell you another thing," Troy continued, sliding the paper off to the side and pushing his glass toward the well to signal he'd have another, "there's an equal chance they'll fuck it all up when it gets to court. Nobody over there knows what the fuck they're doing. I'll be amazed if that Frantelli asshole ain't in here sippin' whiskey next month, free as a bird."

"Never know, I guess."

Steve watched him walk away. *Never know.* Well fuck him, too.

A few minutes later, Dave came back and topped off Troy's whiskey, then leaned against the back of the bar. "So how's the new job?"

Steve chortled. "The fucking job. The babysitting job, you mean?"

He shrugged.

"It's a boring piece of shit, that's how it is. These fucking guards out there call themselves cops. They ain't cops, they're fucking guards. But guess what, you can't call 'em that. They get all butt-hurt over it if you do. Well, let me tell you, they ain't fucking cops, that's for sure.

"I've got more respect for some of the convicts, at least the ones where I'm assigned. I kind of have a plush job up in the hospital ward, which isn't just for the sick, lame, and lazy. They house some of the keep-aways there too, these guys that can't be out on the yard because they'd get shanked or raped, maybe both.

"I've got this one guy, was a cop back east—New York or some goddamn place—who came out here and ended up dumping some asshole during a robbery. Yeah, the guy's a retired cop, working at a market when some punk comes in to rob the place. This guy dumps him, puts two in the ten-ring and that's the end of that. Well, he can't walk the yard, cause he used to be a cop—"

"Wait, why'd he go to prison for that? I mean, he was within his rights, wasn't he?"

"Yeah, he was within his rights when he shot the one asshole, but then he ran outside and shot the other kid who was waiting in the car

—the getaway driver. The jury gave this cop a second-degree murder for that one, if you can believe it. Fucking juries."

Dave shook his head.

Troy took a long pull on his whiskey and wiped his mouth with the back of his hand. "Anyway, my point is, this cop, he ain't a bad guy, you know what I mean? Hell, I'd rather hang out with him than half the idiots I work with, all these wannabes. I play checkers with him sometimes when nothing's going on cause it beats reading a book or looking at a magazine. That's all I was trying to tell you."

Dave nodded. "You having another?"

"What, are you keeping track? Yeah, pour me another, for Christ's sake."

54

A fter the funeral of J.P. Long, the first federal agent killed in Idaho since Ruby Ridge, Jeremy sat solemnly at his desk, feeling a bit overwhelmed with the mountain of paperwork filling dozens of files before him. There were files from six murders: Lacy Jane Lewis, Elwood Johnston, Tanika Edwards, Santiago Salazar, *AKA: Lil' Chongo*, Reginald Jackson, *AKA: Chino*, Ladarius Love, and J.P. Long of the Federal Drug Enforcement Administration. The sheriff's office had agreed that Tanika was likely killed in Boise and dumped in the county, so they were happy to pass that one over to Boise PD.

Jeremy didn't know where to start. All he knew was he had a list from the prosecutor's office of what they needed in the way of discovery: copies of reports, evidence logs, photographs, transcripts, search warrants... copies of recorded interviews and interrogations, plus transcriptions... all of the same documentation from the Mineral County Sheriff's Office in Nevada, the Inyo County Sheriff's Office in California, and the Reno Police Department.

Well, there was only one way to eat an elephant—one bite at a time.

After another hour, he decided the work would be here for him

317

tomorrow, and with a fresh brain it might seem a little less imposing. He decided to head home and go for a run, have a nice dinner in and spend the evening with his family. He'd go at it hard tomorrow. He pushed out of his chair and was slipping into his suit jacket when his cell phone vibrated on his belt. He picked it up and saw it was Rich.

Rich slurred, "Jeremy, my friend..."

"Rich, are you okay?"

"Oh yeah, yeah... I'm great, couldn't be any better. How'd the funeral go? Never mind, I know how it went—they all go the same way. Listen, the reason I called... well, one of the reasons I called—"

"Uh-huh"

"—is, wait, Jeremy?"

"Yeah, Rich, I'm here."

"Jeremy, I miss you, brother. I just wanted to tell you that I enjoyed working with you. It was good to be on a case again."

He could hear the sadness in his friend's well-lubricated voice, and it was difficult to know where he was emotionally. "Have you heard from her?"

"Who, Odessa?"

"Yes, Rich, Odessa."

"No, I haven't."

There was a long pause, an awkward silence. Jeremy didn't know what to say, but after a moment, he said, "Rich, listen, I was about to head out. Can I give you a call tomorrow, or later in the week? It's been a long day."

"Yeah, yeah... no, that's fine, man. You have a nice evening, partner."

"Was there something you called about, Rich?"

"Ah, yeah, no, nothing, man... nothing. Just, I was thinking about you, that's all, wondering how you did today, having the funeral and all. Just thought I'd check in on my friend."

"I appreciate it."

"I'll let you go, partner."

"Okay, Rich. You get bored, come and see me. Maybe I'll put you to work, get you to help me clean up this mess you left me with."

Rich chuckled. "Yeah, now comes the fun part, huh? I'd offer to give you a hand, but, well, I've got... I've got..."

Jeremy waited.

"I've got Orlando here to take care of."

"Orlando?"

"Yeah, he's my good friend."

"Oh, I never—"

"I can't lie to you, Jeremy... Orlando is dead."

"What? Rich—"

"He was my fish, but he's gone. He's been gone for a while now, but for some reason, I was missing him today. And you guys too, and Lizzy. There's no one now."

Silence.

"Hey, Jeremy—"

"Yeah, Rich."

"I love you, man, but I gotta go."

"Rich? Are you there?... Hello?"

Jeremy stared at his phone as the screen faded into darkness, *Rich Farris* disappearing before his eyes.

———

RICH SET HIS PHONE DOWN ON THE COFFEE TABLE NEXT TO THE SCOTCH and his Glock nine. He wiped the moisture from his eyes and said, "Jesus."

55

N early a year later, Jeremy walked out of the District Court in downtown Boise with complex feelings about the outcome of the trial. One of the two men who had turned his quiet little city into a crimewave-driven blood bath had just been sentenced to death, the one-armed outlaw named Buddy Frantelli. It had only been a few weeks earlier that the other man received his sentence. The college football player, who had seemingly had everything going his way in life before essentially becoming a serial killer of sorts, had received his death sentence as well. It was almost ironic that he had survived being shot eight times and now the state would try to kill him again—eventually.

Two men were headed for Death Row in part due to the work of Boise Police Detective Jeremy Cross. He wasn't sure how he felt about it, but he was pleased that neither would ever be on the streets again, and he was proud of the work he had done to contribute to the successful prosecutions.

He stopped and waited on the steps as the cameras and reporters converged on him, insisting on a statement.

Odessa sat in her car, bored to death. She was scrolling through her Twitter feed, thinking this wasn't nearly as much fun as it had been with Rich and Jeremy. She wondered if working as a private investigator was really something she'd stick with. Of course, her parents had just about given up hope with her, career-wise. First med school, then the ministry, and now, after her whirlwind adventure chasing killers throughout the west, she had returned to Louisiana only to announce her plans to take criminal justice classes and learn to be a private investigator.

She found out she could do both, so she enrolled in college and took a job with a local private investigation company. Her experience, she had told them, had been working with two top-notch homicide detectives to solve a series of murders and put two killers in prison.

Now she sat for the third day in a row, watching the home of a man who was suspected of committing workers comp fraud. She had a video camera set up to capture any activity that conflicted with his claims of disability, but the claimant rarely showed his face. When he did, there was little to no *activity* to record. It seemed most cases went the same way, and she couldn't help but think that the insurance companies were wasting their money. These people didn't claim to be injured so that they could work hard in their yards or see how active they could be; they did so in order to lay around and watch television in sweatpants or pajamas while they waited to collect their checks.

Maybe she would look into the FBI. Or call Jeremy, see how you get to be a detective in Boise. She loved that town and would go back in a heartbeat. It was something to think about, and she was due for another change.

In Los Angeles, a psychologist by the name of H. Arthur Williamson, Ph.D., a recognized expert on Post Traumatic Stress Disorder and its effects on police officers specifically, and first-responders in general, had just finished his report detailing his findings related to the case of Richard James Farris, Los Angeles County Sheriff's Homicide, Retired.

His findings came as no surprise. Farris had suffered the typical effects from long-term, ongoing exposure to traumatic incidents found in cops who worked in high crime regions and challenging assignments such as homicide, and who often encountered violence themselves. The suicide rate among cops was bad enough, and Doctor Williamson believed that if there were ever a study focused on only those who worked in high crime areas, or who held assignments such as homicide or child abuse investigation in major metropolitan districts, that the rates would likely rival that of military combat veterans. At least that was the expert opinion that Doctor Williamson had recently published in a psychology journal.

Williamson tossed his report of Farris onto his desk, exhibiting his distaste for the matter in general. The doctor leaned back in his plush leather chair and nibbled at the end of his pen. Farris reached across the desk from the other side and picked up the file.

Doc cut to the chase. "You're fucking nuts, Richard."

Rich smiled. "That's what you came up with? All those years of college, that's all you got? Your mother and I are very disappointed, Doc."

"You leave my mother out of it," he said, "or I'll have to reconsider whether or not you're a danger to yourself or others. I check one box, and you're stripped of your concealed weapons permit."

"Mamas are off the table then."

Dr. Williamson watched as Rich thumbed through the report. He admired the man and was glad he had been able to help him through a rough patch in his life. It was these cases that made his work seem worthy of the time, the study, and the ongoing efforts to change how cops dealt with the all-too-often crippling effects of the job. There were many he hadn't been able to help, and most he had never been able to bond with the way he had bonded with Rich. He had found Rich engaging and honest and easy to like, and it hadn't taken long for them to lower the barriers of professionalism and work together as friends while addressing a serious health issue.

"How's your love life?"

Rich chuckled but didn't look up from the report. "What's that?"

"Don't bullshit me, man. A good-looking guy like you, single, and living in Los Angeles. It's not like there's a shortage of available women out there."

"Yeah, well…"

"What about that flight attendant?"

Rich glanced at him and grinned. "We're talking."

Doc nodded. "And the little southern belle?"

Rich stopped smiling and lowered his eyes to the report, perhaps trying to avoid the topic. If there was one thing Rich never seemed open to discussing, it was the young woman named Odessa.

"Well?"

"I haven't heard from her."

"That's a two-way street."

"She's too young."

"That's perspective, and relative."

"She's a long way away, living her own life."

"That's an excuse."

Rich looked up with pleading eyes. He might have been searching for an answer, or maybe hoping for direction. But Doc knew he didn't really need it. He was smart, smart enough to follow his heart if he'd just let the regimented, old-fashioned side of his brain get out of the way. Doc said, "Love has few boundaries, and you're not anywhere near crossing any of them with her. What you are doing is denying yourself—*and her*—the chance to see if it was meant to be."

Rich nodded but it was nearly imperceptible.

"Call her, Rich. Better yet, go see her. Quit being such a pussy, for Christ's sake."

They both smiled, and as if on cue, got up from their chairs and faced one another for a long, silent moment. Dr. Williamson walked around his desk and met Rich near the door. They embraced as old buddies might, and they held it for a long moment.

"You're going to do great things, Richard Farris. Follow your heart, my friend."

STEVE TROY HIT THE BUTTON TO ALLOW THE TWO GUARDS INTO HIS module, the hospital section of the prison where the cripples and snitches were housed. They were bringing him new fish—a term used for the prisoners just coming into prison—three of them total. Troy recognized one of them, and smiled widely. "Well look it here, Boise's own famous outlaw, Mr. Frantelli."

"You know each other?" asked the older of the two guards who had escorted the prisoners into the module.

Buddy stood silent.

"Well let's say *I* know him." Troy stopped grinning and looked Buddy in the eyes. "I was working Homicide when you killed that poor little colored girl behind the bar. It's a small world, ain't it, boy?"

The condemned man said nothing.

"Nothing to say, huh?" Troy huffed to show his disdain for the man, and then turned his attention back to the guards. "I have a special place for that one."

"They're all yours," the one officer said. "Do with them as you please."

The guards departed and Steve Troy addressed the first two of the three inmates, the ones in whom he had little interest, directing them to cells where there were open beds. All of the cells were configured to house two inmates, and these three would bring the module to capacity. He turned to Frantelli, and chuckled. "You're going to love your cellie, boy." Then he sent Buddy down the row and called out to his back, "Last cell on the right, back there where nobody can hear you scream."

Some of the inmates chuckled. Others made catcalls. Troy pulled the lever to open the gate to the cell where Buddy would be housed. Once it opened, the other resident of that cell peeked out to see his new roommate. Then he stepped all the way out of his cell onto the tier—rather, he limped out—this big man dressed only in white boxer shorts and gray socks, his numerous scars from being shot multiple times on display.

Buddy stopped, took in the sight of the man who would be his new cellie, and then he looked back at Officer Troy.

Troy smiled and winked at him.

He turned back to meet the big man's gaze.

Tank said, "Welcome home, bitch."

EPILOGUE

The City of Boise needed another private investigation firm the way Vegas needed another casino, or Nevada another brothel. It was an unlicensed state, one of only seven in the nation. Alabama, Alaska, Colorado, Mississippi, South Dakota, and Wyoming were the others.

Without licensing, anyone could hang out a shingle and call themselves an investigator. A private eye. A private detective, or simply a dick. Which meant there were wannabes everywhere, people with no experience, no training, and no credentials. Others with questionable backgrounds. Some, Farris had discovered, with criminal histories.

But what was lacking in the saturated industry of Boise's legal community was a retired homicide detective from L.A. who had investigated hundreds of murders and thousands of cases. Boise also didn't have a single black investigator.

Much less a pair of them.

Until now.

INSIDE A NEWLY REMODELED COTTAGE LOCATED IN THE FASHIONABLE north end of Boise, a phone sitting on an old wooden desk rang, and a young woman with lively brown eyes snatched it up before the man at the desk had a chance. The man, renewed and content, leaned back in his chair and watched, admiringly.

She stood with a hand on her hip, the other holding the handset against a halo of deep brown hair that encircled her face. She winked at her partner and said, "Farris and Associates, Odessa speaking. How may I help you?"

REVIEW

Independent authors count on word-of-mouth and paid advertising to find new readers and sell more books. Reviews can help shoppers decide about taking a chance on authors who are new to them.

I would be grateful if you took a moment to write a review with whichever retailer you purchased the book.

Thank you!

Danny R. Smith

Also Available by Danny R. Smith

THE DICKIE FLOYD SERIES

- A Good Bunch of Men
- Door to a Dark Room
- Echo Killers
- The Color Dead
- Death after dishonor
- Unwritten Rules

SHORT STORIES

- In the City of Crosses - A Dickie Floyd Detective Short Story
- Exhuming Her Honor - A Dickie Floyd Detective Short Story
- Harder Times: A Cop Goes to Prison

AVAILABLE ON AUDIBLE

- A Good Bunch of Men
- Door to a Dark Room

AFTERWORD

I love staying connected with my readers through social media and email. If you would like to connect, find me on BookBub, Amazon, Goodreads, Facebook, Instagram, and Twitter. You can also sign up for my newsletter and receive bonus material, such as the Dickie Floyd short story, Exhuming her Honor.

As a newsletter subscriber, you will receive special offers, updates, book releases, and blog posts. I promise to never sell or spam your email.

Danny R. Smith

Dickie Floyd Novels

ACKNOWLEDGMENTS

I am eternally grateful that my very good friend and editor, Patricia Barrick Brennan, carefully scrutinizes every word I write, and that some of those words are allowed to remain unaltered. Thank you, Patti, for all that you do.

My all-star team of beta readers are appreciated more than they could imagine. A heartfelt thanks to: Scott Anderson, Jacqueline Beard, Michele Carey, Teresa Collins, Andrea Hill-Self, Henry "Bud" Johnson, Phil Jonas, Michele Kapugi, Ann Litts, William "Moon" Mullen, Ralph Kay Reeves, Dennis Slocumb, and Heather Wamboldt.

Danny R. Smith spent 21 years with the Los Angeles County Sheriff's Department, the last seven as a homicide detective. He now lives in Idaho where he works as a private investigator and consultant. He is blessed with a beautiful wife and two wonderful daughters, and he is passionate about his dogs and horses, whom he counts among his friends.

Danny is the author of the *Dickie Floyd Detective Novel* series and The Murder Memo, a true crime blog. He has appeared as an expert on numerous podcasts and shows including True Crime Daily and the STARZ channel's WRONG MAN series.

He is a member of the Idaho Writers Guild and the Public Safety Writers Association.

CPSIA information can be obtained
at www.ICGtesting.com
Printed in the USA
FSHW020727071220

9 781734 979435